ONE FLOWER IN MY GARDEN

BY

WAYNE BROWN

PROLOGUE

Another slap.

How? Why?

Craig!

Pain!

Someone on top of her, thrusting, again and again.

The awful, salty taste in her mouth.

Terror!

The thoughts ran through Sara's mind as the boys used her, hurt her.

Panic!

Occasionally opening her eyes, she would see them smiling, laughing.

Then, one would finish, another would begin, over and over they would swap, sometimes more than one at a time.

She'd never known how much she really loved him, why had she forsaken him?

Craig!

Now, she knew. She realized as the brutality was taking place, as her body was being used, she realized how much she loved Craig. His heart would be broken.

Sara wondered, could this be her punishment for forsaking the love she knew Craig had for her?

More pain, more slimy liquid on her face, it burned her eyes, it gagged her.

Would it ever end?

Darkness began to descend upon her, then light, beautiful light.

Gently, hands reaching to her.

Beauty surrounding her.

The angels, Sara saw the angels.

Warmth and love surrounded her.

Sara glanced back and saw the girl, she saw the boys, she saw what the boys were doing,,to the girl.

Sara saw the girl's face.

Sara saw herself.

An angel spoke softly, "Do not look there, come with us, for a while"

The angel pointed, at a boy, he was smiling.

Craig!!

***

How had it all happened?

A man in the crosshairs of the rifle scope.

Thoughts.

Memories.

Heartbreak.

Love.

Sara.

So many miles ago.

The little boy sitting under the tree, he was eating green apples.

Craig heard singing, hymns, old hymns.

The little boy sitting on top of the old piano, a lady playing.

The man seen in the rifle scope smiled.

He loved Sara, beautiful Sara.

On a blanket beside the river, making love.

Her smell, how her scent was so sweet.

Green eyes.

The terror she'd lived through.

Now, a jungle, half way around the world.

A man in the crosshairs of the rifle scope.

A loud noise.

The man fell.

CHAPTER

1

It had been a long time coming. Time to begin the ending. The time was right.

Oscar had been drafted right out of high school. It didn't work out.

Oscar just couldn't seem to help being a bully and an asshole. "Bred into him," many who knew his dad would say. But, as with most bullies, most of the time if someone stood up to him, he backed off or wimped out. The Corporal who'd caught him selling a small bag of weed to another soldier weighed eighty pounds less than Oscar, in seconds he had him on his knees, crying like a baby. Charges filed and snitched on by two others in the barracks, Oscar was presented with a Less Than Honorable Discharge, put on a bus and sent back to South Creek, Georgia, a place he was despised by almost everyone except his daddy.

He developed contacts over the years, and it became well known to those who used the stuff that Oscar was the man to see if someone needed a joint or two, maybe a small bag, he had the good stuff. One evening he was approached by a sweet young thing he'd noticed around the party scenes; she was going to a party and needed a couple of joints. Oscar made her a deal; she could give him some time in those panties and get what she wanted for free or she could pay double. Two months later her

daddy would inform him he would sign for her to marry Oscar or call the police and file charges of statutory rape, she was pregnant. After the court house wedding he moved her into his mobile home, after the baby, a girl, was born and every time it cried, Oscar would slap his wife and tell her "put a tit in that thing's mouth, shut it up."

It took a while, but Oscar finally found a job on a farm a few miles outside of South Creek. If good for nothing else, Oscar could work, he quickly learned the ways of the farm life. The owner had several chicken houses, cattle and two hog parlors where pork was raised for market, also 200 acres of soybean fields. Oscar was taught all aspects of the farm and within two years was made foreman.

Far across the other side of the soybean fields the owner had built a barn with an apartment above it. The apartment was offered to Oscar and his family as a part of his pay. The old gentleman wasn't generous, he just liked the idea of his foreman being close by in case something was needed. Oscar accepted the offer, he moved his family in.

Saturday nights became what was referred to as Oscar's Night, his wife instructed to take the kid and go spend the night with her parents. She knew things were taking place on Saturdays, drugs being used and dealt, sexual things happening, she had twice found used condoms in the bathroom trashcan. But Oscar's wife said nothing for fear of a beating.

***

He came into town unnoticed, just another traveler passing through. Gary Wayne Graham, sporting a neatly trimmed beard, stopped at the diner and asked directions to the nearest motel, he was going to spend a few days in the area enjoying the local scenery. Bill, the owner of the diner inquired as to what kind of scenery?

2

"All kinds. A while back my uncle died and left me a tidy sum of funds. I was born in South Carolina, he lied, and enjoy photography. I decided to travel around the south and take pictures of things that interest me. I like it all, landscape, architecture, people. I just meander around and shoot random photos."

Bill laughed, "Must be the life!" He gave directions to the motel, "It ain't award winning, but Miss Anne keeps it real clean and tidy. Clean sheets and towels every day."

Gary thanked Bill, as he was walking out Oscar was walking in, loudly stating, "Gimme a large black coffee to go and be quick about it, I got business to take care of."

Sitting in the beast, loading a camera, Gary watched. Oscar came out of the diner and walked across the street to the feed store. Leaving the feed store Oscar headed east out of town, Gary decided he needed to see what was east of town and followed Oscar, from a distance. A few miles out of town Oscar turned onto a gravel road, Gary continued the main road.

Gary drove on for a while, the country really was very pretty. Having stopped a few times and used three rolls of film he decided to head back to town and get checked in at Miss Anne's Motel.

Anne Childers was in her late-fifties, attractive with the looks and figure of a much younger woman, and very pleasant. Gary checked in as Robert W. Brown and produced a South Carolina Driver's license issued to the same. Anne showed him to his room and asked how long he would be staying. "Honestly, I'm not sure, I drove out of town some today and the country is very pretty, how long I stay will be determined by what I find interesting to shoot photos of. Full moon tomorrow night, I always enjoy the effects of the moon in the background of things, I may go out at night a few times."

3

"Do you photograph people?"

"Yes, on occasion, with their permission of course."

"I really am embarrassed to ask, but if you find time would you mind photographing me? My daughter has been bugging me, wanting a recent picture."

"Robert' smiled, "Mrs. Childers, It would be an honor to assist you."

"Oh, call me Anne. I was Mrs. until my husband passed on."

"I'm sorry, how long?"

"Five years ago, aneurism. It got lonely out in the country where we lived, I sold the place, bought the motel and the little house next to it," she pointed to the neat small frame house. "It and the motel needed fixing up, my daughter and I worked hard to get it in shape. Finally turned a profit last month, not much but it was nice having more coming in than going out," Anne laughed.

Opening the door to the room, Robert was shocked, he'd stayed in much pricier places that weren't as clean and well kept, the place was spotless. Speaking to Anne, "The room is so nice I feel bad about messing it up." Both laughed.

Another customer drove in, Anne said good evening, Robert began unpacking his truck, he would stay in tonight and rest. He had noticed the area around the motel was nice, maybe he would stay close during the day, concentrate on photographing what he could find within easy walking distance. Tomorrow night would be a different matter, he would be out most of the night.

***

The next day was a Saturday, Oscar's favorite day. On the farm there were still chores to be done, but the hired help knew, pretty much, what to do. Oscar would make his rounds and be

sure everything was being taken care of. About five this afternoon the wife and kid would leave, he would begin setting up the alcohol at the bar in the lower area of the barn where he had built a place to party. Oscar smiled as he wondered which of the local girls and women his friends would be bringing, all of whom were willing to give blowjobs or pussy for a few drinks and tokes on joints, for anymore "special action" he would be happy to provide Quaaludes.

***

Robert woke just after seven the next morning, refreshed but hungry and wanting a cup of coffee. He showered, trimmed his beard, grabbed one of the camera bags and walked to the motel office. Anne was there and greeted him with a smile, her perfume filled Robert's head and was more than pleasant, he found himself admiring just how very attractive this lady really was, she was really very beautiful. Finally, he asked where the closest place he could get breakfast and coffee. Anne smiled, "Right here," she stepped into a small room behind the counter and produced a mug of coffee with a plate of donuts, "Some places call it a Continental Breakfast, we call it Coffee and Donuts." Both laughed.

"So, Mister Brown, what do your plans for the day include in lovely town of South Creek Georgia?"

"Well, Anne, I thought I would stay within walking distance my first day here and see what I might find interesting. If you have time, I would be happy to get those photos you asked for. Know a place with a nice background?"

Excited, Anne said, "Oh this is perfect, my help, Maria, will be here at 10 and work the afternoon. Will that be OK?"

"You bet."

5

Anne continued, "I know the perfect place, about a quarter mile through the woods there is a small pond on my neighbor's property, he recently built a pretty little bridge over the stream that feeds it. I think that would be a great place, I'll call him and let him know we will be there for a while, he and his wife are very nice and won't mind. Will 11 this morning be fine? It'll give me time after Maria gets here to put on something nice and touch up my makeup and hair."

"Eleven will be good. Meet you here?"

"No, come to the house and make yourself at home on the patio out back."

***

The chicken houses had feeders that were driven by a belt from the electric motors to the augers that carried the feed down the trough, a belt had broken. This was nothing new and Oscar had prepared by keeping extra belts on hand, he told Chuck, one of the hired men, what tools would be needed and sent him to get them from the toolbox on his pickup truck. Fifteen minutes later the belt was replaced, feed was filling the trough. Oscar thought to himself, "hope this is as bad as it gets today, I need to be rested for this evening."

***

Robert had been on the patio only a few minutes when he heard the door open. Anne stepped out, she was wearing a sleeveless casual front button dress that reached halfway between her knees and ankles, makeup was done to perfection with bright red lipstick accentuating her full lips, her hair was pulled back and held into place with a nice bone comb, she was stunning! The only thing out of place were the work boots, she had on work boots and socks.

Robert had to ask, "Anne, boots?"

6

"OH, I almost forgot!" She rushed back into the house, returning with a pair of nice wedge heels in her hand. "These are next to useless for walking through the woods, I'll change when we get there."

"Well, you're absolutely beautiful, but the boots did have me concerned." Both laughed

"Shall we go?"

"Lead the way Milady."

Conversation was easy with this lady; unlike any he'd ever experienced with someone he'd known less than a day. It was almost as if they had known one another for years. Following the path, they arrived at the small bridge, Anne had been correct, the place was perfect, very beautiful and with no wind the pond was as slick as glass. Anne began looking around, Robert asked what she was hunting, "somewhere to sit down while I change shoes without getting my dress dirty."

"No problem, go to the bridge where you can hold the handrail." She did, Robert knelt and removed the boots, and helped her into the heels.

"Thank you, it's been a while since a man helped me into my shoes, it was very nice."

The next hour was spent taking photos of a very beautiful lady. Anne knew how to pose and needed very little instruction. Both enjoyed themselves, they laughed and joked. Robert told Anne they really needed at least one picture of her with her boots on, she stuck out her tongue, he captured the moment on film. Robert wanted one more picture, one of Anne's reflection on the smooth water of the pond, he chose a place and held her hand for balance as she walked on the uneven ground still wearing her heels. Finishing the shot Anne stood, turned and lost her balance, heels and tree roots are a bad combination. Robert quickly

stepped forward and caught her in his arms. Anne looked up into his eyes, Robert looking into her eyes, faces inches apart, Anne's perfume once again filling his mind. Neither said anything for what seemed an eternity, Anne spoke first, "I want to kiss you." Robert spoke, "and I want to kiss you." Slowly, gently, their lips met, lingered, separated. Still staring into one another's eyes, Anne slowly closed hers and moved toward Robert's lips again, this kiss was more passionate, lips parted, this kiss lasted longer. Separating again Anne said, "Oh My, it's been so long since I kissed a man, I had almost forgotten how wonderful it is."

For the next several minutes they held and kissed one another many times, some kisses with the passion both people had missed for so very long.

Finally, Anne spoke, "I'm thirsty, there's cold beer at the house, and I'll fix sandwiches."

"Sounds great."

He helped her change back into her boots. Not much said as they walked to the house. Anne took off her boots and put on a pair of comfortable house slippers, she washed her hands, opened two beers and began preparing sandwiches at the cabinet. It had been several minutes since either had said a word.

Robert stood, walked behind her, he placed his hands on her shoulders. Without looking back Anne asked, "How old are you?"

"Twenty Five"

"I am fifty-three years old, old enough to be your mother. I have a daughter a year older than you and a grandchild three years old."

He moved his hands slowly down her arms, when he reached her hands he stopped and enjoyed their softness. "You

are one of the two most beautiful women I have ever held in my arms."

"You've been in love?"

"Yes."

"Are you still?"

"It was a few years ago, I still am but it can never be, she married a while back. She married a very nice man, I'm happy for them."

"It's hard, letting go of someone you love."

"Yes, it is."

Anne repeated, "I am fifty-three years old."

"I know."

She continued, "But I want you, need you in my bed."

Without a word Anne took a step, then, without turning, she reached back. He took her hand and followed.

Robert could never have believed Anne was fifty-three, both her face and her naked body appeared to be no older than possibly a woman in her middle thirties. They made love, slowly, gently, softly. It was beautiful.

Twenty minutes later they had sex, sex with all the fury of what they had been missing, of lost loves, it was raw, furious sex from two people who were both letting out the pain they'd experienced! The emotions held in for so long, they fucked like wild people, sometimes crying, sobbing, other times breathing hard and moaning from the pleasure. They used one another and both screamed when they orgasmed.

Exhausted, they lay next to one another, not a word said for over ten minutes. Anne spoke first, "Damn! I can't do that again today."

Robert laughed "I can't either!"

Anne rolled onto her side and looked at the young man beside her, "There may very well be twenty eight years difference in our age but that was beyond great. I don't know how long you intend to stay but you are not to leave town without showing me a replay! Do you understand me, young man?"

"Yes Ma'am!"

***

He loaded his gear and pulled away from the motel around 4 PM, he needed to find someplace to hide his vehicle before beginning his recon. By 5:15 he was in a position located in the woods across the soybean field, his only weapons were a Colt .45, a camera with a telephoto lens and a spotting scope. He would wait, observe and mentally take notes. This being the first of three missions he had planned involving this subject. There was no fourth mission planned unless something unexpected came up. Always expect the unexpected and plan for it.

On his way in he had seen a car leave, in it was a young woman. The assassin set up his high magnification spotting scope, ate a small box of raisins, careful to place the empty box back in his pack, took a sip of water from the canteen. He waited, he watched.

***

Oscar knew nobody would arrive until around 7, he poured a drink and turned on the TV installed on the wall behind the bar. The assassin had a clear view of the TV and could see it was tuned to a popular game show. Twice Oscar stepped outside to relieve

himself, he was turned facing the scope. Now he knew one reason Sara had suffered the injuries. Craig, during his military days had showered with and seen many men naked, what he saw Oscar holding in his hand was huge, most women porn stars would have refused to work with him. The visual in his mind of such an abomination being thrust into Sara both vaginally and rectally angered the assassin, he wanted to rip the man's throat out, and could do it. Calming himself, he remembered an angry person is a person who makes mistakes Craig stopped looking through the scope for a few seconds, lay on his side and cleared his mind.

Shortly after 7 PM cars began arriving, a couple with loud exhaust and one Cadillac, a jeep arrived half an hour later. All the cars carried more than one man and multiple young women. The women were all dressed skimpily, tight shorts, and tops that showed plenty of cleavage. Drinks began being poured, beers from the refrigerator available to anyone who wanted them, a while later people passing what appeared to be cigarettes from one to another, marijuana, the assassin had seen this take place in Nam. About half an hour into the festivities Oscar was observed walking around the room with a small sandwich bag half full of something. Zooming the scope revealed the contents of the bag to be pills. None of the men accepted, over half the women did. Not long after, the event morphed into a full-blown orgy. Girls passed from man to man, girls with girls, girls with multiple men at the same time. Lights were turned on upstairs, the party had spread throughout the entire barn, even into the apartment. One girl was on the pool table, one man under her, one on top of her and one standing in front of her. Oscar had a young woman on the trunk of the Cadillac, naked and legs spread wide, she was alternating between screaming, "YOU'RE KILLING ME", to, "FUCK ME HARDER!" She would bleed and hurt for a week and have no recollection of why nor what had happened. The assassin had never witnessed anything such as this, and he'd seen a lot.

11

Around 3AM people began leaving, drunk men helping drunk, stoned or drugged, maybe a combination of, women into the cars.

The assassin had witnessed things taking place he had never imagined; he knew then that much of what he'd seen had taken place with his sweet Sara while she had been incapacitated by a mind gone into self-preservation mode. When he saw Oscar use the large end of a cue stick on one young woman who was so stoned she was begging for more, he remembered the broom handle, now he knew who had used it.

Oscar Tomlinson was short for this world.

* * *

Robert arrived at the motel before dawn, he quickly showered and went directly to sleep, he would sleep until noon.

Waking, Robert brushed his teeth, got dressed and went directly to the motel office. Anne greeted him with a smile, "Hello Mister Sleepy Head! Out late?"

Robert smiled and asked, "Wouldn't have any of that good coffee, would you?"

"Put on a fresh pot as soon as I saw you come from your room, it'll be ready in a minute or two. Get any good shots last night?"

"Got some I hope turn out well, took them at several different exposures, different lenses. One I think will be especially good."

"So. Where you off to today?"

"Thought I'd take in the business district of your town and concentrate on the local architecture."

"Try just outside the business district, if you can call a town this small having a business district, some of the homes are over a hundred years old, many are absolutely gorgeous."

"Will do, thanks for the tip."

"Given any more thought to how long you'll be staying with us?"

"I'll be here through tomorrow night and check out early day after tomorrow."

"You know, I think I might call Maria in tomorrow afternoon and ask her to fill in for a while. I'm sure she can use the extra hours."

"I think that would be a very good idea."

Anne looked around and saw nobody where they could see, she reached across the counter and pulled "Robert" to her. They kissed, she giggled and asked, "1 o'clock tomorrow afternoon?"

"See you then."

Both would enjoy a replay they never thought possible. The memory would last their entire lives.

***

Two weeks later the assassin would again be close, staying at a dump in the next town, driving a rental car. Beard shaven, wearing a wig, hopefully this would be the last recon. He wished he could have stayed at South Creek, but the risk was simply too high.

The last recon had been filled with valuable information. Oscar liked to party and it had been on a Saturday night. Having a hunch the man liked to party so much, this might be a weekly event. This recon would also take place on a Saturday.

The assassin was in his hide earlier than last time. At 5 PM he saw the same young woman carrying a small suitcase to the same car he'd seen leave on his first recon. Going back into the house momentarily she came out holding a toddler, got in the car and left. Same as last time. Craig thought, Oscar must make her go somewhere else on Saturday nights so he can entertain his friends.

Oscar again was alone for a while, he set up the bar, poured a drink, and turned on the TV. A man of habit.

The killer had brought along one of the specialty items he'd found in one of the gun safes, a range finder. The device could accurately measure distances up to 1000 yards, he figured the techs had played with it, possibly built it. Right on time, Oscar stepped out of the party barn to pee. The distance, according to the device, was 899.25 feet. Three hundred yards, close enough.

Close to 7 PM, cars began arriving, same men, many of the same women, a few new ones. After one hour the assassin had seen enough to know this would be the same as last time, he whispered, "See you soon Oscar", and slipped from the woods.

***

Weeks passed, the 4th of July came around and Gary enjoyed plenty of fine Barbeque with the good people of Lexington Virginia. He had made many new friends in the area. The little league was helped with new equipment thanks to the well to do young man, he tithed each week to the church and attended many church socials. Gary had met several lovely women his age and dated a few, he always made sure they knew he was a confirmed bachelor, most understood, some were one date only,

those were the ones looking for a husband. A couple had stayed over for breakfast. It was a good life.

July became August. On Wednesday of the first week of August Gary loaded his truck for a trip. This time, hidden in a secret compartment, was the Winchester Model 70 he had carried in Viet Nam. Having shot the rifle as many times as he had it was almost an extension of himself, he knew it, it seemed to know him.

* * *

From the time the trigger is squeezed many things happen in a certain sequence which all must happen in order that a bullet can successfully leave the barrel of the weapon from which it is fired.

Squeezing the trigger releases the spring-loaded firing pin mechanism, driving the pin toward the primer at the rear of the cartridge. The primer ignites within the cartridge with a small explosion, this in turn ignites the propellant, gun powder. If the brass cartridge was not located snuggly within the steel housing of the weapons breech it would simply split open, the brass alone could not contain the pressures involved. Not being able to move rearward because of the locked bolt behind the cartridge, nor being able to expand because of being surrounded by the steel breech, the only direction the pressures of the explosion can travel are forward, toward the weakest link of the assembly, where the bullet has been pressed into the brass cartridge. The bullet is violently blasted from the cartridge. Once the bullet leaves the cartridge and enters the barrel it begins spinning, this caused by rifling, grooves machined into the inner wall of the barrel. In the case of the 30.06 caliber, for each 10 inches the bullet travels inside the barrel it is spun 360 degrees. The spinning of the bullet creates much better accuracy than if not spinning.

From the instant the 165 grain boat tail bullet left the muzzle of the barrel at 2800 feet per second many things begin to affect it. Gravity, air friction, wind and at some point, bullet drift caused by its own spinning. Gravity pulling downward causing the bullet to drop, lose altitude. Air friction slowing the bullet's speed. Wind moving the bullet to one side or another depending on wind direction. Drift caused by spin, at 300 yards this is minimal but considered, not forgotten. All must be taken into consideration and equated in order to make a successful shot.

At 300 yards the 165 grain hand loaded boat tail 30.06 bullet drop is 13.38 inches and would slow to 2218 feet per second, spin drift approximately ¼ inch to the right, Any effect by the wind would require an EWAG (Educated Wild Ass Guess). The bullet would travel 300 yards from muzzle to target in 0.36 of a second.

***

The assassin carried 5 handloaded 30.06 rounds of ammunition, he hoped to use only one. There was no handgun, only the Model 70 Winchester. He had no desire to get into a gunfight with anyone if anything went awry in his mission. There was one target and one only, nobody else would be harmed.

In his hide at approximately 4 PM, rifle loaded, he waited, hoping this Saturday would again be party night. It would be.

On time at 5 PM the young woman loaded the suitcase and toddler into the car and drove away. Oscar went through his pre-party routine.

At 5:20 PM Oscar stepped outside and relieved himself, walked back to the open doors of the barn, stopped and stretched, he had 0.36 of a second to live.

***

The projectile struck the back of the skull slightly to the right of where the left and right parietal bones met and approximately 1 ¼ inch above the juncture of the parietal bones with the occipital bone. Hair, skin and connecting tissues were hardly any resistance and were easily penetrated. The skull resisted, but lacked the structural integrity to stop the 165 grain bullet, although the resistance did have the effect of misshaping, slightly mushrooming, the soft lead and its brass jacket, parts of the penetrated skull would also have the effect of small shrapnel and would enhance damage within the skull. Cerebrospinal fluid which cushions the brain instantly began leaking, then expanding, vaporizing. The projectile continued its path into and through the brain, moving faster than tissue could tear, simply pushing it violently aside. The projectile met further resistance at the front of the skull, this time from within as it struck the intersection of the nasal bone, upper maxilla, ethmoid bone and the glabella. The projectile exited the head at the inside corner of the right eye, where it met the nose. Everything it met made of bone shattered like glass under a hammer, the right eyeball deflated, other smaller facial bones were broken. None of this killed Oscar.

What killed Oscar was the creation of what could only be described as an earthquake taking place within the confines of his skull. Tissues pushed apart attempted to rejoin but were moving too fast and overshot one another, this set off a rippling effect, back and forth, back and forth, increasing in violence, this action combined with the expanding of liquids in the skull were more than the already fractured bone structure could stand. It burst!

First hit in the back of the head, Oscars head moved forward, slightly. Once everything exploded within his skull, the weakest area of the head effected by the projectile, the face, exploded outward, forced outward by the jet of brain matter, cerebrospinal fluid, blood, even snot from his sinuses. This jet forced the head backward, violently.

17

Oscar William Tomlinson fell. He hit the ground on his back, arms spread, he never moved.

Oscar William Tomlinson was as dead as any man could ever be. Dead from a bullet, fired from a weapon he never heard.

***

7 PM, the first car arrived at Oscar's Party Barn.

The young woman opened the door of the car and ran to the barn.

She screamed.

Oscar lay on his back, the upper right side of his face completely gone. Oscar's left eye was on his left cheek, held there by sinew and what was left of the muscles that move the eyeball, his nose was flopped over into the left eye socket.

There would be no orgy at Oscars Place tonight.

His funeral would be closed casket.

The man had died exactly eight years from the date of the assault of Sara Blackmon.

***

Two months later two things happened.

Sandy Tomlinson and her baby had moved into her parent's home. An attorney knocked on the door. It seemed there was an anonymous benefactor who had set up funds in trust which would care for Sandy and her baby. Sandy cried tears of thanks.

***

Gary received a letter in the mail.

Dear Gary

I have recently learned of your successful venture. Congratulations on a job well done.

Dyke

CHAPTER

2

The little boy approached his mother, "Mom, I'm in love."

"Oh really, Craig? Who are you in love with?"

"She's beautiful."

"I'll bet she is, but who is she?"

"I don't know her yet."

"That's interesting. How do you know you love someone you never met?"

"Because I watched all the grownups yesterday."

The day before had been the annual Fourth of July family celebration. Always a big event, all Craig's uncles, Aunts, Cousins, his Grandparents, the whole family always got together on July 4th.

Minnie knelt to her son's level, "Craig, I don't understand. What do the grownups have to do with you being in love with someone you never met?"

"Did Papa know Mama when he was a little boy?"

"No."

"Did you know Daddy when you were a little girl?"

"No, we met in high school."

"Aunt Sally, has she always known Uncle Wilbur?"

"No, they met when he came here to work."

"How about all the other grownups? Did they know the people they're married to now when they were like me? Little?"

"As far as I know, no, they didn't."

"But they all knew something.'

"And, what is it they all knew?"

"That they would fall in love. They just didn't know who they were."

The little boy had always been a thinker, now Minnie was beginning to, somewhat, understand what it was her son was trying to convey.

"I guess they did. I knew someday I would fall in love."

"So, you knew you would fall in love with Daddy?"

"I knew I would someday fall in love with someone and have a child, he would be your Daddy. At least I hoped I would."

"See? Now you understand."

"Son, I'm not exactly sure I do understand."

"Well, I've already fallen in love, I just don't know who she is. I just know she will be beautiful and I will always love her."

"Craig, you are telling me you are in love with someone you will someday meet?"

"Yes Ma'am."

"Son, that might be the most beautiful thing I've ever heard." Tears formed in Minnie's eyes.

"Mom, did I make you sad."

"No, son, you made me very happy."

Abruptly, as children will do, the little boy changed the subject.

"Mom, the green apples on the tree are big enough to eat. May I take the old salt shaker with me and play under the apple tree?"

"Yes, baby, go play. Don't eat too many apples."

Craig went to play as Minnie went back to doing the ironing on the screened in back porch. She watched her son and was in wonder at how the child thought. Minnie looked forward to someday meeting the beautiful girl her son was in love with, whom he'd not yet met.

***

Howard Craig Kirkland was born in April 1946, his fath hard-working construction man, his mother, the daught coal miner. First name the same as his father, middl friend of the family, he was called Craig in order confusion of two Howards in the same hous never very healthy, he seemed to always intestinal issues and suffered from c he was a skinny little boy with a k

Craig's grandparents lived two doors up the street, he would spend many hours with them. Always an early riser, by the time he was three Craig would wake many mornings before anyone else, tuck his teddy bear under his arm, sneak out of the house and walk to his grandparents' home. The neighbors had learned the little boy's routine and watched after him on his early morning stroll. Jesse, Craig's grandfather, could be found sitting at the kitchen table enjoying his coffee. In that time coffee would be served into a cup sitting on a saucer, Jesse would pour his morning brew from the percolator on the stove, mix in just the correct amount of sugar and milk then pour some of the coffee from the cup onto the saucer, cool it by blowing across the liquid, he would tip the saucer to his lips and sip. When Craig would arrive Jesse would take a cup and saucer from the cupboard, pour a liberal amount of milk, mix in plenty of sugar then add a small portion of coffee, the little boy would then imitate his grandfather. Papa and grandson would share fine conversations as they drank their coffee.

From the time he could open the door Craig would listen for his father to arrive home from work. The instant he heard the car turn into the driveway Craig would stop anything he was doing and rush outside and ... h a hug and kiss. Craig
lo... ..., a lot. Drinking coffee
... g his Daddy in the
... ne of his most

... e older sisters. A few
... and her sisters might
... se occasions all the
... regated at the old
... well-worn Baptist
... e rack above the
... me running and
... he sisters would

... r a
... er of a
... name from a
... o avoid the
... As a child Craig was
... have stomach or
... viruses more than most,
... d disposition and sweet smile.

21

pick him up and sit him atop that old upright piano. He loved those special occasions and knew the lyrics to all the old songs; it was his most special of times. Years later, halfway around the world, the memory of those hymns would come back to him.

By his 4th year Craig found a new joy, the solitude of playing under one of the apple trees in his parent's back yard. He would take his toy cars, a garden hoe to use in making roads in the dirt, often his little plastic army men and always, always, comic books and a shaker of salt for those delicious green apples. Craig would spend many hours reading, playing, contemplating life and eating green apples in the shade of an apple tree. It was during his times under the apple tree that Craig began giving thought to his parents, his aunts and uncles, even a few of his older cousins, he came to realize they all had partners they loved and who loved them as well, and he also fell in love. Craig fell in love with a girl he didn't know, nor had ever seen, he simply knew he would someday meet the girl he was already in love with and she would be pretty. Eleven years later Craig would see her at a party, the next year he would meet her.

The Christmas Season of 1954 brought Craig two gifts which would forever shape his future, a BB gun and a Best Friend. A new couple moved into the neighborhood. The Jacksons had a son, Charles, who was so much like Craig it was remarkable. The two boys instantly hit it off and would become so close it was as if they were brothers. For the next several years, as their bond grew, the two boys would be almost inseparable. Craig and Charles would share their most intimate thoughts with one another, they would expand the areas of exploration outside the neighborhood. The boys would both come to love target shooting, books and the outdoors. A few miles from home were large areas of forests Craig and Charles would spend countless hours exploring and learning the ways of the woods. Both boys would learn how to stalk, and the patience involved in becoming a part of the surroundings. They could sit for hours moving nothing but

their eyes as animals would come so close they could have taken them with one quick grab.

Charles got a BB gun on his birthday after Craig had gotten his for Christmas. The boys, together, would shoot thousands of BB's at cans and paper targets. It became something very amazing to watch as they became proficient with those BB guns. By the time they were 10 years old both had advanced to .22 rifles. As good as Charles became as a shooter he was never quite as good as Craig, who could regularly hit a match stick at 50 yards, with open sights, no scope! At the time Craig had eyes like an eagle, the patience of Job and could sit motionless for hours, the marksmanship ability of someone with years of professional training. All this by his 11th year. Charles admired his best friend's abilities and worked hard to do the same things; he could just never quite seem to be up to the same standard. There was no jealousy, Craig would try to help Charles, but some things just are natural to some people while not natural to others. Charles appreciated the help and loved that his friend could do the things he could do. Charles returned the favor by tutoring Craig with his classwork. Neither boy could realize what was taking place at the time were skills that, in just a few short years, would carry them both in different directions. Charles academic skills would carry him to pursue law and engineering, he would earn degrees in both. Craig's skills would be used in a much more violent way.

It was another day of exploring the forests in the Summer of 1958 that Craig would discover something he'd never seen. Sitting against a tree, practicing and refining his ability to remain completely motionless, he was also learning to control his respiration and heartrate, Craig would notice, on the side of a hill, a bush that seemed very peculiar. Staring at the bush, studying it for over an hour he suddenly realized it wasn't the bush that was out of place, but the area immediately behind it, a cave. Blended into the hillside, camouflaged by the bush was an old mine entrance that had not been sealed as all the others he and Charles had discovered in their many hours of exploration. This opened an entirely new chapter of things to explore and learn. Craig went to tell Charles of his new discovery.

Craig had been practicing his tracking skills and self-teaching himself how to silently move through the woods. Charles was usually the victim of these practice sessions and more than once Craig had come up behind Charles and frightened him. From books Craig had learned when walking as quietly as possible a person shouldn't walk heel-toe but rather should very slowly reach the next step and put the toe of the foot down first, then ease body weight onto the foot, repeating the next step the same way. By observation he had also learned to be aware of everything around in order to successfully "track" that which he was following, a broken twig, a green leaf knocked off a bush and laying on the brown leaves, a little deeper indention in the forest floor, all the things that might be out of place, disturbed by something, or someone who had been moving in the woods. Using all these things he had practiced so diligently, Craig spotted Charles leaning with his back to a tree. Charles never knew Craig was anywhere close until he was grabbed by his ear. Charles almost fainted.

Once the laughter and boyish grab-assing had subsided Craig told Charles to come with him, he had a surprise to show him.

25

They arrived at the mine entrance and both became very excited at this new development. Taking a few steps inside, it became quickly obvious they needed light. The boys would return the next day with two lights each, extra batteries, a rope and overwhelming curiosity of what might be waiting to be discovered in the damp, dark hole. Charles academic mind would think to bring along a pencil and pad with which to make a map.

Charles would keep his maps among his most cherished childhood mementos. The old shoebox would be filled with wonderful memories of his and Craig's times together, of times he and his "brother" had done so much exploring. Neither boy could possibly know how important the maps would be many years later.

By the time the boys were thirteen they had both become healthier, although still too skinny for their heights. Perhaps it had been all the time outdoors, maybe the support of one another had caused the improvement. Charles was on crutches and had a cast on his leg, the result of a bicycle mishap, his exploration ability was severely limited, so the boys sat many hours under the old apple trees, talking and just being together, eating those delicious green apples. It was during one of those visits that Charles came up with the idea of a secret code, something each would instantly know if the other ever needed help, or to simply identify one to the other without anyone else knowing. They bounced around different words for a while, "green apple", "grey roof", etc. They were drinking their favorite soft drinks, Craig picked up the bottle and looked at the label, there were numbers on the label, 10-2-4. Many years later Charles would receive a letter, the opening page would read only three words, TEN-TWO-FOUR.

Charles' leg healed and over the next year the boys would visit the old mine many times, each time going deeper into the tunnels, discovering many intersections with other tunnels,

Charles would pace off distances and was creating a very remarkable map, especially for a boy of only thirteen years old and would often sneak into his Dad's office to make updated copies on the copying machine. Charles always saw to it that Craig had a fresh copy of the map. What Charles didn't know, while his leg had been healing, was that Craig had been making several solo trips into the mine and had discovered, behind some abandoned machinery, an opening leading into another tunnel which was cut off from the rest of the mine except for that one opening. Craig would keep his discovery a secret.

As happens with all children, usually in their early teens, some possibly younger, nature brings the age of puberty. Boys voices deepen, hair begins to appear where there was none, some boys begin to develop a more muscular physique and, boys begin to take note of the opposite gender and how they are changing, Craig and Charles were no different, except neither boy's body's seemed to be keeping up with the physiques of others their age, they both remained skinny. By Craig's fourteenth birthday, while target shooting one morning, he noticed everything at a distance seemed just a little out of focus. A trip to the local optometrist found him to be mildly nearsighted, a prescription was ordered, Craig became the owner of black plastic framed glasses. Those glasses combined with his skinny, lanky build caused Craig to have the appearance of the ultimate geek, he was anything other than a geek, the girls seemed to just give him passive looks and move on to any better-looking boy who would show them attention. This isn't to say Craig didn't have friends, he was a nice boy, well-mannered and had many friends, his next best friend was the girlfriend of a buddy, Cindy was a cheerleader, popular, she and Craig spent many hours just talking, being friends, he had even taught Cindy to shoot.

Charles was the lucky one who, by his fifteenth birthday, had begun to fill out and was becoming very handsome, his personality had changed along with his appearance, Charles

became very outgoing and popular. Most friends would have been jealous, but Craig was very happy for his best friend's newfound popularity, although they spent less time together. Craig missed not seeing his friend as often as he had. But Craig still had the forests and the mine to explore and perfect even more his already incredible woodsmanship skills. For some reason the mine continued to tug at his curiosity, as if to plan for something.

As Charles became more handsome, Craig was dealt the ultimate insult, braces on his teeth at the age of fifteen. Already somewhat timid, the braces drove him further into the forests. Craig had a few dates, usually set up by Cindy or Charles, but nothing ever lasted more than two dates.

The Summer of 1961 Craig would attend a party, he would see the most beautiful girl he'd ever seen. The girl had no idea Craig existed; he never spoke to her that night. He would remember her, vividly.

Almost exactly one year later, Craig would fall in love.

Sara Imogene Blackmon was born in June 1947 on a Military Base in Alabama. She was a tiny baby, just over 4 pounds, not premature, simply a tiny, beautiful baby girl. She would always be small, and beautiful.

Out of high school in 1943 Sara's father enlisted in the military. America was at war, James Leon Blackmon wanted to do his part. Having survived polio early in his life had left James with a leg that was less than perfect, he struggled through basic training but passed. It was obvious that he would never be up to the physical requirements for combat but could still be very useful to the military, James had a brilliant mind that more than made up for his bad leg. Following the war there was much work to be done, the world had been torn apart, it required being put back together. Although he could have taken his discharge James was asked to reenlist, he accepted.

Through his time in the military James had stayed in touch with a hometown girl two years younger than himself, he had managed twice to see her while home on leave and they corresponded weekly. They were in love and in one of his letters James asked her to marry him, Cynthia Leigh Johnson accepted. The wedding would take place in January 1946, six months following the proposal letter. Knowing how badly Cynthia would be wishing for an engagement ring, James planned a surprise. A ring was mailed to his younger brother Gerald who would perform a proper proposal, standing in for James. It came as a total surprise to Cynthia the following week during church services

when Gerald stood and asked the minister, who had been informed what would take place, to allow him just a moment with one of the other parishioners. Request granted, Gerald came forward, took Cynthia by the hand and led her to the front of the congregation where he dropped to one knee and asked, "Cynthia Leigh Johnson, would you honor us, the Blackmon family, by accepting our request that you marry my brother James?" Cynthia said "Yes!" As she cried, the congregation cried, the minister smiled, as Gerald placed the engagement ring on Cynthia's finger.

The wedding was small with immediate family and very close friends attending. James had only a three-day leave, the wedding night and night after were spent at a small cabin located in a nearby state park. James caught a bus the morning of the third day and reported back to duty. Cynthia arranged to move into a small apartment just off the base. Sara would be born seventeen months after the wedding.

James, wanting to get on with the life of a family man, and further his education, requested and was approved for discharge. James Leon Blackmon received his honorable discharge in April of 1948. Life wasn't easy for James and Cynthia, James worked part time for a trucking company while also attending college classes, Cynthia worked part time wherever extra help was needed. The addition of another baby girl in 1950 was welcome, but made paying bills even harder, somehow, they managed. A son would arrive two years later, he would be given James name. Six years after James Junior, another son would be born. It would take James five years to graduate with a college degree, he took a job as a high school teacher, teaching his passion, history, at a high school in Anniston, Alabama. Cynthia applied for a job at the same high school, she got the job and would perform clerical work in the office. James began taking correspondence classes, attended classes in the Summer and earned his Master's Degree in 1962. The man had worked hard, but finally, with all the effort, he was earning a decent living.

Cynthia, as it would reveal itself a few years later, had a mean side to herself, a side James would be too cowardly to confront.

James loved the beach and he swore to himself that the first Summer after he was finished with school, he would take the family to his favorite place, Tybee Island. That year was 1963. What would happen on that vacation would devastate several lives, futures of many would change.

***

Sara was born small and would remain so all her life. Smaller than all the other kids at the school bus stop, by the time she was entering the second grade the other kids had given her a nickname, "Shrimp", a common nickname of the time, often used to describe those smaller than other people of the same age group.

When all the other girls were just beginning to develop Sara was entering that stage in life when a young person's teeth seem the biggest part of their face. Small, skinny and with big teeth and no breast to speak of she was teased unmercifully, especially when her sister, three years younger, had begun developing and was being noticed by boys. But she was smart, smarter than most.

By the time Sara was four years old she could read very well. Very well was not good enough for her mother, if Sara missed a word her mother, Cynthia, would slap her and call her "stupid". Sara would cry and apologize, promising to do better. James, being a coward, would remain quiet and allow the abuse to continue.

It was during her 5th and 6th grade years that Sara became what one might describe as "homely", most children go through such a period in their lives, and when it happens classmates as well as some adults can be very cruel. While her sister was being doted over by almost everyone, Sara was called "ugly", the worst

pain was when she heard It from her mother. Through all the abuse, the jokes about her appearance, self-esteem very low, Sara would go through most of her life never thinking she was pretty, she would be so very wrong.

During the Summer of 1960 Sara turned 13 years of age. It was during that Summer her entire body began to change, her face changed, her hair seemed to become fuller instead of the limp blonde mass that had previously grown from her head. Sara's body was being introduced to the hormones it had begun producing, she was very slowly being transformed, breasts began to develop, her hips began to widen, buttocks became rounder, face filled out perfectly, making her teeth seem not too big, Sara Imogene Blackmon was becoming a very beautiful young woman, because of her very low self-esteem she would never accept how very beautiful she was and would always be. No matter how many times people would complement her, Sara always thought of herself as being homely.

Other changes were taking place in Sara, with the introduction of hormones her interest in reading material changed and she would often sneak away to read her aunt's romance novels and risqué magazines, gone were the little girl fairy tale books. Sara began noticing boys in an entirely different manner, thoughts of childhood games hide and seek, tag and playing marbles with the boys were gradually being replaced with desires of a different nature. Sara was beginning to wonder how it would feel to kiss a boy.

Her friend was two years older and had become a girl with a "reputation", Sara had been told she wasn't to hang out with her, something she would disobey. Visiting her friend when she could the two talked, mostly about boys and Sara confided she had never kissed a boy, her friend agreed to help change that. Two days later her friend called, asked if Sara could drop by around noon for a surprise. Sara knocked on the door and was invited in,

32

she was introduced to two nice looking boys, one of which was her friend's boyfriend for the day, the other, Ricky, had come along to keep Sara company. The girl and her boyfriend went into the bedroom and it wasn't long until sounds Sara had read about in her aunt's books began to be heard, the effect on her was something she had never experienced, Sara was getting turned on. Sitting next to Ricky they both looked at one another, he was grinning, she was breathing more rapidly than normal, they kissed. For the next hour Sara awkwardly enjoyed her first "make out session", kissing, necking, she liked it!

Sara had, thankfully, inherited her father's intellect, her mother never having been very bright. Although not being of high intelligence Cynthia could be cagey and learned a different tactic following having slapped Sara so hard one afternoon it drew blood and caused swelling in the bottom lip. Cynthia found a new use for hairbrushes and would often hit Sara and her sister on the head, never hard enough to bring blood, but the hair hid the bruises, and using the brushes saved harm to the user's hands.

James knew the abuse to both girls was taking place, he never stepped in, never had the courage to confront Cynthia. James' mother knew what was going on and threatened to say something to her daughter in law, she was told, by James, "leave it alone or it'll just get worse". It wasn't long after that James's father suffered a fatal heart attack.

Imogene Blackmon, Sara's grandmother, had never liked living in Alabama, she missed her childhood home of Knoxville, Tennessee. Not long after the death of her husband, Imogene set to the task of selling her home, purchasing a new place just outside the city she loved most. Imogene, with her daughter, returned to Knoxville.

By her 14th Birthday Sara had become what some boys would define as a "Little Knockout", they stopped calling her names, the transformation had been amazing. A local boy named Randall

took notice and began flirting with Sara at the skating rink, Randall had his driver's license, but Sara wasn't allowed to car date until she was 15. She could, however, invite Randall to visit her at home one night of the weekend and bring her home from Sunday night church services, stopping for a soft drink or ice cream. Taking advantage of the extra few minutes they were allowed for refreshment, a couple of times they would skip it and use the time to stop in a secluded area and neck.

By now the transformation was almost complete. Petite, standing at five feet, from the back Sara had the most well rounded buttocks in school and legs that would take any male person's breath, she was "pear" shaped but with the broad end of the pear not being overly wide, just right. From her front her breasts were not very large, high on the end of a "B" cup, perky and still growing (those breasts would become a firm "C" cup by the time she became 15). But it was her face that stood out, the most perfectly shaped dazzling green eyes, perfect cheeks, perfect nose and a smile that would make the darkest day seem bright.

July 1961, Sara would attend a party at a friend of her best friend's home. Sometime during the evening someone would say something that struck Sara as very funny, she would laugh. Across the room a 15-year-old boy was talking to his friends when he heard laughter, looking to see who it was he saw the most beautiful girl he had ever seen.

Not long after the Summer of 1961 Randall stopped seeing Sara, she would never allow more than kissing and necking. Randall wanted more than Sara was willing to give, he moved on.

The following year Sara would meet a boy who was very nice. That boy would almost instantly fall in love with her.

CHAPTER

4

The Summer following Craig's fifteenth birthday was spent as he had spent most of the previous summers, in the forests, in the mine, sometimes, not often, hanging out at the local swimming pool, there was really nothing different other than he was doing most of these things alone instead of having Charles with him very often. Charles new good looks and popularity was keeping him occupied with the young ladies. Of course, there was also target shooting, Craig could never get enough of shooting his .22 and had progressed to throwing bottle caps into the air, hitting them nine out of ten times. Timid, skinny, horned rim black plastic glasses and braces caused Craig to keep to himself a lot.

Charles' parents had recently purchased a Cushman Super Eagle and presented it to their son, scooting all about town he was a sight to behold, often with a girl on the back sitting on the throw pillows he'd taken from his mother's sofa. Charles was living the dream, but he had not forgotten his best friend and would drop by to visit. It was on one of those visits that Charles told Craig about the party and suggested they go check it out.

Joe was a classmate and would occasionally invite a few friends over to his home where he would set up one of those silly parties that teens coming of age enjoyed attending. Supposedly a social event where the record player was always too loud, it never failed that someone would always suggest a game of spin the bottle, girls would usually attend with one of their girlfriends and boys would show up to check out the girls. As was normal, word always spread about a party and more people would show up

36

who hadn't been invited than those who had. Craig had attended a few such parties and usually stood to the back of the room or just outside and did what he did best, he quietly observed. The parties were pretty much always the same, those invited would arrive, later the older guys who were driving would show up in their cars with loud exhausts, some of the older guys had girls with them, others showed up to prey on the some of the younger girls who were infatuated with guys with cars, as the night would progress a few of those girls would spend time in the back seats of a few of those cars. As usually happened a couple of boys who had a beef with one another would show up and there would be a fight in the yard, if you could call it a fight, usually chest bumping or wrestling, occasionally a good punch would land and the fight would end. Girls would sometimes dance with their girlfriends, most guys thought it too cool to dance, honestly most just didn't know how. Craig could have written the script to one of Joe's parties, they were all the same.

So it was that Charles told Craig about another party scheduled for Saturday night at Joe's and suggested they drop in, Craig was reluctant but finally agreed.

Saturday rolled around. Joe lived a mile from Craig's home, he and Charles walked to the party. Cindy was there and greeted the boys with a hug. Charles always loved the parties and having developed an outgoing personality walked on in and began his usual socializing, especially with the girls. Craig chatted with Cindy a few minutes then found himself a place he could remain unobtrusive and observe. Everything began happening pretty much on schedule, other people began arriving, the sound of loud automobile exhausts indicated the older boys had arrived as they parked in front of the house and gunned their engines, the music volume increased, the bottle began being spun, girls began to dance. The script was being followed perfectly.

Jean lived next door to Joe, she and Craig had met a couple of times, they'd chatted but didn't really know much about one another. On this night Jean's best friend, Sara, was sleeping over at Jean's home. Sara loved Jean's mother who treated her as another daughter, always sweet and kind, something Sara never experienced from her own mother, she always enjoyed being invited to stay over. Jean had been invited to the party, she brought Sara. Sara's boyfriend, Randall, would also be dropping by sometime later, the two would slip out to his car for a few minutes of necking. As always, she would slap his hands several times when they attempted to touch things not to be touched.

As the room became more crowded Craig would move in order to have a different perspective from which to observe. It was just after one of his moves that he heard a laugh, a girl's laughter. Leaning to his left Craig spotted where the laughter was coming from. Sitting on a stool next to Jean was a girl whose laughter was the sweetest sound Craig had ever heard, she had the most perfect face he'd ever seen. It was as if his mind became a camera and his eyes the lenses, his brain snapped a photo of the girl. Craig asked the boy next to him who she was, "Blackmon", is all he said. "First name?" The response was "Sara, she's got a boyfriend". By her having a boyfriend Craig decided it would be better if he not bother introducing himself, as badly as he wanted to.

At the age of 15 years, Craig Kirkland first saw 14-year-old Sara Imogene Blackmon. She was the most beautiful girl he'd ever seen.

**

Absolutely amazing how rapidly changes take place with a person in their teens. About half way into his 15th year Craig began gaining weight and grew to his full height of six feet. His weight had gone from 135 pounds to around 150, still too thin,

but not as bad. Craig's face filled out and he became somewhat handsome. Craig would never be the best-looking boy, he was more handsome than many, above average. The braces and black framed glasses still gave him a geekish appearance, he was self-conscience and still somewhat timid, but a few of the girls began taking note of him, it was nice.

As nice as the attention Craig was beginning to receive from the opposite gender, the mere thought of Sara Blackmon would open the camera of his mind and he would see her as if looking at a photograph. Each time his memory brought the sight of her back to him, Craig would smile. Although he wished her no bad luck, he hoped someday, when she might not have a boyfriend, he would have opportunity to meet her.

By this time Craig's father's boss had decided to retire and sold the business to Howard Kirkland. Timing couldn't have been better, the economy good, commercial construction was booming, Howard's business was growing and doing very well. A new subdivision had opened not far away, still in the same school district, Howard moved his family into a nicer, larger home.

Having gained the attention of a few girls, along with his friend Cindy always trying to arrange dates for him, Craig realized he required the funds needed to treat a girl to a nice night out he approached the owner of a local gas station for a job and was rewarded to his first real employment other than the few lawns he would continue to mow twice a month. Although not driving yet, most girls didn't mind riding the bus to the movies, usually walking to a soda shop afterward. A couple of times Craig and his date would go out with Cindy and her boyfriend, her current boyfriend being old enough to drive. It was a fun time for Craig, but he could never get serious about any of the few girls he dated and rarely dated the same girl more than a time or two, he couldn't get serious because of the memory of Sara Blackmon.

The next April 18th, Howard Craig Kirkland became 16 years of age, he took the driver's test and received his license, a good day which would get better following the birthday celebration that same evening. Following dinner and cake Howard presented his son with a set of keys, Howard grinned and pointed to the front door. Outside a pretty, white, two door, hardtop "58" Chevy was just pulling to a stop in front of the house. The doors to the car opened, the still 15-year-old Charles was driving, Charles parents were with him. "Hey Brother! This is as far as they would let me drive it but", he teased, "at least I drove it before you did!" Laughter filled the night, Craig hugged and thanked his parents, he hugged Charles' parents, then he hugged Charles. "We gotta go cruise man" Charles said, then stopped, looked at the four adults and humbly asked "we can go cruisin', can't we?" All the adults looked at one another, Howard said, "If you get a ticket, bring me the keys. Be very careful, be home by 10." The two best friends, "brothers", as they had so many times before in their lives, again experienced another first adventure together, the boys went cruisin'!

Having transportation opened an entirely new world to Craig, no longer would he be riding the school bus, he could run errands for his mother, go cruising and no longer had to catch the city bus to the library where he'd spent so many hours reading books on shooting and survival. Having a car also helped Craig become more popular with the girls, some of whom he took to the local lovers lane where he learned the art of making out, a few girls encouraged him to learn more about the female anatomy although none wanted to go further than petting and necking, he was learning many nice new things.

Cindy had given up on her older guy and was dating a boy her age who wasn't yet old enough to drive, she would arrange dates for Craig, so she and her guy would have transportation. Many Saturday evenings Cindy and her boyfriend, Craig and some

40

girl Cindy had set him up with, would double date. Craig jokingly began referring to Cindy as his Dating Service.

The automobile also allowed Craig the opportunity to expand his search for new forests to explore and practice his skills of observation and woodsmanship in varying terrains. As much as he enjoyed the new areas he was visiting Craig would still return to the old mine, it was almost as if he were drawn to it, compelled to learn more about it, he didn't understand why. The reason would be revealed to him some years later.

The end of his sophomore year of high school, his first Summer with his own transportation, Craig was living the dream. His schedule, although hectic with working at the gas station, mowing a few lawns, still allowed time to enjoy being a teenager. One of the things Craig found himself doing was driving to the local swimming pool where he would park and hang out with several other people at a shaded area just off the parking lot, Cindy would often come out of the pool area and sit with him, sometimes they would drive to the store for a soda. Cindy would also line up a date for Craig. Anytime she would come sit with him he would always tease her and ask, "Who has my Dating Service got me a date with this week?" The two would laugh with Cindy usually responding, "Now that you mention it!"

Craig had a day off and decided to go hang out at the pool, Cindy was there and came out to sit with him. As the two were talking Craig looked toward the pool and spotted the girl he'd seen the year before at Joe's party. This was the first time Craig had seen her standing and was in awe at how gorgeous she was in her swimsuit. Cindy was talking when Craig abruptly interrupted her and while pointing, he asked, "Do you know that girl?"

Cindy was startled by Craig's reaction and asked, "Which one?"

Pointing again he answered, "The short blonde walking away from us with the terrific butt!"

Giggling, Cindy replied, "That's Blackmon, she's a sweet girl."

"She got a boyfriend?"

"I don't think so."

"Think you can get me a date with her?"

Cindy laughed, "I can go see!"

Leaving the car and giggling at Craig's sudden interest in one particular girl, something she'd never seen him do, Cindy went to talk to Sara Blackmon. Craig, trying to be as nonchalant as possible, watched as the two girls talked, and Cindy pointing toward his car. The girls moved inside where Craig couldn't see them, then Cindy came out of the girls dressing room with something in her hand. Returning to the car Cindy presented Craig a piece of paper with a phone number, "She said she would like for you to call her around 6 this evening if you want a date with her." Craig was highly impressed!! Not only was this girl beautiful, she also had class!

He didn't eat much that evening at dinner, much too excited about the phone call he would be making to the girl whose picture lived in his memory. Just before 6 PM Craig's mother called her sister, these conversations could often last a long time, all Craig could think was that his chance for a date with Sara Blackmon might end in disaster. Around 6:20, following much looking at his watch and signaling he really wanted to use the phone, Minnie Kirkland told her sister "I think Craig has lost his mind, he keeps looking at his watch, pointing at the phone and acting weird!" Craig's favorite, and very astute, aunt replied to his mother "Minnie, he's a good-looking boy and he is either expecting a call from a girl or he wants to call one. Now let him have the phone, we'll talk later!"

He was sweating when he dialed the number. "What in the world is a geeky looking boy like me supposed to say to the most beautiful girl I've ever seen?" On the third ring someone on the other end picked up.

"Hello", a lady's voice.

"Uh, may I speak to Sara?"

"Who is calling"

Thinking she'd told her mother she wouldn't be talking to anyone who was not punctual enough to call on time, Craig's heart began to sink.

"Craig Kirkland"

"Hold please."

The person covered the phone, but not very well, Craig heard them yell, "Sara, some boy named Craig "something or other" calling." He heard the response, "Tell him to hang on, I'll be right there."

"Hang on, she'll be here in a minute."

The person never heard Craig say "yes ma'am" as they put the phone down all he heard was a "clunk".

Suddenly a voice said, "Hi Craig, I was about to think you weren't going to call"

"Sorry, my mom had to use the phone."

The next half hour was spent with Craig stuttering his way through teenage chit chat, trying to work up the courage to ask Sara out. She finally said she had to get off the phone, Craig blurted out quickly, "Would you care to go to the movie this Saturday night?"

Sara said "yes, but can we talk about it tomorrow evening, I really have to go now."

"Sure, I'll call same time tomorrow, Bye."

"Bye, Bye"

Minnie had been listening, eaves dropping would be a better description. She smiled when Craig said to her, "Mom I really need to use the phone at 6 tomorrow evening."

"OK, son, I promise to not make any calls at that time."

The next evening went easier, the call was made at 6 PM exactly. Sara informed Craig she couldn't single date until she was sixteen and since they didn't know one another she would really like her best friend, Jean and a date to double date with them, Craig readily agreed. A time was agreed upon, Craig knew where Jean lived and would pick her and her date up first, Jean would then direct him to Sara's house.

The young man who had spent so many hours, countless days and nights alone in the forest, found himself literally a nervous wreck in the days leading to his first date with the girl of his dreams.

***

Halfway through the movie Craig offered his hand for Sara to hold, she accepted.

What Craig felt next was completely unexpected, the instant his fingers closed around the smallest, softest, most feminine hand he had ever touched, he experienced a simultaneous warmth and chill, his respiration and heart rates increased, his mind was spinning and it was the combination of it all that resulted in the most wonderful, beautiful feeling he'd ever experienced, he had no idea what it meant.

Craig lost track of the movie; he couldn't keep himself from looking at the girl sitting next to him.

***

It wasn't until the third date that Craig finally worked up the courage to kiss Sara Blackmon. Even then it was a very gentle peck when he walked her to the door. Craig had a mission to somehow convince Sara to have the same feelings for him as he had for her. He set the goal and went to work on achieving it.

As time passed Craig found himself totally consumed with Sara, she filled his heart every waking moment and even his dreams were of her beautiful smile and sparkling green eyes, he could never get enough of seeing her and wanted her in his life forever so he, every day, for the rest of his life could take in her beauty.

Three months went by, Craig asked Sara to go steady, she accepted. Craig placed the sweetheart ring on her finger. They kissed. Craig looked deeply into Sara's eyes and told her, "It's taken me a while to figure it out, but now I know what it was that affected me on our first date, it was your hand, touching your hand. I fell in love with you the first time we ever held hands."

Craig would know Sara Imogene Blackmon as the girl he had been in love with since he was sitting under an apple tree when he'd been just a little boy. He'd been right, she was beautiful.

***

Along the way, as happens with teens, the making out became petting, touching, exploring and learning. Sara and Craig were no different.

In the Spring, April, Sara offered herself to Craig. At the ages of 17 and 16 they both lost their innocence on a blanket spread

on the soft grass next to the river. The sky was filled with stars, it was the most beautiful experience of their young lives.

And so it was, two teens in love, lusting for more of one another. They would seek places and times to be alone, still learning lessons each were far too young to know.

The night before Sara left for vacation Craig made gentle love to her. It was beautiful.

Neither knew it would forever be the last time they would make love.

CHAPTER

5

Oliver entered the world as what could only be described, and was by all who saw him, as the most beautiful baby boy anyone had ever seen. A head full of very dark hair, olive complexion and the most perfect face any newborn could possess. There wasn't a girl or woman in South Creek who didn't want to hold "that new Watson baby", he was that perfect.

His name was chosen carefully by his parents, first name, Oliver, chosen by his father and taken from his grandfather. His middle name, Calix, chosen by his mother of Greek descent. "Calix" Greek meaning "Very Handsome".

It was obvious from early on that Oliver possessed a high IQ, he walked early, talked early, could quote the alphabet by the time he was three and by three and a half was reading sentences. By the time Oliver started school he knew how to use his intellect, charm and extremely good looks to have anything he wanted, the combination, plus money, and he became the greatest of manipulators. As he grew, he also had one more advantage, Oliver's dad was one of the wealthiest men in the state and had become that by shrewd, most often shady, business deals and manipulation. By the time Oliver was ten he was reading correspondences of his father, even reading and learning how to interpret contracts, he would listen to his father on the phone

during business calls. The boy was a genius, with a dark side which would reveal itself in his early teens.

Due to his parent's wealth Oliver could have easily been educated in any private school but his father, wanting his son to know the real ways of the world, and his mother wanting him to have a normal childhood, decided to place him in the local public-school system. Oliver did well through his elementary years, only once performing less than perfect on his exams, that grade was a 98. In class and on the playground, Oliver would watch and study the other students. It became a hobby to choose one and learn a person until he could define their strengths and weaknesses, it was their weakness that interested him above all else which he would use to his advantage in some way, then move on to some other poor unsuspecting sucker.

Being ahead of his classmates in almost every way by the time he reached puberty Oliver had already discovered the wonders of the female anatomy. As girls had begun developing, he made note of it and there were only a few in his class he hadn't charmed, or manipulated, partially out of their clothes and allowed him to touch in places that would have made their Mother's faint. He was so good at his game there had also been no less than three girls two years older he had done the same things to. By the time testosterone hit him in full force Oliver's hands had explored enough that he knew how to touch just the right places to cause most girl's eyes to roll back and their throats to bring a vocal moan. There was just one thing left to learn and at the age of 14 he would be taught that lesson.

As with most males, Oliver had his preference in what he liked best about how a female was built. He preferred petite girls with nice round butts, not particularly large breasts, small but perky were his favorite, and he liked blondes. Exactly like his friend Sam's mother.

48

By now Oliver had grown to his full height just a fraction over 5'9", he would never be as tall as his father who was just over 6', but thru good genes and playing sports his body was already developing a well-defined muscular physique, not heavy, lean and well cut. What he inherited from his mother was her Greek beauty, curly black hair, olive skin and his face had the classic Greek lines. His blue eyes from his father's family. Oliver wore his hair longer than most boys in South Creek, over his ears and down just past his collar. By 1961, at the age of 14, Oliver was the most handsome boy in town, girls and women could not resist the urge to stare at him whenever they saw him. So, it was with Sam Jackson's mother.

Lilly Jackson was a very lovely 34-year-old housewife, she and her husband Steven, along with son Sam, lived in a sub-division not far from town. Steven worked as a sales manager for national pipe manufacturer and his area covered most of the southeast, he traveled a lot and was away from home at least two weeks a month. Oliver knew this, and although neither Lilly nor Sam knew, for two years, from his age of 12, he had been watching, studying, searching for any weakness he might observe in Lilly. There was only one reason Oliver had befriended Sam, to have opportunities to get close to his mother. Having a desire to do research, one morning Oliver got on his bicycle and rode to Sam's home. Sam wasn't home, his bike was gone. As Oliver was approaching the door, he heard a noise coming from the open bedroom window, he stopped and listened, the sounds were moans. The curtains were not quite pulled together, he looked inside, Mrs. Jackson was alone on the bed, nude, she was masturbating, he stood and watched until she orgasmed, he waited.

Relaxing for a few minutes, catching her breath, calming herself, Lilly sat up. Looking toward the window she saw Oliver. She smiled, walked toward the window, her beautiful 34-year-old

49

body filling Oliver's eyes, she spoke. "Soon" is all she said, she gathered her clothes and walked out of the room.

Two years earlier Sam had introduced Oliver to his Mom, she had prepared the boys sandwiches for lunch and served them both cold glasses of iced tea, it was a hot Summer day and they were sweaty from riding their bikes all morning. Lilly immediately liked Oliver, he was extremely well mannered, pleasant, could carry on a conversation better than any boy his age she had ever met. When Lily mentioned to Sam the grass needed cutting Oliver instantly offered to help, she even laughed at Oliver mildly fussing that Sam needed to clean his room, and he was a beautiful boy. Over the next two years Oliver would often drop by to visit and if he saw her doing her daily house work would offer to help. What Lilly didn't realize was that Oliver would often plan his visits when he knew Sam wouldn't be home. On more than one occasion Lilly had caught him staring at her but tossed it off as mere childish infatuation, until she realized there had been several times she had found herself staring at him.

Lilly had never seen a boy's body mature so quickly as Oliver's had. He had, before her eyes, physically become a young man by the age of 14. She knew she shouldn't, knew it was wrong, but sometimes during her private times she would fantasize about the very handsome, olive skinned, blue eyed boy. She would imagine kissing his full lips while running her fingers through that beautiful black curly hair.

Late on the afternoon she had been seen pleasuring herself by Oliver, Steven arrived home, he took Lilly and Sam to dinner at the diner in town. Sam was asked to stay in town and play basketball, one of the other boy's dad agreed to bring him home later. It was Summer, no school the next day, Sam could stay. Steven and Lilly returned home and made love. Lilly enjoyed her fantasies.

Oliver didn't last very long his first time but for the next hour he learned quickly. Twice more they had sex, each time better than the last. Lilly taught a genius things he had only imagined while he was with the girls his age, he caught on very quickly. There were two months until school would begin and those months would be spent, when circumstances allowed, teaching and learning. What Lilly failed to realize was something Oliver had already thought about and researched, she had committed a felony. Lilly had committed statutory rape, and she would do so several more times that Summer. When the guilt of all she had done and was doing finally overcame her lust, it was too late. Oliver had planned for this and told her there would be no stopping, or, he asked, would she rather he take the information to the police? By now Oliver had learned many things very well but there were many things he wanted to experience, things Lilly knew took place between men and women but never had any desire for, considering those things to be too dirty or extreme. Oliver taught her things she didn't want to learn.

Oliver had a best friend, Andy Bohannon. The two thought a lot about the same things and had discussed them in depth. They talked about different girls in their class, and some of the older girls, they confided with one another about who they had been with and what had taken place, except, Oliver kept Lilly his secret. Andy told Oliver of his desire to have a threesome someday, two guys showing one girl a good time. What Andy had no way of knowing was that Oliver had already been planning a surprise.

Stopping by Sam's house one morning while on his way to football practice Oliver told Lilly to find an excuse to go to town the next Saturday evening, she was instead to meet him next to the creek where they had met a few times before.

Andy and Oliver arrived early. Andy was excited and asked several times what the surprise was, Oliver simply smiled. Then, headlights appeared to slow down at the turn from the main road,

Oliver instructed Andy to stand still while he was blindfolded with a towel. The car came to a stop a few seconds later. Leaning in the driver's side Oliver whispered to Lilly that she was to get in the back of the station wagon, she unfolded and placed the blanket as she had done before, removed her clothes, and lay down, waiting, she closed her eyes. Oliver led Andy to the rear opening of the car and removed the blindfold, all he said was, "Surprise".

For a brief few seconds Andy had no idea who it was, all he could make out in the darkness were two well shaped legs, spread and waiting, he climbed in. Eyes finally adjusting to the light of the moon, Andy recognized Sam's mother. Andy became more animal than human as he penetrated Lilly. For over two hours Lilly was, multiple times, taught everything a threesome from two high on testosterone male teenagers could teach her, could do to her. As humiliated and frightened as she was, she orgasmed twice, then came the acts she thought would rip her in half.

Lilly washed as best she could in the shallow creek before going home that night. Little did she know, the same thing would take place several more times before the boys would be through with her. Another thing she had no way of knowing was that by the time the boys were 15 years old there were at least two other women in town who were being treated to the same hell she was living through. Oliver had been busy.

***

From the time he was six Oliver had enjoyed sports. By the time he was 10 he had a new respect for sports and that they offered another way to observe more people. At age 12 Oliver began attending the local high school football games and began studying how the teams would line up, how they moved when the ball was snapped, he absorbed the information and by the end of the season knew every play, and more often than not which play would be called for by the coach before the coach called it. He

took in everything, including how the women and girls acted at the sight of the strong young men who played the game.

Aware he had the intellect, Oliver knew he had been born with more brain power than most, he began working on his body. Trips to the library where there were books on nutrition, using his father's weights and workout machines, riding his bicycle, walking, jogging, pushups and sit-ups by the dozens plus the little league workout routines, within only a few months Oliver could see and feel the transformation. Although he wasn't big, and his physique wasn't bulk, he was lean and becoming muscular in the correct ways to enhance the natural good looks he had been born with. By the time he was fourteen he was a more perfect male specimen than most boys at the age of sixteen. The next two years would be the greatest years of his teenage life.

The one place Oliver discovered he was never best was on a ball field, except for one thing. No matter how hard he worked, no matter how much he studied the game, he was very good, but not the best at any position he tried, except end. Although not the fastest on the field, he could somehow manage to catch the ball if it could possibly be caught. Oliver would study the defense and somehow make himself open for a pass. Once the reception was completed, he rarely gained much more yardage, and often would sacrifice himself and take a big hit, but the workouts had helped him be able to absorb the punishment. Completed passes gained yards on the football field, and popularity off the field.

Oliver made many friends on the football team. Andy was already his best friend with whom he had enjoyed many "adventures", Oscar, who played defense and was a huge brute of a boy, and David who wanted so badly to be popular but couldn't seem to understand how to be. Oliver, Andy, Oscar and David became very close, the first three allowing David to tag along because they liked him, he was a good kid and handled the jokes they played on him very well.

Oliver turned sixteen in May. By his looks, charming personality, intellect, manners and ability on the football field Oliver finished his first year of high school as a member of the Honor Society, a member of the Student Council, he had earned a letter for his athletic ability and had been laid more times, by more girls, and women, than any boy in school. It was no wonder he was voted Most Popular Boy in his class.

Through the years Oliver's father had become owner of many properties, most of his land holdings had come by less than honest deals. A portion of Thomas Watson's holdings were several cottages, some unimproved property, along with commercial properties, at Tybee Island, a growing beach community on the Georgia coast. The family had vacationed several times at the cottages and Oliver very much enjoyed hanging out on the beach, checking out the girls.

Talking to his older cousin Ginny one afternoon she informed Oliver her family would be using one of the cottages for a week the first week of August, Oliver had an idea. He and his friends had all recently celebrated their 16th birthdays, he thought it would be a great way to extend the celebration by inviting them all to the beach. Because Ginny would be close by to watch after the boys, Thomas agreed and arranged for Oliver and his friends to stay at another cottage, he had no idea Ginny had recently become Oliver's source for beer.

CHAPTER

6

The trip had been long and hot in the unairconditioned car. But to Sara, when she breathed in her first breath of air coming off the salt water, it had been worth it. There was no place on earth she loved so much as the beach. The sounds of the surf gently rolling in, the feel of the sand under her feet, the sun in all its splendor, and the smell, the wonderful smell of the clean air, it was her heaven.

The house was a block off the water, Sara helped unpack the car then, anxious to be on the beach, she and Brenda quickly changed into their swimsuits. They got their towels, suntan oil, and walked quickly toward the sound of the surf.

***

Day Two of vacation the girls were up early, anticipating their first full day of beach time. Quickly finishing breakfast, they cleaned up the dishes, once again grabbed everything they would need for the day, out the door the laughing sisters went. James and Cynthia would bring Giles to the beach later for a while, they wouldn't stay long, Giles tender 4-year-old skin would burn too easily if exposed to the midday sun. James would usually stay a while after Cynthia took Giles back to the house, he would walk along the surf, feeling the water he loved so dearly running across his feet, he would sit with his daughters and enjoy their company, when at the beach James was an entirely different personality, almost a different person.

***

As much as Sara had inherited her build from her Grandmother, Brenda had just as much inherited hers from her mother, she had also developed very early. By the time Brenda was 13 she could, from a distance, be mistaken as the older of the two girls. Both girls were beautiful, Brenda was beautiful and much more buxom than one would think a girl her age would be. Sara was very astute and had noticed boys and young men checking out her younger sister's figure as they walked past. It was when the boys and young men looked at her face that they realized Brenda was too young to be approached.

It was afternoon when the four boys decided to walk at the beach and begin checking out the girls, in search of a few who might enjoy the kind of fun they were hoping for. From a distance they spotted Brenda. Andy saw her first, she was with another girl who had very short blonde hair, "Check out the boobs on the girl with the long hair!"

Oliver had seen Brenda, but what caught his eye was the figure of the short haired girl, "You check out the boobs, I'm checking the butt on the one with short hair." Oliver decided it was time to meet the girls, he also had a plan to use his wit and tease the one with short hair, he and Andy came up with a plan.

As they approached the girls, Sara heard a voice, "See Oliver! I told you that wasn't a boy!"

Sara turned and saw a boy talking and pointing at her.

"I swear Andy, maybe I need glasses. From off back yonder I would have sworn she was a boy, I guess the short hair fooled me." The hair was perfect for the petite girl, she was gorgeous, and built in every way perfectly to Oliver's preference.

When Sara saw Oliver she was absolutely stunned by his looks, she had never seen a boy as handsome and perfect, his black curly hair was gorgeous, it was longer than average for the

style of the time, his body was astonishing, not bulky, but muscular, his full lips looked as if something an artist would draw, facial features appeared Greek and the tan on his already dark skin was flawless. Sara caught herself staring, she couldn't help it, Oliver was that perfect.

Suddenly, realizing she needed to stop staring, Sara stood, placed her hands on her hips. The beautiful Sara Blackmon proceeded to turn slowly, very slowly, flirtatiously, so all the boys could closely examine, visually, her body. Finishing her 360 degree turn, "Do you still think I'm a boy?" Sara smiled, she winked.

"Oh no, I apologize for my mistake." Oliver grinned, he winked back.

Sara by now had noticed the redheaded boy with dimples. He, too, was very handsome, but his looks paled while standing next to the black headed one. The other two, one was very big, not ugly, not handsome, the last one was not at all good looking, he was homely.

Conversation began, the boys from South Creek, Georgia, the girls from Anniston, Alabama, all the boys 16 years old, Sara had thought Oliver a couple of years older. The boys learned Brenda would be 14 in six months, they instantly decided to leave the younger girl alone, Sara had turned 16 in June. The guys all played football at the same school, Oliver was also a member of the Honor Society, this impressed Sara even more. Everyone enjoyed talking, getting to know one another, several times Sara's and Oliver's eyes met, they would linger as they stared. Without saying, both knew they were attracted and wanted to see each other again.

It was time for the girls to go in for dinner, they said goodbyes and hoped they might all see one another again. Just before losing sight, Sara turned, she waved. Although all the boys waved back, her wave had been intended for only one.

"Give me another few visits with her and I'll get some of that. Hell, I might even convince her to give some of it to y'all. What say David, want to lose your virginity with her?"

Although embarrassed by the question, David responded, "You Bet!"

By the time they'd finished dinner and cleaned the kitchen the sun had gone down. Nighttime at the beach was always family fun, even Cynthia seemed in a better attitude as they all took flashlights, chased and captured crabs, saw the tiny fish at the edge of the surf. Sara kept looking around, hoping she might see Oliver.

Just before turning off the lights at bedtime, Sara looked at her left hand, at the sweetheart ring Craig had given her. She felt a moment of guilt, but then when she remembered the handsome boy on the beach, the guilt left as quickly as it has come. She fell asleep wondering how it would feel to kiss a boy named Oliver.

***

Day Three, Sara woke earlier than usual, she wanted to get to the beach as quickly as possible. Just in case Oliver might happen by again, she didn't want to miss him. Not wanting to wait for Brenda, Sara left the house alone. Brenda would come later.

Sitting behind a dune a hundred yards away, Oliver was waiting. He knew where Sara and her sister had been the day before and would probably be again today. Sure enough, he saw her, she was alone this time. He waited another 15 minutes and watched as she seemed to be looking for someone. It was when she opened a book that he stepped from behind the dune and began walking toward her. Halfway there she looked up again, saw him, smiled a beautiful smile, they waved at one another.

"Good morning, Sara."

"Good morning to you, Oliver. Sleep well?"

"I did, thanks. Had a nice dream."

"Really? You remember it?"

"Yep, I dreamed of a short haired girl I had mistaken for a boy."

"I wonder who that may have been?" Sara smiled her sexiest smile.

Wanting him to touch her, wanting to feel his hands on her, and wanting to somehow let him know he could touch her, Sara reached into her beach bag and found her suntan oil. "Do my back please? Brenda usually does it for me but she's being slow and lazy today."

"Happy to help!"

His hands felt good to her as he slowly, almost romantically moved them over her back, even very briefly letting his fingers enter the back of her bikini bottom, not far, but just enough that it turned her on. Sara was bent over, her hands on her knees, she opened her eyes and once again saw the ring on her left hand. With Oliver's hands on her back, this time she felt no guilt.

Handing Sara the bottle of oil Oliver tapped the ring with his finger, "I see you have a boyfriend."

"Yep."

"Tell me about him. Any guy with a girlfriend as pretty and sweet as you must be a special kind of guy."

"He's OK, well, he's very nice. His name is Craig, he treats me very nice, takes me to nice places. He is a year older than us, but you wouldn't know it, he's kinda silly, makes me laugh."

"He play ball?"

60

"Oh, no. He's more the kind of person who likes the woods and forests. He has a part time job at a service station and enjoys working on cars and such, he can build things and he loves to shoot his gun, a pretty good shot too."

"So, if he walked up right now would he shoot me? Maybe beat me up?

Sara laughed, "Shoot you maybe but no way he could beat you up, he's skinny, not at all into physical exercise. Honestly, he looks sort of dorky, wears black framed glasses and has braces on his teeth. Once he gets the braces off and takes off his glasses, he will look nice enough."

"What in the world is a girl with your looks doing with a boyfriend like, what's his name, Craig?"

"Yes, Craig. Like I said, He is very nice, he's very kind, treats me nice, and is very courteous. Giles loves him to pieces."

"Who is Giles?"

"Oh, I'm sorry, Giles is my baby brother, he's 4. Hang around a while, my parents will bring him out here to play."

"Can think of nowhere I'd rather be."

"Where are the other guys?"

"Off somewhere else up the beach, I told them to stay away so I could have time to talk to you without them interrupting."

"I'm flattered! Your friend Andy is cute too, love his dimples."

Oliver laughed, "Yeah, all the girls at home are wild about Andy's dimples."

The rest of the family arrived at the beach; Oliver was introduced to Sara's parents. Even Cynthia was amazed at how

61

handsome this boy was and wondered what he saw in Sara, she still had not accepted how beautiful her oldest daughter was. Sara and Oliver played Frisbee with Giles for a while, then helped him build sandcastles.

**

Day Four began much the same as the day prior, except this time Oliver was waiting for Sara. Suntan oil was once again applied, this time his fingers reached a little further into the back of the bikini bottom and stayed there a little longer. They also reached around a little further, brushing the sides of Sara's breasts. She knew what he was doing and she liked it.

By the time the family arrived Sara and Oliver were playing in the water, swimming and chasing one another, each time Oliver caught Sara he would toss her into the air, they would laugh as she splashed back into the sea. Sara had never had any boy as handsome and strong show her so much attention.

Giles was fussy, James and Cynthia took him back to the house. Brenda had met some girls her age and they had gone walking. Once again Sara and Oliver were alone, he mentioned getting back in the water, Sara agreed. The two teens swam out until the water was neck deep on Oliver. With Sara being short, she had to choose between holding on to Oliver or treading water, she chose to hang on, he kissed her, she returned the kiss. When he kissed her the second time, his right hand slid inside her bikini bottom and cupped her butt, she made no move to resist. Knowing he now had permission to play, Oliver turned Sara around with her back to him and held her. Hidden from view by the water he slipped his hands under her swimsuit top. Sara loved every second of the attention she was receiving from the most handsome boy she'd ever seen.

62

Walking alone on the beach that same evening, Sara was startled by someone rushing from behind her, grabbing her and picking her up, spinning around as if they were going to throw her, she screamed a little scream then realized she was being held in Oliver's strong arms, they kissed. In the moonlight Sara saw the glint of the ring, she felt absolutely no guilt. Oliver put her down, they walked further down the beach to a more secluded place. Oliver's hands explored all of Sara Blackmon, his fingers reached into a place only one other boy's fingers had been, his lips tasted the nipples only one other boy's lips had tasted, Sara's hands felt and fondled only the second erect manhood they had ever touched.

***

Day Five she arrived on the beach early but saw nothing of him, she wondered if last night was the end and would ever see one another again.

James and Cynthia brought Giles to play. James asked, "Where's your friend? Seems like a nice young man, I like him."

"Haven't seen him today. He and his friends might be off somewhere doing something together."

Sara and Brenda walked to the house for lunch then returned to the beach. Oliver was waiting, "I found something I want to give you." He reached out his cupped hands. "Close your eyes and hold out your hands."

Doing as told, Sara felt something drop into her hands, she was told to open her eyes.

In her hands were two perfect sand dollars, "Wow, I've never found a whole one, only pieces, Thank You!!!" She hugged Oliver's neck.

Brenda went to play with her new friends.

Oliver asked, "Wanna go for a walk? Maybe find some shells or another sand dollar."

"Sounds like a great idea."

They walked for almost an hour, slowly looking for shells, finding a few but no more sand dollars. The day was hot under the afternoon sun. "I'm thirsty, could use something to drink. How about you?"

Sara responded, "I sure could, I've got some drinks in my little cooler if you're ready to head back."

"Well, from here we're closer to where I'm staying, we've got plenty of drinks if you'd rather go there. We can sit in the shade on the patio for a while."

"Sounds good" Sara smiled.

It had been only five months before that Sara had lost her virginity with Craig. It had been both their first time. Since then they'd had sex as often as they could but still both lacked experience, they were learning things together. Sara loved it but she knew there had to be more.

After making out and both having removed the other's clothes, he asked her, "Are you a virgin?" Oliver had never before cared and wondered to himself why he'd bothered to ask.

"No, I'm not a virgin, not very experienced, but not a virgin."

"Want to have sex?"

"You have a condom?"

"Yes."

"Yes."

"Not very experienced you say?"

"Not very."

"Before we do it, let me show you something."

Sara learned for the first time what a real orgasm felt like as Oliver's did things to her with his mouth and tongue she never had any idea could be done. It was the most amazing, wonderful feeling of her life.

As Sara lay still, trying to catch her breath from the most wonderful experience of her life, Oliver spun around and put his erection close to her face, "Have you ever?"

"No."

"Want to?"

"More than you know." Sara took Oliver into her mouth, she learned very quickly and loved it. Not knowing what to expect she first tasted his precum, next she felt the hot stream of semen hit her in the throat. At first it gagged her, then she swallowed. Both teens lay resting, holding one another. Oliver had a very short recovery period; he was ready in less than 10 minutes.

For the next two hours Oliver taught Sara more than she'd known possible, different positions she hadn't even read about in books, more oral sex. Sara experienced multiple orgasms, until this day she had never realized how good one real orgasm might feel, much less how several could feel. Oliver had three more.

"I never knew a boy could orgasm more than once a day, much less four times in one afternoon."

"That boyfriend of yours must not be much man."

"I guess he isn't."

During their walk back they talked about the next day being their last vacation day, both would be returning home the day

after. "I won't be on the beach tomorrow but can meet you tomorrow night. If I can get rid of the guys, would you want to go back to my place again?"

"Yes."

"7:30? I can walk to your place first."

"OK."

"Sara slept very little. She was excited and filled with anticipation.

***

Day Six, August 7.

Leisurely day on the beach, it was difficult for Sara to not show her excitement for what would be happening later that evening.

She showered and put on the best outfit she had brought. Sara spent extra time with her makeup, wanting to be as perfect as she could be for Oliver, lastly, she used the perfume Craig had given her. If there was any remorse, she never felt it. Sara was ready at 7, she stood at the door, watching.

"What are your plans for the evening?" It was Cynthia who'd asked.

"Oliver is coming here, we're gonna walk on the beach a while."

"It isn't right."

"What?"

"You going off with that boy when you're wearing your boyfriend's ring. It is not right, and you know it."

"It's just a walk on the beach, MOTHER!"

"You sure got awful fixed up for just a walk on the beach, and isn't that the perfume Craig bought you?"

"Yes!"

"What time do you plan to be home?"

"10:30, maybe 11"

"Make it 9:30."

"MOTHER!!"

"Sara, you can be home by 9:30 or not go at all. I still don't like this, and you know it isn't right! You and I may not get along very well, but I like that boyfriend you've got at home, he treats you good and you know he does."

Sara was angry at her mother, and although she didn't realize it, she was also angry at herself because she knew this time her mother was right. The day would come when she would understand all her anger that night had not been at her mother."

"I see him, no need in him having to walk up here. I'm gone."

"Remember, 9:30."

Sara left without another word; she was seething.

Oliver saw her coming, she wasn't smiling, "Hey, what's up."

"Just my mother being the bitch she can be. Do I smell beer?"

"Yeah, had a few beers with the guys a while ago. Don't tell anyone but we smoked a couple of joints, too."

"Are they there now."

Oliver laughed, "Why? You want us all?"

Sara playfully punched him, and teased, "No, you and Andy might be fun, but not ALL!"

Oliver never answered her question about the guys being there. Sara had a surprise coming. If she thought yesterday had been fun, she was in for a big treat tonight.

He was different tonight than he'd been yesterday. The day before Oliver had been very attentive to her, made her feel great before mentioning sex. Tonight, he kissed her a couple of times, he kissed her as he lay her on the bed. Then, without a word, he undid her shorts and pulled them off, he immediately dropped his shorts, put on a condom and while standing at the edge of the bed, thrust into her, hard.

Sara grunted loudly, "You're hurting me. Go easy, you didn't give me time to get wet."

Oliver continued to thrust. Sara continued to tell him to slow down.

After a few minutes, she managed to get her feet up onto the bed rail, it gave a better angle and felt some better, still not good yet she again asked him to slow down.

"You some kinda tease?"

"Huh?"

"Give a guy some one day, let him start again the next day then bitch about it?"

"No, but this is different than yesterday, please slow down. I can tell I'm getting wetter but still need a little more time before you go fast."

Oliver slowed, finally.

"That's better, oh yeah, lots better. Oh God, that feels good." She closed her eyes and was enjoying.

Andy had told the others to stay put for a few minutes, he eased out of the bathroom from where they had all been watching. Tiptoeing to the bed he very gently reached down her top and began fondling Sara's breasts, then he kissed her.

For a moment Sara had no idea there was anyone there except Oliver and herself. Then, suddenly, she realized there were hands on her legs, and hands on her breasts, there was no way it could be Oliver kissing her, not from the position he was fucking her, she opened her eyes. A handsome dimpled boy was smiling at her, first she smiled back, briefly excited at what was happening. Then, suddenly, reality struck her! The reality of what she was doing, of what she had been doing all week. How wrong it had all been. "OH MY GOD, WHAT HAVE I DONE!!?"

"NO! STOP! PLEASE!"

She saw the other two boys looking. Just before Andy covered her mouth with his hand, Sara screamed, "CRAAAAIIGGGG!"

***

All week Sara had been consumed by her desires for Oliver. She had never met a boy who had seemed so perfect in every way, charm, charisma, looks, intellect, he had it all and she had stupidly fallen for it. Why, oh why, had she been so stupid? She had a boyfriend who treated her so good, so gentle, waiting for her to come home, but she had allowed her lust to overcome thoughts of him. She felt dirty, filthy. Sara felt unworthy of Craig's love. The week had finally come to this, she lay with Oliver's dick pounding in and out of her, another boy, Andy, holding his hand over her mouth, and two other boys watching it all take place. For the first time in her life Sara had been a slut, she knew it, realized

69

it. And now, as she was being raped, she realized how much she was in love with Craig. Sara not only realized her deep love for Craig, Sara also realized she could possibly die this night at the hands of four half drunk, half stoned teenage boys.

He slapped her, hard! Andy told her, "You scream again, bitch, and I'll hit you harder. Understand?"

Crying, Sara nodded.

***

The assault on Sara Imogene Blackmon would last over two hours. During that time her body would be subjected to more vulgarities than she, or most people, could ever imagine.

Sara would experience the helplessness, humiliation and pain associated with a gang rape. Her beautiful petite body would be used for nothing more than self satisfaction by a group of four strong, young athletes turned animal. Sara prayed for death.

Sometime during it all Sara would feel a sudden calmness, a comforting feeling of warmth.

Sara would see them, the angels. She would feel their hands as they lifted her. The angels took her away from the pain and fear, the humiliation, the horror and the shame of all she had done the previous days.

As she was being taken away Sara turned and looked back. Sara saw herself; she saw what was happening. An angel spoke, "Look not at the evil. Come with us and behold the good."

Sara slowly looked forward, she saw Craig, smiling, his arms open, awaiting her embrace.

***

Sara would later wake, she would remember her prayers and thank God for having taken her away from the pain.

For the rest of her life she would give the same thanks. Every morning of every day, every prayer before she closed her beautiful eyes at night was that Craig would, could, forgive her for the heartbreak she had brought upon him.

The Tybee Island vacation week, culminating with the assault, would result in destroyed futures, changed lives and, ultimately, deaths.

She was supposed to have been home no later than 9:30. At 10 her dad was getting worried; her Mom was getting mad. James Blackmon got in his car at 10:30 and went looking for his daughter, twice stopping and walking to the beach in hopes of seeing her. It was midnight when he called the police. A formal missing person report couldn't be filed for 24 hours but a description could be called to the officers working that night and they would be on the lookout for her.

***

Harry Dobbins and his wife, Millie, really didn't need to be spending the money on a day trip to the beach but Millie loved it. They'd packed the ice chest and picnic basket, beach towels, Harry's fishing rods and three children into the station wagon and left early for Tybee Island. Several months earlier Harry had taken a fall while working on a new house construction, he'd broken his leg and was off work while the leg mended, times had been tough. Having recently gone back to work there were finally paychecks coming back into the household, most of which were being spent to catch up on past due bills.

Driving along the main beach road Harry felt the car start feeling strange and noted the rear end felt lower on the right side, that darn old "May Pop" tire was going flat, the spare was in the same condition, he hoped it would hold. Harry pulled onto the shoulder of the road and began the process of changing the tire.

The day was hot, it gets hot early in August at Tybee Island. Harry let the jack down, threw the flat tire in the back of the wagon, picked up the lug wrench and jack, tossed those in the back and walked back around to snap the hubcap on. Standing up, Harry leaned back against the car and wiped the sweat from his eyes with his handkerchief. About 15 feet from where he was standing, he saw a small hand raise up from the high grass, the hand dropped back out of sight. Harry walked to where he'd seen the hand. "OH MY GOD, CHILD!" What Harry saw was a petite female, her face bruised and swollen, one eye swollen shut and her lip bleeding, the crotch of her shorts stained with blood. Harry Dobbins leaned down and spoke softly, "It's OK honey, Harry and Millie gonna take care of you and get some help." The girl opened the eye she still could, Harry saw it was a beautiful color of green, He screamed, "MILLIE, MILLIE, TELL THE KIDS TO STAY IN THE CAR AND YOU COME HERE QUICK! I NEED HELP, NOW! BRING THAT JUG OF ICE WATER AND A TOWEL!! Millie did as told, when she saw what the ruckus was about she dropped beside the girl, "Oh My Lord." Harry held the girl up a little so she could sip the water from the jug, then lay her back down. "Wet that towel and wipe her face off, I'm going back to the service station we passed and have somebody there call the police and an ambulance, I'll be right back." Millie nodded.

Gone only a few minutes, Harry returned. Within minutes sirens could be heard in the distance. The girl was unconscious, Harry asked if she'd said anything. Millie looked at her husband and told him, "All she said was, "Tell Craig I'm sorry. Tell Craig I love him". Each time she woke up that's what she would say." "One time she did tell me her name when I asked, she said Sara." Millie began to pray. Harry didn't have a clue who this girl was, but he wanted to kill whoever had hurt her.

***

Jack Wilson MD. had a small practice at his home, every resident on the island knew him as Doc Jack. Doc heard the familiar sound of the ambulance growing louder, it was in a hurry. He stepped to the small waiting area and told the two people there that if the ambulance pulled up to his place they might have to wait a few minutes, it did. Doc and a man who had a cut on his hand both walked to the front door and saw the attendants taking the gurney from the back, the man went to help, Doc held the door.

The men knew where to take Sara, they gently lifted her off the gurney and placed her on the exam table. Doc came in and told the rest to wait outside, for the ambulance to not leave. The old doctor gently began taking care of business, first he checked for head wounds , checked her pupils, then as carefully as he could began cutting her clothes off, he saw the bruises on her breasts and that one nipple was bleeding slightly, it had been bitten, there was what appeared to be a burn, possibly from a cigarette, on her belly. Doc removed her pants and discovered the washcloths someone had put there, he found she'd bled from both her rectum and vagina. Heart rate was good, respiration was good. Sara woke and screamed. The good, kind doctor held Sara as if she were his daughter and calmed her, he covered her, she'd gone through enough indignity. Sara talked a little before she returned into the stupor, awake, but not. While he'd been examining her privates, he had smelled semen and used a swab to take a sample, he would send this with the ambulance attendants. Not having the proper facility to thoroughly examine and give the care he knew the girl required he called the ambulance attendants back in and ordered her to be transported to the hospital in Savannah. She had been dehydrated; Doc had started an IV. All the information he could give the police, other than what little he'd found in his examination, was her name was Sara and there was somebody named "Craig" she loved a lot. Doc called the hospital and gave a description of what he'd been able

74

to determine, the girl appeared to be in her middle teens, petite, had undergone what appeared to be rape, vicious rape, with both rectal and vaginal injuries, one eye badly bruised with severe swelling, facial x-rays would be required, he went on to say she might or might not be conscious and that due to the emotional trauma may not be capable of communicating. The ER physician thanked Doc Jack and began assembling his team of nurses, he called in a colorectal specialist and an ob-gyn, her mental needs would be met later to address her emotional care. The team was waiting when the ambulance arrived, she was rushed into the exam room, suddenly she screamed, "CRAIGI I LOVE YOU CRAIG! HELP ME!!" This would happen several times over the days until Sara finally regained full consciousness.

Doc Jack had cleaned the small exam room and went to call in the next patient, the man with the cut on his hand who'd helped bring Sara in the house, the man was crying. Doc knew the man had a daughter about Sara's age, he'd delivered her. The man had seen her face, he knew behind the bruises and swelling there was a very pretty girl, he looked at Doc, "Doc, who the hell could do such a thing to that girl? Who the hell could be that mean? Who?! Why?!" All Doc could say was "I don't know". Both men cried. Finally, Doc spoke, "C'mon back here Jeff, let's see how many stitches you need this time. You must be the most accident prone patient I have."

***

The police car stopped in front of the house, Officer Tilly walked briskly to the door and knocked, he was invited in. "A girl has been found who meets the description you gave of your daughter, she says her name is Sara, she has been transported to a hospital in Savannah where she is currently being cared for and evaluated." James Blackmon asked, "Hospital? How bad?" Tilly knew some, but it was not his place to answer such questions, those answers should only come from the doctors. "Sir, I don't

know, the doctor will fill you in at the hospital. I need someone to come with me now who can positively identify the young lady as your Sara or not. I would also expect someone will need to sign papers giving the doctors permission to treat her if she is indeed your daughter."

James turned to Cynthia, "I'll go, you stay with the kids, I'll call you when I know more."

Cynthia started to speak. James pointed his finger at her, "You WILL do as I say." For the first time since they had been married, James Blackmon showed some spine, Cynthia backed off.

"Officer Tilly, let's go!"

The drive from Tybee Island to Savannah was somber, it was quiet, neither man said much. The one question James asked was what had happened to her. Officer Tilly responded, "Sir, an investigation has begun to determine what happened, anything I were to tell you would only be speculative, and I will not do that. Once we arrive at the hospital and you identify the girl, if she is your daughter, the doctors will tell you everything. Sometime in the next few days a detective will visit you." There was no more conversation.

Tilly escorted James into the Emergency Room entrance, the men stopped at the registration desk where Tilly explained to the young woman who he had with him, she picked up the phone and made a quick call, "Dr. Sykes will be with you in a few moments." The police officer knew Dr. Sykes well and that he was a very good physician, he'd saved Tilly's life the year before in this same ER after Tilly had been shot while answering a domestic dispute call. Tilly was glad Sykes was caring for the girl.

The doors opened, Sykes saw Tilly and the man with him, he introduced himself, "I'm Doctor Sykes, and you are?" James stood, "Doctor Sykes, James Blackmon." The men shook hands.

"Mister Blackmon, do you have a daughter by the name of Sara?"

"I do."

"Follow me please, let's see if the young lady we have is your daughter."

There were two nurses tending to Sara in the curtained enclosure, they looked up as the three men entered. Seeing his daughter's face, swollen, bruised, one eye very black and extremely swollen, James took a step toward her, his knees buckled, Tilly caught him. "OH GOD, OH GOD! SARA WHAT HAS SOMEONE DONE TO YOU, OH GOD, OH GOD!!" James was set in a chair next to Sara, he held her hand and cried as no man should ever have to cry. The nurses consoled him as best they could, Tilly and Dr. Sykes stepped just outside the enclosure.

Sykes spoke first, "You're looking well Don, glad I've not had to see you in a while. Is his reaction answer enough?"

"Doc, I know the answer, but I still have to ask him."

"I understand. We'll give him a few minutes to get over the initial shock of what he's just seen then take him to my office."

"OK, Doc." Tilly continued, "Doc, I really should wait and let the detective ask you, but how bad is this?"

"It's so bad I would not describe what was done to that girl as having been done by anything society would define as human beings, they are crazed animals with no feelings for life other than their own."

"You said they, more than one?"

"Doc Jack sent a sample of semen he swapped, we did a more thorough exam and got more from her. There were at least

three people involved, we determined three different blood types. Could be more, some may have the same type."

"Oh my God."

"Don, it's my job to try and preserve lives. My feelings about this are such that when y'all find who did this, and I know you will, I wouldn't mind reading in the paper that they were killed while trying to evade arrest. In fact, it would do my heart good. Let's go get Mister Blackmon."

In doctor Sykes office James was brought coffee. Tilly spoke first, "Mister Blackmon, I already know the answer but am required to ask, please forgive me. Is the young lady you just saw your daughter Sara Imogene Blackmon?"

"Yes."

"Thank you, sir. I'll leave you and Doctor Sykes to your conversation. After I make my call I will remain close in case you need anything." Tilly left the room and closed the door.

"Mister Blackmon, I hate having to be blunt but sometimes there is no other way, your daughter has been raped, it was very vicious. She has sustained injuries which will require further testing to determine how bad and what needs to be done to repair, this could require surgery, we just do not know at this time. Injuries include tears to the rectal area, bleeding there has stopped but we need to further examine her to be sure there are no internal injuries associated with the lower intestine, she is still bleeding from her vagina, we've managed to slow it but we need to find why she is still bleeding. She has bruises all over her body where she was slapped, hit and pinched, one burn to her torso that appears to have been done with a lit cigarette. Her eye was another concern, she has been x-rayed and we found no broken facial bones, thank heaven, the rest of her facial swelling appears to have been caused by being slapped multiple times. Her eye has also been examined and we feel her vision will not be impaired,

again, thank heaven. The cut on her lip required a few stitches. Sara was first taken to a physician on Tybee Island, we call him Doc Jack, good man, your daughter was dehydrated, he began an IV then had her transported here, we are still giving her fluids and she required one unit of blood due to the vaginal bleeding, more may be required. We discovered at least one injury to her breast that appears to be made by a human bite. There is a young lady waiting just outside with papers giving us permission to treat Sara, all needed will be your signature and filling in a few things you can tell us about your daughter. Shall I have the lady step in?"

"Yes sir."

Sykes opened the door and motioned the lady in.

"When you all are finished, I will come back in, I have another few questions."

The young woman was pleasant, she detailed everything and explained the things James questioned. Doctor Sykes was making calls and ordering tests.

Once finished the lady stepped from the room, Sykes re-entered and sat at his desk across from the very distraught father. Sykes asked, "Who is Craig?"

At first the question stunned James, it was the last thing he would have expected to be asked, "Sara's boyfriend, surely he had nothing to do with this, he's at home in Alabama."

"No sir, I don't think he had anything whatsoever to do with this, your daughter loves him."

"Then,,what?"

"The human mind has built in protection mechanisms; they work differently in everyone. When a person is being emotionally or physically traumatized the mind can, in a sense shut down, removing the person from that which is causing pain or trauma,

79

rape is exceedingly emotionally traumatizing. What can happen is that the mind can go into a form of suspended animation, the person can go into a stupor, not feel physical pain as it is being inflicted, detach itself from reality. There are many cases where rape victims have done this. I believe this is what is happening with your daughter. Understand?"

"Yes sir, what's this have to do with Craig?"

"Your daughter was in such a stupor when she was brought in. But occasionally she would snap out for a few seconds and scream Craig's name, she would scream she loved him, a couple of times she screamed that she was sorry and at least once asked him to help her. Sir, the only sounds that girl has made have had to do with a boy named Craig, the only name she has spoken. Tell me about him."

"He is a real good young man, courteous, treats Sara very special. To be honest I have seen his eyes, how he looks at her, he's only seventeen but I can tell from his eyes he is head over heels in love with Sara. If not for those black framed glasses and the braces on his teeth he would be a handsome kid, not nearly as handsome as that boy, Oliver, she met this week on the beach, but handsome."

"We'll get back to the kid she met this week in a few minutes. First, is there any way you think possible we can get Craig here? I feel it would be very helpful if he is one of the first people she sees when she comes around."

"His family is very nice, I know his dad loves Sara to pieces, calls her his "little girl", they only have the one son, no girls. I think they would understand and let him come."

"I need the number if you have it, and his parents' names. Also need your permission that I may call them."

80

James took the business card Howard had once given him from his wallet and gave it to the doctor, "Their names are Howard and Minnie."

"OK, Mister Blackmon, I ordered some very mild sedation for Sara before you arrived. Although still in her stupor I didn't want her waking up screaming and thrashing about possibly causing any further injury. I am going to leave you here and go call the Kirkland's. I feel the call would be better from me as I can explain, without too much detail, why we need Craig here. I am also going to send Officer Tilly back in here, please tell him everything you know and can remember about this "Oliver" kid, it could be important."

"I need to call my wife."

"Use my phone, call anyone you need, don't worry about any long distance charges on any calls you may need to make."

***

Officer Tilly talked to James, he called in and asked who had been assigned lead detective on the case.

The detective answered, "Brighton!"

"Jake, this is Don Tilly."

"Hiya, Don, How you doin'?"

"Fine thanks, hey I hear you've been assigned to the "Sara" case and I might have something for you. I'm currently at the hospital, babysitting her Dad."

"What ya got?"

"I got a description of a boy the girl met this week, Dad said he hung around the girl a lot on the beach and they went walking last night. Kid's name is Oliver, collar length black curly hair, deep tan, muscular but trim, about the Dad's height, I'd say 5'9" to

81

5'10". Dad says the kid was very courteous and extremely good looking, oh, had blue eyes."

"OK, I got it."

"Jake, the girls last name is Blackmon, positive ID by her Dad, middle name Imogene."

"Got it, Thanks Don."

"Jake?"

"Yeah?"

"That sounds a lot like the Watson kid. Wonder if he was down here using one of his Dad's places this week?"

"Oh Shit, the description is dead on. Hey, stay with the dad and help him. I was just about to come over there, but I need to go check out the cottages to see if the Watson kid, or anyone by the same description has been seen there this week. Tell Mr. Blackmon I'll be talking to him later, maybe tomorrow."

Down the hall, in another physician's office, Dr. Sykes was making a call to Alabama.

CHAPTER

8

Craig had been so excited the night before, he'd found it difficult to go to sleep. Waking early today, August 8th, he was almost beside himself, Sara would be home tonight! He planned to take her to the movie and to her favorite restaurant, then to their favorite secluded place and surprise her with something he had been paying on for months.

He was downstairs putting the finishing touches on cleaning his car when his dad called down and asked him to come upstairs.

***

Howard Kirkland was working from the office located in his home, Minnie was in the shower when the phone rang, Howard stopped working and picked up the receiver, "Hello."

"Mr. Kirkland?"

"Yes."

"Sir, my name is Sykes, I am an emergency room physician in Savannah, Georgia. Do you have a son named Craig?"

"Yes sir. Has someone with the Blackmon family been hurt? They've been vacationing the last week on Tybee Island."

"Mr. Kirkland, Sara has been hurt and is currently undergoing test and treatment here. For legal reasons I cannot go into all the details I'm sure you would want to know. There are a few things I can tell you and I hope you may be able to help me help Sara."

"Oh Lord, Little girl. Go on doctor."

"Since Sara has been here, she has been in a semi-conscious state of mind, but would occasionally arouse and say one name, your son's name, Craig. She has more than once said she loved him, then she would slip back into her current state. I believe it would be very beneficial to Sara if your son could be with her, be one of the first people she sees when she becomes fully aware of her surroundings. Is this possible?"

"Doctor Sykes consider it done. Wild horses couldn't keep my son away from that wonderful girl. He'll be on his way as soon as possible. May I have an address and any other information he will need, please?"

Writing down all the information, Howard went into the bedroom where Minnie was dressing, "We have a situation, Little Girl is hurt and is in the hospital." Howard explained all he knew. "Minnie, I can't go, I have two bids due in two days and absolutely have to get them prepared." Howard continued, "Call the Jacksons and tell them we have an emergency, ask them if they and Charles can come to the house right now. Craig cannot go alone, and I can think of no one better to go with him than Charles. Hopefully they will allow it."

The Jacksons arrived within minutes, Howard explained and asked if Charles could go with Craig. Charles dad said, "Absolutely!" Then told his son to go home, pack, hurry and come back. Within half an hour Charles had returned, all he said was, "Ready." Craig had hastily thrown some clothes in a suitcase; it was sitting by the door.

Howard kept a small safe in the house, he'd removed $2000.00 from it, half he handed to Craig, the other half to Charles, he also gave his credit card to Craig. "I know damned well neither of y'all packed everything you'll need, buy what you need once you get there", he tossed Charles the keys to his Buick. "Take

my car, there is an Atlas in the back seat and both of you know how to read road maps, Charles you drive as far as you can until you get too sleepy, Craig is not to drive for a while, at least until he has some time to calm down." All the parents hugged both boys and told them they loved them and to call when they got to Savannah.

It was a long drive to Savannah, twice the boys got lost and had to backtrack, they arrived at the hospital shortly before dawn the next day.

The lady at the information desk had instructions to send the boys straight on up even though it wasn't visiting hours, they were told to check with the head nurse at the nurse's station.

The woman looking up at the two boys appeared to be the kind of person who would bite a rattlesnake's head off just for the fun of it, "Who are you? What do you want? It's not visiting hours."

"Craig Kirkland, my friend Charles Jackson, the lady downstairs sent us up, said to check in with the head nurse here." The lady softened, "I'm head nurse of this unit, you can call me Nurse Janet," she stood, pointed at Charles and said, "Wait here."

Walking with Craig, nurse Janet had some things to tell him, "Dr. Sykes told me to be waiting for you. I am to let you in the room and allow you to stay there. What you will see will shock you, you may not even recognize her immediately, her face is swollen. Do you understand?"

"Yes Ma'am."

"I want you to be very strong, try to maintain your composure, Sara desperately needs you to be strong for her, OK?"

"Yes Ma'am."

"OK, her Daddy is in there, but he's had a sleeping pill and won't know when we go in. We will pull a chair to beside her, you can hold her hand if you want. I'll stay a few minutes in case you need me. Young man, are you ready?"

"Yes Ma'am."

Craig was indeed shocked, he gasped and tears began to flow. Nurse Janet hugged him, "Be strong honey, you have to be strong for her." They moved a chair next to the bed, Craig reached out for the hand, the tiny beautiful hand, he kissed it and laid his head on it. Nurse Janet waited a few minutes until she knew Craig was OK, she closed the door as she left.

Charles saw the lady walking up the hall in his direction, she was wiping her eyes. Nurse Janet asked Charles if he was thirsty, he was, she stepped away for a moment and returned with a soft drink. Taking Charles by the arm she began leading him down the hallway, then into an unoccupied room, Janet asked, "What does Craig mean to you?"

"He is the best friend I've and ever have had; I love him like a brother."

"Good, he is going to need you. You are no good to him if you aren't rested. Drove all night getting here, didn't you?"

"Yes Ma'am."

"Well alright Mr. Jackson. I am ordering you to finish your soda then climb your young ass in that bed and get some rest. Have I made myself clear?"

"Yes Ma'am."

"My shift is over at 7. I will leave orders that you are not to be disturbed for a while. Call me at 2PM, here is my number. I know the lady who runs the motel across the street, she will fix

you and Craig up with a room. I will make the arrangements. Understand?"

"Yes Ma'am."

"Charles, Craig is really going to need you, Sara too. She mean anything to you?"

"Ma'am, Sara is terrific. I never knew Craig could be so happy until he met her. Yeah, I love her too."

"Good, sounds to me Sara has two things going for her, Craig and YOU! Now, get some rest."

"Yes Ma'am."

***

Once that night Sara briefly regained consciousness.

Craig, asleep with his head on her hand, felt her stir, he looked up into the one eye she could open, a very beautiful green eye.

"Craig, please forgive me, I love you."

Before Craig could reply, she returned into the place her mind had taken her. Sara returned to where there were angels.

***

Following consulting with one another, the physicians determined Sara required surgery. A team of nurses came into the room, James and Craig were told to check with the nurse's station for instructions on where to wait. Charles was waiting at the station, he shook James' hand and hugged Craig, "You OK?"

"Yeah." Craig's lips quivered, his voice broke, "They're taking her to surgery."

"I heard em talking about it. They wouldn't let me come see her and see about you. But I'll tell you one damn thing, I'm waiting right here until they bring her out of that room and I damn well will see her before they take her to the operating room! You know I love her too! Different than you, but I still love her, she is my friend!"

One of the nurses at the station heard the boys' conversation, she walked down the hall and entered Sara's room, she spoke to the nurse in charge, "Alice, up at the station there is another young man who drove all night getting Craig here, he is Craig's best friend and a very good friend of Sara's, he wants to see her before you take her upstairs."

"We've given her another shot to keep her sedated, she won't know he was here."

"No, but he will know he was here. I think it will be good for him, and who knows, somewhere deep in her mind she may gain some comfort. His name is Charles."

"OK, bring him down and wait with him outside the room. Once we finish here, I will let him in for two minutes, no more, then we must go. The doctors are scrubbing as we speak."

The nurse walked to the station and spoke to Charles, "You come with me." Craig was instructed to wait.

The door to the room opened, Charles entered, one of the nurses in the room motioned him to come to where she was. "You're Charles?"

"Yes Ma'am."

"Two minutes then we have to take her."

Charles looked at Sara, he cried. Leaning over he whispered in her ear, "I'm here with Craig, Sara, I brought him." Charles

kissed Sara on the forehead, "I love you Sara, Thanks for being my friend and for making Craig so happy, he needs you."

Two of the nurses saw Sara's hand move ever so slightly, they looked at one another. Both women knew, somehow Sara knew Charles was there.

The nurse in charge gently touched Charles, "Its time."

"Yes Ma'am."

Craig had instructions where to go, the boys got on the elevator, neither said a word, each knew the other's thoughts.

***

The Blackmon family were supposed to check out of the rental house the morning Sara had been found and head home. While James had gone to the hospital Cynthia had the responsibility of packing the kids and loading the car on her own, she had bitched about it the entire time. Once leaving the rental she followed the instructions James had given her to the motel across the street from the hospital. At the registration desk all she did was gripe to the person checking her in about the money she was having to spend all because of her daughter having had the hots for some boy.

Finally, getting to the room, she instructed Brenda to take care of Giles while she went to the hospital.

Little did she know, Grandmother had already arrived.

***

James, Craig, Charles and Grandmother were in the surgical waiting area when Cynthia came in with her bad mood. She briefly hugged her husband and the boys, nodded at Grandmother, who simply nodded back. Cynthia flopped down in a chair and crossed her arms.

89

Grandmother had questions but didn't want to talk to her son in such an open area where others could possibly hear, she especially didn't want to talk to James with Cynthia close. She made small talk for a few minutes. The hospital chaplain came into the area, he had a list of each patient and called out for their loved ones as he made his way down the list. The chaplain would visit with each group of family members and have prayer. This was done with the Blackmon family.

Craig was in a chair directly across from Grandma, elbows on his knees, face in his hands. Charles was sitting beside his friend, he had a hand on Craig's back, patting, gently. Charles saw her looking at him, she smiled and mouthed the words, "Good Job", Charles offered a small smile in return.

Grandma stood, "Boys, what have you had to eat since you left home?"

"Crackers, chips, peanuts, soft drinks."

"Well, both of you come with me and let an old woman buy you a decent meal."

One boy on either side of her she took their hands and led them to the elevator. While waiting Mrs. Blackmon looked at Charles, "Until now there has only been one person ever allowed to call me anything other than Mrs. Blackmon or Grandmother, Craig is that one person, he is allowed to call me Grandma, there are now two. Charles, you are to refer to me as Grandma, understand?"

"Yes Ma'am, I feel honored."

Craig looked at his friend and told him, "You should! Trust me, it's a high honor."

Although subdued, they laughed.

The hospital cafeteria food wasn't as good as home cooked, but it was still nice to eat a hot meal. Both boys went back for seconds, Grandma had always enjoyed watching men enjoy a meal, especially young men who she knew could eat a lot. She smiled as the boys ate heartily.

Grandma also had alternative motives for taking the boys away from the waiting area. First it was doing neither of the boys any good just sitting there worrying, and Second, she knew James and Cynthia would be needing to discuss plans for the near future. James needed to be at school in one week to make preparation for the beginning of the next school year and Cynthia needed to be there as well and start helping get the office in order. She didn't know about the boy's plans, those would be left to their parents, but she would be willing to help in any way possible. She also wanted a few moments alone with Craig.

"Charles", Grandma spoke, "would you mind waiting here for a few minutes while Craig and I step outside, I'd like to have a word with him, just us."

"I'll be right here."

Craig and Grandma walked to a grassy area away from prying ears, "Craig, do you love my granddaughter or are you IN love with her? There is a difference."

"Ma'am, I've never been more in love with anything or anybody in my life. And I do realize the difference."

"I believe you; I've seen how you look at her."

"Grandma, can you keep a secret? Promise to never tell a soul what I tell you?"

"Absolutely."

"I had something on layaway for a while and have been making payments on it. Last week I worked extra hours and had

enough to pay it off. It's something I knew I couldn't give her for a couple of years but I wanted to at least show it to her, it's something she picked out a while back and we joked about. She had no idea I went back and put it on layaway. I was gonna show it to her the night they came home, I took it out of layaway on the same evening she was hurt."

"What in the world is it?"

"An engagement ring, wedding ring set. Please remember, our secret, I want to surprise her when we get back home."

"Oh My! You just confirmed all my suspicions concerning your love for her."

"Yes Ma'am."

"How much do you know about what happened to her?"

"Not much other than somebody hurt her badly. Nobody has told me much. What do you know?"

"Honey, I don't know much more than you, only a little more, I'm sure we will find out more later."

"Yes Ma'am."

"Although I may not know much more, I know something you need to know and you need to hear it from someone who cares deeply for you. It will hurt but I am here for you"

"OK."

"Sara was raped. By more than one person."

His knees gave way, he fell into the fetal position and screamed.

Grandma dropped to her knees and held the 17 year old boy as if he was a baby, she had never seen a teenage boy cry so hard,

she wept with him, "Its OK honey, Grandma's got you, Grandma is with you, Let it out."

Charles had lied, he didn't wait in the cafeteria, he'd followed and was watching from the exit door. He couldn't hear what was said but he did hear his "brother" scream. It was more than he could handle, seeing his friend hurting so badly, being held by the wonderful lady he now knew as "Grandma." Charles burst from the door and ran to aid the friend he loved so very much. He too held Craig.

A few minutes later, everyone began to calm.

Grandma looked at Charles, "You told me you would wait in the cafeteria."

"Grandma, I lied."

"I'm glad. Now take him into the men's room and help him wash his face, we need to get back upstairs. Wash yours too!"

***

Nobody kept up with the time, nobody knew how long the surgery lasted. All anyone knew was that two nurses came into the waiting area and asked James and Cynthia to come with her to speak with the surgeons. Grandma stood, "May I come? I'm Sara's grandmother." The nurse looked to James, he nodded yes, Cynthia rolled her eyes. Grandmother would be allowed.

Craig and Charles stood, one of the nurses told them they had to stay in the waiting area, family only.

Everyone was seated and offered coffee or a soft drink, all said no. There were two surgeons.

The colorectal surgeon, Doctor Davis, spoke first. "Sara has suffered trauma to her lower digestive tract. The rectum has suffered tears, these were repaired, deep bruising of the area, all

93

this will cause her a lot of discomfort in the coming days. There were internal tears, but none had penetrated the outer wall, these tears were cauterized and should heal very well. We will continue to monitor her for a few days, possibly perform another scope and see how everything is doing. She is very fortunate there were no total penetrations.

Next the OB/GYN, Doctor Carter, spoke, "Before I give you my report I want you to know there was also an ophthalmologist in the operating room, he'd asked for opportunity to do a thorough exam while Sara was under anesthesia. According to what he told me and asked that I convey to you is that he found no reason Sara's eyesight should be affected. This is good news, but he wants it checked again once Sara is home. Now, what I must tell you all is most distressing and not something I'm looking forward to. I've no idea what was inserted into your daughter but it was done so in a most vicious way. Damage was done to her reproductive system which could not be repaired to the point she will ever be able to have children. Sara will never have any babies. I am so very, very sorry.

James cried, Grandmother wept, Cynthia said, "Well, she asked for it."

Doctor Carter stood, pointing his finger at Cynthia, "I have no idea what happened on y'alls vacation week which may have led up to that beautiful young woman having been hurt in such a vile, vulgar way, but I can assure you she never asked for what she received. Her physical injuries can be repaired so she can live a somewhat normal life again, except for not bearing or giving birth to any children. But she has already been emotionally traumatized the point her mind has gone within itself and I've no idea when it will escape back to reality, nobody does. And now, what was a very healthy teenage girl a few days ago will have to be told she can never do something most women dream of, carrying and

giving birth to her own child. By God Madam, That Girl Never Asked For Any Such Thing!"

The doctor calmed himself and sat down, he continued, "We have an excellent psychiatric staff in this hospital, they've already been filled in on Sara's condition and as soon as she is able to communicate they will send someone up who is knowledgeable on how to treat rape victims. Once Sara can go home, they will also refer a doctor in your area and send her files. I can only hope and pray Sara will receive the kind of support from her family that she needs." His last sentence directed toward Cynthia. "Are there any questions?"

There were no questions, he continued, "I understand there is a boyfriend and that he is here. Is this correct?"

"Yes."

"I want to speak to him. I should get it in writing, but I trust you will give me verbal permission to let him know of Sara's condition. Especially since I have learned his is the only name she has spoken since she was hurt."

All James said was, "Tell him."

The Blackmon's left the room, a nurse went to bring Craig. When Craig stood, so did Charles, he was told to wait, "No Ma'am, where he goes, I go. I am here to help and support him and that's how it is."

Both boys entered the room, together.

Following introductions, the doctors held no punches, he spoke frankly as he gave the same report as he'd given the Blackmon's. Both boys wept. "Craig, she must love you a lot, you are the only name she has said, I hope you love her as much. She will need that love, she will need you to be tender with her

95

feelings, you can be a major part of her overall recovery, especially her mental recovery. Son, do you understand?"

"Yes Sir, whatever it takes, I'll do anything for her."

Charles spoke, "WE WILL."

Detective Jake Brighton loosened his tie as he stepped from the car, another hot August day. He walked toward the cottages, all nicely landscaped, patios with very nice furniture, Jake was thinking Watson probably charged more than a month's detective salary for a one week lease. But there were those who could afford it, and those people spent money on Tybee Island that helped provide many jobs. He saw the older couple, maybe in their 60s, enjoying lunch on the patio of a cottage down the way, as good a place as any to ask a few questions.

Jake smiled at the couple, "Hi folks, how y'all doing?"

The gentleman spoke, "Good Sir, hope you are." The lady nodded and smiled.

Frank and Sally Beam had been vacationing at Tybee Island every Summer for the last ten years, they loved the people and location.

Jake introduced himself, "I'm Detective Jake Brighton, may I ask you folks a couple of questions?"

Frank stood and shook Jake's hand, "We're the Beams, my wife Sally, I'm Frank. Please have a seat and tell us how we might be of assistance."

Sally stood, "Detective Brighton, it's a hot day, may I bring you a glass of iced tea?"

"Yes Ma'am, that'd be wonderful."

Sally returned with the tea; it was delicious, just what Jake needed on such a hot day. "Thank you, Ma'am."

"There has been an incident on the island, and I am looking for a boy about the age of sixteen I need to ask a few questions, wondering if you may have seen him? I don't have a photo, but I do have a description."

"Go ahead Jake. May I call you Jake?"

"Yes sir. Let's see, around sixteen, 5'9" maybe 5"10", black curly hair, very dark tan, slim but muscular, blue eyes, very handsome."

Sally's eyes suddenly developed a bright twinkle, "Yes! I can't say it's the same boy you're looking for but there was a boy meeting that description who was staying in the cottage across the street. And, OH—MY—GOODNESS, If I was only a girl again!! Whew!!"

Frank chuckled, "Calm down Dear, remember your blood pressure."

Suddenly Jake remembered something. "Folks, can y'all wait here? I will be back in fifteen minutes or less with something I want you both to look at. Please."

"We'll be here."

Jake ran to the car, spun the wheels as he hit the main road. Stopping at the marina he ran inside to where Cap'n Chuck's wall of photos were. Finding what he was looking for he took the thumbtack from it and yelled to Chuck, "Chuck, I need this for a while."

"Take what you need. See Ya, Jake!"

Jake showed the picture to the Beams of the boy posing with the very large fish.

"Damned nice fish!" Frank exclaimed

"That's him, his name is Oliver," Sally said. He was outside with the other boys when we arrived, came over introduced himself and helped us get the bags out of the car, very courteous young man." Sally grinned a mischievous grin and winked, "I got a REAL good look at him then. That cute little girl we saw him with may be the luckiest girl in the world."

Jake asked, "Can you tell me about the girl you saw him with and the circumstances when you saw them together, please?"

Frank spoke, "It's my turn to give a OH—MY—GOODNESS! She was a little knockout, middle teens, petite, maybe five feet tall, 90 to 95 pounds, blonde with her hair cut very short, not many girls or women could wear their hair like that and it be attractive, she made it look adorable, she had a terrific tan. As much as Oliver made Sally wish she was young again, I feel the same about Sara." Frank turned to his wife and laughed. Sally winked.

"The girl's name was Sara? You're sure? How do you know?"

"Oh, Sally and I like to walk on the beach and hunt shells, we saw she and Oliver hanging out a few times. One morning we stopped to chat, he introduced us to his friend, Sara, and her sister, can't remember her name. Saw them a few more times, once with some folks I guess were the girl's parents and a little boy who could have been a little brother, nice looking family. We saw Oliver playing with the little boy, he seemed the kind of kid who would do such a thing, you know, spend some time with a little kid. We also saw them making out on the beach one night."

Sally spoke up, "Oh Frank, don't forget about last evening. Right around sunset Oliver and the girl, Sara I mean, came walking to the cottage, they had their arms around one another, at least

she had her arm around his waist, he had his hand on her butt, I thought, Lucky Girl!"

"Yes Ma'am, go on please."

"Anyhow, I figured they were going to do what hot to trot teens do when they get a chance." She giggled, "I would these days, times have changed from when I was a teenager."

"Yes Ma'am."

"So, they went in and were there quite a while. What I saw later makes me believe she really must be a little slut, another one of the boys came out, a little while after that Oliver and the other two came out, they were all laughing and drinking beer. The first boy who'd come out went back in, a few minutes later the other three went in but weren't there long until back out they came, still drinking and laughing. Can you even imagine, one girl with four boys? Even on my wildest days, and I had a few wild days, I would never do that!" Sally turned to Frank and grinned, "Two maybe, but never four." Frank looked at his wife, winked and laughed.

Jake was speechless for a few seconds. He looked at Sally, then at Frank, they were an attractive couple, even in their sixty's. He could only imagine the wild times they must have experienced together.

Snapping out of it, Jake asked, "Anything else?"

Frank answered, "Yes, she must have gotten very drunk, or stoned, one of the boys came out with her, he was having to help her walk. He walked off with her and was gone a while. While he was gone the other boys started loading stuff in their car. The boy returned and loaded his stuff, they all left, haven't seen hide nor hair of em since. Any of this help you?"

100

"Yes Sir. I need to ask y'all to stick around for a while. Another officer will be here shortly and will get some information on how we might get in touch with you again once your vacation is over. Thank you, you've been more help than you know."

Once again Jake ran to the car and spun the wheels. The radio in his car was on the blink, he drove back to the marina. "Chuck, I'm keeping your photo for a while, need your phone."

"Help yourself, Jake."

"Chief, I need a search warrant, NOW, for Cottage number five at the Watson Complex. Please call the Judge, tell him it's very important concerning the Sara Blackmon case, I'm sure he already knows about it, he and Doc Jack are buddies. Send a car to pick up the warrant and another car with two officers to the complex."

"Jake, I talked to Tilly and know what they did to the girl. You got a good lead?"

"Yes Sir!"

"Making the calls now. I'll also be down there in a while."

***

The two officers arrived on scene, Jake stationed one at the cottage with instructions nobody was to enter without his authorization, NOBODY! The next officer was introduced to Frank and Sally Beam. After introduction Jake asked the Beams how long they planned to stay, Frank answered, "The rest of this week and the week after, we always stay a full two weeks."

"Sir", Jake said, "Once I get back to the office, I will type up a report on what you've told me from the notes I took during our conversation. I will drop by in a day or two and let you and Sally read it for accuracy. If no changes need to be made, I will ask you both to sign the report. OK?"

"Happy to help. Jake, what's this all about? If I may ask."

"Sir, I really can't say, at least not now. I hope you understand."

"Completely."

While Jake was looking around the cottage patio, he heard a car drive up, it was Chief Adams, he had a paper in hand. "I went to visit the judge myself, he was happy to help." Adams handed Jake the warrant. "I also talked to Tilly. The doctors are still trying to figure out why she's bleeding and if it doesn't stop soon, they will operate."

"Chief, I feel bad about not having already talked to her parents but felt I needed to come here as soon as Tilly gave me the description of the boy."

"You did the right thing, Jake. Let's go see what we can find."

The door lock was cheap, the officer picked it easily. Chief Adams told him, "I do not want to know how you know how to do that!"

Before anyone entered the cottage Jake gave some orders, the officer was instructed to get the camera and extra film from Jakes car, and to take photos of everything he was told to. "Nobody touches anything, not even you Chief, the only fingerprints I want left inside other than the people previously here will be mine, mine only, I do not want the area contaminated and confused. Got it?"

Everyone agreed, they entered the building.

The place was a mess, something one would expect to find after four teenagers had been partying. The sink was full of dirty dishes with more piled up on the cabinet, beer cans sitting everywhere, most empty, some half full. Sheets had been stripped from the bed; the mattress was stained. Jake pointed; the officer

photographed it. Entering the bathroom Jake saw blood on the floor and on a towel, more photographs. Back into the bedroom, Jake knew how to examine an area, he stood in one place and allowed his eyes to careful scan every square inch, he saw a potting trowel laying in a corner, a broom with a mostly yellow handle leaning against the wall, the end of the handle was covered with stains, he closed his eyes and let his nose go to work, the scent of sex was detected, urine and feces, a very strong scent of sweat and beer. Opening his eyes Jake moved to the small utility room, there was a metal trashcan, he removed the lid, Jake turned his head away from the odor as his sense of smell rebelled. Recovering, he investigated the contents of the can, there were sheets. Jake motioned for a few more photographs then told everyone to go back outside.

"Chief, we're not set up to perform the kind of forensics we need on this kind of crime scene, and it is a crime scene. I would like the State Police to bring in their people and perform a very thorough forensics examination on both the interior and exterior of the cottage. I will want to be here while they work."

"Jake, you need it, you got it. I'll make the call."

"Chief, we already know the Watson boy was with Sara this week, we know he brought her back here last night and that she could barely walk when she left, got eyewitnesses. We also know who his father is and the power his money has in this state. And though I can't prove it, I have a good idea he has a lot of powerful politicians in his pocket."

"What are you trying to say, Jake?"

"Sir, I think we may just be in for one hell of a shitstorm! Do you have my back sir?"

"Jake, we've both survived hurricanes here, to hell with a shitstorm, I got your back all the way! Between me and you, I

never liked Thomas Watson anyhow, he's a crooked sonofabitch who gained most of his wealth by manipulating, running over and using people! From the looks of it, the apple didn't fall far from the tree. You bet your ass, Detective, I got your back!"

Jake set up an around the clock watch on the house. Absolutely nobody was to enter without him. He headed to the office; a report needed to be typed.

***

"Hello Mr. Blackmon, I'm Detective Jake Brighton. I hate to intrude at a time like this, but I need to ask you some questions, please."

"It's fine Detective Brighton, I've been expecting you."

"Sir, please call me Jake."

"And I'm James"

The men shook hands, a nurse escorted them to an empty conference room and provided coffee.

"James, may I record our conversation?"

"Yes."

"I need you to tell me all you can about Sara's movements and people you may have seen her with this past week, everything you can remember."

For the next 10 minutes Jake allowed James to talk uninterrupted. James told of his daughter spending a lot of time on the beach and how much she loved it. He told of a boy she'd met named Oliver who seemed to be a very nice kid and that she had gone for a walk with him the day before. Sara had also met Oliver's friends; they were all on the same football team. James

told of the argument Sara had with her mother and that she was angry when she left the house.

"Sir, have you talked to Sara yet?"

"No, her mind, as the doctors explained, has gone into a form of neutral, it removed her mental state from the fear and trauma, she cannot talk yet. Although the doctors and nurses say she will occasionally come to long enough to scream for her boyfriend. Then she goes blank, almost hypnotic, again."

"Yes sir, I've heard of it happening."

"It was that Oliver boy and his friends, wasn't it?"

"James, all I can tell you now is that we have a suspect, possible suspects, and a location of the assault. I wish I could tell you more, but at this time I cannot."

"I understand."

"Most importantly, Sara is alive and in the best of care. The staff here are outstanding people."

James began crying, "yes" was all he could manage.

* * *

Having spoken to the ER staff and gotten a copy of their initial report, next stop was Doc Jack's place.

"Come in Jake, I knew I'd see you soon."

"Thanks Doc", the detective handed the ER report to the physician, "Tell me what you think."

Doc Jack read the reports carefully before handing them back to Jake, "About what I expected. I wish I could have done more for her here, just not equipped to handle the kind of care she needed. Any idea who did it?"

"You're my Doctor, how far does that doctor patient secret stuff go?"

"It goes as far as anything you tell me as long as I charge you for the visit, that'll be two bits, give me a quarter."

"Jake handed Jack a quarter, "I have very good reason to believe Oliver Watson and some of his friends are involved."

"Damn, that arrogant little son of a bitch! Why am I not surprised?"

"Yeah, I feel the same. Jack, I got a bad feeling about this, Thomas Watson's money and such."

"Do the best you can to present the best case possible. Other than that, there is only one more thing you can do."

Jake looked quizzically at the good doctor.

"Protect the girl the best you can. When she comes to her senses, and she will sooner or later, be as gentle as possible with your questions. Pretty little thing, she didn't deserve this, no woman does. What is coming will be very hard on her emotionally, I hope she can survive it. Frankly, I wouldn't care if the people who did it suddenly met with tragic accidents."

***

The State Police forensics report was delivered by courier. Jake the report, placed it back in the envelope, he took the rest of the day off.

Sandy Brighton had done laundry and was in the process of pressing Jake's shirts when her very pale husband walked into the house and sat down at the kitchen table.

"Are you OK Jake?"

"Would you hand me a glass of ice water please?"

Sandy sat the water before her husband then sat next to him, he handed her the envelope, "Read this." Sandy was in tears by the time she had finished reading the report. She looked at Jake, tears were streaming down his face, he spoke, "A potting trowel handle? A broom handle?? Those bastards crammed a fucking potting trowel handle and a damned broom handle into that girl. Damn!! I want to nail their asses to a wall. I want those animals, BAD!"

She had never seen her husband this way and she knew some of the cases he'd been assigned had been bad. This one affected him in a way she had never seen. She also agreed, she wanted him to nail their asses to a wall!

"Jake, you get em, you get em good!"

***

"Chief, we have witnesses who saw four boys, including Oliver Watson, at the cottage with Sara Blackmon. I have the State Police Forensics report which also includes fingerprints, blood types and all other information they could ascertain. Now we need warrants."

"OK, I'll personally take the information and request to the judge. I see no reason he won't issue warrants."

"One more thing sir. I know the chief of police at South Creek. He is an unpleasant, boisterous, card carrying member of the Klan, and is probably neck deep in Thomas Watson's back pocket. Is there any way we can circumvent him and his department? I had also rather him not know about the warrants until the arrests have been made."

Chief Adams agreed, "Let's get the warrants then I'll make a call to the county sheriff over there, he's a hunting buddy, his power of jurisdiction supersedes the chief's. He also enjoys

surprising people, especially those he doesn't like, and he likes neither the chief nor Watson. I know this to be a fact."

CHAPTER

10

"JESUS CHRIST, Oliver, What the hell went on at Tybee?"

The company who performed cleaning at the cottages had called, the police were not allowing anyone into Cottage 5, the same one Oliver and his friends had just occupied. Overheard was something about a girl having been there two nights before. Thomas thanked the person for the information, he then called Oliver.

"What do you mean Dad?"

"The cops are not allowing anyone into the cabin you stayed in last week. What went on there? Specifically, two days ago?"

"We, uh, had a little party."

"We, who?"

"The guys, me and a chick we met on the beach and I spent some time with."

"Four guys and one girl? You fuck her?"

"Yes sir, all of us did, she loved a good party."

"Oh Jesus. Was she hurt?"

"Not so I could tell, she was half stoned when we got there, then she started drinking beer. She was totally drunk out of her head when she left, but she could walk, David walked with her a

little way just to be sure she'd be OK. We loaded up right after and came on home night before last, got in pretty late."

"Damn, wild ass kids. I'll call you later. Right now, I've got to make some calls and see what's going on and what damage control may be required. You stick around the house. Understand?"

"Roger and Ten Four, Sir."

***

Ted Anderson, major with the Georgia State Trooper Office picked up the phone, "Ted, this is Thomas Watson."

"I've been expecting your call. Let me call you back in half an hour."

"I'll be waiting."

Ted Anderson was a well-liked officer in the State Police who had worked his way up through the ranks, he was also bought and paid for by Thomas Watson's money.

Watson answered the phone; the caller was Anderson. "They hurt the girl, she's in the hospital now, may be looking at surgery. I'm not sure how much I can do, Colonel Wilson has taken a special interest, he has a 16-year-old daughter."

"What do they know now?"

"Forensics is going over the place. Oliver brought a girl to the place, he and his friends, or at least he and two of them, maybe more, had their way with her. Mr. Watson, I think they raped her, all of them. Oliver may have gone too far."

"Shut-up Anderson and keep your opinions to yourself. I pay dearly for what you can offer and provide for me, not for what you think, I can do the thinking."

110

Anderson knew he was in too deep, he sheepishly responded, "OK."

* * *

He was on his boat enjoying the company of two very young women, he heard his call sign come over the CB radio. Only one person knew the call sign, when he heard it, he was to call the person via telephone as soon as possible. The attorney allowed the young lady kneeling in front of him to finish what she'd begun. It was full throttle back to the dock.

Samuel Bartolli 'Esquire' had one client, Thomas Watson. Samuel was kept on retainer and took care of legal issues Mr. Watson may have that his other attorneys deemed too dirty to touch. He called from a phone booth. Lunch the next day was arranged.

For the most part, Bartolli had initially been put on retainer in case Oliver ever got in trouble, he was also to keep a close eye on the boy and report back to Thomas. He had reported Oliver's actions with the Jackson woman and two others. What nobody knew was that Bartolli had invested in very expensive equipment capable of recording on 8MM movie film or 35MM still photos in very low light and/or from long distances if required. He had a safe at his home containing hours of 8MM and hundreds of still photos of Oliver, and sometimes his friend Andy, having sex, often deviant sex, with some married women and many local girls. That wasn't all, there were also films and stills of both Thomas Watson and Alena Watson in compromising situations with people, often multiple people, none of whom were their respective spouse. All this was Bartolli's insurance in the event Thomas Watson ever turned on him.

* * *

The meeting took place at a nice little cabin an hour's drive from South Creek. Alena had wanted a peaceful place in the woods, located on its own lake, Thomas had seen to it. Alena always got what she wanted.

Bartolli had picked up fried chicken, both men were hungry, conversation was casual as they ate. Bartolli knew Watson never liked to discuss business while eating, always afterward.

"Bartolli, Oliver and some of his friends may have taken their fun a bit too far. I need you to get on top of it and start damage control as soon as possible. I mean the instant we leave this cabin."

"No problem sir. Tell me what you know up till now."

Watson talked a few minutes and gave the lawyer what he could, which wasn't much yet. A few names, location of where it had happened, a couple of phone numbers to people that might be happy to provide information and the hospital the girl had been taken to. "Oliver told me the girl is from Anniston, Alabama, that might be helpful."

"Might be, we'll see. Anything else?"

"Not at this time. If I learn anything, I'll contact you, you do the same."

"Will do."

***

Watson heard the boy come in the house, "Oliver, come to my office and close the door."

"Sir?"

"I've spoken with a couple of people about looking into what took place at Tybee. They are also to continue checking out the

girl, possibly in her hometown if need be. Last word I got was that she isn't able to talk."

"OK."

"I want you and your friends to keep quiet about this but be sure everyone is on the same page as far as what happened, but under no circumstances should it be discussed with anyone who was not there. I also expect soon there will be cops around asking you all some questions, be damned sure everyone's answers are the same. Understand?"

"Yes sir."

"Good."

"Mom know?"

"Yes, she told me to protect her baby boy at all costs. From what little I already do know; the costs may be considerable."

* * *

Bartolli had a few contacts at the hospital, what he heard from them wasn't good for the girl, the boys had really done a hell of a number on her. Bartolli was pissed off about what he'd heard, but he had a job to do, and would do it. He reported to Watson what he knew and warned him to be expecting the cops soon.

* * *

Twice Thomas had seen a county sheriff's car pass the house, he knew they were keeping an eye on Oliver's movements. Time to call Anderson again.

"Tell me what you know."

"Forensics found blood, urine, feces on the mattress, sheets, a potting trowel handle and a broom handle. They used a fucking potting trowel handle and broom handle on the girl, Watson!"

113

"Just tell me what you know and keep your emotions in check!"

"She has had surgery, the kid will never be able to have any children. I want nothing more to do with this."

"You will continue to do as you're told or suffer the consequences. In your case that will probably mean a prison term. DO YOU UNDERSTAND?"

"Yes, damnit, I understand."

What else?"

"They beat her up bad, at least one of them bit her titty and somebody burned her with a cigarette. Her rectum was torn and some injury's inside her backside, and vaginal tears. They fucking beat up a beautiful, tiny 16-year-old girl, raped her, sodomized her, God knows what else, and left her on the side of the road like nothing more than garbage when they finished with her. It's been determined that at least three of them screwed her, three blood types determined from semen, I'm betting two of them have the same blood type. THAT IS WHAT I KNOW!"

"You will keep all that too yourself. Is that clear?"

"Yes."

***

Now, it was a waiting game. Waiting for what the cops would do next. More help might be required, Thomas called the bank and had money transferred into a cash account. This was going to be expensive.

CHAPTER

11

Through the inner workings of her own mind and the slow reduction of drugs meant to keep her calm, it was a week before Sara became fully aware of where she was and who was around her. For the rest of her life she would recall the first person she recognized, Craig. All Sara could say when she saw him was that she loved him and to please forgive her. She would then say no more to him, simply turn her head and cry. He would try to hold her hand, but she would slip it away. Craig knew he should not press the issue, give her time.

The puffiness in her face was gone, the swollen eye was almost back to normal except for the remaining bruises, those would fade away soon. Sara was recovering nicely from her surgery although still sore. With discomfort when she sat up, this too was getting better by the day. It was her mind now that required the most treatment. The trauma of the rape had left her almost emotionless. There was more, there was something she was obsessed by, for some reason she needed Craig's forgiveness, she had not said what it was.

The phycologist who specialized in treating rape victims would soon discover Sara's secret.

***

James had grown weary of Cynthia's attitude; he'd sent her and the children home. He'd also called the school, the principal

was very understanding and told James to take all the time he needed. James mother had informed her son she was staying as long as she wanted to and that he, the psychologist and herself needed to sit down and have a long talk concerning Sara's future. Put bluntly by the wise older lady to her son, "Sara will only suffer if she returns home and has to listen to Cynthia's belittling! You think about that!"

***

"Hi Sara" the nice lady said, "I'm Zoe Brewer, I work in the mental health department here and I wanted to drop by to meet you. May we talk a little?"

"Hi, sure." Sara's voice was bland in her greeting.

Opening the file, the lady read aloud, "Says here you are Sara Imogene Blackmon, sixteen years old, live in Alabama, you recently underwent surgery and some other things we will discuss in due time. What it doesn't say in here is that you are very lovely, cute beyond words, have a handsome boyfriend who is sitting outside the room, he refuses to sit in the waiting room, says it's too far, he wants to be close. By the way, there is another boy with him who flat refuses to leave your boyfriends side, he's cute too! Oh, I love your hair!" Already knowing the boy's names but wanting to start a conversation with Sara, Zoe asked, "What are their names?"

"Craig is my boyfriend, the boy with him is his best friend and good friend of mine, Charles."

Zoe Brewer was in her mid-thirties, herself petite and attractive, married, mother of a six-year-old son. Zoe had been raped when she was 18 years old and while undergoing treatment had decided she wanted to help other rape victims.

"So, Sara, everyone here treating you well?"

116

"Yes Ma'am."

"Whoa! First, I'm Zoe, not ma'am. Deal?"

With just a brief, ever so slight smile, Sara said, "deal."

"The surgeons reports say you're healing up very well, that's good. How do you feel right now, physically?"

"Still pretty sore but I remember coming around a couple of times, I don't know when. I remember screaming, it all hurt very badly."

"If you had one wish right now, what would it be?"

"That Craig can somehow, someday find it in his heart to forgive me."

"For what?"

"I can't say."

"Why?"

"Because I am so ashamed of myself." Sara began to cry, Zoe let her.

The tears slowed after a while, Zoe leaned over and hugged Sara, "Sara, I am here to help you, I want to help you. You have gone through something no female should ever experience and although physical injuries can heal, the emotional injuries can sometimes take longer, I know. You will be seeing much of me and we will confront the demons within you, together we will devise a plan to defeat them. I will ask only one favor of you, be open with me, tell me what you feel, no matter how badly it might hurt. Sometimes we must hurt before we can get better. I'm going to leave you now but will be back soon. OK?"

"OK."

The boys stood when Zoe came from the room, "Craig, I have to make some rounds but will be back in a couple of hours. When I get back, I need to talk to you." Looking at Charles she said, "No offense, but I need to talk to Craig alone. You may wait just outside, OK? I promise I won't beat him up or anything!"

She put the file down on the desk, pointed at it and asked, "Craig, this file contains up to date reports from every Doctor, nurse and even the ambulance attendants who have cared for Sara in one way or another, do you know the one common thing every one of those people put into their reports?"

"No Ma'am."

"Each and every one of those people have reported that YOU, not her mother, not her father, not her grandmother, who I happen to like a lot by the way, YOU are the only name she ever mentioned. Have you any idea how damned special that makes you in her life? That even in a state of bewilderment, self-hypnosis, call it a stupor if you like, that YOU, ONLY YOU, are the person she could think of?"

Craig sat and looked at Zoe.

"Real damned special! You remember that! How old are you?"

"Seventeen."

"Craig, she wants your forgiveness."

"For What? I mean, she woke up once and asked me to forgive her then slipped back into her stupor. I have no idea what I'm supposed to forgive her for. If I knew, I would!"

"I don't know, but I will find out. Craig, we will learn things together, Sara and me, which will be discussed with her father, I understand her mother has returned home with the other children. I am going out on a limb just talking to you now, any

118

further discussions between you and I will be with the permission of her legal guardian, who at this time is her father. Damned legalities often get in my way of helping people, but I am bound under the law. Understand?"

"Yes Ma'am, and ma'am?

"Yes."

"Thanks for taking what appears to be a special interest in Sara. I really mean it when I say I appreciate it."

"You're welcome. Sara and I have some things in common. Let's say, she and I are kindred spirits."

Craig nodded.

"Now get out of here, I've got to call a detective who has been bugging the hell out of me for several days."

Zoe made the call, "Detective Brighton please."

***

Sara improved daily, by the end of the third week following the assault and subsequent surgery she could walk with very little pain, only mild discomfort. Grandma Blackmon had purchased the makeup and shampoo Sara had requested, she also purchased new clothes, Cynthia had taken EVERYTHING back to Alabama. In some ways Sara was returning to normal, in other ways she needed more time, her heart, mind and soul were being tormented terribly.

James tried talking to his daughter but her desire to converse with him was very limited, she wished he had shown this kind of concern for her in previous years when her mother had been so abusive. But he hadn't and she could only imagine, once home, things would be the same, probably worse because of the decisions she'd made the first week of August.

Craig spent many hours visiting Sara, he brought gifts, snacks he knew she liked, flowers, the brand of root beer she preferred, she thanked him but would still not talk much, wouldn't hold hands and turned her head when he tried to kiss her. Each evening, when visiting hours were over, Craig would tell Sara he loved her. Each evening as Craig was leaving, just as he got to the door, Sara would tell him she loved him and hoped someday he could forgive her. She would say no more.

***

Zoe never bothered to knock, she simply walked into the room and learned much from the facial expressions of anyone, everyone, who were there. Smiles always were good things, they meant improvement was taking place, blank expressions or frowns meant just the opposite. Tears could go either way, good or bad. Today there were blank expressions on Sara's, James' and Craig's faces.

Zoe smiled when she spoke, "Hi guys, good to see you and all that, now get lost, Sara and I are going to chat a while."

Once the door closed Sara looked at Zoe and began to cry, "I can't go home, I don't want to go home, I will not go home!"

Zoe knew today's session would be a long one, that Sara had finally gotten to the point she was ready to open her soul, maybe not completely yet, but more than before. She called the nurses station and requested they not be disturbed, if any medications were due to please knock on the door and allow her to administer the meds. Every nurse had come to love Sara and they knew Zoe was damned good at her job. It was agreed, other than meds there would be no interruptions.

Putting down the phone Zoe looked at Sara, "Honey, there must be reason's you don't want to go home, it can't be because

the food here is great, it isn't. Talk to me girl, I listen very, very well."

For two hours Zoe sat silently as Sara told of her of the abuse, somehow, she could remember so much of it, even from her very early years, in detail. Things came back to her that she'd long thought forgotten, the slapping's when missing a word while learning to read, the verbal abuse, being told she was ugly, the busted lips, knots on her head and all the different times it had all happened. She told of how her father knew but did nothing about it, how he simply looked the other way and let it continue because he was such a coward.

Sara told of how until she'd met Craig her only escape from the abuse were the times she spent with her Grandmother, it had been her Grandmother who'd taught her proper table manners, how to walk like lady, dress like a lady. It was the older woman who had read to her and allowed Sara to read and when a word was missed would gently, kindly point out how it should be. The saddest times in her life were when she had to walk the path from Grandmother's house back to her own and when Craig would take her home following a date. She hated the idea of ever going back to that place and would not.

There were several times Sara couldn't talk; she'd had to take a few minutes to cry. Zoe patiently let it happen. At the two-hour mark Sara suddenly said, "I'm hungry."

"Me too. You like milkshakes? The lady in the cafeteria makes some good ones."

"Chocolate please."

Zoe made the call, "Jane please. Hi Jane, I have a very special patient up here that I've bragged to about your milkshakes. Think you could send up a large chocolate and one of those famous strawberries?" Jane asked the patient's name, Zoe told her.

Every employee in the hospital knew about Sara and what had happened to her, people talk, even when they aren't supposed to. Every employee was pulling for Sara, many included her in their nightly bedtime prayers. These milkshakes would be extra special.

"Sara, where will you go?"

"I don't know, but I'm not going home."

"What about your friends? Charles cares a lot about you, what about him? More importantly, what about that boy out there who loves you so much that when he isn't in here, he sits in a chair just outside the door? What about Craig?"

Again, Sara cried.

Having recovered, "Sooner or later everything about that week will be revealed, everyone will know all that took place. If they've not already been, the boys who hurt me will be identified and arrested, I know this. There will probably be a trial. Once everything is known those who once called me their friend will shun me, they will talk about me behind my back, they will consider me, in their eyes, to be a slut. I can't blame them. The less than honorable boys in school will think I'm an easy lay and will do all they can to get into my pants, many will lie that they managed to do so just to make big talk."

"Sara, understand this, what happened to you does not make you a slut in any way shape nor form!"

"Zoe, you don't know everything."

"Ready to talk about it?"

"No. I am trying very hard to figure out how to say what I know I need to say. I'm just not ready yet, not ready."

"And Craig?"

"He is the worst of it. I will break the heart of the person I love most in this world, the person I know loves me more than anyone in this world. I only hope he can someday forgive me. I'm very tired now."

"OK, it's been a long session. I need to tell you a couple of things before I leave. You're right, there are four suspects, they've not been arrested yet pending talking to you and you identifying them. I've held off the detective in charge of the investigation from questioning you, he has spoken to your father, I don't know what was said. The detective will not be allowed, if I have any say, and I have say but also have a boss who can override me, to question you until you and I both determine you are ready, do you think you are?"

"No."

"I agree."

"You said there was something else?"

"Yes, I need to talk to your father about what you and I discussed today."

"I understand."

Although trained to avoid any emotional connection, in this case it was unavoidable, Zoe couldn't fight it off, she had developed a very strong bond with Sara. Standing to leave, Zoe looked once again at the pretty young woman who deserved better than she'd been dealt. Sara was reaching her arms out, as a small child does, for a hug. As they hugged, Sara whispered, "Thank You Zoe, thank you for being here for me."

Zoe left the room, walked past Craig and Charles without speaking. She hurried to the stairway, not wanting to wait for the elevator, and rushed the two floors down to her office. Zoe fell into her chair, lay her head on her desk. Zoe cried.

CHAPTER

12

He sat down across from her, Zoe poured them both coffees, "Good morning Mr. Blackmon."

"Mrs. Brewer, how are you?"

"I'm well Thanks. Mr. Blackmon part of my treatment for Sara also involves knowledge of her family life and the people surrounding her there. Do you understand?"

"Yes, much of my education includes having studied psychology."

"So, you know much of what I may ask and what I need to know."

"Yes."

"How is your relationship with your daughter?"

"Not nearly as good as it should be. Regrettably and admittedly I feel, no, I know I have failed at being the father to her I should have been."

"And her relationship with her mother?"

"Mrs. Brewer, if I may be blunt I can save you, us, a lot of time. At the risk of saying something unbecoming of a gentleman, may I be blunt?"

"Absolutely!"

"My wife Cynthia is an abusive bitch to Sara, and sometimes her sister, but mostly toward Sara. She has never done anything other than belittle her, she has hit her, slapped her and if you look at Sara's legs you will find scars from a beating with a belt her mother gave her when she was only 3 years old. The last time she hit Sara with her hand it hurt, she started using hair brushes and occasionally a wooden spoon and would hit her on the head, not hard enough to break the skin, but the knots and bruises would be hidden by the hair. Mrs. Brewer, I repeat, my wife is an abusive bitch! But that isn't the worst of it." He paused.

"Mr. Blackmon, continue when you're ready."

"I knew what was happening and turned a blind eye to it. I could have stopped it, but I was a coward, less than a man. Things are changing the moment Sara and I get home."

"We need to talk about something Sara has told me."

"What?"

"Sara has told me explicitly that she has no desire to return home, in fact, that she will not return home."

"She is a minor, I am her father. Once I talk to her, she will obey me."

"Sir, you may believe that, but I've seen things like this particular case, of a child refusing to return to the environment they were raised in. I can also tell you that in not one of those cases, sadly, has it ever worked out. Somehow the child found a way to leave, a couple waited until they were of age to join the military, most others ran away, some with disastrous consequences."

"What would you recommend?"

126

"Is there any family member Sara would be comfortable living with who would give her the support and love she will need for a long time and see to it she continues her therapy?"

"Only one I know of, my mother."

"I met her briefly, a lovely lady. Do you know where she is now?"

"Just before I came to this meeting she was in the room with Sara, Craig and Charles. She may still be there."

"Mr. Blackmon, may I call and have her come down here if she is still there? If so, I will ask you to wait outside for a few minutes while I speak with her alone, then have you come back in and we will all talk. Before I go any further, I want you to know something. My priority is Sara, but I am also here to help you and your wife, as well as Sara's grandmother."

"I understand, thank you."

Zoe made the call to the nurse's station. Yes, Mrs. Blackmon was still there, she was given directions to Zoe's office and would be along in a few minutes.

***

"Thank you for meeting with me Mrs. Blackmon, would you care for coffee?"

"No thank you dear, and you're welcome. How may I help you help my granddaughter?"

For the next several minutes Zoe went over her conversations with Sara and James. Grandmother sat patiently and listened to what the young psychologist had to say. Once finished Zoe waited for the stately woman's response.

"Mrs. Brewer, nothing in this world would give me greater pleasure than to have my beautiful granddaughter come live with me in Knoxville. I absolutely adore that girl and will see to it her every need is met."

"Mrs. Blackmon, that's music to my ears. And she really is beautiful but doesn't seem to realize it."

"I call that "whipped puppy syndrome." She's been told so many times, and it's been beaten into her by her mother, that she is not beautiful. She doesn't know how very beautiful she really is."

"Whipped puppy syndrome, I'll remember that for future reference. May I call your son in so we can all discuss this?"

"Please do."

The next hour was spent discussing the details of how Sara would come to live with her grandmother. Legalities would be required giving Mrs. Blackmon guardianship so she could make decisions concerning Sara's best interests. The question of any issues with Cynthia signing over guardianship to Mrs. Blackmon came up. The women didn't like one another, Cynthia could possibly create issues for no other reason than to spite the elder woman, Sara's wellbeing be damned. James looked at his mother with a look she had only seen once, "There will be no problems from Cynthia, I can assure you both."

James' mother had often wondered if her son would ever grow a backbone and become the head of his house. She got her answer in the look she saw that she'd only seen one time, once was all it had taken, from James' own father! Cynthia had no way of knowing, yet, but she had just lost her place in the pecking order of the Blackmon household.

Zoe spoke, "Until all this is legally worked out, I need both of you to keep it under wraps. The last thing Sara needs now is to be

built up and have her legs pulled from under her if something goes awry. Understand?"

Both agreed.

Mrs. Blackmon asked if there was a phone she could use. It seems she had befriended a widower at church who also happened to be an attorney and owed her a favor, or two, and could very well take care of any papers which would be required. She failed to mention why the favors were owed, she simply winked at Zoe.

Offering her desk and phone to Mrs. Blackmon, Zoe took James by the arm, they left the office.

***

Next day, change of venue. Zoe called up and told Sara to get dressed in street clothes, "Be ready at 10 AM. We will be talking today at a more pleasant place than a hospital room."

Unbeknownst to Sara, behind the hospital and across the street was a park. Zoe entered the room pushing a wheelchair, "Hop in kiddo, let's go!" Once they crossed the street and entered the gate to the park Sara asked if she could walk. Zoe allowed it, thinking it would be good for Sara to get a little exercise. The day was beautiful, still a hot late August day, but very lovely, they talked little as they simply let Sara enjoy being outside. After a while Sara began to tire, they found a bench and watched two boys skipping stones on the pond.

"Sara, you know sooner or later you have to, need to, talk about it, don't you?"

"Yes, I know. Just not sure how to, or where to start. And there is so much I don't remember."

"Let's begin with how you got to the place you were assaulted, do you remember?"

"Yes, I walked."

"OK, nobody forced you. Were you going there of your own will? Why?"

"Yes, nobody forced me, it was my decision to go."

"Why?"

Sara hung her head, "I'm so ashamed." She cried, Zoe provided tissues and soothing words of comfort.

Sara raised her head, looked into Zoe's eyes and said, "I went there to have sex with Oliver. I cannot express how very ashamed I am of myself, but I put myself in position to have what happened to me because I wanted to have sex with some boy I met on the beach that week. I was acting like a tramp, a slut."

Stunned by this sudden revelation, Zoe sat back and took a deep breath. "OK, I'm going to back up, First I am assuming the night of your assault was not the first time you ever had sex. Second, we need to go back to the entire week and how you and this, Oliver, came to get acquainted. From there we will go as far as you want to talk."

"You're right, it was not my first time. Craig and I took each other's virginities last April and have had sex several times since, as often as we could without being caught. And, I also had sex with Oliver the day before. It was the best I ever experienced, he knew more than Craig knew how to do and it was great, I wanted more. Words cannot describe what a slut I feel I am, I am so ashamed, so ashamed."

"OK, continue as long as you want." Zoe took two soft drinks from her pack, Sara began to talk.

Sara began with the day, early in the week, when Oliver and his friends had shown up and teased her about her short hair. She instantly was attracted to him and how he came back alone

130

several times during the week, flattered by the attention she was receiving from the best looking, most handsome boy she'd ever met. He was smart, witty, funny, courteous, honor society and played football, he was perfect. Sara told Zoe about the entire week and every day she was with Oliver and what had taken place, and how amazed she was to have someone like him paying attention to someone like her, there were much prettier girls on the beach, he could have had any one of them. Zoe stopped her right there.

"Honey, you really have no idea how beautiful you really are, have you?"

"No, the only people who ever told me I was pretty are Grandmother and Craig, but I've been told otherwise by other people, especially my mother. I really didn't believe Grandmother nor Craig, I thought they were just trying to be kind."

"Well, let me inform you, they were not just being kind, they were being honest. I can't tell you how many times the people in the hospital, people who work there, have told me how gorgeous you are. Now, continue."

Sara continued and gave as accurate an account of the events of the week as she could, right up to the point her mind went into neutral and everything went blank. Sara spoke of seeing angels then she could remember only bits and pieces. Something about someone washing her, then someone helping her walk and telling her over and over that he was sorry. She vaguely remembered a nice man and woman giving her water and wiping her face. She remembered a continual dream, in the dream she always saw Craig and told him she loved him, asked him for help and begged him to forgive her. Once again, Sara cried.

***

The teenager was visiting his grandfather who had recently had surgery and had wheeled the older gentleman to the park for some sun and fresh air. The walkway coming into the park sloped slightly downhill, not a steep slope but it was long, leaving the park meant walking uphill. He saw a lady pushing a girl up the long slope, the one pushing wasn't any bigger than the girl in the wheelchair and was beginning to struggle.

"Gramps, I'll be right back, I'm gonna go help that lady."

"Good boy, Go!"

"Excuse me Ma'am, looks like you're having a tough time, please allow me to help."

"Whew! Thank You!"

At the top of the hill the young man pushed the chair across the street then turned it back over to the lady. "Thank you again, I'm Zoe and this is Sara." He shook Zoe's hand and reached for Sara's. Sara looked up and it was obvious she'd been crying, eyes bloodshot and slightly puffy, "You've been crying."

Zoe cut her eyes at the young man.

Sara answered "yes."

"I don't mean to be forward, but may I say something?"

"Sure."

"A face that pretty should be smiling, tears should never find their way out of those lovely green eyes. Just my opinion. Gotta get back now, I left Gramps sitting in the park. Nice to have met y'all, God Bless!" He turned to leave.

It was Zoe who stopped him, "Wait! What's your name? You didn't say."

"Oh, I'm sorry, Kenneth, Kenneth Allison." He waved then turned and jogged back to his Gramps.

Zoe looked at Sara, "See? I told you so."

***

Grandmother's friend must have owed her some very big favors, the papers arrived early the next day by special courier who was also a notary public. Once signed, the courier took the papers and headed to Alabama where he and a relief driver would witness Cynthia's signature then return the documents to the lawyer. Another church friend was a local Judge who would read over the items and place his signature, he would also contact a Judge in Alabama and make any arrangements which might be required there. Within three days it was official, Sara would be moving to Knoxville.

At first Cynthia had balked and her smart mouth spewed its venom. James stopped her and made it very clear she would sign the papers or be dealt hell once he got home, a kind of hell she had never realized could exist.

***

Zoe and Sara talked, both agreed it was time to call Detective Brighton.

Jake Brighton had been working overtime and finally took a day off to catch up on some things needing done at home. He was on a ladder replacing a pane of glass in the kitchen window, a foul ball off his son's bat was the culprit. His wife let him know he had a call, "They say it's important."

He left the house still in his jeans, sneakers and tee shirt, wearing a ball cap. Jake walked into the hospital less than an hour after talking to Zoe. Knocking on the door and being told to enter, Jake removed his cap as he opened the door. Zoe met him, "I'm

133

Zoe Brewer, if I see this get to a point where it needs to stop, I will ask you to stop, and you will. Agreed?"

"Nice to meet you, Mrs. Brewer, I'm Jake Brighton. Agreed."

"Fine, allow me to introduce you to Sara."

"Sara, this is Detective Brighton, he will be asking you questions and listening as you give him the account of events as you gave me a few days ago. He has pictures he needs to show you, you will be asked to identify the people who hurt you. If at anytime you feel you must stop or at any time if I feel you need to stop, Detective Brighton has agreed to stop. His work is very important but not important enough to cause you any setbacks. OK?"

"Yes. Nice to meet you Sir."

"Sara, please call me Jake."

Sara nodded.

"Do you know what a lineup is?"

"I've seen it on TV shows, they bring in the bad guy along with several others and the witness has to pick the right guy."

"Exactly. What I've done is much the same thing. I have ten photos for you to look at. The photos were taken from three different high school yearbooks. I asked my wife to shuffle the photos and place them in this envelope and to mark the envelope so I would know how to open it with the photos face down. Are you with me?"

"Yes sir."

"Without my knowing which photo I am showing you I will remove them one at a time and hold them up for you to see. I am doing this because I've seen the suspects photos and do not want

to sway your answers by any kind of personal facial expressions. Understand?"

"Yes sir."

Jake slid the first photo from the manila envelope and held it for Sara to see.

"It's upside down."

Apologizing, Jake turned the photo to the correct position.

Sara shook her head. Jake lay the picture aside.

On seeing the second photo she said, "His name is Oscar, I don't know his last name." Jake lay this photo at the foot of Sara's bed.

"Please get that off my bed, please!"

Once again Jake apologized and moved the photo.

She didn't recognize the third or fourth.

On seeing the fifth, Sara said, "David, his name is David. I can't be completely sure, but I think he is the one who tried to clean me and helped me to the road, just not exactly sure though. At least not yet."

Six was a negative, as was seven.

Eight, "Andy."

Nine was a no.

On seeing ten Sara gasped, put her hands to her face and stared at the photo.

Zoe had been looking at the photos as they were shown, when Jake held up the tenth, she realized how right Sara had

been in her description, the boy was absolutely the most handsome sixteen-year-old boy Zoe had ever seen.

"Oliver, his name is Oliver."

Jake returned six of the photos to the envelope he'd taken them from and put the other four in a new envelope. He wrote something on the outside and placed it in his file.

"Sara, I know this is hard, want to take a short break before we proceed?"

"Yes please."

Zoe called the nurses station and asked for soft drinks for all. A nice Candy Striper delivered them.

For the next fifteen minutes the three casually chatted, Jake apologized for his informal attire and explained why he was dressed as such. Sara apologized for taking him away from home on his day off. He assured her it was OK.

Zoe asked, "Sara, you ready?"

"Yes."

Jake told Sara to start at the beginning and tell the entire story as best she could remember; he would only stop her if he needed clarification on anything. He placed a small recorder on the table before the girl and told her to begin.

Sara gave the same description of the entire week, almost word for word, as she had told to Zoe when they were in the park. Jake never had to stop her. Sara was smart and articulate, the only times she stopped talking were when she would become emotional, but those times were few and brief.

In ending, Sara said, "That is all I remember until I finally came to my senses a week after surgery.

Jake turned off the recorder, "Sara, you did very well. Thank you."

With the recorder now off Jake looked at her, "Sara, I need to ask you something very personal."

"OK."

"Had you ever had sex prior to the evening of your assault?"

"Yes sir, with my boyfriend, Craig."

"He the only one"

"No sir, Oliver and I had sex the day before."

"OK. Keep that too yourself as long as possible."

"Yes sir."

Jake stood and asked Zoe if he could speak with her. He Thanked Sara again and told her he and his wife wished her all the best and were praying for her.

Zoe and Jake stepped into the hallway, she told Craig he could go in. Charles was like a shadow and followed Craig into the room.

"Somewhere we can talk in private?"

"Sure, let's go to my office, its two floors down."

* * *

"Jake, before you say anything please call me Zoe"

"Zoe, do you know who Thomas Watson is?"

"High roller, big in all kinds of real estate, a lot of money."

"That's him, he is also Oliver Watson's father, the same Oliver Sara just identified. He is one of the wealthiest men in the

137

Southeast. The man owns more politicians and judges than most people know the names of, he has on retainer one of the most crooked attorneys you could ever imagine, and he is very damned good.

"Uh Oh, where are you going with this, Jake?"

"The boys will be arrested, they will be indicted, hell a grand jury will indict someone for spitting on the sidewalk. Then it will go to trial, that is where it will not be good for Sara."

"How so?"

"At the trial Sara will be put on the witness stand, the defense lawyer will come at her like a wolf after raw meat. Because she went to the place voluntarily, to have sex, and having already been sexually active with her boyfriend, which they will find out sooner or later, and then having sex with Oliver the day before, they will literally rip her to shreds. And there isn't a damned thing anyone will be able to do to stop it. It wouldn't surprise me if they were to subpoena her boyfriend as one of the defense witnesses so he can attest to the fact he and Sara were sexually active with one another. Sara is in store for some major emotional pain. And, even if the jury was prone to find them guilty it's a good bet plenty of Watson's money will be made available to purchase a not guilty."

"Oh My!"

"Yeah. Sara seems a sweet girl, she's beautiful and smart, she just did one stupid thing and look what it got her. She will be needing a lot of help in that courtroom. I will keep you abreast of all that goes on before the trial but there is one thing I'd like you to consider doing."

"That is?"

"I've seen the kind of work people in your profession do, y'all work miracles. While waiting to see Sara I did some other research, on you. You have firsthand, personal knowledge on how a rape victim is treated at a trial by defense attorneys. I'm right, aren't I?"

The memories flooded back to Zoe; it was all she could do to hold back the tears.

"Yes."

"Then you know what that girl upstairs is facing, except this time it may even be worse than your experience. I want, no, let me rephrase that, SHE NEEDS you in that courtroom and I am begging you, when the time comes, to drop everything and be there for her."

"I'll be there, that's a promise!"

"Zoe, those boys will never spend a day in prison. They will be arrested but won't even spend the night in a jail. Watson will bail them out. I fear nothing they have coming to them ever will. I have never had a case with so much positive evidence of guilt as this one, hell, people I've investigated are serving time now when I had much less evidence. I still have every intention of trying to help the DA offer a case that will put those animals away for a long time, but I really fear it will never happen, I'm almost positive it'll never happen. Damn!"

***

James, Grandmother and Zoe came into the room together. Sara was informed everything had been arranged that she would be moving to Knoxville with Grandmother. All matters had been taken care of and Grandmother was now her legal guardian. Sara watched as her father began to cry.

James voice cracked as he spoke, "Sara, I need you to forgive me, to forgive me for never being the father I should have been, for never being a real daddy. If I could turn back time things would be much different now. I know what your mother did to you and that I allowed it to continue, I was a coward. If I could only turn back time. I realize you and I never had any father daughter talks. If I had invited you to walk with me on the beach that night and talk, for just you and me to talk, then you wouldn't be here. I love you; I always have. Please someday find it in your heart to forgive me. Be good for your Grandmother, she will care for you much better than I ever have."

"Daddy, I love you too."

James hugged Sara and his mother, shook Zoe's hand and thanked her. The man walked from the room, out of the hospital and caught a cab to the bus station. He had some things to change in Alabama. No way in hell he was going to lose another child because of a mean ass woman!

Craig and Charles had permission to stay in Savannah through the second week of September. Although school had started their parents had called the board of education and received permission for both boys to start two weeks late, no more, but they must make up any missed work.

Sara had been moved to another floor and had begun group sessions along with her private sessions with Zoe.

***

"Zoe, what day is it?"

"Tuesday."

"Date?"

"September 10th."

"School started last week. I've been here a month."

"Yes, and you've come a long way in a month."

"Where is Craig?"

"He can't sit outside the door on this floor, he and Charles are down the hall in the waiting area. They have to go home this weekend; school would only allow them two weeks from the first day of school."

"How much does he know about things you and I have talked about?"

"Very little. He still doesn't know you're moving to Knoxville."

"I need to talk to him."

"I agree."

"I'll ask you to stay with us, he may need you as much as I will."

"I'll be here."

"Call the waiting room please, ask him and Charles to come to my room."

"Both of them?"

"Yes, please."

Both boys ran down the hall and entered the room, Sara was standing, waiting. She reached her arms to Craig, he rushed to her, they held one another. Turning to Charles, Sara hugged him and kissed his cheek. "Charles, I can never thank you enough for being my friend, I love you so much. I can never find words to tell you how much I appreciate the love you've shown me and the kindness it takes in a person to have done all you've done standing by and supporting Craig."

Sara continued, "I am so sorry it has taken me so long to talk to you, I simply could not find the words. Craig, Charles, when I leave the hospital I'll be going to live with Grandmother in Knoxville, she and my parents have signed the papers making her my legal guardian. Grandmother has already been in touch with the school board there and been told which school district she lives in and where I'll go to school, she's been making arrangements and having my records transferred."

Both boys were shocked, Craig said, "Well it's a long way, but I'm willing to make the drive."

Zoe sat quietly and allowed Sara to handle things.

"Craig, there is more you and I need to talk about. Charles, always remember how much I care for and love you, but I need to talk with Craig now." Charles hugged Sara again and left the room.

"I've asked Zoe to stay here while we talk, OK?"

"Sure."

"Please, let's sit."

Facing one another at the small table, Zoe to the side, Sara began. "I have much to tell you, things I should have already told you. I have thought and prayed so very hard to find the words that might make it easier on both of us. My biggest prayer has been for forgiveness, not only from God, but that someday you will find it within yourself to forgive me for what I am about to tell you. What you are about to hear will hurt you deeper than anyone should ever be hurt, and I hate myself for being the one who has done it."

Craig waited for Sara to continue. He didn't want to interrupt. Although he already had questions, he let her talk, he knew she needed to.

Zoe kept a close eye on both Sara and Craig, she knew what was about to be said and how badly it was hurting Sara to say it and how badly Craig would be hurt by hearing it.

For the next half hour Sara gave a day by day, hour by hour account of her time with Oliver, from how they met, their first kiss, the infatuation she had, the sex the day before the assault and the sex she wanted and was having with him, up until the others appeared and they all began hurting her. Her account went right up until she blanked out and even then, the bits and pieces, she could remember afterward. "I have never and will never, be more ashamed of myself for what I did that week and what I know

it's doing to you right now. All I can say is, I love you and ask that you please, someday, will forgive me."

As Zoe watched, she was witnessing a young man emotionally destroyed before her eyes. But it was better he was hearing it from Sara than to learn it later in other ways. Zoe watched the young man lay his head down, he cried so many tears they began to run off the table. Sara was also weeping but nothing like Craig.

It took a while, but Craig finally raised his head, stood and went to the bathroom to wash his face. Sara and Zoe sat silently.

Coming out of the bathroom Sara asked Craig to please sit back down, "There's more."

"Craig, every time I look at you, I feel my shame. I believe for the rest of my life I will always feel it, especially anytime I think of you or look at you and know what I've done to you. I also feel that anytime you look at me, I will wonder if you are thinking about what I did to you. Because of that I think it best if we go our separate ways."

Zoe was shocked, she'd not seen this coming.

Craig said nothing as Sara handed him the sweetheart ring he'd given her when they began going steady. He stood and walked toward the door.

Craig opened the door, then stopped, closed the door and turned to face Sara. Walking back to the table he knelt next to her, "Please kiss me. Then I have something to say."

Zoe watched as the two teens exchanged the sweetest kiss she'd ever seen. Soft, gentle, it was a kiss of love, love in its purest form.

Craig stood and laid the ring on the table, "This is yours, it was given to you, only you, yours to keep. I want you to keep it as

a gift, a special gift from me to you, the most beautiful girl I've ever seen. I hope sometimes you will look at it, and when you do, I want you to remember these words, nobody has ever, does now, nor will ever love you, as I have, do and always will." He left the room.

* * *

The nurses had run Charles away from the door and back to the waiting room. Hearing Craig's footsteps, he knew the sound so well, Charles stood. Craig stopped at the doorway, "Let's go home."

Charles didn't know what had been said in Sara's room, all he knew was that his friend was suddenly a different person, he saw it in Craig's eyes. For the first time since they had met, Craig's eyes seemed empty, as if his soul had simply left his body.

Nothing would ever be the same.

CHAPTER

14

In an instant the person who had once been the seventeen-year-old Craig Kirkland died. A new one replaced him. Not only had he lost the person he loved more than even he had realized, his heart had been shredded, his soul felt as if it had been torn from all he had ever been, his entire life felt as though it were nothing more than a void. But, somehow, somewhere deep within him was just barely enough God that he knew he couldn't hate the person who had hurt him as no other ever could, she would always be with him and he would always love her.

Charles and Craig checked out of the motel and headed home to Alabama. Charles tried to talk but only received yes or no answers to his questions or statements. Craig sat, face blank, no

expression, with his eyes looking out the window as Charles drove. Craig trusted no one and wanted to distance himself from everyone.

Arriving home Charles pulled the Kirkland's car into the driveway. Craig's parents had not been expecting the boys for a few days and rushed out to greet them, Craig's mother spoke first after having hugged both boys, "Y'all are home early, everything OK?"

"Yes Ma'am, fine."

"Howard then asked, "Sara, Little Girl, how's she doing?"

"Good."

Craig thanked Charles for all he had done, picked up his bag and walked into the house. Howard and Minnie turned to Charles, both had confused expressions. Charles had no good answer for them but did the best he could. "We were in the waiting room and got a call to go to Sara's room, she greeted us with hugs, we both thought, this is great, she's finally come all the way back. The psychologist was there. Sara then told us she will be going to live with her Grandmother in Knoxville, that was a downer, but Craig said they would work it out somehow."

Charles paused, "I really don't know what happened next."

"Its OK son, just tell us what you can."

"Sara asked me to let her talk to Craig, so I stepped outside the door. I tried to eavesdrop, but a nurse ran me off, I had to go back to the waiting area down the hall. A little while passed, not sure how long, and I heard Craig's footsteps. I stood up expecting him to come in smiling and ask me to come back to Sara's room, all he said was, "Let's go home." He didn't speak half a dozen words all the way home, just stared out the window."

Howard told Charles thank you and hugged him, "I'll talk to him, I'm sure whatever is on his mind will pass in a few days."

"Mr. Kirkland, I don't mean to disagree, but I don't know if Craig will be himself ever, at least not for a long time. I've never seen anything like it, his eyes."

"What you mean son?"

"His eyes are empty. I'm not sure how to explain it, it's as if his body is alive but his spirit has left him. I swear sir, the person we just watched walk into the house isn't the same Craig, he's a different person now."

"You have no idea what happened in Sara's room after you were asked to leave?"

"No Sir, no idea."

"OK, come on, I'll take you home."

Few words were said at the dinner table. Usually a place filled with conversation and happiness, the Kirkland's ate their meals in near silence. Nobody pressured Craig, it was obvious he had no desire to talk, his Dad observed his son closely and saw exactly what Charles had described, empty eyes. Craig finished and excused himself, placed his dishes in the sink and went to his room.

***

Howard Kirkland was usually up at 4 AM, well before anyone else in the house. This morning as he stepped from the bedroom he saw lights in the kitchen. Craig was sitting at the table sipping coffee, "You're up early this morning, Son."

"Yes sir, needed to wash a few clothes and get ready for school, need to get there early."

"Why early? You know you don't have to be there until next Monday."

"Need to pick up this year's schedule at the office and pay for a locker. As far as waiting until Monday, I'm home, no need to wait."

"What happened?"

"Told me we didn't need to see one another anymore. There was more, I'm sure it'll all come out, but it isn't something I want to talk about, Dad."

"OK, no pressure from me, just know I'm here if you want to talk, your Mom too. Charles know you're going to school today?"

"Didn't mention it to him."

***

He was sitting on the steps to the front door of the school when Mrs. Simpson arrived to open the doors. Mrs. Simpson had worked in the office for as long as anyone could remember, she had been there when many of the student's parents had attended the same school, "Hi Craig, wasn't expecting you back until Monday. How is Sara?"

"I got back home yesterday, thought I'd come on in today and pick up my new schedule and pay my locker fee, if any are left. Sara is good."

"Good to hear she's doing well but I hate she's transferring. I spoke with her Grandmother and helped get Sara's records together. You're a senior this year, right?"

"Yes Ma'am."

"OK, let me get the lights on and I'll pull your file."

Finishing in the office Craig found his new locker, tried the combination on its lock, it worked, he closed it and walked down the hall to Mr. Albert's room. Mr. Albert would be his homeroom teacher this year, he hadn't arrived yet. Craig leaned against the door and waited.

The man arrived and arrogantly asked, "Who are you?"

Craig handed the man a paper stating he was to be in Albert's class for homeroom. He was told, "Out of desks, you can get that folding chair and sit at the table over there."

"Thanks."

The man was not pleasant, Craig had heard nobody in school liked him, not even any of the other teachers.

"Kirkland, Kirkland, Oh, now I remember. Aren't you the boyfriend of that girl who got raped?"

"Her name is Sara and frankly I neither like your attitude nor tone of voice. May we please just not talk to one another unless absolutely necessary?"

Albert raised his voice, "Exactly who are you to not like my attitude nor tone?"

"The person who just told you!"

"Come with me, we're going to the office."

Principal Edwards was sitting calmly at his desk when Albert stormed in, Craig in tow. The man ranted for several minutes then left, slamming the door.

"Your first day back at school and this is how it begins? Bend over the desk," the man was reaching for a paddle made from a hardwood 1X4, "three licks."

149

"Mr. Edwards, I respect your position of authority, that being principal of this school, other than that sir, I neither respect you as a man nor as a human being. And nobody, not one person at this school will ever be allowed to hit me with a board. I will accept suspension, detention, you can send me back to Mr. Albert's class and I will probably be back here in less than fifteen minutes, or you can change my homeroom, but SIR, YOU WILL NOT HIT ME WITH THAT PADDLE!

Edwards was seething, standing abruptly to his feet he pointed his finger and began, "Just let me explain something to you, Boy!"

The door opened; Mrs. Blankson stepped in. Placing her hand gently on Craig shoulder, "Craig, why don't you go get a drink of water and wait in the hall please. I have something very important to discuss with Mr. Edwards."

Edwards said, "You didn't knock."

Ignoring the man, she sat, then asked, "May I sit?" She was smiling sweetly, as only a well-mannered lady in her early sixties could.

Exasperated, Edwards responded, "Sure Mrs. Blankson, have a seat."

"Mr. Edwards, as you know, Craig has been through a very rough time the last few weeks and I think a bit of patience with him might be exhibited where he is concerned. If you don't mind my saying so, please." She smiled sweetly again.

"Mrs. Blankson, I realize that. But we cannot have our students talking to us the way he spoke to Mr. Albert and myself."

"May I offer a solution? At least to this particular issue."

Knowing she would anyway, "Yes Ma'am, please do."

"Homeroom is nothing more than a 15-minute period by which we learn if a student is in the building on time or not, I suggest you assign his homeroom to be in my classroom. Albert's homeroom is full anyhow and I have a few empty desks, problem solved."

Reluctantly, "Yes Ma'am, I can do that."

"One more thing, please."

"Ma'am, I'm sure there is. Please, continue."

"I looked at his schedule and saw his English class is to be with Mrs. Sanders. Do you think you can have that changed to my class? Please?"

"I shouldn't, but may I ask why?"

"Surely. He was in my junior class last year and I got to know him, really, to more understand him. He is a nice young man and he has a lot on his mind right now. He is much more intelligent than his grades show him to be. But all that aside, what he needs right now is kindness and understanding instead of being hit with a board. I think he and I already knowing one another might be good for him."

"I have had excellent results from that board."

"You won't with that boy, and from what I heard, I eavesdropped, and saw in his face when he was leaving, I would highly suggest you not attempt to ever use it on him. He isn't big or muscular, but he has a fury in him right now that could make him dangerous if pushed. I've seen such before."

"I'll change the schedule."

"Thank you, sir."

Mrs. Blankson left the principal office, she saw Craig standing in the hall, "Come with me, you are now in my homeroom. Also, where your schedule shows you to be in Ms. Sanders class, change that to my class. Now, I heard some about what happened, how is she?"

"Fine, moving to Knoxville to live with her Grandmother and go to school there."

"I'm sorry."

"Thank you, Ma'am."

Craig's first day of school had been miserable, he'd known it would be. Too many people asking too many questions. He really didn't want to talk to anyone, simply get this year over with. Later, Craig only spoke in class if called upon by the teacher, and because he didn't want to talk his normal answer became, "I don't know." He avoided people he'd once enjoyed spending time with. Each morning he was first at the school and would go directly to Mrs. Blankson's room, no pre-class socializing or chit chat. He wanted to be left alone and do what it would take to graduate and escape this town and all its people. Craig Kirkland had built around himself an almost impenetrable armor.

***

It was a Saturday, Fall was rapidly approaching but Summer wouldn't let go, not yet. The leaves had begun to fall but grass still needed mowing, same Alabama Summer/Fall transition as every other year. Craig was taking a break from the yard work, cooling off with a glass of iced tea while sitting on the front porch steps. He was there when the car pulled up, it was Cindy and her boyfriend, she got out, her boyfriend drove on. "Hey Craig", Cindy leaned over and hugged him, Craig didn't return the hug, she sat down. "I asked Billy to let me talk to you. He'll be back after a while and pick me up. How you doin'?"

"Fine, thanks."

"Just fine?"

"Yep, fine."

"Where's my friend gone?"

"Who?"

"You. Where've you gone?"

Craig said nothing.

Cindy continued, "I really miss my friend and would like to know where he is and when he might come home."

"Cindy, I don't want to hurt your feelings. How long did you tell Billy to stay gone?"

"Long enough for you to talk to me."

"I don't want to seem mean, but I really just want to be left alone. Getting close to people leaves nothing but pain. I'm going in now; you're welcome to wait here until Billy comes back."

"I want my friend back damnit!

"Cindy, your friend is dead."

Craig closed the door slowly as Cindy cried.

***

He'd begun waking at 4 AM, getting dressed then jogging until time to get ready for school, longer jogs on the weekends. The evenings when he wasn't at work were filled working out with his cheap set of weights, sit-ups and pushups, Craig had attached a pipe to the floor joists over the basement and began doing pull-ups. His body was changing, becoming stronger. He never went out with friends, never dated, all his spare time was spent

conditioning his body or reading. Charles would come by on occasion, but it was obvious Craig had no desire to talk. Craig meant no harm, he just no longer wanted to be close to anyone.

Grandma called in November, she'd asked for Craig, he was working that night, she and Minnie talked for a while. Grandma told Craig's mother that Sara was coming along nicely and was seeing the psychologist Zoe had referred her to, but she still had a long way to go. Sara was doing well in school and had made a few friends although she still had no desire to go out much except to church events for young people. Detective Brighton had called, the boys had been indicted, trial was set for February in Savannah.

"Minnie, tell me, how is that wonderful son of yours?"

"Mrs. Blackmon, I never believed any person could change as much as he has, he just is not the same Craig he once was. He rarely speaks unless spoken to, I don't think I've seen him smile since he came home from Savannah. He never goes out except to school, work or to jog, maybe the library every now and then. One of his teachers called and told us he almost got in trouble on his first day of school, that isn't like Craig. He does everything he is asked to do here, most of the time gets things done before having to be asked. But he has become such a loner, he and Charles have barely spoken and that cute little friend of his, Cindy, called me and told me of a talk she had with him, it was so sad. I pray for him every day."

"Minnie, you know Sara still loves him, don't you? She hasn't said it, but I know."

"I figured she did, I believe he still loves her. I just can't imagine what happened his last day in Savannah that has had such an effect on him."

"Honey, Sara broke his heart, I know how but she has asked me not to discuss it with anyone. Sara told me everything and she is working with the therapist on it. I can't tell you what she told me, but I will tell you it will all come out at the trial. I hope it doesn't shatter her to the point of no return, it's that bad. And another thing, you can bet he still loves her, boys don't look at girls the way I've seen him look at Sara and not be in love with them. I don't know if they will ever be together, but I can tell you, the love they have for one another will always be there, no matter what."

"I understand."

"Well, I need to get off the phone and get busy with some laundry. You all take care, and may I call again sometime?"

"It was so nice to hear from you Mrs. Blackmon, yes please call again soon. Bye."

An hour later Craig got home from work, Minnie gave him the report on Sara, that she was doing well.

"That's good, hope she's happy, I know Grandma is glad to have her living there. Going downstairs for a while."

***

Walter Bradberry was big, at least 6' 5", weighed close to 300 pounds, he was a bully. Walt was smarter than he looked and would feel a person out for any weaknesses. He was also very strong; Craig had once seen him lift a boy who must have weighed 200 pounds then throw the boy to the floor as if he were nothing more than a rag doll.

Craig, these days, typically walked with his head down, not wanting to make eye contact with anyone who might consider it an opportunity to talk. Walt saw this as a weakness, a shyness, and in some ways it was. It all began with Walt occasionally thumping Craig on the ear. It hurt, Craig would react by rubbing his ear while Walt laughed and called him a "pussy." Next came knocking Craig's books from his hands, once again calling him a "pussy". All this continued into pushes or tripping Craig and laughing when he fell. By now others had joined in as some teens will do. Charles would witness some of these episodes and try to help Craig get back up, Craig simply told him not to help.

Mrs. Blankson asked him to stay after class for a few minutes, "Craig what I'm about to say was never said, if asked I will deny ever having said it. Do you understand?"

"Yes Ma'am."

"I've seen how that Bradberry boy and those other thugs push you around. I promise you it will get worse until you stand up for yourself."

"I don't want to get in trouble Ma'am, and those guys will beat the crap outta me."

"Maybe they will, maybe they won't, but it will get worse if you do nothing about it. I've been a teacher for nearly 40 years and have seen a lot, much of it the same as what is happening to you right now. Handle it before it gets too bad. Now go to your next class and remember, this conversation never took place."

The bullying continued for another couple of weeks, nothing changed, ear thumps, knocking of books from his hands, being pushed and tripped. Craig continued to take it. Cindy saw it and had to be held back by Billy or she might have gotten hurt trying to stand up for Craig.

Unknown to anyone, including himself, Craig had a line.

157

Walter Bradberry crossed it.

At his locker Craig was approached from behind by Walt. Walt reached out, poked Craig in the back with his thick finger, then, speaking loudly, "Hey boy, I hear it takes four men to satisfy that cute little girlfriend of yours, you just couldn't handle business." Of those who heard it, most gasped at the lowest of insults, a few laughed. Craig would discover later that Walter had a cousin who worked at the hospital in Savannah.

Turning around quickly, with no warning, Craig kicked Walt in the balls, the bully grabbed his groin and bent over at the waist, groaning, mumbling. Before he could recover Craig hit him dead center of the nose with a very strong upper cut, he felt the nose break. The blow was so vicious it stood Walt straight up, another kick to the balls folded him again. Craig spread his arms, cupped his hands and brought both hands, as if trying to clap as hard as possible, simultaneously together on Walt's ears. Walt went down, Craig fell to his knees astraddle of the bully and began pummeling his face with both fists.

Unseen by Craig was Walt's friend who had been attempting to help Walt, Charles had stepped in and was taking the beating the other boy had intended for Craig. Cindy joined the fray and jumped on the boy's back, once this happened Charles got in a couple of good punches until the boy threw Cindy off. Billy arrived just in time to see Cindy hit the floor, he looked at a girl and told her to take care of Cindy. Billy joined in, he was a big boy himself, shoving Charles aside he beat the shit out of the boy he'd seen throw Cindy down.

Sometime during it all Mr. Albert had run to the fight, he grabbed Craig's left arm just before it was about to land another blow to Walt's already very bloody face. Craig turned to see who had hold of him, "Get your motherfucking hands off me!" Mr. Albert released his grip.

It required two male teachers, Charles and Billy to get Craig off Walt. As they were standing him up, he managed one more kick to Walt's nuts.

Craig, Cindy, Charles, Billy and the thug who Billy had beat up were all suspended. Walt was taken to the school nurse who called an ambulance. Walt would also be suspended but he first needed medical attention.

It had all taken place just outside Mrs. Blankson's classroom, she'd heard every word and managed to see some of what had taken place before the crowd had forced her back. She returned to her classroom, grinning. She would ease out of the school after next class and make a phone call. Mrs. Blankson would call Howard and Minnie Kirkland and explain what had happened, and why, before Craig would arrive home. She hoped they wouldn't be too hard on him.

An hour after Craig arrived home Charles, Cindy and Billy pulled up, Cindy was first out and came strutting up the walkway looking pissed off. Sitting on the steps, Craig looked at her as she came toward him. Cindy snapped at him, "I just want to know if my friend is still dead, from what I saw today a dead person doesn't fight as hard as you did. I am going to ask you one time, once only! If you are still dead, I will leave here and forget you exist! Otherwise, well, we'll see! But let me tell you one thing Buster," Cindy was pointing her finger, "if some damned good friends hadn't stepped in today you would have gotten your head kicked in. You remember that!"

"Damnit Cindy, until just now I never realized exactly how cute you really are!" Craig grinned for the first time since coming home from Savannah.

Cindy jumped into Craig's lap, put her arms around him and playfully kissed him on the lips, "See what you've been missing?" She winked, laughed and hugged Craig's neck. Craig looked up to

see if Billy was upset. Billy and Charles were both laughing. Everyone hugged.

Craig went into the house and brought everyone a soft drink, "Guys, I know I've changed. I also know I may never be the same again as I was, well, before. But as far as yall are concerned, I know you all have my back, I hope you all know I have yours. Thanks for sticking by me when most everyone else wouldn't have. I swore I would never again say this to anyone else except my parents, but I love yall, a lot."

***

Walter had served his suspension while at home recovering and waiting for the swelling in his eyes to reduce so he could see again.

Once again Craig was at his locker when he heard a familiar voice, "Hey, You." All Craig could think was, "oh crap, here we go again." He turned to see Walt looking at him. Walt still didn't look so good, both eyes still somewhat swollen and blackened, tape still holding his nose in place, stitches in both lips, "Hi Walt, you're looking good these days."

Walter Bradberry let out a laugh unlike anyone had ever heard come from him, "Looking good these days, my ass." He laughed more. Craig was suspicious and cautious, wondering what Walt's next move might be.

Laughter subsiding, Walt spoke, "Boy I want to thank you, you taught me some things. While I was laying at home and couldn't open my eyes I got to thinking about some stuff. I started to realize what an asshole I've been to people, especially to you. Thing is, what I said to you about Sara was way the hell out of line, it was crude and vulgar. It was the line you had that I crossed and let me tell you, aint nobody ever kicked my ass like you did. How's ya knuckles?

160

"Still sore but not bleeding anymore."

"Glad they're better. So, like I was sayin', I've been a bullying asshole most of my life because I was bigger than everyone and it was easy, at least till you jumped on my fat ass. Well, all that is over, I'm gonna change my ways. And one more thing, if anyone in this school thinks they gonna mess with you anymore they better know right now they will answer to me."

Having heard that Walt was back and had found Craig, Cindy, Charles and Billy had all come running, they were all watching, stupefied at what they were hearing.

Walt put out his big right hand and asked Craig, "Can we be friends? I want to be your friend."

Craig smiled, took the bigger boy's hand and shook it, "Friends it is."

Walt smiled, "I gotta tell you, whatever it is you did to my ears sent my head spinning, I couldn't tell up from down, left from right, made me dizzy as hell. Doc at the ER said I was lucky it didn't bust my eardrums. You owned me, well actually you owned me from when you kicked me in the nuts, but you had the title to me when you did that thing to my ears."

Everyone laughed. As the crowd dispersed there was only one person still looking on, Mrs. Blankson. She was standing with her arms crossed, head tilted to one side, grinning a wicked little grin, she winked at Craig, turned and walked into her classroom.

Life got better, somewhat, for Craig, the very small spark of life that had been left within him following his last conversation with Sara had grown to become an ember. He still had no desire to date or hang out, but it was nice when Charles, Cindy, Billy or even his new friend Walt would drop by. Craig introduced Walter to his parents. Once the boys had left Howard looked at Minnie

and exclaimed "Damn, that is one very large young man our son chose to fight!"

Craig continued his daily jogging/workout routine, it had become a part of his life, he continued to grow stronger. His braces were removed and he got new glasses, wire frames instead of the black plastic. With his always improving physique came much better posture, he carried himself well. Along with no longer having the braces and wearing more stylish eyewear, he had become a very handsome boy, girls took notice. Craig wasn't interested, he just wasn't ready.

He once again entered the forest he loved so very much. Practicing his woodsmanship and for some reason visiting the old mine. He could not explain to himself why he continued to be drawn to the mine.

***

Minnie hadn't heard from Mrs. Blackmon in a while, she decided to call, Sara answered.

"Sara this is Minnie Kirkland, how are you dear?"

Sara sounded very happy to hear from Minnie," I'm good Mrs. Kirkland, it's so nice to hear from you. How are y'all?"

"Howard and I are good. Craig got into a bit of trouble a while back, but it's all worked out."

"What kind of trouble?"

"Some boy said something about you and Craig got into a fight, he beat the boy up pretty bad."

"Who was the other boy?"

"Oh, we just met him, a very big boy, he and Craig are friends now, let me think a second."

"How big?"

"Biggest high school boy I've ever seen."

"Was his name Walter?"

"That's it, Walter! From what we can gather through conversations with Cindy, Charles and one of Craig's teachers, he had been bullying Craig. But Craig just took it, until he said whatever he said about you. They said Craig was like a human possessed when he lit into him. I don't think Craig had a knuckle that wasn't bleeding."

"Craig beat up Walter Bradberry? Oh My God! Walt is a giant!"

"Well, so was Goliath."

"Yes ma'am. Mrs. Kirkland, I hate not being able to talk very long, but I was just about to leave for the library and do some research for a project. Grandmother went to bible study tonight, but she should be here tomorrow if you would like to call back."

"No honey, just tell her I called, hadn't heard from her in a while and she is so nice to chat with. Have her call me when she gets a few moments."

"I will. And Mrs. Kirkland, tell Craig I said hello. I think of him every day."

"Surely."

Goodbyes were exchanged.

Sara hung up the phone and sat silent with her thoughts for a while. Craig had taken on Walter Bradberry in defense of her because of something the huge boy had said. That confirmed it, as badly as she'd hurt him, he still loved her.

The County Sheriff's affinity for surprises was well proven the night of the arrests. He had handpicked four teams of deputies who would simultaneously begin banging on the doors of four homes at precisely 2 AM.

***

The boys had already talked about the possibility of being picked up and questioned. None of them expected it to go down as it did. And none of them had given thought to their parent's homes and cars being searched.

***

Lee and Selma Tomlinson were shocked from their sleep by the pounding at the front door. First, Lee gave thought to the pistol in his bedside table, then he heard the word "Sheriff" and decided better of it, he quickly put on his pants and went to the door.

The Sheriff had chosen his men perfectly for the locations they would be assigned. Knowing Lee Tomlinson to be a big, strong bully and Oscar Tomlinson to be a very strong, large young man, the team assigned to the Tomlinson house could all have been defensive linemen for a pro team, the biggest, meanest deputies on the county roster.

As soon as the knob turned, two large deputies pushed the door open, shoved Lee backwards. One deputy rushed in, slapped

a search warrant against the chest of Lee as he pushed him against the wall. Lee had never been manhandled by anyone in his life and the man doing it was doing it easily. The Second deputy held up a paper and stated, "Arrest Warrant for one Oscar William Tomlinson!"

The deputy found Oscar in his bed, eyes wide, quivering in fear, crying. The bully he was melted away at the sight of what he was seeing and being confronted by, a very large, mean looking man pointing a very large caliber revolver at him, screaming he was under arrest and to put his hands up.

Two more men as large as the first entered the bedroom. Oscar was handcuffed, a pair of sweatpants pulled roughly onto him, he was led away.

***

Andy Carlton Bohannon was well known all over the county for his speed in the sports he'd played. What Andy didn't know was one deputy who still held the U.S. Army records for the 100 yard dash and 1 mile run had been assigned to his home. There would also be two well trained K9's on hand if needed.

Ciara Bohannon had married twice more after Bart had been killed in Korea, neither marriage lasted. Still a handsome woman, she had a certain benefactor who would occasionally meet with her in some secret place where both could satisfy the other's needs. Thomas Watson would always leave a very nice cash token of his appreciation.

The pounding of the door and screaming coming from the porch startled Ciara so badly she jumped from her bed and went to open the door wearing only her very skimpy, very revealing nighty.

Ciara opened the door. The deputies knew the only male in this house was the suspect and were, therefore, gentler in their

166

approach. Ciara was handed the search warrant and told they also had an arrest warrant for Andy, two began the search for young Bohannon.

Entering Andy's room, the bed was empty, the window open. In his fright by the sudden pounding on the door Andy had jumped from the window and ran. Looking out the window the deputies saw two people running across the open field behind the house, the second very rapidly gaining on the first. One deputy left the house the same way Andy had and began walking to the field to assist, the other found a housecoat and house slippers in Ciara's room, he took the items to the very frightened woman.

Andy could hear the steps behind him getting closer, it was surreal to him that anyone could be gaining on him this quickly, nobody ever had. Suddenly, he found himself face down in the grass, his arms roughly being pulled behind him and handcuffs placed on his wrists. Rolled over, Andy found himself looking at the deputy, "How the hell did you catch me so quick? Nobody ever caught me if I had an open field!" The deputy responded, "Are you Andrew Carlton Bohannon?"

"Yes"

"You are under arrest."

"For What?"

"All information will be given to you later tonight."

"How did you catch me?"

The deputy smiled, "Boy, you're fast, I'm faster."

By now the second deputy had arrived. Andy was led away.

***

167

Other than the initial shock and fright of being awakened by the loud banging and screaming at their door everything else at the Clements residence went very calmly.

Both Joseph and Winnie went to the door and let the deputies in, papers were served to search the home and arrest David.

David had heard it all and had quickly gotten completely dressed, he stepped from his room with his hands above his head and in plain view. Walking to the deputies he was frisked and handcuffed.

Just before being led away, David looked at his parents, both were crying, as was he.

**

When you are one of the wealthiest men in the state there are many precautions in which you invest, one of those things is a very good security system. Thomas Watson had heard the alarm announcing someone coming up the driveway. Stepping into his office Thomas switched on the TV and set the dial to the security cameras, he saw deputies surrounding his home and staging themselves. Thomas walked to the door and opened it, waiting in a rather arrogant posture as the lawmen approached. "Something I can do for you?"

"This is a search warrant authorizing us to search these premises. We also have an arrest warrant for Oliver Calix Watson. Is he here?"

"Yes, I'll go wake him."

"No Sir, just tell us which room."

"Oh, alright! Upstairs, second door on the right."

The deputies entered the room with weapons drawn. Oliver, being a light sleeper, had been awakened by the alarm, he was dressed and sitting at his desk. A deputy handcuffed Oliver and as all the others had been, he was read his Miranda Rights.

As Oliver was being led to the awaiting vehicle his father spoke to him, "Don't worry Son, you won't be there long. Probably be home before the sun comes up."

***

All the homes had been searched. Nothing of any consequence had been found at any, except the Watson residence. Photographs, a lot of photographs, had been found hidden behind a concealed panel inside Oliver's closet.

Upon the photographs being handed over to him, the Sherriff's reaction was one of quiet shock, "Oh My God, I know a couple of these women."

"Yessir, I know one of them."

"Anyone else see these?"

"No sir, When I found them, I wanted only you to know. I showed them to nobody else."

"OK, I want you and only you to come to my office and go through the pictures with me, nobody else. We will take those we deem possibly relevant to the "Sara" case and lock the others in my safe until I figure out what to do concerning the other women. If it can be helped, I do not want their lives destroyed, the two I know are very nice, hell, one's son has spent a couple weekends hunting with my nephew at my hunting club. I cannot fathom how they got themselves involved in such a thing."

"I'm with you sir."

"By the way, I intend to hold the ones of the Blackmon girl and hope neither the DA nor the defense find out we have them."

***

Attorney Samuel Bartolli was waiting at the jail.

As each boy was brought in Bartolli would inform the officers in charge that they were to ask no questions without him being present.

Each boy was photographed, fingerprinted, booked, reread their rights and told what the charges were. One at a time they were placed in separate interrogation rooms, alone.

Once each boy had been charged and booked Bartolli made one phone call. Within minutes bail had been set. Bartolli asked, "One check cover all of them or do you need a check for each?"

The old Sargent told him, "One for Each." The old officer was pissed off and didn't mind showing it. He had a 16 year old granddaughter.

Bartolli saw the Sheriff and walked over to speak to him. "You can interrogate but it will be done at my choice of venue and at a time we can agree upon. And not before!"

Checks written, paperwork done, each boy was loaded into the waiting station wagon and transported home. They were all told to be at Bartolli's office at 10 AM the next day.

Sherriff Jeff Edmunds felt as though he'd been bitch slapped. He didn't like it. A lesson had just been painfully learned about how much weight Thomas Watson's money and influence really carried. Edmunds felt nauseated.

Above all, Edmunds felt sorrow and pain for what he knew Sara Blackmon would soon be put through. He prayed later that night, down on his knees, that somehow the young Blackmon girl would survive everything she would be facing soon.

Jeff Edmunds asked something else in his prayers, something most would find hard to understand, he asked the Lord to bring down his wrath upon those who had inflicted pain on someone who was incapable of fighting back. To bring death upon them in a most horrendous way.

The good man, the good sheriff, had no way of knowing that someday his prayers would be answered.

CHAPTER

17

Two days after the arrests.

Sheriff Edmunds and his deputy had gone through all the photographs, separating them by the person identified in each. Many only showed sections of the people in the pictures and couldn't be placed with any of the faces, those were placed in another stack.

"I've no idea how I need to handle this and keep it discreet."

"I understand Sir, but the women will have to be questioned about the photos. We may be able to keep it hush hush, but first we need to hear their stories."

"No doubt about that. OK, you said you knew one of the women, which one?"

Pointing at one of the stacks of photos the deputy replied, "This one, Sally Gillespie. I went to high school with her."

"OK, I know the other two, Lilly Jackson and Marie Sanders. Here's what we'll do. Take 3 of the less graphic photos and place them in a plain envelope, contact Mrs. Gillespie and somehow arrange to meet her where nobody will see you, show her the photos and question her. Please make it clear we, you and I, are the only ones to have seen the pictures and are doing everything possible to keep this under wraps. The last thing we need or have any desire to do is harm their family lives in any way. But, also make it clear that this is not over yet. Damned if we do, possibly

damned if we don't. I will do the same with Lilly Jackson and Marie Sanders. And lastly, none of the women's identities will be revealed to any of the other women."

***

"Hi Lilly, this is Jeff Edmunds, Jack's Uncle."

"Good afternoon Sheriff, how are you?"

"I'm well, I hope you are."

"Very well, Thank you. What can I do for you?"

"Lilly, there is something of importance I need to discuss with you, something that requires nobody else know about. Is your husband in town today?"

"No, he's gone for a few days. Has this anything to do with the arrests of those boys' day before yesterday?"

"Yes Ma'am."

"I was afraid it might. Where is best to meet?"

"Get a pen and paper, I'm going to give you directions to my hunting club, it's about an hour out of town and nobody will be there this time of year."

***

Edmunds had stopped and purchased a box of tissues and some soft drinks, he sat in a rocker on the porch and waited. The man hated what he was about to do.

Lilly Jackson arrived, got from her car and was already crying. She knew she'd been photographed, and she knew Edmunds had seen those photos.

"Hello Jeff, I know what this is about. I also know you can arrest me. Are you?"

173

"Lilly, I can promise you, I intend to do everything within my power to keep it all a secret. I can't promise you it won't all become known, but I have absolutely no desire to ruin yours or your family's lives. Nor the lives of the other women involved."

"There were others?"

"Two that we know of. Please do not ask who, I will not answer."

"I don't want to know. I just hate it for them as badly as I do for myself that we were all so stupid."

Edmunds invited Lilly inside, he handed her the box of tissues and got her a soft drink. On the table was the envelope containing the photos.

"Before you open the envelope, I need to tell you something. Only one other person in my office has seen the pictures. The ones in the envelope are the less graphic, there are many more which are much more graphic. The rest of the pictures are locked in my personal safe and only I have the combination. The other person who has seen them is the deputy who conducted the search, he is, as we speak, talking to one of the other ladies, he knew her."

"I understand."

Lilly Jackson opened the envelope, looked at its contents, she began to cry.

"Take all the time you need, then we'll talk."

Half a box of tissues later, the tears subsided. "What do you want to know?"

"Everything. But first, my deputy and I both decided that we would neither take notes nor would we record any of these conversations on any form of recording device. There will be no

record of anything you say today. If in the future something happens that requires it, you will be questioned at my office where it will all be recorded. It is, as honestly as I can say it, my hope that we can find a way to destroy the pictures and allow you and yours to continue to enjoy a happy life together. Frankly, it's one helluva risk to my deputy and me, but one we feel is well worth it to protect you and the other two women."

"Thank you, Jeff. I cannot tell you how much I appreciate it."

"You're Welcome. Now, you talk, I listen."

For two hours Lilly Jackson talked. There were times of crying, nose blowing and near hysteria as she told the entire story of her "sessions" with Oliver, and later Oliver and Andy. She spoke of loneliness, infatuation, curiosity, sexual fulfillment and then humiliation. Simply speaking, she spilled her guts, held nothing back. Every word Lilly spoke was the gospel truth.

Lilly shook Jeff's hand just before she got in her car to leave, she thanked him, then drove away.

Looking back at the waste basket Jeff was glad he'd brought the tissues, although one box had been barely enough. He'd bring two boxes when he met with Marie Sanders, just in case.

It had been a long, hard day.

Jeff went home.

* * *

The stories of the three women were all so close they could have been taken from the same chapter of the same book. Time would tell if the photos could be destroyed and lives could be unaffected.

CHAPTER

18

"I've got a sick feeling about this one."

It had been the chief prosecutor, Al Foley, who'd spoken. His Boss, District Attorney Robert Allen was all too familiar with the feeling, having experienced it on more than one occasion, Allen spoke next. "I've read the reports, studied your game plan, you have a good case, but I also know what and who we are up against. I also know who the judge is, I've never trusted him. The jury looks iffy as well. Have you explained everything to the girl?"

"Yes"

"She knows what the defense will ask her and all that will be revealed, including her past relationship with the boyfriend?"

"I've explained it."

"And she still wants to continue?"

"Bob, I've never seen anyone show such resolve. When I finished telling her that she would be dragged through the mud and ripped to shreds by the defense you know what she said to me?"

"Tell me."

"I wrote down her exact reply so I could precisely quote her, verbatim." Foley removed a paper from his file and read from it, "I am Sara Imogene Blackmon, I am my Grandmother's grandchild and am proud that I have inherited some of her traits. As my

grandmother, I will not back down from what I know is right, even when the odds are against me. I have a firm understanding it is my own fault that I made the choice of putting myself in a place I should never have been, with a person I should not have been with, including the day before the assault. I know my past will be revealed and I live every minute of every day in shame because of the person's heart that has suffered, and will suffer, most by all this, Craig Kirkland. But I am willing to face everything, face the humiliation of having my reputation destroyed, of knowing I will be made to look like nothing more than common white trash. I am willing to face all of this because I know there are still more good people in this world than bad, and I want those good people to know exactly what was done to me, by whom and that those four boys are capable of doing it again to some unsuspecting girl. But, even if there is no more than 1% chance of those animals going to prison, I am willing to take it!"

Allen Responded, "Tough Kid."

"No doubt. I just hope she's able to emotionally survive."

***

In another room Thomas Watson asked, "Is this handled?"

Sam Bartolli smiled, "Piece of cake. With the girl's past with her boyfriend and having had sex the day before with Oliver, plus the jury and judge in your pocket, it's all nothing more than an embarrassing formality."

"Bartolli, listen and listen close. You are right about it being embarrassing, and for that reason I want you to rip the girl to shreds. I want the impression given that she is nothing more than a dime whore who would spread her legs for anything that can achieve a hardon. I also want her emotionally destroyed. Get it?"

"Got it Boss!"

178

* * *

All the defendants had been read the charges and had entered pleas of not guilty at the arraignment. Judge Milton Isbell set the trial date for February 14th, St. Valentine's Day.

* * *

The deputy, a friend of Howard's, arrived late in the day, he asked for Craig. Craig accepted the letter. It was a subpoena; he would be a witness for the defense and was required to be at the courthouse in Savannah on February 12th to be interviewed by the defense attorneys prior to the trial. Howard had invited the deputy in for coffee, they both read the papers and the deputy offered his opinion, "Howard, all I know is that if it's the defense who want Craig to testify, it can't be good for Sara."

Craig walked to Howard's office later that night, "Dad, do I have to go?"

"Yes, Son, you have to, and you have to tell the truth no matter what they ask."

"What will they ask?"

"I don't know, but your Mother and I will be with you this time."

"Thanks Dad."

Craig closed the door to the office, he lay awake all night, scared.

* * *

Craig was in a small room located on the second floor of the courthouse, it smelled of cigarette smoke, Howard and Minnie had to wait outside. A person with a bible came in and Craig swore he would tell the truth to any questions, the person left.

179

Next came a person with some small machine with typing keys, then a man entered the room and asked if everyone was ready, all said yes.

"State your name please."

"Craig Kirkland."

"Full name."

"Howard Craig Kirkland."

"Are you aware you are under oath to tell the truth and anything other than the truth can result in being charged with perjury, a penalty punishable by incarceration, going to jail?"

"Yes sir, that was explained to me earlier."

"Good, I have two questions. Your answers will be the determining factor on whether you will be called upon to be a witness at the trial, or not.

"OK."

"Do you know Sara Imogene Blackmon?"

"Yes."

"Did you and Sara Imogene Blackmon ever engage in the act of sexual intercourse prior to August 7th, 1963?"

Craig knew he didn't want to answer; he knew this would be bad for Sara. He dropped his head and said nothing.

"I'm waiting."

Craig looked at the man, Craig's eyes were cold, empty and without soul. For a second the man felt a chill, this boy frightened him.

"Yes."

That's all. Trial is in two days, you can go home but a subpoena will be waiting for you when you arrive. I would suggest finding somewhere locally to stay. Laying a card on the table the man told Craig to report where he would be staying.

The attorney hurriedly left the room.

Howard and Minnie instantly knew Craig was upset the moment he stepped from the room. "Mom, would you mind waiting here for a few minutes, I need to talk to Dad. It won't take long." Minnie patted Craig's cheek and nodded.

Craig told his dad everything that had taken place and the questions he'd been asked. Howard was told the answers to the questions.

"Son, I guess I never even gave any thought to the possibility you and Sara were sexually active. I should have, I was young once, so I guess I'm not surprised. You know they will ask you those questions again in the courtroom, don't you? In front of everyone."

"Yes sir."

"You have to answer them, truthfully. They will probably ask other questions such as how long, how many times, any other sexual acts. This will not be good for Sara."

"They're gonna do all they can to make her look like a slut, aren't they?"

"That's exactly what they are going to do, Son."

"Dad, you and Mom are going to learn some things about the whole week she was on vacation, things I already know, things that broke my heart, changed me. We all make mistakes, y'all taught me that, please remember it when you hear all you will hear. And when you hear it, please don't judge Sara too harshly in your heart."

181

***

The Kirkland's were walking into the courthouse when Grandma Blackmon saw them. Walking to the family she greeted them warmly with hugs. There was brief small talk concerning everyone's wellbeing and the weather, typical southern chit chat. Grandma asked them if they would please sit with herself, Sara and Sara's parents during the proceedings.

Howard spoke softly, "Mrs. Blackmon, Thank you, but that may not be a good idea".

Before any other words could be exchanged Craig took Grandma's hand and asked to have a private word with her. She agreed and the two walked away a short distance.

"Grandma, a couple of days ago I was brought in and questioned by a lawyer, the other side's lawyer. I think it was called a deposition, something like that. I had to answer his questions truthfully or they could have put me in jail."

Craig dropped his head, there was a long pause.

"Go ahead Dear, you know I love you and you can talk to me."

"I was asked questions about Sara and me, and if, if we,," Craig paused again.

"Honey, I already know about yours and Sara's relationship, even that y'all were, well, sensual at times."

"Then you probably know the other lawyer will most likely put me on the witness stand. He will use me to make Sara look bad. You know this, right?"

"I do, as does Sara, we all do."

"And you still want us to sit with y'all?"

182

"Yes, and by the way, it was Sara's idea that I ask you. I'm glad she did."

Grandma's answer stunned Craig for a moment, all he could say was, "OK."

Sara was allowed to sit with her parents and grandmother. Having no desire to sit next to her mother she was between her father and grandmother, then Minnie Kirkland, Howard Kirkland then Craig.

Slowly, Sara leaned forward and looked to her right, she saw Craig looking at her. Sara whispered, "I'm so sorry", she leaned back, wiping tears from her cheeks. Howard, having seen the exchange, placed his arm around his son's shoulder, reached inside his jacket and handed Craig the handkerchief. His son needed wipe the tears from his own cheeks.

CHAPTER

19

Jury selection shouldn't be any problem, but it would be expensive. Between Bartolli's list of potential jurors, his contact at the courthouse and Thomas Watson's money, no problem at all.

He'd been busy since Oliver and his friends had vacationed at Tybee Island, Bartolli knew a trial would in all probability become a reality. He had made a part of his defense gaining as much dirt on and making a list of people he would prefer to be on the jury. Entering this trial would be much the same as walking into a poker game knowing the dealer would deal Bartolli a Royal Flush.

Even better was the fact that Thomas Watson owned The Honorable Judge Milton Isbell. Although Bartolli had provided Watson with enough information concerning Isbell's preference for young women still in their teens, along with pictures which had been presented to the Judge, Watson also threw in monetary tokens of his appreciation whenever Isbell's services were required. The Judge was a bonus.

***

If you've enough money you can afford to have a Governor, or two, and as many Mayors as you want see things your way, you can also afford a few state legislators to do the same. A county clerk is pocket change.

Shutting off the car engine and stepping out of the vehicle, Bartolli reached in and picked up the brown paper sack. Having had many dealings with Chatham County, it was time, once again,

to pay a visit to Mrs. Rebecca Powell Garland, County Clerk. Bartolli grinned as he walked up the front steps, inside his jacket pocket was a pint of the Widow Garland's favorite whiskey. After two drinks the Widow Garland could, and willingly would, do things that would make a 20 year old New Orleans street walker blush.

Two hours after arriving, Bartolli got in his car to leave. Behind, he'd left one very satisfied naked Widow Garland laying on her bed counting each of the twenty dollar bills which would total five grand. There was also an envelope containing a list of names to whom jury notices would be sent.

Of the twenty five persons who received summons to serve on jury duty two were in the hospital, one was recovering at home with a broken leg and one was recovering from gall bladder surgery. All four were excused.

Of the twenty one left on the list, all were paid visits by either Sam Bartolli or some very serious looking men with bulges under their jackets.

Juror # 1.

Lilliam Conway was an attractive, very personable lady, married to a church deacon, three children, Sunday School teacher, active in the PTA and in charge of the concession stand at the local Little League ballpark. Lilliam only had one problem, her past.

Bartolli had done his research and found that Lilliam had once been known around Kansas City as Blue, a high end hooker who was doing well in her profession until she'd chosen to expand her enterprise into the world of illegal drugs and been busted. Due to the Judge's intimate knowledge of Lilliam, something he'd just as soon nobody else know, she received a very light sentence

On her release from jail, Lilliam began life anew, moved to Savannah and started all over. She joined the local Baptist Church and met her husband there; her life was wonderful. Until Bartolli knocked on her door.

Juror # 2.

Ray Jordan had been an amateur boxer, almost went pro, he was that good. The problem was, he had a temper, that temper could easily become out of control after his third drink. Ray had liked to drink.

In a Mobile, Alabama bar one night a guy had recognized Ray and began buying him drinks. Nobody ever knew what the guy had said to Ray to set him off. The only thing anyone knew was the boxer had hit the man with one punch, it was enough. The man died.

The best thing that ever happened to Ray was going to prison, he dried out and swore to never again take another drink of alcohol. Upon his release from prison, Ray withdrew all he had in the bank and headed East, to Georgia. He fell in love with Savannah and used his last money to open a hardware store. Ray became active in the community, joined the church, got married, he and his wife adopted two children. Ray became a pillar of the community.

Bartolli showed up one day at Ray's store, he helped himself to a cup of coffee from the pot that was always there for the customers. He asked Ray to help him find something and once they were away from the others in the store Bartolli showed Ray the arrest record.

Juror # 3.

Wanda Genry's daughter was a cheerleader, the same as Wanda had been during her high school years. It was during those years that Wanda had learned to enjoy the attention she received from the football coaches; some things had not changed.

Wanda had taken care of herself, she jogged, ate right, and exercised, she still had the same terrific legs and ass the coaching staff had found so attractive when she'd been in her teens. The present coaching staff also liked what they saw and played with.

Bartolli watched the house and waited until the rest of the family had left home, husband to work, daughter to school, he knocked on the door.

The photos revealed Wanda in the boy's locker room, in many compromising positions. Sometimes with one coach, more often with two or more.

Juror # 4.

Luther King was a humble man of color who worked hard as janitor of the high school. His job also required keeping the boiler in good working order, a dirty job.

The mild mannered Luther had installed a shower in the boiler room and would often bathe before leaving the school, not wanting to carry soot and ash into the home his wife kept so very clean. He was also very endowed.

The principal's sweet 16 year old daughter, Jenny, stayed late with her Dad one afternoon and was asked to take Luther his paycheck. What she saw made her hormones take a jump, she wanted it. She got it, many times over the remaining school year.

Bartolli was passing by the school one afternoon and happened to see Jenny leave the exit to the boiler room with Luther leaving the same door only a few minutes later. Bartolli set

up camera equipment he'd had specially designed to be easily concealed. He would later show Luther the pictures.

Juror # 5.

Larry Hanvey was a happy go lucky kind of guy, always smiling, he got along with almost everyone he ever met. Larry and his wife never missed a church service at the Methodist Church and he loved playing on the church league softball team, he was an excellent hitter and played center field very well.

What Larry wasn't good at was gambling, he found himself in too deep at a local night spot game of craps and it was made clear what would happen if he didn't cover his bets within a week.

Hanvey emptied his savings account, but that was a drop in the bucket to what he owed, he contacted Thomas Watson. A loan was made.

Juror # 6.

Albert Stanton had quit school when his Dad became sick and gotten a job to help his mother support his siblings. He was a pretty good self taught mechanic.

Stanton would later marry a nice young woman and they lived in a very modest home with their two children, he owed nobody but could never get ahead. Once household bills were paid and groceries bought, Stanton would have to take on side work to buy his kids new shoes or clothes.

One evening two men dropped by, both had bulges under their jackets, and a sack containing five thousand dollars. The money would come in handy; Albert knew better than to not accept it.

Juror # 7.

Harwell Berry enjoyed his position as pastor of the New Way Church of Eternal Life. He was well liked in the community and coached the church league boys' basketball team; they'd won district championship the prior year.

Harwell also had a dark secret, his passion for young boys. He was careful and would prey on the more vulnerable boys who might not have good lives at home, perhaps by poverty or divorced parents. Harwell would do unspeakable things to the boys and have the boys do unspeakable things to himself.

Bartolli met with Harwell one evening, showed him the films and called him a sick sonofabitch.

Juror # 8

William Ingle was a contractor who had made mistakes, wanting two sizable projects he'd taken both too cheap with his low bids. His business was in financial trouble.

Three visits to three banks earned Ingle three denials for loans, he was at a loss as to what to do next. Everything appeared he would close his business and probably lose his home he'd mortgaged.

The next day Thomas Watson called William and made him an offer, an offer that would save his business from bankruptcy and pay off his mortgaged home.

Jurors # 9 and # 10

189

Frank and Pamela Beecham were very good friends with Jack and Carolyn Odom, the couples spent much time together, out for dinner, going to ball games, playing gin rummy, and swapping wives.

Bartolli learned of the Beecham's and Odom's way of life through a friend who, along with his wife were involved in the swinger lifestyle, he set up his equipment and captured some very explicit pictures.

On top of the juror offer Bartolli also explained that Thomas Watson and himself would, for one year, anytime they chose, be having threesomes with either Pamela or Carolyn.

To prevent the pictures being made available in a magazine, there were no objections from either couple. Pamela and Carolyn would suffer a miserable next twelve months.

Frank Beecham and Carolyn Odom would prove to be excellent jurors.

Juror # 11

Owen Simmons was a jerk; nobody liked the man. Put simply he was a loudmouth who used vulgar language around anybody, men, women or children. Half of Simmons teeth were rotten and he rarely bathed, he stank.

Two men pulled Simmons into an alley one night and with the barrel of a large revolver shoved up a nostril, they made him a deal.

For a set of dentures, a decent new wardrobe and a bag of cash totaling five grand he would promise to bathe each day of the trial. Simmons happily agreed.

Juror # 12

Sandra Tucker was just unlucky, life had dealt her a tough time.

While she was pregnant her truck driver husband had been killed in an accident and the child had later been born with serious health issues.

She could have been pretty, but never invested the time trying to be, Sandra could only be described as "plain".

Two men dropped by one evening and over iced tea made Sandra and offer.

The offer included five thousand dollars cash, something that would go a long way toward the medications and treatments for her little boy. Sandra also knew who the men represented and that the offer should not, could not be refused.

Alternate #1

Hank Southard had been known to do some less than scrupulous work from time to time, Work that pushed the line of legalities, but never crossed it. He liked cash.

Alternate # 2

Stanley Crider gladly took the money and accepted the promise his used car lot wouldn't be revealed as a front for the chop shop he operated.

CHAPTER

20

The defendants were brought in and seated at the defense table. All had recent haircuts and were dressed in new suits. Oliver was wearing a necklace with a diamond studded crucifix outside his shirt for all to see, he had a rosary in his hands.

Each boys' expressions were different. Oliver sat erect, but with his eyes down appearing to be in prayer. Andy chewed gum and wore a slight smirk on his lips. Oscar couldn't keep his eyes still and was continually looking about the room, paranoid. David's face was truly sad, he'd made brief eye contact with Sara when he entered the room. David's expression was the only one among the boys that showed real and true remorse, he hung his head in shame and prayed that somehow God and Sara might someday forgive him.

Oscar William Tomlinson

Oscar could be defined as average. Average looking, average student, average personality of a 17-year-old boy. He was average in every way except his size, Oscar stood six feet four inches and weighed over 250 pounds, big boy!

Oscar did have one talent where he excelled, he was strong, football was his claim to young fame.

Born to a working family, blue collar people. Oscar's Dad, Lee, worked as a heavy machinery mechanic. Lee was good at his job and worked long hours keeping the earth moving equipment

of McKinney Construction in good working order. Lee was a brute of a man, hands so strong they could cause most grown men to flinch with pain by something as simple as a handshake.

Lee enjoyed the pain he would see in another's eyes when he shook their hand.

Oscar's mother, Selma Jane (Pugh) Tomlinson. Tall, slender, Selma could have been attractive, she just no longer had any desire to be. She had once been a pretty young thing. In high school Selma had always paid very close attention to her makeup, her clothes always fit perfectly, her smile beautiful, hair just "so" and she had "Movie Star" legs!

Selma had her share of requests for dates and accepted many. There wasn't a boy in South Creek High School that didn't want to date "Selma Jane." For most boys a date with her was akin to winning a prize, to be seen with her put a boy at the top of the list of winners. Although Selma accepted many dates, she was very picky about the boys she saw. Most dates were either very popular, older than she, a couple were already in college, or they were star athletes at South Creek. She had her eye on one boy, star quarterback of the South Creek Tigers, Lee David Tomlinson. Selma was a Junior, Lee a Senior. Lee had already signed for a football scholarship to college, he was the prize she wanted and actively sought.

In her own way and with her ability to be subtle she began slowly. Selma would catch Lee looking at her and move in a way that makes a boy take notice, she would occasionally give him a quick glimpse of those gorgeous legs and when catching him admiring the view would offer a quick smile and fake a blush. Selma was stalking her prey. Her hunt was working. It was something she would regret.

For several months she played her game, most moves played with the expertise of a chess master, some improvised quickly to

fit the circumstances of the moment, she was very good at the game. She was also was slightly confused at how long it was taking, little did she know but Lee was already in the game, making his own moves, he was very astute and had picked up the signals, showing mild interest but biding his time. Lee had a natural ability to read the opposition's strategy while looking across the line and could change a football play in an instant, make it all work to his advantage. Chess Master vs. Football Strategist. Game On!

Two weeks before graduation ceremonies Lee made his move.

Selma was at her locker between classes when she suddenly sensed the presence of someone behind her, she turned. Lee was smiling. He had just finished a workout in the team room and taken a quick shower, a shower so short it didn't effectively wash away all the odor of his having worked out. Her nostrils were filled with the sweetness of soap mixed with the pungent smell of male sweat, pheromones! Selma was instantly more turned on than she had ever been.

Conversation was short as Lee walked Selma to her next class. It was only two short weeks until he graduated and he had been noticing her, trying to work up courage to ask her out. His planned lie was working on the girl who had begun the game. Excited but trying to hide it, she accepted his request for a date the following Friday night.

She was sweet but not innocent, Selma had lost her virginity the year before to a handsome friend of her cousin. Since that time, she had enjoyed several more sexual exploits, but never with any local boys, and learned more about the sensual arts. She was a natural and learned quickly. One date with Lee made her realize what an amateur she really was.

He picked her up in his Dad's "39" Chevy Sedan. They went to the local Shake Shop for ice cream then, as the sun was on the horizon, drove to a private place on the edge of a nice creek where Lee had often gone swimming. He kissed her, gently at first, warming her up, she responded to his advances as he had hoped and as she had wanted, the kisses became more sensual, sexual. Without asking he moved his hand to her breast, she liked it, then lower, much lower, her breathing became faster. They moved to the backseat and within seconds both were nude. Lee spread those gorgeous legs and entered her, his whole demeanor changed, it got rough, something Selma had never experienced. For the next hour Selma did things she was told, not asked, to do, things she never thought she would ever do. Dirty things she had only read about in cheap novels and her brother's girly books. Then, he took her home. Selma was sore all over from the experience but what she had no way of realizing at the time was, a baby had just been conceived.

She missed her next period, two weeks later she had the test, three weeks later Selma Jane Pugh married Lee David Tomlinson, it's just how things were done in small southern towns in 1946. There would be no college scholarship for Lee, no further education, no more star quarterbacking. There would only be a lifetime of hard work, spite, abuse and hurting people he shook hands with.

A son was born nine months later, the Summer of 1947. His name would be Oscar William Tomlinson.

Oscar would inherit traits from both parents, but mostly from his father.

Andrew "Andy" Carlton Bohannon

Andy was fast. From the first time he played tag as a child it

was obvious all the other children his age were outclassed. Not only was he fast but he had moves, cutbacks, turns none of the others could match. Later when children's games became sporting events everyone wanted to pick Andy to be on their team. At baseball he stole more bases, on the basketball court he outran the opposition, track was nothing more to him than another day to be awarded a trophy. But nothing was more meaningful to him than having a football in his hands and being unleashed to run against another team. By Andy's junior year of high school he held the school record for kickoff return touchdowns, and still had another year to play.

Young Bohannon was tall, slim and handsome, he was above average in his grades, mostly B's with plenty of A's tossed in. Standing at 6'2", weighing around 170, red headed with deep dimples, Andy never had any problem having a date for any weekend.

Andy's father, Master Sgt. Samuel Bartholomew "Bart" Bohannon, had been born in a time and place of very little hope, born to what southerners describe as "piss poor" sharecroppers. The landlord, never being satisfied with his share of the crops, would visit Bart's mother when his father was working the fields and collect more "rent". She never complained, what she was getting from the landlord was better than the beatings she received from her husband and it helped keep a roof over her children's heads. Any time Bart's mother saw the landlord coming down the road she would run Bart and his baby sister out of the house, walk to the kitchen for a small amount of lard, she would reach between her legs and deposit the lubricant. She knew the man would be in a hurry and without the lard the pain was almost unbearable.

Bart's father made moonshine in the woods, he never profited by his illegal venture, himself drinking any profits he may have used to better life for his family. The man was a drunk, a mean one.

What neither Bart's mother nor the landlord knew about was the knot that had fallen out of the old pine plank wall. Bart learned things no child should ever see while he peeked through that hole in the wall. Bart was educated that women should bend over, lift their dress when told to and later at night submit to being slapped around by a drunk husband. Something deep inside his young mind told him it was all wrong but in his confused youth it somehow seemed the thing to do.

Big for his age and having a heavier beard than most sixteen year old boys would have, Bart looked old enough to legally sign the Army enlistment papers. Nobody gave any thought to requiring a birth certificate, the recruiting officer was happy to make his monthly quota.

Bart savored basic training, sure, he grumbled with the rest of the guys about how tough it was and he bitched with them about the drill instructors. In reality, he loved every minute of the abuse. Already a tough kid, he was learning to refine that which he had been taught all his life. Bart excelled in all phases of his training and graduated top of his group. Within two years he had achieved the rank of Sargent and was stationed at Fort Bragg, North Carolina.

Ciara Aileen O'Higgins, a red-haired Irish beauty with full lips and a pinup "hourglass" figure. Her eyes as green as the fields of her homeland, skin as smooth as the finest silk, she had the looks, smile and personality every man dreamed of and at the age of eighteen she knew it. She was also wild as a mustang running

198

across the plains with a tailwind. Her one mission in her life, have as much fun as she could before age caught up and slowed her down. Ciara had learned something at the age of fifteen, sex was fun, she wanted all she could get. She liked her men big, strong and with a domineering attitude.

Miss O'Higgins would soon meet the man of her dreams, or so she thought!

The event was a birthday party, same as most, girls dressed to a "T", boys in their sports coats and ties. The guest of honor was Sally Anne Peters, she was celebrating her eighteenth birthday. Sally's parents, members of the local country club, had reserved the clubhouse for the evening. One of those invited had been Sally's friend, Army Sargent Alan Joseph Carpenter. Sgt. Carpenter brought a friend, Sgt. Bohannon.

Ciara was there, more because of her popularity than friendship, she instantly spotted the tall, handsome Sgt. Bohannon and she wanted him.

In her casual manner, Ciara worked her way through the other suitors to Bart's side and waited to be introduced. Sally was close by and performed the introduction. After all, the two looked as though they were meant for one another.

Conversation was pleasant. Bart wanted a smoke and asked Ciara to join him in the garden. They shared a cigarette and Bart asked if he could see her the next time he had leave, she agreed.

For the next few weeks all Bart could think of was the red headed beauty with the most fabulous full lips and body he had ever seen. She had been flirtatious, but mysterious, moved in a way that beckoned his desires, but would then turn away and taunt him. Ciara knew he had taken the bait.

Things were hectic at Bragg with new recruits arriving daily, Bart had to first break them down, then bring them back up to

make soldiers out of them. He was working his ass off but loved every minute of every day. Bart called Ciara twice, the second time to let her know of his coming leave. Both were excited, although Ciara was more reserved in her excitement. Never let em know!

Borrowing a car from a friend Bart picked her up at 8 AM, they drove to Carolina Beach. Ciara had brought her bathing suit, Bart had rented a room for the day. They never got sand on their feet.

Entering the room where Ciara had expected to change, Bart took charge. He wrapped his arms around her and kissed her the way he knew she wanted to be kissed, roughly. Within seconds they were naked, groping, grabbing and feeling for what they wanted. As Bart has seen through the knothole, he bent Ciara over the table, she had never experienced the rawness, the sheer animalistic side of sex, and she was crazy about it. Not waiting for her to get ready Bart spit in his hand and used the saliva for what lubrication it would provide. He entered her, not slowly, not gently, Bart rammed himself all the way into her with one hard, solid thrust, she screamed from the pain. Thrusting again he slammed into her, then again, and again. By now her screams had become pleasure from pain. Within five minutes Ciara had orgasmed as she never had before. He pulled from her, turned her around and kissed her, gently, then slapped her. Ciara was shocked, but she liked it, he did it again and told her, "get on your knees, bitch", she obeyed. Bart reached down and took a handful of that beautiful red hair, he leaned her head back and thrust into those gorgeous full lips. Gagging, but not caring, Ciara took all he had, and he had a lot, she choked as she swallowed. She was exhausted, but the day had only begun.

By the time they headed back home Ciara was used up, she didn't know how many times they had "done it", hell, she didn't even know all they had done, what she knew was she was sore

200

between her legs, her nipples so sore her bra hurt her, extra makeup was required to cover the redness of her cheeks. Ciara had absolutely loved it all.

Nine months later Ciara delivered a beautiful baby boy, Andrew Carlton Bohannon.

Bart had married her. Not for love, but to give the baby his name. At least he did this one proper thing.

Bart requested and was approved for transfer, he wanted to distance himself from both Mother and child. He was promoted and finally earned the rank of Master Sgt. He bounced from base to base, going where he was told and doing as ordered, for all he lacked as a husband and father, he excelled at as a soldier.

His last assignment was Korea.

The Chinese guns were well camouflaged from the bombers, when they opened fire it was as if hell had been unleashed.

Somewhere on a nameless hill in Korea, Bart was leading his men when a shell came in.

There wasn't enough of Bart to properly identify.

All that was left were The Government Letter, The Bronze Star, the Purple Heart, all of which came in the mail. Bart also left behind strong genes, the genes Andy carried in quantity!

David Edward Clements

David almost didn't begin life. He was born with asthma and weighed only five pounds at birth. Sickly most of his childhood he still loved sports and would try his best at any of the games his friends would be playing. As David grew so did his love for

baseball and would sit alone for hours throwing a ball against the front steps and catching it, he would do this until the stitches would fall out then his Dad would buy him another ball. By high school David knew the girls fell more for the football players than for the baseball players, he tried out for the team.

David never did well, as hard as he tried. Sit-ups, pushups, running, blocking, he never was up to the same standard as the other guys. But everyone loved his spirit, his desire to never give up gave the others a boost to work harder.

He made the team, not because he was good enough, he wasn't, but because nobody had ever seen anyone try as hard as he had. The coaching staff rewarded David, figuring he would be good for the team even if he only practiced, dressed out for the games and cheered from the sidelines.

David wasn't at all handsome, he was pimpled and skinny, wore thick glasses and his teeth were crooked. But he smiled a lot, and everyone liked him. His grades were tops, all A's, smart kid, the teachers liked him, and his manners were impeccable. David was a good kid.

Joseph Edward Clements Jr., David's dad, came from a family of physicians, Father a doctor, Mother a nurse. Joseph decided upon pharmaceuticals and earned his doctorate in pharmacology.

Joseph was not handsome, not ugly, he was plain. Tall at 6'4" and lanky, he wore a bow tie and jacket every day. He was polite, held the doors for any female who might be entering the same building, he was pleasant and would tip his hat to everyone. Anyone who met Joseph liked him, but he rarely had a date, keeping himself in his studies while others were out partying.

On graduation day Joseph wasn't the top of his class, he was close, close enough to earn a few nice jobs offers. Joseph chose a job at one of the bigger hospitals in the area and went to work.

Two years later Joseph was invited to dinner at a colleague's home.

Winnie Ann Cornelius was a very petite freckle faced girl, she wore well fitting clothes, glasses and was cute. Although not pretty in any form of classical way, she had a smile that would warm the heart of anyone. Winnie, being a friend of the hosts, was also at the dinner. For the strangest of reasons Joseph and Winnie instantly hit it off and spent the evening in the deepest of conversations. By the end of the evening Joseph had timidly asked Winnie out for a proper date, she accepted.

For a year they dated, Joseph a perfect gentleman and Winnie the perfect lady. Both had desires, but neither would make the first move, fearing it would offend the other.

At the dinner they attended one pleasant Saturday evening was a man who had brought some extra refreshment in a few Mason Jars. The clear liquid burned as it passed the back of the tongue, on its way to the insides where it would work its evil ways. The more Joseph and Winnie drank, the easier it was to drink.

Sometime later in the evening Joseph and Winnie found their way to the apartment over the boathouse belonging to the hosts. Warmed by the liquid from the jars, they took one another's virginities.

The wedding was nice but very reserved for the few friends who were in attendance.

Later that year a sickly child was born. David Edward Clements was born.

Oliver Calix Watson

The boys referred to themselves as "The Team".

The team leader was Oliver Calix Watson.

CHAPTER

21

"All Rise" the bailiff ordered. The Honorable Judge Milton Isbell entered the courtroom and took his seat. Picking up his gavel, banging it once, Isbell told everyone to be seated and ordered the jury brought in. The twelve jurors entered and took their seats, two alternates sat to the side. Bailiff Johnson was then ordered to read the charges.

"The State of Georgia Versus Oscar William Tomlinson, Andrew Carlton Bohannon, David Edward Clements and Oliver Calix Watson on charges of Rape and Assault of one Sara Imogene Blackmon."

And so it began, the greatest injustice in the history of the good state of Georgia. The wheels of justice put askew by money, power and lies. All directed to destroy a beautiful, petite teenage girl. A girl who had already survived the unspeakable, the humiliation of rape and the physical, mental injuries associated with it.

It began.

***

Judge Isbell addressed the jury.

"Ladies and gentlemen of the jury, during these proceedings you are charged to remain attentive and listen closely to both the defense and prosecution statements and questions. You are to consider the answers to questions presented to the witnesses and any evidence which may be presented. Each of you were chosen based on questions from both the defense and prosecution and are expected to base your vote, either guilty or not guilty, solely on the law and your evaluation of all you will hear during this court proceeding. During your deliberation, following all evidence and testimony, it is your job to decide the fate of those being charged, take this responsibility seriously."

"Now, I will add, if any of you need a break please signal the bailiff and we will address your need as quickly as possible. Thank you."

"Mr. Foley, Opening statements?"

"Yes, Thank you Your Honor".

Foley stood, walked across the room and stood before the jury. "Ladies and gentlemen during these proceedings we will prove that the four defendants did willingly entice a beautiful young woman into the seclusion of the cabin they were staying and did savagely rape and assault her. Sara Imogene Blackmon's small body was used, abused, beaten, bitten, and burned. The physical injuries inflicted on her were such that she will no longer ever be able to carry a child, she cannot ever become "with child" due to having had her insides torn apart by objects never intended for sexual pleasure having been roughly and savagely inserted into her body. Sara was treated in such a way that night that her mind mercifully caused her to lose consciousness. After having lost consciousness, the assault on her continued, each defendant continued to have their way with her even after she had passed out, continually raping and abusing her."

Foley turned and asked Sara to stand. She did, turning to the jury so they could see her.

"The psychological injuries Sara suffered have been overwhelming. Think about it, try, in your minds to picture four strong athletes holding down one very petite beautiful young woman while they animalistically had their way with her, as she begged them to stop while they hurt her. Sara Imogene Blackmon has for months been under the care of a psychologist and remains so to this day. Imagine the absolute terror of what took place that night, the horror she must have undergone. Unimaginable, isn't it? Nobody knows how far reaching the effects of that night will be for Sara, but that night will always be in her mind, for all her days."

"Ladies and gentlemen, look at her, beautiful isn't she? Sixteen years old, petite and beautiful, and she can never give the world any children, her parents will never have grand children from her. All because four young men took that away, four athletes against one beautiful, petite young woman. Sara Imogene Blackmon never stood a chance. Thank you".

Foley turned and motioned Sara to sit, he returned to his table.

It was during Foley's opening statement that Zoe had quietly entered the courtroom. She stood silently inside the door until Foley had finished. Once he was done, she walked down the aisle and stopped next to Craig. Craig stood and hugged her, she noticed he had been crying. Zoe eased past everyone to Sara, the two hugged and Sara thanked her so much for being there, asking Zoe to sit with her. Zoe sat to Sara's left, where James had been. Sara now sat between the two people in the world who gave her the strength to continue, her grandmother and her psychologist. Sara held both women's hands, bowed her head and silently thanked God they were in her life.

***

Mr. Bartolli, opening statements?

"Thank you, your honor."

Bartolli approached the jury. "Ladies and gentlemen, Thank you for being here, I know serving takes you away from your jobs and families, but your civic duty is very much appreciated."

"What you will discover during these proceedings is that four fine young men have been wrongly accused of heinous crimes. All the young men sitting before you are outstanding athletes and good students, it is a travesty that this has befallen them. All the defendants are guilty of is having been tricked into having a good time with a girl known for her loose and wild ways, a party girl if you will who has a reputation with the boys. Frankly, these 16 year old young men are only guilty of teenage boys being teenage boys."

It will be proven that the girl went to the cabin of her own free will, not once, but twice. The first time with only one defendant, but wanting more, she freely returned the next day in hopes of a bigger party."

"All the defendants feel deep remorse that they didn't stop her before she got too wild and caused injury to herself which has resulted in her never being able to become pregnant. Surely a sad thing to have happened. Tis a terrible thing, but the unhappy result of drugs she brought with her that night mixed with the alcohol she also consumed."

"Thank you all again."

"And thank you, your honor."

Sara lowered her head and whispered, "He's lying, they held me and made me drink a beer, it could have had something in it."

Both Grandmother and Zoe put their arms around Sara to comfort her. Cynthia, not being able to keep her thoughts to herself, she whispered, "Never did I ever believe one of mine would become a little slut druggie." James wanted to slap her.

Foley, having heard Cynthia, turned and whispered to her, "If you cannot keep your damned mouth shut, I can have you removed."

What would take place next would be a massacre of a mind reaching down into the very soul, it would push Sara to the brink of an emotional breakdown a weaker person could never overcome.

The trial would be short, only a few days. All that would take place in that courtroom would create something of a very nice seventeen-year-old boy that nobody who knew him could ever have thought possible.

***

As is normal when any powerful person or a member of his family is involved in something, especially if a criminal trial is involved, the news media will be on scene asking questions, half of which are stupid. Ratings, it's all about ratings.

Because Thomas Watson's son was one of the defendants, the courtroom was half filled with news reporters, both local and national. Outside, cameras were set up, reporters stopping anyone who would be willing to speak into a microphone and get their face on TV.

Opinions varied among those who were asked about the trial from, "I think she's a little slut" to "I hope they nail their asses to the wall," and anything in between.

It would be after a day during the trial that Craig would come to Sara's aid. All the running, working out he had been doing since coming home from Savannah would pay off.

***

"Mister Foley call your witness."

Harry Dobbins was called and sworn in.

"Mr. Dobbins, What can you tell us about the date of August 8th?"

Well, me and Millie was taking the kids to the beach and had a flat. I changed the tire and was catch'n my breath when I seen a hand reach up above the weeds next to the road. I went to see and found a girl lay'n there. I yelled for Millie to come help me.

"And, sir, what kind of condition was the girl in?"

"She was out of it and all beat up. Her clothes was a mess and her pants was all bloody. Somebody had beat that girl up bad."

"OBJECTION! "Speculation on the part of the witness." Bartolli spoke.

Isbell replied, "Sustained. The witness will not further speculate on what had happened to the person in question."

"Go ahead Mr. Dobbins."

"Anyhow, I told Millie to stay with her, then I drove to the closest phone I could find, at a service station. I come back and Millie told me the girl come around a time or two and said her name and something about somebody named Craig. That's about it, then the cops and ambulance got there, and they took her away. We went on to the beach, kids had a good time but mine

and Millie's day was purty much shot, we was worried about the girl.

"Sir, do you see the girl in question?"

"Yes sir," Dobbins pointed at Sara, "it's that pretty little girl sit'n right yonder."

Sara and Dobbins eyes met, she said quietly, "Thank You." Dobbins smiled and nodded.

In the back of the room a woman stood and began walking down the aisle. Isbell hammered the gavel and told the woman to return to her seat. Millie Dobbins looked at the Judge, pointed her finger at him and said, "You can just hold yore horses. Last time I saw that baby she was a mess and, with me being a momma and all, I'm gonna go and hug that child. So, you just hush for a minute."

Mild laughter came from the jury box and courtroom.

Isbell once again brought down his gavel and ordered "Order in the courtroom. Lady, please get your hugging done, we are attempting to hold court."

Millie met Sara and the two embraced, Sara kissed Millie's cheek and thanked her. Millie told Sara, "My, My, I couldn't tell before how purty you really are, so glad to see you feelin' better."

Isbell arrogantly asked, "Are we finished hugging?"

"YES!"

"If anyone else in here feels the need to hug someone I would appreciate it if you would do it now, get it done so we can continue these proceedings!"

Nobody felt the need to hug.

Foley, "No further questions." He looked at Bertolli, "Your witness."

Approaching the witness stand, Bartolli asked, "Mr. Dobbins, you said the girl "was out of it," did she appear to be on drugs?"

Foley was about to object but Dobbins spoke first.

"No Sir!" Pointing a finger at the defense table he continued, "She appeared to be out of it cause those four assholes had beat hell out of her!!"

Bartolli, "Your Honor!"

Isbell, "The witness will refrain from making such statements or will be held in contempt of court. Do you understand, Mr. Dobbins?"

"Yeh, I understand. I ain't no doctor, I don't know about no drugs."

Bartolli grinned, "No further questions."

Mr. Dobbins, you may step down.

Dobbins stood, stepped from the witness stand, he turned and spoke to the Judge, "Contempt or not I'm gonna step over there and speak to that girl. Iffin' you have me arrested I'm betting I got enough friends that'll have my bail paid before the key is turned on my cell."

Isbell simply looked at the man in disgust.

Dobbins stepped behind the DA's table, leaned over the rail in front of Sara where he took her hand and kissed it. A tear fell from each of Sara's eyes as she stood and kissed the man on his cheek. "Thank You," was all she could say.

Millie was waiting for her husband as he was headed toward the door. Just before exiting, Dobbins muttered the word, "Assholes", not loud, but everyone heard.

Harry and Millie Dobbins walked out of the room.

***

"Mr. Foley, next witness. And Sir, I do hope things go smoother."

"Doctor Jack Wilson."

Doc Jack took the stand.

"Dr. Wilson, were you the first physician to examine the victim?"

"Yes."

"Can you describe her injuries"

"She had a contusion to her upper face, at the right eye, bruises about the rest of her face and scattered all over her body, her bottom lip had an open wound, a bite mark on her right breast and what appeared to be a cigarette burn on her midsection. She was bleeding from both her vagina and her rectum and was in a semi-comatose, mostly comatose, state of mind, waking only once, briefly, and she was severely dehydrated."

"Sir, did she say anything when she woke that one time?"

"She screamed the name, "Craig" and that she loved him."

Craig slumped, put his head in his hands and began to cry, softly. Sara, Zoe and Grandma saw him, they too cried. All Howard and Minnie could do was console their son with pats to his back, Minnie softly whispering a prayer in his ear.

"Dr. What then?"

"While examining her groin area I smelled the odor of semen and swabbed for a sample, then started an IV and had her transported to the hospital in Savannah where she could be better cared for and have tests run, I lack the proper equipment and lab."

"Anything else?"

"No, I'd done all I could."

"Anything you'd like to add?"

"There is a lot I'd like to add. But after seeing how Mr. Dobbins was called down, I will reserve my opinion."

"Thank you, Doctor Wilson,"

Isbell called on Bartolli, "Your witness counselor."

Bartolli had performed extensive research on Jack Wilson, even had him followed, searching every aspect of the man's life in an attempt to find something, anything, to offer as a threat to the man's character. He'd found nothing, the man had never even had a traffic violation.

"Doctor Wilson, you mentioned a bite on the right breast."

"Yes"

"Can you be sure it was a bite injury?"

"Yes."

"How can you be so sure?"

"I have probably treated in excess of a thousand human bite injuries in my career, people fight, they bite, children get angry, they bite. It was a bite on her right breast."

"But, Doctor Wilson, how can you be sure it was human and not animal?"

"It was an animal bite, a bite from a two legged wild beast that wants to define itself as a human being. It is wrong in its self definition!"

This took Bartolli aback, "No further questions your Honor."

Isbell told Dr. Wilson he could step down.

Doc Jack walked to the gate between the defense and prosecution tables, he stopped and turned, looking at Judge Isbell, Doc spoke, "As Mr. Dobbins did, I too want to speak with the victim, and intend to. I know damned well I've enough friends to make my bail before the key is turned on any damned cell you might have me put in."

Isbell looked at the doctor with a detest that could borderline hate. Doc returned the glare, then stepped to face Sara across the rail.

"You're looking much better than the last time I saw you" he whispered.

Once again, Sara stood and embraced a person who had helped her, a person she didn't remember. Doc Jack Wilson returned the embrace, Sara thanked him. It was the second time Doc had held the beautiful young woman, he embraced her as if she might have been one of his children, the same as he had on August 8th.

***

Judge Isbell called to recess for lunch, "Court will reconvene at 1:30 this afternoon."

Bartolli had been watching the jury during the morning's proceedings and had read the facial expressions of Sandra Tucker

and Carolyn Odum. Not liking what he had seen and wrote notes on two small pieces of paper. Two men were handed the notes and instructed what to do.

Carolyn had stepped outside to smoke and was sitting on a bench when a man sat down and laid a note next to her. Sandra was sitting at a table in the courthouse dining area when a man passed by and dropped a note on her tray. Each of the women experienced the same sudden feeling when they read the notes, the feeling was of extreme fear when they read the words, "BE VERY CAREFUL."

"Prosecution calls Detective Jacob Brighton."

Foley began, "Detective Brighton, are you the lead investigator concerning this case?"

"Yes."

"When and how did you learn Miss Blackmon had been located?"

"Around 11 AM, August 8th. I was at my desk when I received a call from Officer Don Tilly who had escorted Miss Blackmon's father to the hospital, Mr. Blackmon had positively identified the victim as being his daughter, Sara Blackmon."

Bartolli objected, "Alleged victim."

Isbell sustained the objection.

Foley continued, "Detective Brighton, what led you to believe the "alleged" assault had taken place at the cabin owned by Thomas Watson?"

"Officer Tilly called back after interviewing Mr. Blackmon who gave a very accurate description of Oliver Watson. Mr. Blackmon also remembered a boy named Oliver who had been hanging out with his daughter on the beach. Most of us on the force have, at one time or another met Thomas Watson and his son, Oliver. We also know Watson owns cabins, I drove to the

cabin location to see if Oliver was there or if anyone had seen him there."

"Was he at the location when you arrived?"

"No, according to witnesses he and his friends had left the night before."

"Did you further question the witnesses concerning his identity?"

"Yes, they gave a very accurate description and positively identified him by a photograph I borrowed from a local fishing guide."

"Is he in the courtroom now? If so, please point him out."

"He is." Jake pointed to Oliver.

"What did you do next?"

"I reported to my chief who called a judge who issued a search warrant."

"What did you find once you entered the cabin?"

"The first thing was the odor, the place wreaked of spoiled food, beer, sex, urine and feces, it stank. I then searched and found what appeared to be blood on the bed. The bed was also soiled with what appeared to be feces and urine. Looking further I located a trash can, inside the can among the household trash were bed sheets and condoms, used."

"Anything else?"

"Yes. Leaning against a wall was a broom, its handle was stained with what appeared to be blood and feces. A potting trowel was located across the room, its handle also stained with what also appeared to be blood and feces."

"Did you then begin a forensics evaluation of the cabin?"

"No, our force isn't equipped to perform in depth forensics, I asked the Chief to contact the State Troopers Forensics Department. I then had the cabin cordoned off and left an officer with orders that no one was to enter except The Chief, the troopers or myself."

"When did the forensics team arrive?"

"The next morning at 8 AM."

Foley held up the forensics report and requested it be marked as "Exhibit A"

"Detective, can you tell us what the report found?"

"First were fingerprints all over the interior and exterior, they matched the four defendant's prints. The "alleged" victim's prints were found on a bed post and on the bathtub."

"Were there fingerprints on the broom handle or trowel?"

"Yes. On the broom handle."

"Whose were they?"

"The prints on the broom handle matched Oscar Tomlinson and Sara Blackmon, I think Sara must have grabbed it trying to stop it from being rammed into her."

OBJECTION, YOUR HONOR. ASSUMPTION ON THE PART OF THE WITNESS!!

"Sustained. The witness will only give the facts, not what he may "think."

Jake knew his statement would be objected to, but he also knew the jury had heard it and might possibly consider it. Foley knew exactly what Jake had done and was glad he'd done it.

"And the trowel?"

"There were smudges of prints, none were usable."

"Continue, Detective."

"Blood samples taken at the hospital proved to match those found on the bed, the broom and the trowel, matching Sara Blackmon. Urine samples also matched Miss Blackmon."

"The substances found on the broom, bed and trowel?"

"All were proven to be blood, feces, semen and urine. Semen testing revealed three other blood types matching the defendants. Watson and Tomlinson have the same type, O Positive, Clements has A Positive and Bohannon has O Negative. All matching the semen samples taken from Sara Blackmon by Doc Jack and at the hospital as well as those taken from the cabin."

"Did Miss Blackmon make a positive ID of the defendants?"

"She did"

"How was this done."

"I had copies made of yearbook photos of the defendants then had six others made of people from yearbooks chosen from other schools. The pictures were mixed, shuffled if you will, by my wife who then placed them into a large envelope. Each photo was shown to Miss Blackmon who positively identified the defendant's photos from the ten she was shown."

"An improvised lineup?"

"Yes, she was still in the hospital and not yet able to attend a lineup at the station."

"Thank you, Detective Brighton." Foley turned to Bartolli, "Your witness."

Jake knew it would be the beginning of an attempt to destroy Sara Blackmon. He also knew he had to be truthful, and at the moment he hated himself for having to be.

Bartolli asked Jake, "Eyewitnesses, Huh?"

"Yes"

"Did they mention what kind of condition Miss Blackmon was in when she arrived at the cabin?"

"They said she seemed fine."

"Detective, didn't they describe her as "smiling?"

"Yes." He hated saying it.

"Well, we will be talking to those eyewitnesses later. No further questions at this time, Your Honor." Bartolli knew this cop and his reputation for being damned good, and honest to a fault. He had read the report and Brighton had been dead on with his description of the investigation and evidence, no need to waste time questioning the man. He had other plans.

Being told he could step down, Jake stood and began walking toward the exit, he stopped and looked at Sara. Nodding at her and silently mouthing the word "Prayers." Sara whispered, "Thank You".

Isbell was beside himself, "This seems to be a pattern I've never before seen in my courtroom, any courtroom for that matter. People stepping down from the witness stand and stopping to exchange pleasantries or hugs with the alleged victim. Well, I have had it, it will stop right now. The next person who thinks about doing such had better understand and understand completely that if they do such they will spend 30 days in our jail on the charge of Contempt of Court!"

"Jurors, you are not to discuss this trial with anyone, ANYONE! You are not to watch anything about it on TV nor read about it in the newspaper."

"This court is in recess and will reconvene at 9AM tomorrow!"

***

Outside the building the reporters were waiting, cameras and microphones turned on. They pounced and had Sara, Grandma and Zoe surrounded in a matter of seconds. The three females had no escape, Craig and his parents were well behind the women and saw what was happening. Sara had frozen and had her hands over her face, Grandma and Zoe were trying to protect the girl.

Looking to his right Craig saw Detective Brighton, he ran to him. "Do you have a car and where is it?"

"Yes, it's down the street, middle of the next block." Jake pointed in the direction of his vehicle. "Why?"

"Go to it now and have the back door open, have it started and ready to go. I'm getting her away from this, now."

"Done! I'm on it."

Craig returned to his parents, "Dad, y'alls car is parked across the street, when you see me move, you and Mom get Zoe and Grandma to it and take them to Grandma's room."

"Son, what are you about to do?"

"Getting Sara out of this, Grandma and Zoe can't move as fast as I can. No more time to talk. Do it Dad!" Craig was hoping the news people would chase him, giving his parents time to get Grandma and Zoe away.

221

Thankful now for all the miles he had been running and the workouts he'd been doing, Craig set out on a dead run.

The reporters never knew what hit them, Craig shoved two aside, moved in and scooped Sara into his arms, he yelled to Grandma and Zoe, "Dad is coming for you." Sara wrapped both arms around Craig's neck, Craig told her, "Hold on tight." The teenager set out and ran harder than he ever had. Reporters tried but couldn't keep up.

He saw the car; Jake had the backdoor open and was behind the wheel. "Sara, I'm gonna put you in a car, tell the detective where you're staying, he'll see to it you get there safely."

"And you? What about you?"

"No time, just trust me"

Craig tossed Sara in the back seat and slammed the door; Detective Brighton spun the wheels as he pulled away from the screaming crowd of reporters.

Turning to the reporters, Craig casually walked toward them. "Hi y'all, what's up?" Craig smiled as all the reporters attempted to ask him questions. He knew by their wanting to talk to him, they had forgotten about trying to chase down the others. "Sorry y'all, I'm getting a little hungry, gotta run." And run he did, nobody tried keeping up, they already knew it was useless to try.

***

The door opened; Craig walked in.

"I've always been proud of you, but never more than today. Good Job, Son." Howard then hugged his son, Minnie hugged both her son and her husband.

"Dad, Are Grandma and Zoe OK?"

"Yep, got em to their room safe and sound. You should have heard Mrs. Blackmon, all she could say was, "Just look at that boy run, look at him saving my Sara." Zoe talked about you too, after she finished cussing those reporters. I swear, I never knew a young woman knew the kind of words I heard coming from her, that girl can cuss a blue streak!"

"Mom, Dad, you both know it's gonna be the same way every day. I'm not worried about me, but Sara doesn't need it. I think I'm gonna talk to Detective Brighton tomorrow morning and see if he can make arrangements to get them into and out of the building."

"Way ahead of you, Son. Detective Brighton, came by after he got Sara to Mrs. Blackmon, he and I had a drink at the bar. He told me every police officer on the force is pulling for Sara and want to help her while all this is going on. He had already talked to a few and had a list of volunteers who will be picking up Sara, Mrs. Blackmon and Zoe every day and taking them back to their rooms until this is all over. The policemen use an underground tunnel from the police station to the courthouse. He also said my son could run like most men wish they could and does it while carrying 90 pound girl in his arms. I think he was almost as proud of you as I am."

"I'm pretty hungry now, we have anything in here to snack on?"

"Your mother and I've not eaten yet, been waiting for you. C'mon, I've heard the food is good at the restaurant downstairs."

Entering the restaurant, the Kirkland's saw Jake Brighton and four off duty police officers sitting at the bar. Each of the men got up and shook Craig's hand, once seated one of the men knelt next to the table and said a prayer. An officer told the family, "We've got this, don't worry about Sara or her people." Another officer

told Howard, "We've got the bill, order what you want, steak here is fantastic."

Finishing dinner, Craig looked at his parents, "I wonder how all of them will feel about me after that lawyer puts me on the stand?"

"Son, every one of those men know you have to tell the truth. They will still be proud of you. And, your Mom and I always will be."

***

The room was dark, it was late and the women were tired. Grandmother was in her bed, Sara in hers.

"Grandmother, are you awake?"

"Yes, Baby, just laying here, contemplating."

"Grandmother, he rescued me today."

"Yes, he did."

"He still loves me."

"I know, dear."

"I still love him, too."

"I know, Dear."

"I wish,, I wish,,"

"I understand, baby."

"Goodnight, Grandmother."

"Goodnight baby, say your prayers."

CHAPTER

23

Al Foley had met again with his boss, DA Robert Allen, "Bob, you know I hate to do it, but I've got to put the girl on the stand and let her give her account of that night, at least what she can remember."

"I know, Al, but you don't have any other choice. Best we can hope for is maybe, by her testimony, some of the jury can be moved to do what's right."

"Bartolli is ruthless. You and I both know he's as underhanded and crooked as they come, and he's mean. Somehow, someday I want to be around here long enough to prosecute him when he makes a mistake and the police catch up to him."

"There is no doubt about it, he's a bad shady character. He is also very smart, it'll be tough for the cops to ever catch him at anything, although we all know he's up to some kind of no good."

"He will destroy the girl on cross examination. Tomorrow will be the ugliest, most sickening day of my career, I know it will be. I am not proud of what I am about to subject that sweet young woman to. By the end of the day tomorrow I know in my soul it will be the first time I will ever experience being ashamed of my chosen profession. God, forgive me."

***

Foley met with Sara, Grandmother and Zoe before court.

225

"Sara, I don't want to do it, please understand, but I need to call you to the witness stand today. By doing this you can give your account of all that happened the night of the assault. But I will only do this if you agree to it. I need to warn you, although I am only planning to ask you about what happened inside the cabin, the defense attorney will cross examine you. The man's name is Bartolli, he is very good at tearing people down, he is ruthless. Bartolli will question you about the entire week at Tybee, he will attempt to make everything about that night seem as if it were your idea. Sara, Bartolli will do all he can to present you to be, for lack of a better word, a slut. Can you stand up to all that?"

Before Sara could answer, Zoe spoke up, "Sara has come a very long way in her recovery, but she is still in a very fragile place, I'm not sure putting her on the stand is a good idea." Grandmother agreed.

"If Sara doesn't think she can handle it, I won't do it. We have no more witnesses who can add to our prosecution. If Sara doesn't take the stand, I will rest our case."

Sara softly spoke, "Grandmother, Zoe, Mr. Foley and I spoke of this on the day I gave my deposition, he knows why my story must be told. Mr. Foley, I know there is no way we can win. I knew it coming into all this, unless at least one juror can be swayed. Honestly, after they hear of the entire week, if I was a juror, I would vote not guilty. It's just the way it is. What I am most guilty of are two things, acting like a tramp that week and hurting people I love. Somewhere there are good people who will believe what those boys did to me. Hopefully my testimony will prevent some other girl from them doing the same thing to her. I pray it will keep another girl from making the same stupid mistakes and decisions I made. Put me on the stand."

Zoe made a point, "I am a medical professional, a psychologist, Sara is still under my care although she has gone home and is seeing another professional, that person reports to me. If I see this getting to a point it needs to be stopped, I can, and will stop it in order to protect my patient. Understood?"

"Understood! By the way, Sara do you know a boy named Randall Harper?"

"Yes sir."

"Who is he."

"He is a boy I saw a few times before I began seeing Craig. Why?"

"I got a message last night that he is being called in to testify for the defense. Sara, were you and he ever intimate?"

"Absolutely not. I mean we kissed a little bit. He wanted more but I never let him go any further than a few kisses. Because I wouldn't give in to his requests for more, he quit calling me."

"Is he capable of lying under oath."

"Yes sir, he is not a nice person. I should have figured that out after our first date, I was naïve. But I swear, I was never sexually intimate with him."

"Well, he is a surprise and I will object because I've not had a chance to interview him. Isbell will overrule."

Randall Harper had been visited by a man driving a nice, brand new Corvette. Randall and the man talked at length. Randall arrived in town driving that nice, brand new Corvette.

***

Foley saw Jake Brighton while walking to the courtroom, "Jake, hold up a second!" Brighton heard the man and stopped

walking. "I heard what happened outside yesterday. I'm told the boy can run like a racehorse."

Jake responded, "Al, short of a pro running back, I've never seen anything like it, he picked her up as if she was a feather and hauled ass toward my car. He was zigging and zagging around people on the sidewalk like a pro avoiding tackles, all while being chased by those vultures with microphones and cameras. It was a thing of beauty to behold."

"Well, I damned sure appreciate you helping him help her. I swear, even after she broke his heart, that boy still cares for her."

"She made a bad mistake, Al. She knows she did and I'm not sure how long it'll take her to get over it, if she ever does."

"I agree. Jake, I'd like you to sit with me at the prosecution table."

"That's a strange request. I mean I don't mind, but would you mind telling me why?"

"The Blackmon and Kirkland families are sitting directly behind me; this you already know. If that boy cares enough for Sara to do what he did yesterday, I have no idea how he will react when Bartolli cross examines her. You've seen him rip people apart. It's gonna be bad on the girl and I may need help protecting Bartolli from the Kirkland kid. Get my drift?"

"You've got a point. I'll be there watching his reaction and help if needed."

"Thanks, See you in a few minutes."

***

"Court in session! Call your witness, Mr. Foley."

Prosecution calls Sara Imogene Blackmon.

Sara stood, straightened the blouse she was wearing and walked toward the aisle. She stopped in front of Craig and held out her hands for him to hold. Craig responded by reaching up, he held her hands while looking into those beautiful green eyes.

Foley spoke softly, "Sara."

"Yes sir, I apologize, I needed a moment."

Sara took the stand and was sworn in.

Foley began, "Sara, how are you?"

"Making progress every day, thank you for asking."

"Sara, what I will ask you do talk about will be very difficult for you, I know that. It will bring up memories you may find difficult to discuss. Are you sure you can talk about the evening of August 7th?

"Yes sir. It will be hard to talk about, but I understand how important it is. I'm ready."

Grandmother and Zoe sat watching closely, each woman holding the hand of the other.

"Sara, I need you to tell, as best you can remember, everything that took place at the cabin on Tybee Island the night of August 7th. If at anytime you need to stop for a break, I will request it from Judge Isbell. Just let me know."

Sara began talking, she talked for almost an hour, going into graphic detail about the events of the night until the angels carried her away from it all.

Sara told of having sex with Oliver and not knowing the other boys were hidden until Andy was kissing her. She told of the pain inflicted, of the gagging on semen after being forced to perform oral sex. Sara talked of the pain when something was inserted into

229

her anus, then of the pain from the anal sex they forcibly did to her. Sara told everything, of being slapped repeatedly, hit in the face with a fist and of having a cigarette being put out on her belly. The girl talked of the pain from someone biting her breast. She told of the humiliation and begging the boys to stop.

Sara talked, the people in the courtroom listened.

Every woman on the jury was crying, as was Albert Stanton.

David Clements had his head on the table, he was crying and praying for forgiveness. David's parents were crying.

Craig was doubled over with his head in his lap, his body quivering.

Sara gave a very accurate account up until her mind had left her body.

All the while Sara was talking, she had held her composure. She had sat with her head high. She would not allow herself to be intimidated by the presence of the four boys looking at her.

Upon finishing, Sara said, "Mr. Foley, THAT is exactly what happened to me the night of August 7th on Tybee Island."

The only sounds in the courtroom were the sounds of people trying to hold back tears. They were failing in their attempts.

"Thank You, Sara." Foley leaned forward and whispered in her ear, "What will happen next will be bad, it will test your very soul. I can't stop it now. Be strong!"

Sara nodded yes.

Al Foley turned and walked to the defense table, he stood directly across from Bartolli and glared at the man for several seconds, "Your Witness."

Upon sitting down Foley turned to the Detective sitting alongside of him, "You ready?"

"Yep, I'm watching him closely." Brighton then leaned close to Foley and whispered, "I have backup in the room if needed. I don't trust those little bastards Bartolli is representing, if hell breaks loose in here, they may try to get to Craig or Sara."

***

Sam Bartolli casually strolled across the room to stand in front of Sara, "Miss Blackmon, Sara, may I call you Sara?"

Sara answered the man, "No sir, you may call me Miss Blackmon."

Everyone in the courtroom were mildly stunned by her answer, eyes widened, a few chuckles were heard. Foley leaned over to Brighton, he whispered, "Girl has spunk."

"For sure."

"Well, MISS Blackmon", Bartolli seemed to almost spit her name, "You've given your account of the evening of August 7th last year, let's talk about the entire week. Then we will once again go over the evening you spoke about a few minutes ago."

Sara knew the storm which was about to hit her. As strong as she was trying to be, she hoped she could survive it.

"Tell us how you first came to know the four defendants, please."

"I was with my sister on the beach when they walked up and teased me about looking like a boy from a distance because of my short hair."

"How did you respond?"

231

"I asked them if I still looked like a boy now that they were closer."

"Now, let's talk about that more. Didn't you stand up, put your hands on your hips and flirtatiously, slowly turn and flaunt yourself so they could all get a look at all of you? "

"Well, yes, but,,,"

"Just yes or no, please."

"Yes." The storm was getting closer, Sara had just heard the first sound of thunder.

"And didn't you give one of the defendants, Oliver Watson, a little "come hither" wink?"

Foley stood, "Objection, your honor. "Come Hither?""

"Overruled."

"I winked at him."

"Just yes or no, please."

"Yes."

"So, you initiated the flirting with Oliver by winking at him?"

By now Sara knew it was useless to add anything other than a simple yes or no. "Yes."

"Let's move on to the next day. Did you happen to see any of the defendants the next day?"

"Yes."

"Which one?'

"I can't answer that unless his name is either Yes or No."

Isbell looked down at Sara, "Young lady, answer the question and stop being sassy."

"Oliver."

Bartolli instructed Oliver to stand, he did, still rolling the beads of his rosary in his hands. "Handsome young man, isn't he, Miss Blackmon?"

"Yes."

Bartolli pointed for Oliver to sit. "Tell us please, did you request Oliver put suntan oil on you?"

"Yes."

"To be clear, YOU asked HIM? He didn't offer first?"

"Yes."

"So, you wanted him to put his hands on you? Right?"

"OBJECTION, YOUR HONOR"

"OVERRULED! SIT DOWN MR.FOLEY!"

"What happened then?"

"We just talked."

"Talk about your boyfriend?'

Sara looked at Craig, she saw the sadness he was feeling. She saw her Grandmother reach across and squeeze Craig's hand.

Softly, Sara answered the question, "yes."

"Did the defendant and you later play with your little brother?"

"Yes."

"Seems like a pretty nice young man who would take from his time on the beach to play with a small child. You agree?"

"Seemed so at the time."

"Yes or no, please."

"Yes, damnit."

Isbell stared down at Sara, "Miss Blackmon, you will not respond in such a fashion again!"

Zoe whispered to Grandmother, "He's getting to her."

The older woman simply nodded her agreement.

"You were attracted to Oliver, were you attracted to any of the other boys? Andy Possibly?"

"I thought he was cute with his red hair and dimples."

"Did you want to have sex with him as well?"

Foley sprung from his chair, "OBJECTION, YOUR HONOR, PLEASE!"

"OVERRULED, MR FOLEY!

Bartolli smiled at Sara, "No need to answer that, we'll address it a little later."

Sara instantly remembered having joked about Andy joining she and Oliver, another terrible mistake she'd made.

Judge Isbell asked Bartolli if it was a good time to recess for lunch. Bartolli agreed it was.

Down came the gavel, "Court in Recess until 1 PM."

Zoe and Grandmother were at Sara's side before she'd stepped from the witness stand, Zoe spoke to the girl whose hands were shaking, "You OK Honey?"

"I'm as good as is possible right now. Did y'all see which direction Craig went? I need to talk to him."

"I heard Mrs. Kirkland say earlier they were going to the sandwich shop downstairs."

"Grandmother, meet us there. Zoe, come with me."

Running from the courtroom Sara and Zoe caught up to the Kirkland family at the elevator. "Craig, I need to talk to you, please."

"OK."

Craig and Sara stepped away a short distance.

"First, Thank you for what you did yesterday, you saved me from all those reporters."

"Your welcome, I couldn't not do something."

"Second, I have an idea why but Randall Harper is here; he will be testifying for the defense."

"I thought I caught a glimpse of him but wasn't sure. Why would he be here?"

"The only reason I can imagine is that Bartolli's people somehow found him and discovered he and I saw one another before you and I began dating. Craig, you know he is no good, he will probably say we had sex, it will be a lie. He wanted it but I wouldn't let him. All I ever let him do was kiss me, and you know when we started dating, I wasn't very good at even that. I never let him touch things he wanted to touch."

"Yeah, he's a thug, never will be any good. I believe you."

"Craig, I want you to know I saved my virginity for the person I love, that's you."

"Sara, I know all that. Don't worry, I know he will be lying. My shame is that I too am testifying for the defense and know what I will be asked."

"And don't you dare lie, it'll get you in trouble. I've already caused you enough pain and this afternoon you will hear more that will cause even more pain. It would all be easier for me if you would hate me."

"Well, that's not gonna happen, ever. You know that!"

The two teens gently hugged and returned to their folks.

***

"Miss Blackmon let's talk about swimming. As I understand it you and Oliver decided to go out into water deeper than you could stand in. Correct?"

"Yes."

"So, instead of swimming back to shallower water you held on to Oliver. Correct?"

236

"Yes."

"With your legs spread and wrapped around him. Correct?"

"Yes."

"And you asked him to kiss you. Correct?"

"No."

"Explain please."

"I was holding on to him to keep from treading water and he made a pass. But I did not ask him to do it."

"Did you resist."

"No."

"Then you asked him to take his hands from your waist and hold you by your posterior. Correct?"

"No, I did NOT!"

"Well, as I understand it from his deposition and in discussions with him, you not only asked, but also took his hand and placed in inside the back of your bikini bottom."

Sara was quivering, not only from fear, but also from anger. She said nothing.

Bartolli asked, "Well?"

"Well what?"

"Are you going to answer?"

"Sir, you have not asked a question. All you did was retell a lie Oliver told you."

Judge Isbell told Sara to answer the question.

In return, Sara looked at the Judge and told him, "Your honor, I will be more than happy to answer Mr. Bartolli's question as soon as he asks it!"

Isbell's eyebrows raised; the very nervous Miss Blackmon was right.

"Counselor, ask a question."

"Did you ask Oliver to put his hand in your bikini and assist him in doing so?"

"I did NOT!"

"Did he put his hands in your bikini?'

"Yes, unassisted."

"Did you resist?"

"No."

"And just a few minutes later, while still in the water, did you or did you not turn around and ask him to put his hands inside the top of your bikini?"

"I did not."

"Did he put his hands inside your top?"

Sara dropped her eyes; her whole body was shaking now as if she was terribly cold. Her answer was barely audible, "yes."

"Did you resist?"

She was crying softly now, "no."

Zoe leaned forward and got Foleys attention, he turned to her. "We need to stop this for a while. Can you?"

Foley said he would try.

"Judge Isbell, sidebar?"

"Mr. Foley. No."

"Judge Isbell,,,,,"

"Mr. Foley, I said no. Mr. Bartolli, continue with your questioning."

"You liked it, didn't you, MISS Blackmon?!"

"OBJECTION, YOUR HONOR!! OBJECTION!!"

"OVERRULED, MR. FOLEY. SIT DOWN!"

"DID YOU LIKE IT MISS BLACKMON?"

"YES, DAMNIT, GOD AND CRAIG FORGIVE ME, I DID LIKE IT!" Sara began to cry.

Zoe wasn't going to ask Foley this time, she knew the judge would deny him, she stood and told the court, "As Sara Blackmon's psychologist I demand the court take a break until I have time to evaluate my patient's ability to continue!"

"Isbell knew better than to argue; his reputation would be destroyed by the media and public opinion."

"Court is in recess until 10 AM tomorrow!"

* * *

Thomas Watson met with Sam Bartolli for a drink later that evening. "Good job today, keep it up."

"Boss I'm just getting warmed up. She'll be a mental munchkin by this time tomorrow."

Thomas Watson smiled.

* * *

"It's going to get worse, much worse"

"Zoe, I know that, but I will not back down now. I will not quit."

"Do you know it could push you over the brink? You could lose all you've gained."

"I know. I also know I have you and Grandmother. But above that, I have an all forgiving God. With all that on my side, if I fall you will all pick me back up."

"You forgot one. There is a boy in that courtroom who loves you."

"I didn't forget him, I never will."

***

"Miss Blackmon, I will remind you, you are still under oath."

"Yes sir."

"Mr. Bartolli, carry on your cross examination."

"Miss Blackmon, I trust you're feeling better this morning."

"Fine, thanks." For the moment Sara seemed more stoic, stronger, she was holding herself up straighter than before. Zoe saw this, she knew it wouldn't last. Sara knew it, too.

"Miss Blackmon, I'm not going to ask questions pertaining to later in the evening after you and Oliver played in the water. I won't ask any questions about how you arranged to meet him on the beach and how you asked him if you could fondle his most intimate body parts after you asked him to fondle yours."

"That's a lie, I never asked him to meet me."

"Miss Blackmon, I thought you didn't give answers to statements, only to questions."

"I occasionally make exceptions."

"So, you're denying it happened?"

"I am denying It was my idea."

"But it did happen?"

"I was walking on the beach and he ran up in the dark and surprised me."

"Is that when you asked him of you could, uh, play with him?"

"I did not."

"Well, regardless of how it happened, did it happen?"

"Yes."

"My, my, you just had one hell of a fun day! Didn't you?"

"OBJECTION! YOUR HONOR!"

Isbell knew he had to call Bartolli's hand on the question. "Sustained! Mr. Bartolli, care to re-word your question?"

"Not necessary your honor. I can drop my last question."

"Good. Carry on."

"Let's move on to the next day, Miss Blackmon."

Sara knew what would be revealed, that she and Oliver had gone to his place and had sex. She slumped, her eyes moved downward, she was afraid that if she looked up her eyes would meet with Craig's and she didn't want to see the pain he would be going through.

"Did Oliver bring you anything the next day? Any gifts?"

"He gave me two sand dollars he'd found."

"And is that when you told him you wanted to be alone with him and have sex in order to properly thank him for his gifts?"

"That is not how it happened?"

"Well, how did you happen to find yourself alone with Oliver that day?"

"I told him I had never found a complete sand dollar, only pieces, and asked if he would show me where he found them so we might find another one, or maybe some shells."

"Ah, so that is the excuse you used to slip away from your sister in order to get Oliver alone with you?"

"It wasn't any excuse, what I had in mind was looking for shells and sand dollars."

"So, a little later is when you asked where he was staying and how far It was."

"No, No, NO, I never asked such."

Bertolli got louder, "Oh come now, Miss Blackmon, isn't it true that you used the shells and sand dollar search as a ruse to entice my client into a place where you could ask him to take you to his cabin, have sex, perform oral sex on him? "

"NO!"

"MISS BLACKMON, DID YOU PERFORM ORAL SEX ON OLIVER THAT DAY?"

Sara said nothing, she looked at the floor, her hands shaking.

"MISS BLACKMON, DID YOU HAVE SEX MULTIPLE TIMES THAT DAY AND ENJOY PERFORMING THE FIRST ORAL SEX ON MY CLIENT THAT HE HAD EVER EXPERIENCED?" Bartolli was screaming!

Foley screamed, "OBJECTION! OBJECTION YOUR HONOR!"

"OVERRULED!"

"MISS BLACKMON, ANSWER THE QUESTION!"

Sara screamed, "WE HAD SEX!"

"HOW MANY TIMES?"

"A LOT!"

"AND DID YOU PERFORM ORAL SEX ON OLIVER?"

"YES!!!

Through her tears Sara looked up, she saw Craig, Sara mouthed the words, "I'm so sorry, forgive me."

Bartolli looked at the judge, "Request a short lunch break Your Honor. I will complete my cross examination this afternoon." Bartolli wanted Sara to have a little while and think about the storm she knew would be coming. He wanted her scared.

"Granted. It is now 11:15, court will reconvene at 12:00."

Craig stood and ran from the courtroom, he needed to be alone.

Zoe saw Craig run, she told Grandmother to take care of Sara. Zoe stood and chased after Craig; she saw him enter a park across the street.

He was sitting on a park bench, Zoe sat next to him, he was crying.

"Hi Craig."

His voice quivering, "Hi Zoe."

"You OK?"

"No, but I will be. I needed to get it out."

"It's good to let it out. But sometimes we need to be with someone while letting it out. That's why I followed you, so I could help you let it out."

"Zoe, after seeing Oliver I know why she did it. He's the best looking guy even I may ever have seen, helluva lot better looking than me."

"Good looking kid, but Craig, he's not you. I will not make excuses for her actions that week, but she knows who it has cost her, you, the kindest, most gentle person who ever loved her. You showed her what love really is."

"Zoe, why, especially after hearing what I just heard, what they did, do I still love her? She and I never did what I just heard she did."

"Because you are Craig, you love completely. I have decided to use a term anytime I need to with any future patients, Craig Love, a love that is all encompassing, total and complete, unwavering and cannot be broken. Craig Love is the best love there can ever be."

Zoe stood, she brushed Craig's hair back from his face, "C'mon, your parents will be worried."

As they walked back toward the courthouse, arm in arm, Craig asked, "Zoe, any of your patients ever tell you they love you?"

"Maybe a few. Why?"

"Add me to that list."

"Got me some "Craig Love", it's the best kind."

CHAPTER

25

Foley and Jake were outside having cold drinks from the vending machine, "Jake, Bartolli has been firing small arms up to this point, he'll fire a cannon this afternoon."

"I kinda figured."

"Watch the kid close, closer than you have been."

"Oh yeah, seeing how emotional he was after hearing what he heard this morning, well, he was bad hurt when he ran from the room. He's used that emotion up; I'm concerned he may move to the next emotion this afternoon."

"Anger?"

"You nailed it."

***

Sara was shaking when she took the stand, she looked weak and resolved to the destruction she was about to face.

"Miss Blackmon, following your sexual adventures on August 6th with Oliver is it true that you and he made a plan to meet again the next evening for more?"

"yes" Sara's answer almost lifeless.

"Is it true you made mention of Andrew, Andy, Bohannon, joining in"

"It was a joke; I didn't mean it?"

"Yes or no, please."

"yes", she hung her head.

"So, after all the fun you and Oliver had, you thought maybe a threesome would be even more fun?"

"No. I never thought that at all, it was a joke."

"Oh, come now, Miss Blackmon, a promiscuous young woman, why not multiple boys to have sex with at the same time?"

"I'm not like that, I didn't think that."

"Well, you had already noted Andy as being cute, liked his red hair and dimples, hadn't you?"

"yes"

"Joke or not, you mentioned Andy joining in, so why not have what I believe is called a "gangbang" with four boys?"

"I never meant that; never wanted that."

"You mean to say that after the fun you had with Oliver, doing all kind of things including oral sex, you mean to say you didn't want to do other things, with multiple people, things that might include anal sex?"

"NO! I NEVER WANTED THAT, THEY HURT ME."

"What about the pills."

"What pills?"

"The pills you brought with you. The pills you said would help you be more "hot."

"There were no pills, I don't know anything about any pills."

"The pills you swallowed with the beer you drank?"

"THEY HELD MY NOSE AND POURED BEER IN MY MOUTH! I TOOK NO PILLS!

"MISS BLACKMON, ONCE ARRIVING AT THE CABIN ON AUGUST 7TH, DIDN'T YOU ASK WHERE THE OTHERS WERE?"

"YES, BUT NOT BECAUSE I WANTED THEM THERE!"

"OH REALLY, MISS BLACKMON!"

Foley objected; he was overruled.

"MISS BLACKMON, HOW MANY MARIJUANA CIGARETTES DID YOU SMOKE?"

"I DIDN'T SMOKE ANYTHING."

"YOU BROUGHT IT WITH YOU, DIDN'T YOU?"

Cynthia Blackmon looked at her husband, "I've had enough listening to our little slut, druggie daughter." She stood and walked out. Half the people in the courtroom heard her.

"WELL MISS BLACKMON, IT SEEMS EVEN YOUR MOTHER KNOWS HOW YOU TEND TO ACT AND WHAT YOU ARE!"

"MY MOTHER IS AN ABUSIVE BITCH!"

"Bartolli lowered his voice for a moment, "Well, Miss Blackmon, maybe she is ashamed of you because she tried to raise you right and you just didn't learn from her."

Sara said nothing.

Bartolli once again got loud, "MISS BLACKMON, ISNT IT TRUE THAT YOU GOT DRUNK, STONED ON MARIJUANA, HIGH ON PILLS AND WHEN YOU ASKED THE BOYS FOR ANAL SEX THEY REFUSED? SO, YOU PICKED UP, OF ALL THINGS, A POTTING TROWEL AND INSERTED IT'S HANDLE IN YOUR OWN ANUS?"

247

"NO! NO! NO! OSCAR DID IT, HE HURT ME,,HURT ME!!

"AND WHEN YOU INSERTED THE HANDLE, YOU TOLD THE BOYS YOU WERE MAKING YOUR ANUS READY FOR THEM?"

"NO! I DID NOT! THEY HURT ME!!"

"NEXT YOU ASKED DAVID IF HE WAS A VIRGIN?"

"NOOOOOOOOO!!

"AND WHEN HE SAID HE WAS, YOU INVITED HIM TO LOSE HIS VIRGINITY IN YOUR ANUS?"

Sara was crying, shaking, "NO, THE OTHER BOYS TOLD HIM TO DO IT, THEY WERE HOLDING ME DOWN! HITTING ME! HURTING ME!"

"MISS BLACKMON, WHILE IN YOUR DRUGED, ALCOHOL AFFECTED STATE OF MIND, DID YOU NOT REQUEST ONE OF THE BOYS LAY DOWN WHILE YOU MOUNTED HIM AND ASKED ANOTHER TO TAKE YOU FROM BEHIND WHILE YOU GAVE ORAL SEX TO ANOTHER BOY?"

"THEY MADE ME DO IT! THEY HURT ME! NO DRUGS!"

"MISS BLACKMON, AFTER A WHILE WHEN THE BOYS KNEW YOU TO BE OUT OF YOUR MIND, THEY ALL STOPPED DOING AS YOU WERE REQUESTING AND WENT OUTSIDE. WHILE THEY WERE OUTSIDE YOU WERE STILL WANTING MORE SO YOU FOUND THE BROOM AND USED ITS HANDLE ON YOURSELF? MASTERBATING ON A BROOM HANDLE BECAUSE YOUR DESIRE FOR MORE SEX HAD NOT BEEN FULFILLED?"

Her screams filled the room, "NOOOOOOOOOO, NOOOOOOOOOO, NOOOOOOOOOOOO!!"

Sara slumped to her side, her body shaking so hard from the emotion she couldn't hold herself up. At first Zoe thought Sara was having a seizure, she ran to give the girl aid.

Having seen Zoe coming, Isbell called, "Bailiff, stop that woman!"

The bailiff in front of her, Zoe faked to his right and ran around him to his left. Grandmother was also up and going to Sara's aid, Bartolli reached out and grabbed the older woman's arm.

Hell Broke Loose!

Craig was up and over the rail before his Dad could stop him. "Nobody puts their hands on Grandma!" He intended to see that Bartolli never forgot it! Jake grabbed Craig, "Calm down son, calm down!" Craig was strong, and with the adrenalin filling his veins, Jake couldn't handle him alone, another policeman saw the struggling detective and came to help. It took both men to get Craig to the floor, and even the two of them were having a tough time keeping him down. Jake had never seen such hate in another person's eyes as he was seeing in Craig's.

It was Minnie who finally got Craig under control. She had eased around all that was taking place and knelt next to her struggling son, she gently spoke, "Baby, it's OK. Settle down, Grandma is fine. Craig, Grandma is fine, it's all OK".

Hearing his mother's soft, reassuring voice, Craig began to calm, sitting up, he reached to the woman who had given birth to him. As Minnie held her son like a child, his body wracked in sobs, she continued to talk gently to him. Minnie talked to Craig as she had when he was little and scared of thunder.

What Craig had not seen was just as Jake had grabbed him, Grandma had spun around and hit Bartolli in the face with her

purse. Nobody had any idea, but Grandma knew a purse could be used as a weapon. Bartolli was rubbing his jaw.

Unnoticed by most during the fray was that Oscar had stood and was easing his way toward Sara. Most may not have noticed him but one very large farmer who had been sitting in the room, observing, did. The man stepped in front of Oscar, "Boy, get your ass back over there and sit down else I'll break your face." Oscar did as he was told.

Zoe had Sara calmed somewhat, she and Grandma were still consoling her.

Between the bailiffs, Jakes backup people and one very large farmer, things rapidly began settling down.

Judge Isbell had been pounding his gavel the entire time. After things were calm he spoke, "Never in my court have I ever witnessed such a crude display by people, and,,,,"

That was as far as the judge got before Grandma stepped in front of him, she pointed her finger at him and spoke in a way nobody who knew her had ever heard her speak, or thought she could, "You just shut up, Mister. You could have controlled all that happened way before it did. You let it get out of hand by not controlling that short bastard sitting over there", she pointed at Bartolli. "You and you alone are responsible for what just happened. What I am going to tell you next is something I have never wished on any other human being, but I hope you burn in hell, you sonofabitch!" She pointed again at Bartolli, "You too, SHORTY!"

The room became eerily quiet. People shocked by what they'd heard from the very proper older lady.

For several seconds not one person said a word, Zoe finally spoke, "My patient is unable to continue."

Isbell spoke, "Mr. Bartolli?"

Still rubbing his jaw, "It's OK your honor. I've completed my cross examination."

"Court will reconvene tomorrow at 9 AM. Adjourned!"

***

Howard Kirkland had ordered room service; the family sat and were quietly having their dinner. There was a soft knock at the door. On opening the door Howard saw Grandma standing there, she was welcomed in.

Minnie stood and asked if she could order Grandma something, she was very welcome to join them. "No, Dear, I came to check on Craig and you all, and to thank Craig for trying to come to my rescue."

Craig stood, Grandma walked to him, they embraced. "I've not had a knight in shining armor come to my rescue in decades, Thank You!"

"I wish I could have done more, but they stopped me before I could."

"Dear, by your actions you began something far larger. By your actions you triggered the emotions of everyone in that courtroom. By their emotions they let it be known whose side they are on, and it is not that pompous short lawyer and his clients. Sometimes people need a shock that will cause them to show their feelings, and they sure showed them today when a seventeen year old boy was willing to take the risk of coming to an old woman's aid. You taught many people in there a lesson, and you served as a reminder to those who already knew the lesson but had possibly forgotten it."

"Lesson?"

"To stand up for who and what you believe in."

"Yes ma'am. Ma'am, Grandma, are you OK? I lost sight of you when Detective Brighton stopped me."

"Oh, yes Honey, I'm fine. That Bartolli man learned better than to grab a lady by the arm ever again."

"What happened?"

"I hit him, knocked him down."

"YOU DID WHAT?"

"Let me show you." Grandma sat her purse on the table and opened it, she reached in and pulled out a half brick. "A few years ago, I began carrying this in my purse, never had opportunity to use it until today. When he grabbed my arm, I spun as best I could and walloped him in the jaw with it. It caught him just right and he went down as if a good heavyweight boxer had landed a punch. I finally know how well it works and would suggest every woman carry one in her handbag. He's probably still wondering what hit him."

As Craig and Minnie sat, stunned at what Grandma had just told them, Howard was laughing, "I'll just bet he is still wondering what hit him! Great job, Mrs. Blackmon!" Everyone then joined in on the laughter.

As nice as it was to enjoy some laughter at Counselor Bartolli's expense, it was short lived.

With a somber voice, Craig asked, "How is Sara?"

"She was in pretty bad shape when we got her back to the room. So very thankful for Detective Brighton arranging all those nice policemen who are volunteering their off time to escort us all to and from the courthouse, one of them had to carry Sara. Zoe called a psychiatrist friend and explained about Sara and that she

is her patient. The doctor has been keeping up with the trial on the news, he called in a prescription for something to help calm Sara, she's sleeping right now. Zoe is watching over her, that young woman is a Godsend."

Craig lowered his head, "Grandma, you know what's coming soon? What they're going to make me say?" Craig sat on the edge of the bed, he put his face in his hands.

Grandma sat next to the boy, put her arms around him and pulled him close. "I know dear. I also know you don't want to do it, and how difficult it will be for you."

"Is there any way she not be there when they make me testify?"

"I don't know. I can ask Mr. Foley and I'm sure Zoe will have some input."

"Grandma, please, if there is any way, keep Sara out of the courtroom when they make me answer Bartolli's questions. It's very important to me that she not be there."

"I think I understand why you want it this way, I'll do what I can, so will Zoe."

Mrs. Blackmon left the Kirkland's a few moments later.

"You OK Son? "Howard asked.

"In some ways I am, Dad. In other ways I'll never be the same."

Craig had no idea exactly what the future would bring nor how it would happen. But one thing was sure, a lot of people would pay for what they'd all done to Sara Blackmon.

***

When Randall Harper had rolled into town, he seemed compelled to not only be a thug, but to look the part. Harper's hair was wild and unruly, dirty, he wore white tee shirts with cigarettes rolled into the sleeves his jeans were stained. The denim jacket with its sleeves cut off and half ass goatee solidified the fact that the kid thought himself to be some kind of tough guy. Bartolli needed him cleaned up and presentable.

The evening of the day before, Bartolli had personally taken Randall Harper shopping for new clothes, two nice suits, two pair of nice shoes, and for good measure a few new casual pants and shirts. He'd also taken the young man to his personal barber. During the time with Harper, Bartolli had personally coached him on what to say and when to say it.

***

Sara absolutely refused to stay away from the courtroom while Craig would testify. "After all I did that broke his heart, he has stuck through every minute of having to hear it all in that courtroom. I know what I did was inexcusable, I know what it's done to him, to us. I will be there if for no other reason than to show him my support."

Court reconvened, "Mr. Foley, have you any further witnesses to call?"

"No, Your Honor, Prosecution rests."

"Mr. Bartolli, call your witness."

"Defense calls Mr. Frank Beam."

Beam was sworn in and sat in the witness stand.

"Mr. Beam, would you state your full name and age please?"

"Franklin Joseph Beam, 63."

"And your occupation?"

"I was an architect previous to my retiring two years ago."

"Where do you reside?"

"Charlotte, North Carolina."

"How is it you managed to retire at the age of 61?"

"Over the years my wife, Sally, and I invested in stocks which did very well, we also hold ownership in several commercial real estates and maintain part ownership in the firm I founded, Beam and Associates, which is currently operated by our son, Frank Jr."

"How is it you came to be at Tybee Island the first week of August last year?"

"Oh, Sally and I have been vacationing on the island every Summer for several years. We very much enjoy the scenery, the

people are wonderful, fishing is very good. It's a place we've always enjoyed."

"Do you always stay at the same place?"

"Yes, the cottages are always very clean and well maintained, close to the beach and there are good restaurants close by."

"Mr. Beam, do you recognize anyone in the courtroom you may have met that week?"

"Yes sir."

"Could you point them out please."

Pointing as he spoke, "I see the four young fellows who were at the cottage across from ours, I also see the young lady we met on the beach, Sara, and there is Jake, uh, Detective Brighton. I also remember seeing Sara's parents, but only briefly, we never met them."

"How is it you met the four defendants?"

"When we arrived, they were sitting on the patio at their cottage and waved at us. We only formally met one of them that day when he walked over and helped us get our things unloaded from the car and into the cottage. My wife noted how handsome he was, she still has an eye for good looking young fellows. I found him to be extremely nice and courteous."

"Which of them was it who helped you and Mrs. Beam?"

"Oliver", Beam said while pointing at the teenager who was rolling his rosary in his fingers.

"And when did you meet the other three defendants?"

"I'm not sure, we would see them coming and going, and on the beach. They would speak and finally we learned all their names."

"And how is it you met Sara Blackmon?"

"Oliver introduced us to her while Sally and I saw them sitting on the beach one day. As good an eye as Sally has for handsome young men, I too have a keen eye for beautiful young women. I mentioned to Sally how beautiful Sara was. We have a running joke, Sally calls me a dirty old man and I call her a dirty old woman." There was laughter at the older gentleman's comments.

"Did you see Oliver and Sara together more than that one day?"

"Yes, several times. More than they realized we saw them."

"Can you explain?"

"Well, one time, from a distance, we saw Oliver applying suntan oil on her back, Sally noted "She's got the hots for him and is letting him put his hands on her. Letting him know it's OK to touch". I got a good laugh at my wife's observation and thought Oliver was the luckiest young guy on the beach."

"And the other times."

"Sally and I like to walk on the beach, both day and night, nothing like preparing a drink and strolling the beach at night, it's a beautiful time. But, one day we were walking, they were sitting, chatting, we stopped for a moment and exchanged pleasantries, then we continued or a mile or so. On our return we saw Oliver and Sara out in the water, they were kissing. They were so busy with one another they never knew we'd seen them."

"Continue Please, Sir."

"The next time, and it may have been the night of the same day we saw them in the water, I'm not exactly sure, we were walking at night and saw them doing more than kissing."

"If it was nighttime, how can you be sure it was Oliver and Miss Blackmon?"

"There was plenty of moon light, and I always carry a small, but very well-made, set of binoculars which pick up more light than the human eye is capable of seeing, although it was light enough to see without them. I was describing the, uh, action to Sally and she finally grabbed the binoculars and saw for herself. I'm positive it was them."

"Sir, what did you and your wife witness."

"They were kissing, her top was pulled up, Oliver had one hand on her breast and his other hand down her pants, she had his erect penis in her hands."

"How long did this go on?"

"I really couldn't say."

"Why not."

Beam grinned, slyly, "Well, it honestly was a turn-on for Sally and me, we both enjoy a bit of voyeuristic tendencies. Sally told me we needed to leave and get back to our cottage. I believe her statement was "Right Now!" It was a delightful evening once we arrived back at the cottage."

"You mean you are some kind of peeping tom couple?"

"No sir, it's no secret to those who know us, but over the years we, Sally and I, have kept company with a circle of friends we would occasionally get together with for more than playing gin rummy."

"Sir, are you and Mrs. Frank, Swingers?"

"Exactly."

"When did you next see Miss Blackmon with Oliver?"

"The next day."

"Where did you see them."

"Sally and I were having a snack on our patio when Sara and Oliver came walking from the beach."

"And then?"

"They entered Oliver's cottage."

"Was Miss Blackmon under any sort of duress?"

"Oh no, she was smiling and giggling."

"Did you see them leave, and if so, how long after they arrived?"

"Yes, it was a couple of hours later."

"And how did Miss Blackmon's demeanor seem to you and Mrs. Frank."

"Actually, Sally said it best, she said, "The look on that girl's face tells me she is one very satisfied young lady! I agreed."

"Was anyone else there at the time, at Oliver's and the other young men's cottage?"

"No, we'd seen the other three boys leave in the car. It was only Oliver and Sara, that time."

"So, you saw Oliver and Sara at the location again?"

"Yes, the next evening."

"How was Miss Blackmon's demeanor that time?"

"Laughing and giggling again except that time she and Oliver had arms around one another, both had their hands on the other's posteriors."

"And the other boys?"

"They were there but their car was parked a couple of cottages down. Someone had taken their parking place, so they had to park elsewhere."

"Would you say Miss Blackmon knew the other boys were at the cottage?"

Foley Objected, "Assumption, Your Honor."

"Overruled. Witness will answer the question."

Beam answered, "Mr. Foley is correct, it would be an assumption. I couldn't say if she did or didn't see the car or even if she knew what kind of car the boys were driving. The others weren't waiting outside, so she wouldn't have seen them before entering the cottage. I can't speak as to whether she immediately saw them once she entered."

"How long was Miss Blackmon there on the evening of August 7th?"

"Again, a couple of hours, give or take."

"Did you hear or see anything during that time?"

"Sally and I both heard, a few times what sounded like muffled screams."

"When you heard the screams, were you concerned for Miss Blackmon?"

"No, Sally and I actually smiled, we assumed we were hearing screams of passion."

"What did you observe next?"

"The one named David came outside."

"What did David do?"

"He sat down and put his hands in his hands. He looked as if he'd worn himself out."

"And then?"

"After a while three of the boys came outside, sat on the patio."

"How were they acting."

"They were laughing, talking. I know they are underage, but they all were enjoying beers. David went back inside."

"Did you hear any of the boys say anything."

"Yes, couldn't tell which one but we heard one of them say that Oliver had really come through, that the girl had been terrific. The big one, Oscar, reached over and slapped Oliver on the back, told him, "Good Job!""

"And what happened next?"

"The three boys went back inside for a few minutes, then came back out and sat down on the patio."

"What did you observe next, sir."

"David and Sara came out; she was stumbling as if she was drunk or stoned or a combination of both. She could barely walk."

Again, Foley Objected, "Your honor, assumption on the part of the witness!"

"Sustained." Isbell knew he had to sustain for Foley at least on a few occasions in order to not appear to be completely biased for the defense.

"Anything else Mr. Beam?"

"No sir, the last we saw was David assisting Sara around the corner, he returned a while later. The other boys were loading up

the car and told him to do the same. They left that night and we didn't see them again."

"Thank you, Mr. Beam. No further questions Your Honor."

"Mr. Foley, Cross Examine?"

"No questions at this time your honor. I would reserve the right to recall if I later feel the need."

"Approved. Mr. Beam, you may step down."

Jake Brighton leaned over and asked Foley, "No cross?"

Foley whispered his answer, "A very credible witness, anything I ask will all be based on assumptions. Isbell is cocked and ready to shoot down anything I bring up."

Sara had numbly sat through it all, knowing everything the man said was true about her times that week with Oliver and that the man thought he knew what had happened in the cottage the second time she'd gone there. He was wrong about that part.

Sara also knew Craig was hearing it all, again, and it was ripping out his soul. She wanted him to hate her, but she knew him well enough to know he never would or could.

***

Upon learning about Randall Harper as a witness for the defense, Al Foley had made a few phone calls to Anniston. He planned to cross examine.

CHAPTER

27

Following a short break for lunch, Isbell called the court to order.

"Mr. Bartolli, call your next witness."

"Defense calls Randall Harper."

Harper stepped forward wearing his new suit and sporting a brand-new haircut, he looked for all purposes to be a teenage executive.

"State your full name please.'

"Randall Allen Harper."

"Where do you reside Mr. Harper?"

"Anniston, Alabama."

"Your age?"

"Eighteen."

"Do you attend school in Anniston?"

"No sir, I dropped out, got a job and earned my GED."

"Why did you drop out?"

"To help my Mother support my younger brother and sister."

Sara and Craig knew this was a lie, Randall's mother had won a very nice divorce settlement and had a good job selling real estate.

"And where do you work?"

"Bill's Automotive Services and Towing."

"What are your duties there?"

"I do oil changes, mount and balance tires, lube jobs, some small mechanic work. Bill is sending me to school to learn to be a mechanic."

"Mr. Harper, do you recognize anyone in the courtroom?"

"Yes sir."

"Would you point them out and say how you know them, please?"

"Sure. There is Craig Kirkland, I know Sara Blackmon and her folks."

"How is it you know the young Mr. Kirkland?"

"We had a couple of classes together when I was in school."

"Miss Blackmon, Sara, how do you know her?"

"We went out a few times."

"You took Sara out on dates?"

"No sir, just out, kinda."

"Explain, please.'

"Well she wasn't allowed to go on car dates until she was 15 and when I was seeing her, she was only 14."

"So, how is it you and she went "out" as you said?"

"Her parents let me take her for ice cream after church services before I would take her home and we have a friend who has a lot of parties. Sara's best friend, Jean, lived next door to the

friend who does the parties. She would spend the night with Jean and go to the parties. We would meet there. It was at one of his parties that I first met her."

"Tell us about the parties, what went on?"

"Loud music on the stereo, guys there looking for girls to hookup with and some girls looking for guys to hook up with. Dancing, spin the bottle, that sort of stuff."

"And what happened the night you met Sara?"

"I thought she was really cute so I introduced myself and we talked a while. Lots of guys were smoking and she said it was bothering her, she asked if we could go outside."

"Continue please."

"Well, we stepped out and she took my hand and walked to a dark place around the corner of the house, she reached up and planted a big kiss on me, I liked it. We started to make out, uh, kiss and neck, she asked me if I had a car."

"Did you have a car?"

"Yes sir, parked down the street, there were a lot of people who got there before I did."

"She asked if we could go to my car." Harper feigned a blush.

"Go ahead Mr. Harper."

"Well, we went to my car and I opened the door to let her in, it's a two door so she leaned the front seat back forward and said, "Big Car, nice back seat". She climbed into the backseat and before I could get in, she had her shirt off."

Sara had leaned forward and was whispering over and over, "Liar, Liar, Liar". Grandmother and Zoe were patting her back,

trying to console the girl they both knew was being lied about. Sara's dad was crying, her mother was whispering, "little slut."

Craig could best be described as seething with anger, but he knew there was nothing he could do to shut the lying thug's mouth. Howard Kirkland noticed his son shaking with his anger and put his arm around him. "Be calm son," the man whispered.

"Then she asked me to unhook her bra, and she pulled off her pants."

"And then?'

"Sara asked me if I had any rubbers, uh, condoms."

"Did you?"

"Yes sir, every boy in school who has a car keeps some in his glove box, just in case."

"Then?"

I got one, before I could open it, she told me to lie back, she opened it and put it on me."

"So, you would say she knew how to place a condom on a male person?"

"OBJECTION, YOUR HONOR, PLEASE!"

"OVERRULLED!" "Witness will answer the question."

"Oh, no doubt, sir, she knew what to do with a rubber, uh, I mean condom."

"Continue, please."

"She told me to stay down, that she liked it on top. Then she climbed on me and darn near fu,,uh,, screwed my brains out."

Sara could stand it no longer, she stood abruptly and screamed, "YOU LYING BASTARD! YOU'RE JUST MAD BECAUSE I NEVER WOULD GIVE YOU WHAT YOU WANTED!"

"ORDER IN THE COURT! ORDER!" Isbell yelled as he banged the gavel. "Someone get control of that young lady or I will have her removed from the courtroom!"

Zoe, Grandmother and Minnie all consoled and calmed Sara.

Zoe told Sara she didn't have to hear Harper's testimony; she could take her out. Sara looked at Zoe and said, "They already think I am a slut, and I was one most of that week at the beach, but never, ever, with him. If I am going to be lied about, I want to hear and see the person doing the lying!"

Isbell told Bartolli to continue.

"So, Mr. Harper, how long would you guess after you first introduced yourself to Miss Blackmon was it until you and she had sex?"

"Less than half an hour."

"Were there any other times?"

A few, but we had to be real quick, most of the other times were when I was driving her home from church. We wouldn't stop for ice cream, instead she just wanted me to drive around some while she gave me a blo,, uh,, oral sex."

"Why did you and Miss Blackmon stop seeing one another?"

"She wanted it so bad every time we were together I was afraid of getting caught. She was wanting us to take some big risks. So, I stopped calling her."

"Thank you, Mr. Harper. I have no more questions Your Honor."

"Mr. Foley, Cross examine?"

"Yes, Your honor."

"Your Witness."

Foley began, "Mr. Harper, how are you today?"

"Fine, thanks."

"Mr. Harper, when I learned you were going to be here, I made a few calls to some friends of yours."

Randall squirmed in his seat, "OK, I got lottsa friends."

"Is a Detective Dennis Wadsworth one of your friends?"

"I know him."

"Yes sir, he knows you as well."

"What about him?"

"It seems Detective Wadsworth was kind enough to answer some questions I had and send me some information concerning his interest in you."

"OK."

"OBJECTION YOUR HONOR"

"Overruled Mr. Bartolli." Once again Isbell had to do something to masquerade his bias.

"Mr. Harper, were you or were you not taken into custody on suspicion of dealing marijuana and LSD a while back?"

"Yeah, but they let me go. None of em could make the charges stick."

"I am a Corvette guy, nice one you're driving these days. How is it you can afford it on your salary?"

"My uncle helped me get it. He owed me some favors."

"Was one of those favors swearing he was with you the night two 13 year old girls claimed they were raped by your uncle?" Foley had no way of knowing the Vette had been a gift from Thomas Watson.

"OBJECTION YOUR HONOR, MR. HARPER IS NOT THE PERSON ON TRIAL HERE."

"Sustained, Be very careful Mr. Foley."

"Mr. Harper, is it true that you were recently arrested on the charge of statutory rape for having had sex with an underage girl not within the two-year limit of your age at the time?"

OBJECTION!

Harper answered anyway, "I was found innocent."

Foley continued, "Actually it was deemed a mistrial because the officers failed to read you your rights! Am I correct Mr. Harper?"

"OBJECTION YOUR HONOR!" Bartolli was screaming!

"SUSTAINED!"

Foley continued, "AM I CORRECT RANDALL?"

"YES DAMNIT", Randall screamed, "THE LITTLE BITCH WANTED IT."

Suddenly, it became very quiet in the courtroom.

Foley spoke, "That's all, your honor."

Isbell adjourned court for the day. "It's been a long day; Court will reconvene tomorrow at 9 AM."

Craig added Randall Harper to his list of people who would pay dearly, someday, for what they had done to Sara.

***

"Grandmother, I want to talk to Craig."

It was dinner time and Mrs. Blackmon had heard Craig's dad saying they would be eating at the downstairs restaurant.

"OK, baby, I know where to find him."

Sara and her grandmother entered the restaurant, spotted the Kirkland's.

Howard and Craig stood as the two women approached. "Good evening, would y'all care to join us." They did.

Conversation was strained, nobody could think of much to say. Craig and Sara were barely touching their food. Finally, Sara spoke, "Y'all, if it's OK, I would like to talk to Craig, alone. Would it be alright with everyone if he and I excused ourselves and took a walk?"

The evening was pleasant, Sara led Craig to the hotel courtyard where they located a bench and sat, she reached out and took his hand.

Craig spoke first, "It's when I fell in love with you, the first time we held hands."

"I know. I wish I had felt what you felt at that same moment, then, maybe none of this would ever have happened. But it took me too long to realize how much I love you."

"Yeah."

"Craig, you know what's gonna happen, tomorrow don't you?"

271

"Bartolli will put me on the stand, I know."

"Exactly, I want you to be strong."

"Do you think this is weird? I wonder if it's ever happened to anyone before?"

Confused, Sara asked, "What do you mean? I don't understand your question."

"That a victim and a witness for the defense would ever be sitting together, holding hands?"

"You're right, it is strange, but for us things are different. So, it works."

"I guess it does."

"Craig, once again, I want you to be very strong tomorrow, tell the truth. Hold your temper, which by the way I'd never seen until this week. Just answer the questions."

"I'm glad we're talking tonight because after tomorrow I'm afraid you will hate me and never speak to me again."

"I can never hate you Craig. You don't know how many times I've wished you would hate me. You should, but you won't. It would be easier for me if you would."

"No, I could never hate the one flower in my garden of life."

The two teens sat, holding one another in each other's arms. Through their embrace they exchanged strength, one to another. And love.

Isbell gaveled the court into session. "Mr. Bartolli, call your witness."

"Defense calls Craig Kirkland."

Craig dropped his head, his eyes were closed so hard his eyelids hurt, fist clenched and every muscle in his body tight, he sat, said nothing. He hated himself for what he knew was coming, what he was being forced to do.

Bartolli looked at the boy, knowing the pain he'd already inflicted on the Blackmon girl and Craig, the man smiled. He wasn't yet finished.

"I repeat, defense calls Craig Kirkland"

Craig stood, he turned to Sara and moved in her direction. Craig Kirkland reached for Sara's hand, he kissed it. Through her tears Sara read Craig's lips as he mouthed two words, "One Flower."

Bartolli spoke, "Craig Kirkland,,,,,,"

The man got no further with is call, Craig turned to him, "I heard you."

Bartolli kept his distance from Craig as the young man walked toward the witness stand. Judge Isbell told Craig to stop where he was. Confused, Craig stopped and stood in place.

"Bailiff, you know what to do."

A threaded fitting was attached to the floor just in front of the witness stand chair. An eyebolt could be screwed into the fitting. Attached to the eyebolt were two short sections of chain. Attached to the ends of the chains were shackles.

"Mr. Kirkland, due to your violent behavior two days ago toward Mr. Bartolli I am having you restrained while on the witness stand."

Pissed off, Foley sprang from his chair, "OBJECTION!"

"Mr. Foley, am I to understand you are objecting FOR a witness FOR the defense? This is highly unusual." Isbell was smirking when he spoke.

"No, your honor! I am objecting to one of the finest young men I've ever met being treated as if he is a violent criminal. Your honor, that is a good young man, he was simply attempting to protect an older lady when Mr. Bartolli saw fit to grab her arm. The only thing Craig Kirkland is guilty of is reminding all of us that chivalry still exists!"

"Sit back down Mr. Foley, your objection is overruled. Bailiff, get it done."

Craig turned to Foley and stepped close enough to reach his hand across the table. Foley stood again and shook hands with him, "I'm sorry Craig."

"It's OK Mr. Foley, Thanks for your kind words."

Howard and Minnie were crying, Sara and Grandma were crying, Zoe was crying so hard she was almost beside herself, James was crying, even Cynthia was shedding tears. All cried as the bailiff attached the shackles to Craig's ankles.

Craig sat, looking down at the shackles. Bartolli reached over and patted Craig on the shoulder, "Sorry about that, kid."

Craig's hand moved almost as fast as a rattlesnake striking when he grabbed Bartolli's wrist with a grip so hard the man couldn't move his fingers, "You can ask your questions, but never make the mistake of ever touching me again." Craig released his grip before the bailiff could get to him.

Jake leaned to Foley and whispered, "Damn, Al, did you see the look in his eyes?" And how fast he was?"

"I saw it, the same look as day before yesterday. And what I saw was something I've never seen before. If Isbell charges him, I will quit my job before I'll prosecute the kid. Hell, I'll even defend him, pro bono."

"Mr. Kirkland, you will not do that again or I will place charges on you. Do you understand?"

Craig simply stared at the man.

"Mr. Bartolli examine the witness". Hearing the Judge speak his name brought Bartolli from his state of shock.

"What is your full name?"

"Howard Craig Kirkland."

"Age?"

"Seventeen."

"Where do you reside?"

"I live with my parents in Anniston, Alabama."

"Go to school?'

"Yes."

"Have a job, too?"

"Yes"

"What kind of work?

"Filling station, oil changes, lube jobs, pump gas and wash cars."

"Do you like it, what you do?"

"I like mechanical things; it puts a few dollars in my pocket for other things I enjoy."

"So, you have hobbies?"

"Yes."

There was a long pause.

"Well?"

"Well what?"

"Your hobbies?"

"What about them?"

"What are they?"

"I hike and explore the forests; I enjoy target shooting."

"Would you define yourself as one of those gun nuts who walks around in the woods shooting at things?"

"No, you arrogant asshole, I would define myself as a student of the forest. A person who enjoys educating himself about the plant life and animals of the forest and how to survive in the forests if I should ever need to. I like learning how to stalk and move as silently as possible in the forest. As far as my shooting, I enjoy the challenge of hitting a matchstick at fifty yards using a .22 rifle with open sights, a skill requiring a lot of practice."

"You just called me an asshole."

"No, I called you an arrogant asshole. Did you hear any of the rest?"

"You seem to have a bad attitude."

"No, I simply have a serious dislike for anyone who would grab an old lady."

"Craig, do you know anyone in the courtroom?"

"Call me Mr. Kirkland, you and I are not on a first name basis. And, yes."

Bartolli waited.

"Well?

"Well what?"

"Who do you know?"

"My parents, Grandma, Zoe, Sara, and Sara's parents. I also know Harper."

"Randall Harper?"

"No, Lying Ass Harper."

Bartolli looked at the judge.

"Mr. Kirkland, you are trying my patience. You will keep a civil tongue. Understand? Mr. Bartolli, continue."

Everyone who knew Craig were seeing something none of them had ever seen in the young man, aggression and an unwillingness to take shit off anybody anymore. His demeanor would quickly change to one of sadness.

"Let's talk about the relationship between you and Miss Blackmon."

Craig had known it was all coming down to this, sooner or later. It was about to begin.

"Mr. Kirkland, is Miss Sara Blackmon your girlfriend?"

"She was."

"So, you broke up with her after her little fling at Tybee Island?"

"No."

"But you aren't going steady now. What happened if you didn't break up with her?"

"She told me it would be best if we didn't see one another anymore."

"So, it was her idea?"

"Yes."

"Did she do it so she could go out with other boys and not be doing it behind your back?"

"No."

"Well, we'll just leave it there, for now at least."

"How long have you known Miss Blackmon?"

"About a year and a half."

"How long have you known about her existence."

"Two and a half years."

"Where did you first learn of her?"

"At a party, I saw her across the room."

"Ah, at a party, seems miss Blackmon likes to party, a lot! But you didn't meet her then?"

"No."

"Why wait a year?"

"I was told she had a boyfriend."

"Do you know who the boyfriend was?"

"Harper."

"Did you see them together at the party?"

"I saw him come in as I was leaving but didn't see them together."

"When did you meet Miss Blackmon?"

"A year later, I asked a friend to arrange a date with her. She came back with Sara's phone number."

Bartolli then switched tactics, "Have you and Miss Blackmon ever had sex?"

Craig was stunned at the sudden change in questioning, he dropped his head, his shoulders slumped.

Bartolli waited.

"Perhaps you didn't understand the question. I'll ask it again, Have you and..."

Craig interrupted Bartolli, "Yes!"

"How many times?"

"I don't know, several."

"Were you aware how promiscuous Miss Blackmon was?"

"That's a damned lie."

"Not according to Mr. Harper and those four boys sitting at the defense table. Each of them have described her as, "easy.""

"They're all a bunch of lying sonsabitches."

"Well now, even Miss Blackmon has admitted to how badly she wanted sex with Oliver Watson. And I believe you heard her admission. Do you not believe her?"

"I heard her."

"How's it make you feel to know your girlfriend wanted someone else sexually?"

"It hurt." Craig's voice was softer, a tear ran down his cheek.

Sara placed her hands to her face, she, too, was crying.

"CRAIG, HOW DOES IT MAKE YOU FEEL KNOWING SHE PERFORMED ORAL SEX ON OLIVER AND THAT SHE LIKED IT?"

"hurts"

"HOW DOES IT MAKE YOU FEEL KNOWING SHE ENJOYED ANAL SEX, THAT SHE WANTED IT, ASKED FOR IT, FROM THE DEFENDANTS?"

Craig looked up at Bartolli with a desire to choke the life from the man, "THAT'S A DAMNED LIE! THOSE BASTARDS RAPED HER!"

"I THINK NOT, SHE WANTED TO BE THERE, SHE WANTED A GANGBANG, SHE NEEDED A GANGBANG. HOW DOES THAT MAKE YOU FEEL? SHE WENT TO THE COTTAGE THAT NIGHT WITH HER ARM AROUND OLIVER, HER HAND ON HIS BUTT, SHE WANTED TO BE THERE! TELL ME, HOW DOES THAT MAKE YOU FEEL??"

Craig began to sob uncontrollably, barely able to breathe. Minnie Kirkland stood and began to walk to her son.

Isbell banged his gavel, "Bailiff!"

Minnie stopped, she addressed Isbell, "If you want a repeat of what happened in here a few days ago I'm damned sure there are enough good men in this room who are willing. Good men who know what has been done during his farce and who will come to my defense."

Several men stood, the very large farmer was one of them, "Judge, it'd be a damned good idea to allow the lady to see about her son."

Isbell looked around the room. He made the decision, "Go see about him."

Minnie held her son and consoled him. After a while Craig calmed. Howard and Jake had joined Minnie and were softly talking to him as well. After calming Sara, who'd been crying for Craig, Grandma went to Craig and kissed him on the cheek, she whispered a prayer in his ear. The bailiff brought Craig a soft drink.

A half hour later Isbell asked Foley if he wanted to cross examine Craig.

"Yes, your honor."

Foley walked to Craig, "You OK?"

"No sir, but I'm better."

"Judge, now that Mr. Bartolli is across the room, with Detective Brighton and me between Craig and him, do you think you could have the shackles removed?"

"Well, I'm not sure..."

The very large farmer stood, "Judge, it'd be a damned good idea to have those chains removed from that boy!" Every man who'd stood before, stood again.

"Bailiff, remove the shackles."

As the bailiff was removing the chains he whispered to Craig, "I'm sorry son, you hang in there."

"Craig, tell us, what do you think every time you look at Sara?"

"Sir, she's the most beautiful thing I've ever seen."

"She is very beautiful. Now tell us what you feel when you see or think of her."

"Love. The kind of love most people only dream of feeling."

"I believe you; I see it each time I witness how you look at one another. Now, tell me why Sara decided that y'all shouldn't be together any longer."

"Sara told me, when she was still in the hospital, she told me that each time she would see me she would remember the sadness and shame she felt of hurting me, and that she felt each time I saw her I would also feel the pain. She felt it best if we went our separate ways. Sir, although I still love her, always will, she made the right decision."

"Did you know what happened on Tybee Island before this court case revealed it?"

"Yes sir, she admitted everything just before she told me we couldn't be together anymore. Told me the whole story about that week, in detail, or at least what she remembered before she passed out that night."

"How did you react? What did you feel?"

"I cried harder than I did a few minutes ago, I felt as if my soul had been ripped from my body."

"But you still loved her?"

"Absolutely."

"I've seen all the reports, while she was still in shock and would briefly wake up. She would scream for you and sometimes for you to forgive her, then her mind would go back into a state of unconsciousness. Did you know this?"

"Yes sir, the doctors told me, Zoe did too."

"But at the time you didn't know what she was asking your forgiveness for. Right?"

"That's right, I didn't know."

"When did you find out?"

"When she told me about her week at Tybee."

"Have you forgiven her."

"Yes, with all my heart."

Sara placed one hand over her mouth, the other over her heart. She softly thanked the Lord. And she silently cried.

"Craig, you know we have to discuss yours and Sara's relationship, don't you?"

"Yes sir."

"Why, do you think, Sara sent her phone number to you via your friend instead of allowing a date to be arranged?"

"Because she's a lady, sir. Grandma taught her to be a lady. She wouldn't allow a date to be arranged, she expected a potential date to be a gentleman and properly ask her."

"And what did you think about it?"

"I was impressed."

"Tell us about that first date."

"Her parents wouldn't let her single date yet, not until she turned 16, and she wanted her best friend to go with us. I had met Jean, so she knew me a little bit, I talked to a friend who called Jean and they went with us."

"Go ahead."

"I picked up my friend, we picked up Jean, then went to Sara's house. I was invited in, introduced to her parents and I inquired as to her curfew. I didn't want to keep her out late. We went to a movie, then to dinner, the rest of the evening we drove around and talked. I had her home a few minutes early, then took the others to their houses."

"No sex?"

"No sir, no sex. Sir we didn't even kiss until our third date, and only then just a goodnight peck when I walked her to the door that night."

"So, nothing happened between you and Sara as Mr. Harper described between he and Sara?"

"Absolutely not! Sara was a perfect lady and I treated her the way a lady should be treated by a gentleman, how I was raised and how my Dad treats my Mom."

"How long did you date before you asked her to go steady?"

"About three months."

"I have to ask you some very personal questions now, do you understand?"

"Yes sir, and I know some of my answers will not be good for Sara. I'll hate myself afterward, but I know I have to be truthful."

"Once y'all began going steady, did the intimacy increase?"

"Yes sir."

"How so?"

"We began making out, kissing and necking with more passion."

"Continue."

"One thing led to another and we started touching, intimately."

"Did you and Sara eventually have sex?"

Craig looked downward.

"Son? Craig?'

"Sir, would you hold my hands and do something with me?"

"I will." Foley stepped forward, took Craig's hands in his. Craig closed his eyes, bowed his head, Foley did the same as Craig softly prayed, "Dear lord, please forgive me my past indiscretions. If Sara and me had never done what we did perhaps what happened to her never would have, I am to blame Lord, I beg forgiveness. Lord please give me the strength to continue and to be truthful, even though I know my answers will be painful to Sara and everyone else who love both her and me. And Lord, please, please, I beg of you, don't let her hate me. Amen."

It was all Al Foley could do to maintain his composure, "Amen."

There wasn't a dry eye in the courtroom. Most of the jurors were weeping, even the very large farmer had a river of tears rolling down his cheeks.

"Craig, would you like me to repeat the question?"

"No need to, a few months later. It was in April that Sara and I gave one another our virginities."

"Neither of you had ever had sex before. Right?"

"Sir, I've gone this far, I might as well describe it all."

"Go ahead."

"Sir, it was awkward and clumsy, I'd never even had a condom on and had to figure it out. We went slow, honestly romantically slow, neither of us knew exactly what to expect. We very slowly undressed one another, gently we touched one another, caressed one another. Then we made love. It didn't last long but it was the most beautiful experience of our lives. Afterward we held one another for a long time."

"No ripping off clothes? Nothing like that?"

"No sir. Slow and gentle."

"Craig, how do you know for a fact Sara was a virgin?"

"Sir, I didn't know what to expect, so I didn't realize until after reading some articles what the slight resistance I first felt was. I found out later that it was when entering her I felt her hymen. Before you ask, I also noticed, on the condom, a little bit of blood. It was from her hymen tearing. She was a virgin, Sir, until she and I made love that night."

Grandmother whispered to Sara, "Sounds a lot like the first time your Pawpaw and I made love."

"Craig your story of you and Sara is much different than the story Mr. Harper told of himself and Sara."

"Mr. Foley, the reason for that is I just told the truth. Randall Harper wouldn't know the truth if it ran over him."

Foley nodded to Craig. "No further questions, Your honor."

"Mr. Bartolli?"

"No further questions, your honor. No further witnesses. Defense rests."

"Court will reconvene at 9 AM tomorrow morning at which time closing arguments will be heard."

Isbell banged his gavel.

***

Randall Harper was known to drop acid on a regular basis, along with smoking his weed and popping pills. It was eight years, to the day, since he had testified at the trial, that he decided to have a drink before leaving to pick up the young lady he planned to party with that evening. Harper's drink of choice was a Screwdriver, orange juice and vodka. About halfway down his drink he began to feel strange, as if he'd taken LSD and was beginning to trip, only he'd not taken anything except a few sips of his drink. Suddenly, all went blank.

Harper was found the next day, he would spend the rest of his life in an institution for the insane, strapped into a wheelchair, drooling on himself and shitting his pants.

***

A few years after the trial Craig had learned things from some extremely knowledgeable chemists about drugs and their effects. He learned there were some things when mixed together

288

made very potent poisons, intended to kill, some chemicals when mixed would cause a person to simply sleep, others could make a person temporarily crazy. But, the one he found most interesting was what could be mixed with LSD that would cause permanent insanity.

CHAPTER

29

Al Foley hadn't slept well. All night he had thought about, wondered about, what he would say to the jury in his closing argument. Al was a seasoned prosecutor and had never had a trial bother him as this one did. Over the year's juries had surprised him, he felt deeply this one would not. Al knew in his heart that Sara Blackmon would not be allowed the justice she so very much deserved. He had one last shot, but he knew, at the end of the day, four animals would walk free from the courtroom.

"Mr. Foley, Are you prepared to address the jury?"

"Yes, your honor."

"Proceed."

Al didn't need to stand at the lectern and read his argument, he had not written anything.

"Ladies and gentlemen, first allow me to thank you again for your jury service."

The prosecutor continued, "This has been the most emotional trial I have ever prosecuted. Many lives have been changed and will never be the same, the effects will be everlasting."

"A mistake was made by Sara Imogene Blackmon; her mistake was allowing herself to be manipulated by the most handsome boy who'd ever shown her attention. You see, I've spoken to Sara on many occasions, she had no idea how beautiful

she really is. The reason she didn't know is because all her life her mother had told her she was homely and would never amount to anything. Look at her, that beautiful young lady had no idea how very beautiful she really is, I don't believe she knows it now. But the fact remains, she was convinced over her lifetime that she couldn't attract anyone as handsome as Oliver Watson. I will admit, Oliver may be the most handsome sixteen year old young man I've ever seen. Sara, was taken by his looks, his charm, his wit. Oliver is highly intelligent, I've seen his school records, he read Sara like a book, learned her weakness and, as any predator does, he manipulated her until he could make his move."

"Oliver charmed Sara all that week, the first week of August, last year, he toyed with her emotions to the point she was willing to hurt the person who loves her most, Craig Kirkland. Once Oliver had Sara emotionally cornered, the rest of the pack moved in for the final attack, an attack on a petite, sixteen year old, beautiful young woman."

"What happened to Sara Blackmon the evening of August 7th should never happen to any woman, no matter their age. The horror which was inflicted on Sara by the four defendants was so vulgar, so terrifying, so painful both physically and emotionally that her mind left her body, she described it to me as, "Angels came and took me away from what was being done.""

"Yes, Sara went there that night of her own accord, she had sex with Oliver the day before, I will not dispute that. We were all once teenagers, we all understand hormones and testosterone and the effects they have on our bodies, our minds. All of us also understand that once we have a pleasurable sex episode, we want it again, there is no disputing that fact. And, that is why Sara went again with Oliver, back to the cottage the night of August 7. She had no way of knowing the others were inside, hidden in the bathroom, waiting to pounce."

"I can only imagine the terror, the humiliation, the sheer pain, the anguish any woman could experience while four young, strong, athletes were performing unwanted sex acts on her. Rough oral sex, rough vaginal intercourse, rough anal sex, at times all performed at the same time. I cannot fathom anybody being subjected to having something such as the handles of a garden tool and broom being jammed inside the vagina and rectum. Items rammed into her body so deeply and roughly that Sara Imogene Blackmon will never be able to conceive a child."

"Sara was beaten that night, beaten by four strong young men. She was slapped, hit with a fist, she was burned and bitten, you've all seen the pictures! Her bruised, swollen face, the bite to her breast, the burn to her midsection, she will carry the scars for all her days, they will be cruel reminders of her night of hell. Sara's body was used, it was abused, she was thrown around like a ragdoll, unable to defend herself against the strength of a pack of wild athletes. I would liken it all to a rabbit being torn apart by a pack of wolves. No way Sara could fight back. This court is the only way she could defend herself."

"Sara's physical injuries will heal, except for never bearing children, that will never heal. Sara's mind remained wherever the angels carried her, waking at times only to scream for the person who loves her most, the only person in her mind was Craig, she would scream for him. Then, the angels would carry her away again. This happened numerous times over several days. The trauma inflicted on Sara's heart, mind and soul was so terrible she may never fully recover. The loving relationship with a young man who wanted to spend his life with her has been destroyed. Sara and Craig will never enjoy the life together they had once so sweetly talked of having someday. Two hearts meant to be joined for a lifetime will never happen."

"Sara Imogene Blackmon made a mistake, and because of that mistake she was viscously attacked and used by four young

men, Oliver Calix Watson, Oscar William Tomlinson, Andrew Carlton Bohannon and David Edward Clements." As Foley called their names, he pointed at each one.

"Ladies and Gentlemen of the jury, the state of Georgia asks you to find each of those four young men guilty as charged for the assault and vicious gang rape of Sara Imogene Blackmon and ask the court to imprison each of them to the maximum allowed sentence."

"Thank You."

Jake Brighton was still sitting at the prosecution table. Once Al Foley had returned to his seat Jake whispered to the prosecutor, "Sara is going to lose, isn't she?"

"Jake, as sure as hell is hot."

***

Sara had asked Craig to sit next to her, he took Zoe's place. They weren't holding hands, but their hands were touching, once again drawing strength from one another. The events of the trial had both young people emotionally drained.

Sara looked at Craig and asked, "What are you thinking?"

He whispered, "I want to kill them all."

CHAPTER
30

Isbell asked if Bartolli was prepared to address the jury.

"Yes, your honor."

"Proceed."

Bartolli positioned himself in front of a jury he knew would turn in the verdict of not guilty. They had all either been paid to do so or were too frightened to do otherwise, some both paid and scared.

"Ladies and gentlemen, I too would like to thank you all for your service here this week. This has indeed been a very difficult and emotional time for everyone in this courtroom. But it should never have happened."

"It should never have happened because all four of the defendants are innocent of the heinous crime of rape and assault."

"What David, Oscar, Andy and Oliver are guilty of is that of being teenage boys with high levels of testosterone and having met a girl who liked rough sex, a young woman who had a reputation of promiscuity. We have already heard the testimonies of two young men who had sex with her and have no reason to believe there aren't more that we don't know about. I can only imagine."

"At the beginning of the vacation, when the defendants first met Miss Blackmon, she immediately began her flirtatious ways,

standing with her hands on her hips, enticingly, sexily turning herself slowly, giving the defendants an opportunity to visually examine all of her beauty. And yes, she is beautiful, no denying that."

"And so, began her week of manipulation of the young men, especially Oliver. Miss Blackmon knew how to entice young men and she used her experience to talk Oliver into being alone with him. During their time alone at the cottage she taught Oliver things he had never done, but things every teenage boy imagines. One of those things was oral sex, not only did she perform oral sex on Oliver, she also instructed him how to do oral sex on her, things he had read about but had no previous experience with."

"Miss Blackmon told Oliver she would like more the next day but wanted to include his friends. It would be her last night of vacation and she wanted it to be very memorable. He made the arrangements with the others and a time was set to meet and go to the cottage. Yes, ladies and gentlemen, the four boys were excited about the opportunity to experience group sex with Miss Blackmon. Upon learning David had never had sex she informed Oliver she had something special in store for David."

Sitting at the table behind Bartolli, David lowered his head, he knew the man was lying. Tears were falling from David's eyes as he silently prayed, for himself and for Sara. All the boys had their heads down, they had been instructed to look very somber.

"Sara had asked Oliver to tell the others to wait in the bathroom until Oliver could get her warmed up. After she took whatever drugs she'd brought with her to help make her more relaxed and more willing, she and Oliver began. It didn't take long; she called the others to come join."

"What none of the defendants knew was that Miss Blackmon liked it rough, she liked to be slapped, she liked to be bitten and she instructed Oscar, while he was kissing her breast to bite it,

hard. He gently followed her instruction, but she relentlessly screamed "HARDER!", no denying, he did as she'd wanted, once tasting blood he stopped and regretted having done as she'd asked."

"Seeing David, she turned her attention to him telling him she had something very special for him but needed to get herself ready. She had already seen the trowel and asked for it and some cooking oil. Lubricating the trowel's handle, she inserted it in her rectum and told the boys to watch, they watched as she masturbated herself in her anus until she orgasmed. She then told Andy and Oscar to hold her legs up, she was at the edge of the bed and told David what to do and where to do it, he followed her instruction. As this was taking place Oliver was told to use her mouth, he did."

"Ladies and gentlemen, Miss Blackmon continued giving the young men instruction on how to have group sex with a girl who wanted it rough. Sara Blackmon mentioned wanting a fantasy fulfilled, she wanted anal sex, vaginal sex while giving oral sex and instructed the young men how to position themselves, her fantasy was fulfilled."

"Sometime later, while they were taking a break, the young men had stepped into the kitchen area and were having beers, Miss Blackmon was lying in bed, nude, smoking marijuana. Somehow the lit end fell of the joint and landed on her belly, one of the boys heard her moan, saw what was happening and immediately put it out by the only thing he had, he poured beer on it, but too late, it had already burned her."

"Finally, it became obvious to David he'd had enough excitement, he stepped outside to rest. Shortly afterward the other boys came out, they joked and chatted about what fun Miss Blackmon had been and hoped they could all get with her again someday. These were boys being boys. Oscar stepped back inside

to use the restroom, what he saw horrified him, Miss Blackmon had not yet had enough and was using a broom handle to masturbate. Oscar saw blood and took the broom from her. He called the others back inside. Miss Blackmon passed out, the effects of a mixture of pills, the alcohol and the marijuana had taken their toll."

"The boys put her into the bathtub and David did the best he could to clean Miss Blackmon while the others stepped back outside. David bathed her the best he could, dressed her and attempted to stem her bleeding with cloths he placed inside her underwear. David then helped her to her feet and walked her as far as she would allow him, finally telling him to get away from her. I realize you've seen the pictures, one of them was of her black eye and swollen face, the swelling was a result of slaps, slaps she'd asked for and received until the young men would no longer do it. Sara's blackeye was a result of her passing out on the side of the road and falling, her face hitting a rock on the side of the road."

Doc Jack was sitting in the courtroom, whispering to himself, "Lying Bastard."

"And so, Ladies and gentlemen of the jury, you've heard the testimony of witnesses who had previously enjoyed sex with Miss Blackmon, including her own broken hearted boyfriend who still loves her, he is a kind, forgiving young man. You've heard from her own testimony how she and Oliver kissed and touched one another in the water and later that night, how she and Oliver had sex the day before the, for lack of better words, desired gangbang."

"Ladies and Gentlemen, there can only be one correct verdict for David Clements, Oscar Tomlinson, Andy Bohannon and Oliver Watson, NOT GUILTY!"

"Thank You"

Sara leaned to whisper in Craig's ear, "Are you OK?"

"I don't know how, or when, but their payback will happen. It will be me who causes it to happen."

Craig turned his head to Sara; all she could think was that she had never seen the look in anyone's eyes as she was seeing in Craig's. What she saw was the eyes of a killer, a look that frightened her.

***

"Judge Isbell looked to the prosecution table, "Mr. Foley, rebuttal?"

Foley answered, "No, your honor." He turned to Sara, Foley softly said, "I'm sorry."

CHAPTER

31

The bought and paid for Judge addressed the jury, "Ladies and Gentlemen of the jury, I also would like to thank each of you for performing your civic duty by your service as jurors. I also

apologize for any hardship or inconvenience it has caused you and your families. Now I must give you your final instructions."

"This case is wrought with emotion; you must not allow your verdict to be dictated by sympathy for either the defendants or the alleged victim. Keep a clear head and base your vote on only the evidence and testimony which has been presented during this trial proceedings."

"Carefully discuss and debate all you have seen and heard in this courtroom, if you disagree, politely say why and discuss it reasonably. Remember, base your vote on the testimony, evidence and the law, not with your heart. Your verdict will effect many lives, a verdict either way will require all twelve of you vote the same, it must be unanimous."

"Many judges give longer instructions, I give the ones most important, I trust you understand those I've given, and you will follow them. Do you all understand? Raise your hand if you have any questions about my instructions." No hands were raised.

"OK, you will now all be escorted by a bailiff to the juror's room where you will deliberate. The lunch hour is at hand, there are menus in the room from the sandwich shop across the street, please give your order to the bailiff and I will arrange lunch be served to you. Due to the importance of this trial, if a verdict is not reached by 4 PM today, you will be sequestered, arrangements will be made at a local hotel for your overnight stay."

"Bailiff, please escort the jury to the juror's room and see that they are all served lunch."

"Court will reconvene at 2 PM, if the jury has not reached a verdict, it will then recess until 4 PM."

Isbell gaveled the court into recess.

***

The good Reverend Harwell Berry was elected Foreman, "I think we need to offer prayer before we begin." Nobody objected, they all bowed their heads. "Dear Lord, thank you for each of these people and be with us all as we make a very difficult decision. We ask you to please offer comfort to everyone this trial has and will affect. Help us Lord to come to a proper decision. We ask now that you bless the food we will soon receive. Christ name, Amen." Berry already knew how he would vote, and why, he'd needed to put on a show for the other eleven jurors, his prayer was a façade. Little did anyone else know that everyone in the room would vote the same way, any discussions would be for show. But the deliberation would be short.

Everyone sat, there were pitchers of ice water and three carafes filled with fresh coffee, everyone opted for coffee as they awaited their meals.

Sandwiches arrived and the conversation was strained, but everyone spoke casually about their daily lives as they ate lunch. Berry didn't believe eating and discussing business at the same time was a good practice.

Finished with lunch, Berry gave the ladies a chance to speak first, he pointed at Lilliam Conway. Lilliam, not wanting to risk her past being revealed, began, "I feel sorry for her, but she was already sexually active, and had sex the day before with Oliver, not to mention the rest of their week together. I'm leaning toward letting the boys go."

Wanda Genry had her own reasons to not cross Bartolli, she knew he would reveal the photos he'd shown her from her locker room escapades with the coaches, "I feel a lot like Lilliam, she went there once before on her own, and she did it again. I think she wanted something and got more than she thought she would.

300

And there are also the drugs, whatever they were. I think the boys were just being horny sixteen year old boys."

Carolyn Odum was next. Carolyn certainly did not want it known that she and her husband were swingers, it would ruin his business. "And the girl is gorgeous, she's a sexy little thing, if she was going to flirt and throw herself at those boys, especially Oliver, wow, that boy is good looking, what normal boy or group of boys would have turned her down?"

Sandra Tucker hated herself for ever having taken the money from Bertolli, she realized the girl had done some bad things that week, but nobody deserved what was done to her. "I've nothing to add." It would take Sandra reading a newspaper article several years later about a body being found that would cause her to locate Sara and write her a letter. In the letter she would detail why she had voted not guilty and that she suspected, but couldn't prove it, all the others had probably been paid, threatened or blackmailed to vote the same. Sara would write back to Sandra, a letter of forgiveness.

All the men had a turn, a couple showed remorse for what had happened to Sara. Most simply agreed they thought Sara wanted it, one tossed out the word "slut", Berry asked him to not say it again.

At 1:30 PM Berry called for a vote. On the small paper ballots were written Guilty, beneath that was Not Guilty. A simple vote, place a check mark in the box next to the vote they chose.

Twelve ballots were marked. Twelve ballots were marked Not Guilty.

When everyone retuned to the courtroom, just before 2 PM, the jury was already seated on the jury box. Foley turned to Jake, "That didn't take long." Jake agreed. Both men shook their heads.

***

Court is now in session; Isbell banged his gavel.

"Mr. Foreman, has the jury reached a verdict?"

Berry stood, "We have, Your Honor."

"Please hand it to the bailiff."

The bailiff passed the paper to Isbell who opened it read it then had the bailiff pass it back to Berry.

"Mr. Foreman, was the vote unanimous?"

"It was, Your Honor."

"Please read the verdict."

"On the charges of Rape and Assault of Sara Imogene Blackmon, We the jury do here and now find the defendants, Oliver Calix Watson, Andrew Carlton Bohannon, Oscar William Tomlinson and David Edward Clements, NOT GUITLY!

Emotionally and physically drained, Sara collapsed into her seat.

For a few seconds, the room was quiet.

Cries of disagreement broke out when the first "boo" was heard from the back of the room. The next thing heard was a very loud, "THIS IS BULLSHIT!"

While the other boys were hugging and slapping one another on the backs, David had jumped from his chair and ran to his parents, "Let's go, now." The Clements family rushed out of the courtroom as they were pushed, shoved and cursed by the crowd.

Craig had sat down, his parents with him, he was softly crying, saying over and over, "It's all my fault."

During all the ensuing chaos nobody noticed Oliver, Andy and Oscar moving to stand in front of the Blackmon and Kirkland

families. Sara looked up, Oliver was in front of her, laughing, he winked, blew her a kiss, "Thanks for a great time, Sweetheart." Andy was beside Oliver, he had his hand on his crotch and was humping at Sara, he was laughing. Oscar was in front of Craig, the big young man was mimicking a small child crying, he had his fist to his eyes, rubbing them as a child would do, and laughing. Jake had been with the other officers having to hold back the angry crowd, he turned and saw what was taking place in front of Sara and Craig.   What Jake saw, but couldn't move fast enough to stop, was Craig suddenly standing and landing the most accurate right cross he'd ever seen landed. The punch hit Oscar perfectly on the jaw, his head snapped violently, the room shook when Oscar hit the floor! Jake and Howard managed to stop Craig as he was going over the rail to get at the other boys. Andy and Oliver had just seen a boy half their friend's size knock the bigger boy down with one punch, something neither had ever seen anyone do to the huge young man. The two boys scurried quickly back to the defense table, real bad asses when a petite girl was involved, cowards when a pissed off, broken hearted young man came at them.

Craig's demeanor had changed from when Jake and his police friend had needed to stop him from tearing into Bartolli, this time he gave up much quicker to Jake and Howard. This time Craig was not crying, "I'm cool, y'all can let me go." Craig leaned close to Jake, "They all just made a decision for me."

"What decision is that, Craig?"

"You'll know someday."

Jake looked into Craig's eyes; the detective's blood ran cold.

***

Not everybody had seen Craig hit Oliver. Isbell had been busy screaming for order, the bailiff had been helping keep the people

from ripping into the jury. But a very large farmer who'd been in the courtroom every day did see it. Making his way to Craig, the man offered his hand, Craig took it, they shook hands, "Son, you just did that asshole the biggest favor anybody ever did for him."

"What's that, sir?"

"You took him down before I could get to him. I saw it all, Good Job!"

"Thank you, sir."

***

Thomas Watson had grinned an evil grin when the verdict had been announced, he slipped from the room and walked down the hall with his bodyguards. Watson waited.

Isbell's courtroom finally calmed, he took care of the formalities of closing the trial and releasing the jury, thanking them again. Sandra Tucker hadn't waited, the instant the confusion had begun, she'd slipped out. Sandra could barely see through the tears as she walked to her car.

Everything finished, Sara, Craig and their families, escorted by two off duty policemen and Jake, were walking to the stairwell that led to the tunnel to the police station. They began to hear laughter.

Turning the last corner to the stairwell door stood one of the wealthiest men in the State of Georgia, possibly in the southeast. Thomas Watson stood there, laughing. "Well, Well, if it isn't the little cunt and her squalling boyfriend."

Howard Kirkland didn't have a mean bone in his body, he could only remember ever being in one fight, high school, it'd turned into nothing more than a wrestling match. But, Howard had worked hard all his life and was strong, even after going into business he kept himself in shape through daily exercise, he'd had

enough of seeing his son belittled and the young woman he still referred to as "Little Girl" being spoken badly about and treated like trash. Howard grabbed Watson before his bodyguards could intervene, the two cops and Jake stepped in front of the guards and kept them at bay. Howard lifted Watson off the floor, slammed him against the wall, looked into the man's eyes and growled, "One more word motherfucker! I want to you open your mouth and say just ONE,,MORE,,WORD. PLEASE! It's all I'll need to finish you!"

Watson was in shock, eyes wide, mouth open, he wasn't accustomed to being manhandled, especially by a man smaller than himself. He said nothing, Howard released him and stood staring at the man.

Stepping away a few feet and closer to his guards, Watson suddenly told Jake, "I want that man arrested for assaulting me!"

Jake asked, "Who?'

"That Kirkland man, you saw it all."

"Him?" Jake asked while pointing to Howard

"Yes, you saw it."

"I didn't see anything except the man pick up some trash and move it outta the way." Jake looked at his police friends, "Y'all see Mr. Kirkland assault anyone?"

"Nope, just moved some garbage."

"I didn't see anything; I was talking to Mrs. Grandmother."

Jake told Watson, "Nothing here happened for me to arrest anyone. See ya later."

All the women were in shock at Howard's reaction to what Watson had said, especially Minnie, she'd never seen her husband show such a side of himself and never knew it existed.

Sara stepped to Howard and embraced him, "I love you so much."

Zoe stepped back and did the Ali Shuffle while faking a couple of jabs.

Craig stared at his father, "Dad, Wow!"

Once at the police station Jake asked Howard for a word, in private. The two men stepped into an empty office. "What would you have done if he'd said something else with that smart mouth of his?"

"Jake, I don't know, but I do know one thing."

"That is?"

"You would have had to arrest me."

Jake smiled, "In that case I'm glad he kept his mouth shut. I always hate arresting people I like. You good for a drink in the hotel bar after while?"

"A double."

"I'll have the desk call you when I get there. Bring Craig, he can't drink, but some people want to see him, they want to tell him they all think he's one helluva man."

***

Doc Jack's phone rang, it was his cousin Bill. Doc thanked Bill for being in the courtroom as he'd asked him to be, along with some of his friends.

Conversation was short. Bill, Doc's very large farmer cousin had livestock to tend.

CHAPTER

32

The drive home was quiet. Following the trial Howard checked them out of the Hotel, all any of them wanted was to be away from Savannah and back in Alabama.

Home and unpacked Craig went to the porch and sat on the steps, his usual place of contemplation. Inside, Minnie told Howard, "I watched Craig very closely today. I saw something in his face, especially his eyes, that I never dreamt possible in our son." Howard waited for her to continue. "I saw hate and death. Howard, it's something I've never seen but instantly knew what it was when I saw it in our boy's face and eyes. He has a hate for those boys, a hate in its purest form. I think he's planning right now how he can kill them, all of them."

"Minnie, all I can say now is, I hope he comes up with a damned good plan!"

***

He was waiting outside her classroom the next morning when Mrs. Blankson arrived. "Good morning Craig, you're here early, nice to have you back."

"Yes Ma'am."

Entering the room, they both sat, "Craig, I have a sister who is retired, she lives in Savannah. My sister is widowed and has no hobbies, to break the boredom she will often go sit in a courtroom and watch. I asked her to specifically watch the trial involving Sara, my sister called me last night. I know what happened."

"I expect everyone will know, sooner or later, newspapers and such. And because Thomas Watson's son was involved there were some TV news people around."

"Craig, I've seen you improve some from that very dark place you were in at the beginning of this school year. Please don't allow this to drag you back into that place. Lean on that cute little Cindy and your friends Charles and Billy. Even that big oaf you beat the hell out of, great uppercut by the way, Walter seems to have become someone you can depend on. And there is always me, come to me anytime you need to talk."

"Thank you."

***

April 18th, Craig Kirkland's 18th birthday. He'd asked his mother to not make a big deal of it, maybe just some cupcakes, no special dinner. Under the circumstances and having seen her son drift back, somewhat, into that dark place he had once been in, she complied with his wishes.

His workout routines had drastically changed his body, he could run for hours on end and lost count anytime he did pushups, pullups or sit-ups. Craig was amazed by all he was now capable of doing, things he'd never thought possible of himself. Cindy and Billy had broken up but were still friendly, she began hanging around the Kirkland house more, Craig even had her lifting weights. Craig enjoyed Cindy's company, she was always perky, never without a joke to tell. If anyone had come close to making Craig laugh, it had been Cindy. She also had a way of surprising him with things she would say when he least expected it. Dropping by one Sunday afternoon while Howard and Minnie had gone to visit friends, Cindy walked in and bluntly asked, "Wanna have sex?!" Craig was shocked!

"With who?"

"Me, now."

"Girl, you have lost your mind. Go to Billy's house, maybe even Charles. For goodness sake!"

"Nope, been there, done that with Billy. Charles would have a heart attack."

"I almost just did."

"So, want to?"

"You know, I might hate myself later, but no. I'm not willing, yet, to screw up a great friendship."

"I didn't think you would. Still love her, don't you?"

"Yes, always will."

"I know."

"What if I'd said yes?" Craig teased.

"We would both be naked right now, probably on that pool table over there, humping like rabbits."

Craig smiled, shook his head. "Lay down on that weight bench, now."

"Suddenly have a change of heart?"

"No, your gonna do some bench presses. We need to work some of your aggressions out of you. Weights will surely do the job."

***

The Marine recruiter was nice, he answered Craig's questions and gave him some papers to read. Craig had also been doing his own research on different branches of military, seeking the one he believed could offer the best training and experience

for something he had in mind. The Marine Corps was currently at the top of his list.

***

Following the trial things were much different for The Team in South Creek, Georgia.

They thought everything would be back to normal after the trial. They were wrong, "The Team" were shunned. Even Oliver who could usually get laid at the snap of a finger couldn't find a date with any of the local girls. The girls who'd before been willing to pay for a date with him, just to be seen with him, would no longer give him even a glance. Times were so bad for him that not one person would stand and applaud when he caught a pass in a game. Because of the boys being on the team, attendance at the weekly fall football games dropped exponentially, few wanted to watch a team any of the boys were playing on. The worst humiliations to the boys were the bumper stickers someone had printed and sneaked onto the rear bumpers of each of Oliver, Andy and Oscar's cars, "REMEMBER SARA". All the boys had driven around for a few days without knowing the bumper stickers were on their cars. Only when Andy was washing his car had he noticed and called the others. So many other kids carried the same bumper sticker nobody could determine who'd had them made. Nobody ever found out who'd had them made, they were simply found in piles around town, stacked atop newspaper vending machines. David wasn't there to witness nor be a part of the persecution, immediately following the trial he'd asked his parents to transfer him to a private Christian school in a neighboring town.

Oliver was getting horny, none of the girls he regularly had sex with prior to the trial would give him the time of day, he remembered Lilly Jackson and decided to drop by one day. What Oliver hoped for was at least a blowjob, what he found was Sam

311

who had grown to be a rather substantial young man in his own right. Oliver rang the doorbell, Sam came to the door and was anything but pleasant. "Oliver you need to leave and leave right now! If you do not leave, I will drag your ass to the street and whip hell out of you! We do not want you seen at our house." Oliver gave thought to telling Sam what a slut his mother had been but thought better of it, he knew Sam would have killed him with his bare hands.

Oliver, Andy and Oscar met one evening at Oliver's parents' home to shoot some pool and drink a few beers Oscar had brought along. The boys had a lot to talk about, mostly how none of them were getting laid, Andy stated, "Hell, it's getting so bad my right hand doesn't even want to beat me off anymore. I tried some 'strange' with my left hand but it's an uncooperative bitch that hasn't a clue what to do." The boys laughed. After a few more beers Andy became very bold, "Hey Oliver, your Mom is a gorgeous dame, she busy this Saturday? I need a date." The ensuing fight would leave both boys knuckles sore and all eyes blackened, even Oscar got hit for having laughed at the question. The alliance the boys had formed was falling apart.

The next day Oliver asked his parents if they would consider transferring him to another school. With his Father's wealth and his own superior grades Oliver was accepted into a very elite private school, his academics would later earn him a scholarship into The University of Georgia.

Andy and Oscar were stuck at home to suffer the consequences of their actions in August of 1963 and the subsequent trial. The boys stopped hanging out together, neither any longer had many friends. The parents of both boys were financially strapped to the point they could not afford any fancy private schools. Even Oscar's own mother showed him nothing but disdain, he would often just look at her and call her a bitch. Times were miserable for the boys. Oscar quit school and found a

job at the local filling station; he would be drafted into the Army at the age of 18. Andy faired some better, at least he finished high school, only his mother, nobody else, applauded when his name was called to walk onto the stage and receive his diploma. Andy too would be drafted into the Army. David would graduate from the Christian School, he applied for and was awarded entrance into the University of Mississippi, he would later study at the Mississippi Baptist Seminary and become a minister.

None of the boys could imagine the wrath being planned for, trained for, by a man who would graduate high school a year before them and serve in the Marine Corps, a man they and Oliver's father had once laughed at. Each of them would someday again cross paths with Howard Craig Kirkland.

CHAPTER

33

Craig would graduate high school the last week of May of 1964, he simply wanted it over and done. His diploma would read "General Form B", nothing spectacular, a diploma given to those who had barely made grades well enough to avoid failure. The intellect being there it was Craig's lack of desire to turn in any homework that didn't help. Although homework represented thirty percent of his final grade, he hated homework, he had managed to pass by cramming for exams and doing his classwork. Craig knew he could have done better, as did his teachers. One very special teacher, Mrs. Blankson, who'd taken note of the changes in his personality attempted to encourage Craig, telling him, "There is more within you than even you realize exists". Craig thanked her for her concern, she hugged him.

Before leaving home the evening of graduation ceremonies Craig's Mother wanted pictures of him in his cap and gown, he posed with his parents as a neighbor took the photos, he never smiled. Just before leaving home he told his parents as soon as he received his diploma he would not be returning to his seat with the rest of the class as he'd been instructed. Instead, he would walk off the stage which had been set up on the football field and walk to the gate behind the stage and exit the field. From the exit, Craig told his parents, he would then walk up the bleachers on the far side of the field and go to his car which would be parked on the next street, then come home. He felt no desire to involve himself in any post-graduation celebrations, his Mother cried, his

Dad simply nodded and told his son, "We'll see you at home later."

Craig arrived at the school on schedule and took his assigned place in line. There was laughter all around, he didn't join in, only smiling meekly at those who patted his shoulder, congratulating him. A few handshakes were exchanged and a couple of girls hugged him. From the speakers the sound of Pomp and Circumstance began being played.

Walking with his fellow classmates Craig followed instruction as the lines began to separate into the seating area in proper order, once all were in place everyone was directed to sit. Sit they did, suffering through all the boring speeches from all the boring guest speakers. Politicians, community leaders, the principal and more than one teacher, the valedictorian and salutatorian had their times at the microphone. Craig would never remember one word of anything said by any of the speakers, it was nothing more to him than wasted time and pain to be endured.

Finally, names began being called, first to receive their diplomas were the Honor Society Members, others followed alphabetically. Hearing his name, Howard Craig Kirkland, he stepped onto the stage. Obediently shaking most of the hands as he was supposed to. When he came to Mrs. Blankson, who had been so kind to him, she stopped him, with tears in her eyes she hugged him and whispered that she hoped he would always remember what she'd said, Craig's lips quivered, all he could say was "Yes Ma'am." The last person he had to deal with was a person Craig had absolutely no respect for, the principal, he refused to shake the man's hand, simply taking his diploma. Craig walked down the steps, other than turning left as he was supposed to, he turned right toward the gate behind the stage. The crowd went silent.

One of the people on the field who was there to help if any graduates missed their seating was a coach, a man Craig detested.

The man saw the graduate and moved to stop him from leaving. The coach stepped in front of Craig and said, "Get back to your seat Kirkland", Craig stopped, looked the man in the eyes and said one word, "No!" Something about the look he saw caused the coach to realize he was dealing with a different person than the boy he had met only the year earlier. The boy had gotten himself in better physical condition than most of the athletes he coached. A wave of fear came over the man, he feared what he saw in the eyes of the 18 year old young man. The coach stepped aside.

Leaving the field Craig turned left onto the running track located between the football field and guest stands, the stairs up the stands were located at midfield. As he walked Craig was removing his cap and gown. Cap under his arm with his diploma he tossed the gown over his shoulder. Craig turned up the stairs and disappeared over the top of the stands. While this was happening, there was not a sound being made, everyone in the stands on the opposite side of the field were silent, everyone watching the boy who was leaving, no names were being called to others waiting to receive diplomas. The principal, realizing the silence, stunned by what had just taken place, once again began the ceremony. Craig started his car and drove home.

Sara was in the stands, sitting with her grandmother. Sara's grandmother loved the sweet boy who had treated her granddaughter so good, she'd driven from Knoxville to see him graduate. A special bond had developed between Grandmother and Craig early on at Thanksgiving dinner when she had told him he could call her Grandmother, as all the other kids did. Craig had stood, looked at her and declared, "I will call you Grandma or Mrs. Blackmon, but not Grandmother." Mrs. Blackmon had raised one eyebrow, looked at the challenging young man and told him to sit back down. The very proper older lady moved behind him, placed her hands on his shoulders and exclaimed to everyone in the room, "He and only he is and shall be allowed to call me

Grandma, the rest of you will continue to call me Grandmother! Is that clear?" It was very clear!

The next day Sara told him of how much her Grandmother had liked him and that she loved yellow roses. A florist was found who could fill the order, a dozen yellow roses were delivered. The card read, "To Grandma, With My Love."

Grandma and Sara were watching intently as Craig received his diploma, they watched him turn behind the stage rather than returning to his seat. Briefly losing sight of him then seeing him again walking toward the steps across the field, he was removing his cap and gown, they watched him walk up the steps and disappear. Sara turned to her grandmother, leaned over and placed her face on the older woman's bosom, Sara said, "I hurt him so badly." The old woman held her granddaughter, both wept. Further down the way, unseen by Sara, were Howard and Minnie Kirkland, all were weeping for Craig.

Craig arrived home long enough before his parents that he'd had time to change into shorts and tennis shoes, he was sitting on the front steps when his parents pulled into the driveway and parked the car in the basement garage. A few minutes later Howard came out the front door with two beers, handing one to Craig, telling his son, "I think it's time you and I had a beer together." Craig was no stranger to beer, having sneaked around and had a few, he took the can, thanked his Dad and popped the top.

Father and son sat in silence a few minutes, Howard lit a cigarette, finally he spoke, "Son, I knew what happened had changed you, but I never realized how much until tonight. I'm so sorry you've been hurt; sorry everyone was hurt. Those bastards!"

Craig took another sip and replied, "It wasn't just them, Dad. Remember that."

"I know, Son. You still love her, don't you?"

"More than anyone will ever know."

Again, father and son were quiet for a few minutes.

Howard broke the silence, "Out of high school now, what's next?"

"Dad, I've been talking to a military recruiter, Marine Corps. I'm going tomorrow and enlist."

"Marines, huh?" Why the Marine Corps?"

"I've been reading some things at the library and believe the Corps can offer the best discipline and training for a mission I hope to complete someday."

"Mission? One mission?"

"Actually, several."

"You realize you will probably go to Viet Nam? Things are heating up over there."

"Hope so, it'll be part of the training. I'll volunteer to go."

Craig continued "Dad, one thing you need to know. It's something I haven't worked out yet, no matter how much thought I put into it."

"What's that, Son?"

"When it begins, I will have to disappear, completely. I will never see you and Mom again. I will have to do this for a couple of reasons. First, for yall's protection, sooner or later someone might figure out who is doing what will be done. You and Mom will be asked a lot of questions, the less you know, the better."

"And second?"

"Self-preservation."

Craig continued, "Dad, all I can say is this, you watch the news and read the papers, you will know when it begins. It will take several years to complete, but when you know it has begun you will also know I am still alive. But I can still never contact you and Mom, ever. You can best explain it to Mom. Just be sure she knows how much I love y'all."

Howard patted his son's shoulder, leaned over and kissed the young man's head, he stood and turned toward the door. Just before opening the door Howard paused, turned back to his son and said, "You know I loved her too, still do, reckon I always will. She will always be my Little Girl." Howard went inside.

Craig sat quietly in the darkness for a few moments. He always thought best while running, he stood and began a jog. He had a lot to think about.

The young man walked into the house as the sun was creating a new day.

Craig Kirkland had done a lot of thinking. He would soon be leaving home, the beginning of a journey which would change the quiet young man who, as a child, had walked with a teddy bear under his arms to his grandparent's home, into a person feared by his enemies.

CHAPTER

34

He had been told what to bring, it wasn't much, packed into a gym bag.

Craig had several visits with the Marine Corps recruiter, questions had been asked, answers given. He'd also spent many hours at the local library studying the training process, training which would help him with missions he was already planning.

It was time to begin.

"I'm ready."

Minnie Kirkland walked to her son. With tears in her eyes, she handed him her Bible, "Take this with you."

"Mom, mine is in my bag."

"I want you to take mine, it has passages I've marked over the years. It will also keep me close to you."

"Yes Ma'am."

Howard, Minnie and Craig climbed into the car and headed for Montgomery, Alabama.

Typically, the Mississippi River is the dividing point determining if a recruit receives his or her basic training at either San Diego or Parris Island. Living in Alabama, Craig would be going to Parris Island.

The drive to Montgomery was quiet. Craig was excited but also scared, he had read enough and talked to enough people to know his very will was about to be tested to its maximum. Howard and Minnie were being typical parents, they were worrying about their son.

***

A few days earlier Charles and Cindy had dropped by the Kirkland's home, the teens shot pool, drank soft drinks and talked of fun times. As teens do, they laughed a lot and poked fun at one another, but they all knew times were changing, life was changing.

Craig racked the billiard balls and told Charles to break. Having had more practice than Cindy, Charles would shoot and manipulate a long shot for his opponent, Cindy would have to lean further than normal over the rail. Craig would grin, knowing what Charles mischievous mind was up to as he watched his friend position himself behind the girl so he could take in the view.

"Wow!"

Cindy turned and asked, "What?"

"Oh, nothing, Good shot! And I do mean Good!" Cindy laughed as she playfully punched Charles in the belly.

Craig's mind began to wander, over the last year. He was amazed how fast time had flown by. How he had come from being a silly, outgoing, fun loving guy to be the quiet, shy young man he had now become. He thought about how his future would change in only a few days from shooting pool with friends today to the chaos he knew would take place at boot camp. One of his Dad's employees had served in the Marines and had warned him of what would happen, then added, "But there is no real way to fully describe it until you live it."

"Hey, you awake over there?" Cindy asked.

"Just thinking."

Cindy and Charles had been watching Craig as he'd been lost in thought. It was almost time for them to go. The three teens all group hugged.

"When's the last time you kissed a girl?"

Craig looked at Cindy, "It's been a while."

"Well, nobody needs to leave for Marine Corps boot camp without having had a good smooch."

Craig smiled.

Cindy reached up, put her arms around Craig's neck and pulled his lips to hers. The two friends enjoyed a kiss that most lovers would have shared. It was sensual, soft, lingering, what it wasn't was passionate, it was a kiss shared by a boy and girl who happened to be the best of friends.

"You better write Charles and me, you hear?"

"Yes Ma'am."

The girl turned and ran at Charles who had been standing by, waiting. Charles grabbed Cindy and playfully tossed her over his shoulder, he carried her to his car as she was screaming to be put down, both laughing.

The car disappeared around the corner.

Cindy asked, "Will we ever see him again?"

"After his boot camp training he will be home on leave. Cindy, I have a cousin who is a Marine, I remember when he came home after boot camp, he was different, Craig will be different, too."

"He already is." Cindy put her head on her friend's shoulder, she cried.

Unbeknownst to the three teens, Howard had been outside enjoying the evening air as Charles and Cindy were leaving. He had seen the three teens share their goodbyes. Howard looked toward the star filled sky and quietly thanked God for the wonderful friends, Cindy and Charles, he'd given his son.

***

Craig had received instruction to arrive at the hotel where a room would be waiting, a room he would share with another person. The next morning everyone would meet in the hotel lobby, there would be a Marine waiting with further instructions.

For the first time in his life Craig was about to be away from his parents for more than a few days, he was scared. Howard and Minnie stayed with Craig until he was settled in his room, the farewells were very emotional, especially for Minnie who kept crying, "My baby, My baby."

Tears flowed, hugs and kisses were exchanged. Craig's parents finally headed back to Anniston. Suddenly hungry, Craig walked across the street to a fast food joint for a burger and fries to go. Arriving back at his room he found his roommate, a young black boy named Otis had checked in.

"Hey, I'm Otis Jackson."

"Craig Kirkland, nice to meet you Otis." Handshakes were exchanged. "Sorry, I didn't think to wait until my roommate got here before getting something to eat. There's a burger joint across the street if you want to get something."

"Nah, no money."

"No problem." Craig took out his pocketknife and cut the burger in half, he halved the fries, got a glass and halved the soft drink he'd bought at the machine downstairs.

"Man, I can't take your meal."

"Otis, my Mom taught me to never let anyone be hungry if I was able to help, and besides, I figure we are about to start sharing more than a burger. What better way to begin a friendship than over a meal?"

Otis smiled, "I appreciate it." The two young men sat and enjoyed their burger.

"Where you from, Otis?"

"Demopolis. You?"

"Anniston. Why'd you join?"

"Got outta high school, had good grades but couldn't afford college and there wasn't much future living where I live. I thought about it a while and decided I want to go on to school, the GI Bill will help."

"Why the Marine Corps?"

"My uncle was a Marine, he told me if I could get through the training it would teach me, I could do anything. So, might as well start this journey by proving to myself I can do anything. You?"

"From what I've read and learned the Marine training will help me with something I plan to do a few years from now."

"Which is?"

"I can't say, you'll have to forgive my not answering."

"No problem, we all have our reasons." Otis laughed, "You ever think you'd be rooming with a black guy?"

"Ha! A first for everything."

The remainder of the evening was spent with the young men talking, telling one another about their homes, sports, things young men talk about. But mostly, they bonded, a friendship was formed.

***

The Sargent was waiting in the hotel lobby as all the young men began assembling. They came from all walks of life, city boys, country boys, black, white, oriental. They were tall, short, chubby, slim, and some were muscular. One was big and very boisterous, he reminded Craig of Oscar. Craig instantly didn't like him; he also saw the Sargent cutting his eyes a few times in the big guy's direction as he frowned.

Speaking loud enough to be heard, but not too loud, the Sargent directed everyone to the bus that was waiting just outside. Everyone boarded, next stop Maxwell Air Force Base.

Pulling into the base the big guy saw the sign, "I thought we was goin to Parris Island, I didn't join no pussy Air Force."

The Sargent called for quiet, "This is where you will fill out your paperwork, be sworn in and then be flown to Savannah. From Savannah you will be boarding a bus to Parris Island." Craig watched as the Sargent made notes on the clip board he was carrying; big guy would soon be catching hell.

Everyone was nice at Maxwell, no yelling, answering questions and giving direction. Otis looked to Craig and whispered, "I thought this was gonna be bad, yelling and getting bossed around. It's not anything like my Uncle told me."

325

"It'll get worse, they know any of us can get up and walk out until we're sworn in."

Paperwork done, time to swear in. Everyone stood, raised their right hands and repeated.

"I do solemnly swear that I will support and defend the Constitution of the United States against all enemies, foreign and domestic; that I will bear true faith and allegiance to the same; and that I will obey the orders of the President of the United States and the orders of the officers appointed over me, according to regulations and the Uniform Code of Military Justice. So help me God."

Following the swearing in everyone were directed to the mess hall and served a good meal. Otis and Craig sat together. "I thought we would be getting on a plane next", Otis said.

"Killing time, they want us to arrive at Parris at night. Otis, it's gonna be a long day, and night, get a nap if you can on the plane, you're gonna need it."

The big guy sat and watched Craig and Otis, he didn't like blacks and whites eating together, much less being chummy. He planned to teach both a lesson.

The plane was a commercial aircraft, Otis had never flown and was shaking as they left the ground. Craig smiled at his new friend and poked him in the ribs, "Calm down man, catch some z's."

"I'm afraid to sleep, I might crap my pants! Almost just did!"

The flight was short, just about the time altitude was reached the descent began. They landed in Savannah around 9PM. Much time had been killed at Maxwell, nobody seemed to be in a hurry after arriving in Savannah. Arrival by bus at Parris Island would take place around 1:30AM, there was no rush, restroom breaks

and time to get a snack was allowed before departing the airport. Craig napped.

The night was dark, no moon, when the bus pulled through the gate everyone was told to bend over and look at their feet. Taking several turns, by the time the bus stopped everyone was disoriented and had no idea which way they had come in.

"Otis," Craig whispered, "We can do this, pay attention, do what they say. Shit is about to hit the fan."

***

The Drill Sargent had been reading the notes taken by the Sargent who had first met the new recruits. There was always one in the group, in this case it was a big one. The DI stepped onto the bus.

"SITUP AND LISTEN TO ME, WELCOME TO MARINE CORPS RECRUIT DEPOT PARRIS ISLAND!"

"FROM NOW ON YOU WILL RESPOND BY SAYING YES SIR, NO SIR OR AYE AYE SIR! DO YOU UNDERSTAND?"

"YES SIR!!"

IF YOU HAVE ON A SHIRT WITH BUTTONS YOU WILL BUTTON ALL THE WAY TO THE TOP BUTTON. YOU WILL ALWAYS DRESS WITH THE TOP BUTTON FASTENED AND WILL DO SO UNTIL TOLD TO DO OTHERWISE! DO YOU UNDERSTAND?"

"YES SIR!!"

"YOU ARE NOT MARINES JUST BECAUSE YOU ARE HERE, YOU HAVE TO EARN THE RIGHT TO CALL YOURSELF A MARINE, YOU ARE RECRUITS AND WILL REFER TO YOURSELF AS SUCH! DO YOU UNDERSTAND?"

"YES SIR!"

All the while yelling at the recruits, the DI gave further instructions about standing on the yellow footprints, placing belongings at the feet, looking down until told to look up, and he could yell Very Loud!

The last instruction the DI gave was, "NOW, GET OFF MY FUCKING BUS!"

As much as Craig had been expecting it, he was still scared and sweating. Otis was wide eyed and shaking like a leaf.

Off the bus other Drill Sergeants began yelling at the recruits, they seemed particularly interested in the big guy and gave him mortal hell, one would scream in his right ear as another would scream in his left. He was told to turn around only to be told to turn back around, over and over this took place. When told to turn to his left he turned all the way around, he was screamed at how fucking stupid he was.

The instant recruits arrive at MCRD their individuality comes under attack, they are never allowed to use the words "I", "Me" or "Mine", once they cease being an individual, they learn to be a team. Being screamed at from multiple directions creates and environment of chaos, the fog of war type of chaos. The recruits are taught to do as told, when told, without question.

Standing at a table recruits empty their pockets and are told what to keep and what not to keep, any weapon of any kind goes in a trash can, any attempt to keep any kind of weapon results in arrests. Next came the phone call home. The recruits call from a bank of telephones, reading the words printed next to the phone. Craig made his call.

This is Marine Recruit Kirkland

I have arrived safely at Parris Island.

328

Please do not send any food or bulky items.

I will contact you in 7 to 10 days via postcard with my new mailing address.

Thank you for your support.

Goodbye for now.

As Craig and Otis, as well as all other recruits, were making their calls there were no less than three Drill Sergeants screaming, "HURRY UP! TALK FASTER!! MOVE!! MOVE!!"

Howard took the call, he had to hold the receiver away from his ear, what he was hearing was very loud. Howard said a word of thanks that it had been he instead of Minnie who'd taken the call, glad the phone was on his side of the bed. "Craig has arrived at Parris Island."

"Aw, I wish you'd let me talk to him just a minute."

"He had to go, there were others waiting to use the phone."

***

Craig's haircut was neat and stylish for the time. In less than 45 seconds his head felt much the same as a peach.

Following the barber shop all recruits were given a bucket, tossed into the bucket were a scrub brush, soap, toothbrush and toothpaste. From there everyone were rushed into the showers, those who didn't use their scrub brushes to wash themselves were given personal instruction by two drill sergeants, several recruits would be sore for days. Uniforms, underwear, boots, socks and bed linen were given to each recruit. Hustled into the barracks everyone was shown how to make their bunks, called "racks" to Marine Corps Specifications.

Sometime between 0330 and 0400 the recruits were told to hit the sack.

Sleep!! Finally!!

0430 Hours every recruit was scared out of their racks by the crashing of a garbage can being thrown across the concrete floor and a Drill Sargent screaming, "GET THE FUCK OFF THOSE RACKS AND FORM UP!"

"YOU BUNCH OF FUCKING MAGGOTS ARE GONNA HAVE FUN TODAY! DO YOU HEAR ME?

"SIR, YES SIR!"

Days begin early for Marine Corps recruits, and abruptly!

"MOVE YOUR ASSES, GET THOSE RACKS MADE AND GET DRESSED, YOU HAVE 5 MINUTES!"

For the first few weeks of boot camp, the word "teamwork" means, if one of you foul up, everybody pays for it, today pushups were the pay. Upon two guys not making their racks correctly everybody did pushups, everyone got screamed at and some had a DI's foot in their backs as they struggled.

It was gonna be a long three months.

CHAPTER

35

He had not begun running to get himself into good physical shape, he had started running to clear his mind, to help heal his broken heart, for the solitude. The fact that running was creating a healthier body was soon realized by Craig and he began working

harder at it, testing his endurance, the more he ran, the further he could run.

Having later added weight training, pushups, sit-ups and pull ups to his routine, Craig was in almost perfect physical condition for a young man his age. Now, Marine Corps Recruit Craig Kirkland was very glad for all those hours of working out and running. It also kept the Drill Sergeants off his back as they screamed at the others who were struggling during physical training or having difficulty keeping up while running.

Otis was also in good condition, he had been on the track team in high school, plus he worked side jobs most of his life at local farms to help his parents with the bills and put food on the table. Otis confided to Craig, "Lifting all those bales of hay and shoveling all that horseshit out of all those stalls is beginning to pay off!"

A Marine Corps Recruit rarely walks, there is always someone yelling in his ear to go faster, run, absolutely nothing is done casually at basic training, everything is done with the urgency of getting from point A to point B as quickly as possible.

The first week of training involves being yelled at, sometimes for no reason other than it's your turn. Running, learning how to dress according to the corps standards, physical evaluation, more running, more getting screamed at, having to do pushups or sit-ups because somebody may have slightly made their rack not quite right, being confused, answering questions there are no correct answers to and being chewed out for answering incorrectly. The Fog of War.

***

Being strong is one thing, being strong with mass is another. The Big Guy was given hell during PT. He was strong as an ox but lifting all that mass was difficult and carrying it on runs was a

chore. The more he was yelled at, the more he noticed how little some of the others were yelled at, especially Craig and Otis. The big guy's hatred for Recruit Kirkland and Recruit Jackson grew.

***

Among the first things taught are honor, integrity and respect for fellow recruits and Marines. Among those things it is especially noted that one never steals from another recruit or Marine.

***

Otis gathered his things and went to the showers. Big guy took note that Otis had not secured his footlocker, opportunity was at hand.

Finished showering, Otis dressed in clean utilities, preparing for evening chow. His 8 point utility cover was missing, he could find it nowhere and knew he had to have a cover while marching from the barracks to the mess hall. Panic set in.

Walking outside with no cover, the DI's wrath instantly descended upon Otis, other drill instructors joined in. Faces so close to Otis he could feel the spit hitting his face as he was being screamed at. Otis lost count of the laps he ran that night around the barracks, stopping in front on every lap and doing 30 pushups. It was raining.

Otis' cover was never found.

"I see your buddy had some trouble." Big guy winked and grinned as he walked past Craig.

Craig's suspicions were confirmed. He knew Otis well enough to know he hadn't lost his cover; his mistake had been not securing his footlocker. Now, there had to be a payback. Craig began thinking about how to make it happen.

***

Although seemingly slow at the time, the first four weeks of basic training pass quicker than could be imagined. Everything taught that first month brings reason for the next month. The lectures, the history, learning to point with a knife hand, the running, the marching, the physical training, everything has a purpose. By the end of the first four weeks what was once a group of individuals are becoming a group of one, a team.

Some couldn't stand the pressure. One member of another platoon who was standing fire watch at night saw a recruit get out of bed and enter the head. After some time, too long, the fire watch went to check and found the recruit passed out, covered with blood, he'd cut his wrists.

Craig also learned the hard way never to miss a step while marching. He only made the mistake one time. A very swift and hard kick to his ass taught him to pay closer attention to his steps. Later, while smiling, Otis asked if it left a bruise.

"I don't know, wanna check it for me?"

"No way! Stay in step, Recruit Kirkland!"

***

It was the third week when Craig found his opportunity. Hand to hand and pugil stick training.

The Big Guy was strong, but lacked speed and agility, both of which Craig possessed. Craig counted off the people in opposing lines and made sure he would be coming up against the Big Guy.

The recruits faced one another. Big Guy with an evil grin, Craig was stoic, focused. The DI told them to "GO!"

Big Guy ran at Craig, he swung. Craig deftly ducked and caught Big Guy with a blow to the back of the head, he went down. On the next charge Craig caught the bigger recruit in the gut and followed with the pugil stick to the head, again, Big Guy

went down. This was followed by two more knock downs. By this time, even with the protective equipment, Big Guy was dizzy. Craig leaned over and told him, "This needs to end you and your friends fucking with me or my friends, grow up, be a Marine, be my Brother!" Craig offered his hand; Big Guy took it and Craig helped him to his feet.

The DI had seen the animosity in the way the big guy had looked at Craig, Otis and some of the others in the platoon. What he saw on Big Guy's face now was a smile, the DI knew the young man had just made a turn for the better.

Twice in the matter of only two years Craig had turned an enemy into a friend.

Big Guy, Charlie Adcock, would become one of the best Marine Corps Brothers Craig ever had.

Two days later there was a brand new 8 point Utility cover sitting atop Otis' footlocker.

***

Bodies had changed, attitudes had changed. There were many who could barely do one chin-up when they had arrived who could now easily do ten. Young men who were skinny had gained weight, muscle weight, and those who had been overweight had lost fat and gained muscle. Everyone stood straighter, everyone paid closer attention to anything and everything. Discipline had been achieved.

The next month would involve different training, the drill instructors would still yell, keep a recruit in line and chew his ass out if a bead of sweat ran down the left side of his nose instead of the right. But things were changing in subtle ways.

The remaining recruits were one third the way to becoming United States Marines.

Having honed his senses over a lifetime in the forests, Craig could sense, by now, the Drill Sargent entering the barracks and was awake before the door closed behind the man who was about to roust everyone from their slumber. Craig was usually hopping from his top rack before the garbage can, the Sargent so amusingly threw, hit the floor. The Drill Sargent had noticed this recruit and his ability to know there was "incoming."

"HIT THE DECK! FORM UP IN TEN MINUTES FOR A FIVE MILE STROLL!" "Stroll", of course meant "run."

With only ten minutes to take a dump, shower and get dressed the recruits were in a dash to get ready. Sargent Sanchez approached Recruit Kirkland, "Go to my office and wait for me."

The recruits, all gone on their five mile run, Sgt. Sanchez entered his office, Kirkland was standing at attention.

"Sit."

"Aye Sir!" Craig sat.

"Kirkland, how do you do it?"

"Sir, Do what Sir?"

"First, relax. Now, tell me how you know when I, or any other DI, is about to enter the barracks? Just talk to me."

"Sir, most of my life, since my parents would allow, I have been going into the forests and teaching myself, learning, how to become one with my environment. The only way I can explain it is that I feel, more than hear or see, the subtle changes around me. I feel the opening of the door, or movement around me more than I see or hear it. I don't know why, or how, I just do."

"It's pretty amazing. You know I will be testing this ability, don't you?"

"Sir, I welcome the test, Sir."

"Dismissed, Go catch up with the rest."

"Sir, Yes Sir!"

***

0100 hours the following morning.

Sanchez opened the barracks door so slowly he thought his arm would cramp before he could wedge himself through the opening. The fire watch never saw nor heard the Sargent, he was that good.

Stepping slowly, silently, it took Sanchez ten full minutes to reach Craig's rack. The rack was empty. Sanchez heard a whisper, "Good morning Sargent Sanchez", the words barely audible.

Sanchez was good, very good, he turned to see Kirkland who was standing behind him, "Get back in your rack Kirkland, I'll see you in the morning."

***

"He's not fucking human; no human can possibly do what he can do! I got $500.00 says none of you who think you can sneak up on him can do it."

There were no takers, they all knew if Sanchez couldn't do it there was no need in losing $500.00 to bet on it.

Another DI asked, "How's he do it.?"

"I've no idea. Not only did I not hear him get out of his rack, I never saw him do it. Next thing I knew he was behind me, told me Fucking Good Morning! The kid moves like a ghost."

Sargent Major Kowalski happened to be listening to the conversation, "Every now and then we will get a very special recruit in here who, for one reason or another, have special abilities. Don't treat him any different, make him earn his anchor and globe, but keep notes on him. He may have something worthy of teaching those who follow him."

***

The fifth week was a break in nonstop training, the recruits help around the island, working in warehouses, cleaning buildings and doing laundry. This week ended with a ten-mile hike. The next week would begin the training every recruit had been looking forward to.

Grass Week!

Recruits spend countless hours at the rifle range and in class learning the fundamentals of Marine Corps Marksmanship as well as how the rifle functions and how to disassemble, clean and reassemble the weapon, the M14 Battle Rifle.

The M14 is a fine weapon, although heavy at 10.7 pounds, loaded. Firing the 7.62 round, the rifle could be switched from semi-automatic to full auto. Although very accurate when firing

one round at a time, the heavy recoil caused the rifle to be difficult to control when fired fully auto.

Craig excelled during Grass Week, he liked the M14. The weight of the rifle felt good in his hands. Already possessing excellent marksmanship skills, Craig was taught things he had never known, much less tried, there were also some habits he had to break and do the Marine Corps way. By the end of Grass Week, Craig knew his skills would be much more enhanced by the training he had received. This was one of the reasons he'd chosen the Marine Corps, what he was learning would help him in his own missions, years later.

Firing Week.

Many of the recruits had never held a firearm before grass week, much less fired one. Even with the prior weeks training, some were still timid and somewhat fearful of the noise and recoil they knew they would experience. It was a fear all would soon realize had been for nothing as they came to enjoy time on the range.

Firing the second round, Craig adjusted the sights on the M14, the next shot hit the target dead center. He proceeded to do this in all positions, standing, kneeling, sitting and prone, the firing range Drill Instructors looked at one another, none had ever seen a recruit as proficient, especially on his first day firing live ammo at the range.

Finishing, the DI told him to stand, they walked to the head Firing Range DI who wanted to speak to Craig. "Kirkland, where'd you learn to shoot?"

"At home sir."

"Who taught you?"

339

"Really, nobody Sir. Just read a lot of books and practiced a lot."

"When did you start shooting?"

"Sir, when I was just a kid, with a BB gun. Later Dad gave me a .22, then a couple of years ago, a Winchester Model 70, 30.06."

"Model 70 is a fine weapon; I have one myself."

"Sir, Yes Sir."

"OK, Kirkland, you're very good. Go get back in line."

"Sir, Yes Sir."

***

On Rifle Qualification Day Recruit Howard Craig Kirkland would end his shooting with a score of 335. Expert!

CHAPTER

37

Entering the 3rd month of basic training Craig, Otis and Charlie were noticing some subtle differences in how the recruits were being treated. Fewer were the random ass chewing's, the drill instructors didn't seem to be screaming as loudly nor as often, there seemed to be a more patient atmosphere. This isn't to say there weren't times when everyone wouldn't be rousted from their racks in the early hours, sometimes the garbage can was still thrown across the room, lockers were still, on occasion, ransacked. But these things happened less frequently than before.

Craig had felt a sadness for those who had failed their swim test and often looked at the empty racks with sorrow for those who had survived all the prior harassment but couldn't qualify in the tank and were sent home. He also realized it was for the best of the entire group, though. A man who couldn't swim might put too many others in jeopardy under some unforeseen circumstances. Craig would feel the same sadness for those who would fail to qualify on the rifle range and would be required to go through the rifle training again, setting their graduation behind and not being allowed to graduate with those they had been with since the beginning. But a Marine is a Rifleman first and the importance of being able to shoot correctly was a priority.

The results of all the marching, the close order drills, proper way to salute, how to left face, right face, about face, all the hours of practicing these things had brought the recruits to the point of moving so perfectly together the group seemed almost as each man was connected to the others by some invisible force.

There was also a rite of passage upon entering the third month. It would seem such a small thing to most people, but to a Marine Recruit it was a high honor.

While standing at attention during morning inspection the Drill Instructor ordered everyone to "at ease" and ordered them to open the top button of their blouse. Once done, they were ordered back to "attention".

Drill Instructor Sargent Sanchez began talking in a loud voice, but not his typical screaming, "Recruits, you have come far and are now two thirds through your basic training. You are not yet Marines, but you have earned the honor of appearing more like a Marine. Having the top button of your blouse open is a high honor, it shows everyone you have accomplished more than most people will ever accomplish. The next month of your training will still be hard, as it was hard for every recruit before you. You are

still expected to put forth maximum effort, nothing less is acceptable nor will be accepted. DO YOU UNDERSTAND?!"

"SIR, YES SIR!"

"GOOD! FULL PACKS, FIVE MILE RUN! ASSEMBLE OUT FRONT IN 3 MINUTES!"

The next week began Warrior Training, Combat Marksmanship and land navigation. There were equal amounts of time in class as well as crawling in the dirt, mud and learning to maneuver in combat. Although hard, everyone was very glad for all the physical training the prior weeks, they were all much stronger than before arriving at MCRD Parris Island. There was still much screaming and if a recruit messed up, he would find himself doing pushups while a DI had his foot on his back.

One day, while crawling across a field under simulated heavy automatic weapons fire, a DI looked at Charlie and screamed, "You're dead!" Pointing at Otis the DI yelled, "Drag him, Marines don't leave Marines behind!" Otis grabbed Charlie's collar and began digging his feet into the sand, pushing with all his might. Charlie didn't budge. The bigger young man found this to be somewhat amusing, he turned his head and grinned at Otis. Otis' feet were digging holes, Charlie still wasn't budging. The DI got louder "DRAG HIM, DAMNIT!"

Craig was a few feet from Otis and Charlie, when he saw what was happening, he chuckled, a DI saw him. "KIRKLAND, YOU FIND SOMETHING FUNNY? LOW CRAWL OVER THERE AND HELP GET THAT MAN OFF THE FIELD! NOW! MOVE!"

It took maximum effort from both Otis and Craig to finally drag the chuckling, "dead" Charlie off the field. Both recruits were breathing heavily, trying to replenish their oxygen starved bodies. Neither had time to catch his breath before a DI came running at them, "YOU FUCKUPS TOOK TOO LONG, GIVE ME 50 PUSHUPS

EACH". Having seen Charlie laughing the DI turned to him, "YOU TOO ASSHOLE, 50 PUSHUPS!"

Charlie rolled onto his belly and got in position to begin his pushups, with his face in the dirt he mumbled, "He called me an asshole, I guess that's an improvement from being a shithead." All three recruits found it difficult to refrain from laughing while giving the DI his 50 pushups.

* * *

The next several days were filled with more running and much more classroom time. Test were given on all the recruits had learned, the confidence course was revisited, climbing all those obstacles one last time. Physical fitness examinations, mental evaluations, more combat training.

Dress blues photos were taken.

Each recruit was fitted for his uniforms, both Alpha Service and Dress Blues. Craig spent considerable time teaching Otis and Charlie how to tie a necktie.

The last few weeks were grueling, longer runs, untold combat situations, land navigation, then more runs, more combat training. Hours on the rifle range until the rifle straps seemed to grow into their skins.

On one especially long run with full packs and weapons everyone's legs were burning, muscles cramping, sweat literally pouring down their legs and into their boots. Charlie stated, "I can't make it."

Otis got pissed, "You muthafucka, you get yourself moving or you're gonna find out how bad a black boy from Demopolis can whip your big white ass."

Charlie raised his head, picked up his pace. Before Parris Island he'd been as racist as any human could be, had a black man

spoken to him in such a way as Otis just had he would have beat him to a pulp. Times had changed, Charlie had changed, one of the two best friends he had now was a black guy named Otis, and he wasn't about to let him down. "Sir, Yes Sir, Recruit Otis Sir."

Craig smiled.

The last night of combat training ended with a nine mile hike from the training grounds to the Iwo Jima flag raising statue at Peatross Parade Deck.

Prayer is given.

A Drill Sargent tells the history of the flag raising atop Mount Suribachi at Iwo Jima.

Recruits line up, stand at ease.

Drill Sergeants approach, one at a time the once recruits are given their Eagle, Globe and Anchor, each hand is shaken, "Good Job Marine."

Charlie was shedding a nonstop stream of tears, a few ran from Craig's and Otis' eyes as well. Every new Marine knew, they were now officially a part of something bigger than themselves.

For the first time since it had all begun, three months earlier, the new Marines could sit and have chow with the Drill Sergeants. Conversation was good, easy, some laughs were exchanged as well as a few stories. Everyone was told not to gorge themselves or they might get sick. Nobody listened, they were all starving.

Sanchez approached Craig, "I'd like to talk to you."

Craig, wondering if he'd done something wrong, followed the Sargent outside.

"Yes, Sargent?"

"Kirkland, I've seen a lot of recruits come through here, seen a lot of em fail, and seen many who were good. But I've never seen one so hell bent and determined to excel as you. I have also seen you break a racist and how you transformed him into a friend, not only to you, but to Jackson as well. You never minded helping another recruit you saw needing help, even at the expense of your own time. The natural qualities you came here with have been enhanced to the point if I was the enemy, I would fear you above all others, you are a helluva warrior. I watched you these last few weeks, especially on combat training, you would be one place, I would look away briefly, look back and you would be somewhere else, I've no idea how you do it. Your grades are as close to perfect as any I've ever seen. So, I am going to talk to some people and see if I can get you your PFC stripe. It might not happen, that isn't up to me, but I can try. I am proud to have been your Drill Sargent."

Craig came to attention; he snapped a salute.

Sanchez didn't return the salute, instead he reached out his hand. Craig accepted the handshake.

The Kirkland's received the graduation packet from Craig.

"Honey, should we let Mrs. Blackmon and Sara know?"

"I've been thinking of that. Yes, I think we should."

"You sure?"

"Minnie, you know how Craig feels about his "Grandma", and there is no doubt about how he feels about Sara. Let them know, give them the details and let them make the decision."

Minnie made the call.

Mrs. Blackmon answered the phone, "Minnie, so very good to hear from you, how is that wonderful son of yours?"

Beaming, Minnie Kirkland answered, "Wonderful he will be graduating boot camp in two weeks, that's why I called you!"

Minnie went through the details as "Grandma" listened and took notes, times and dates.

"I'll tell Sara and let her make her own decision. Only an act of God could keep me away. I do love that boy so very much."

***

"Minnie called today."

"Oh, Good! How are everyone?"

"Everyone is well, she gave me some news about Craig."

"He's OK, isn't he? Nothing wrong I hope!"

"He's doing great and will be graduating from boot camp soon."

Sara looked somber. "I'll worry about him."

"We've been invited to join them for family day and graduation. I accepted for me but told Minnie I would let you make your own decision. She needs to know so she can make reservations with Parris Island, they have to know how many people will be attending."

"Grandmother, should I?"

"Dear, it's your decision."

Sara looked down, "I know."

"But, if it'll help you decide, I will offer something you can think about, just don't take too long to make your decision, Minnie needs to know. You and that young man have been through hell, there is no doubt. And every step of the way he has supported you any way he could, remember him rescuing you from those reporters? How he tried to get to that asshole attorney who grabbed me in the courtroom? All those days he sat at the hospital? Besides, you and he may not be together but everyone who knows y'all know you love one another. Just a few things to consider while you're thinking."

***

The last week of boot camp the new Marines are inspected by the Battalion Commander, final administrative tasks are completed, and they are all given more insight as to what it means to be a United States Marine.

Rehearsal for graduation is performed until every step and action is perfected.

Family day begins early with a motivational run. Family members line the street as the new Marines run past. The anticipation by families is high as they search for their loved one, hoping to see their Marine for the first time in three months.

***

Craig noticed Charlie wasn't happy and appeared to be concerned about something.

"What's on your mind Big Guy?"

"My Dad is here. I saw him earlier, when we ran."

"Isn't that good?"

"No, I sent the packet to my Mom, she and Dad are divorced. She must have told him. I really didn't want him here."

Craig didn't ask why; he gave Charlie a moment.

"Craig, I've changed, hell you and Otis helped me change. My Dad is a Klan member, so is my cousin I saw with him. They're gonna shit when they find out Otis is one of my best friends now."

"So, how we gonna handle this? Want me to ask Otis to keep his distance from you?"

"Not no, but hell no. I love Otis a hell of a lot more than I love my Dad or my cousin, Otis is a brother, same as you! I just hope my old man doesn't create a scene. You remember how I acted before you kicked my ass with the pugil sticks? How I was an asshole?"

"I remember."

"Well I learned how to be that way from my Dad. He taught me everything there is to know about racism, hate and how to be an asshole. He is what I was."

349

"What you want to do? I'm behind anything you decide."

"First I'm gonna talk to Otis, then I'm gonna talk to Sargent Sanchez, he will advise me."

Craig watched from a distance as Charlie spoke to Otis, the conversation ended with smiles, handshakes and back pats. Charlie then walked to Sanchez's office, knocked and was invited in. The door closed. Several minutes later Charlie exited the office, he gave Craig a thumbs up.

Sanchez gathered all the DI's in a group and informed them of Charlie's dad and cousin, he wanted at least one DI close to Charlie at all times during the times the families were with their Marine. One very large DI said, "Only person allowed to mess up those men's day is Jesus if he so chooses to, a couple of redneck Klan good ol boys might just find themselves squashed."

Sanchez stood, "I need to report this to the commandant."

***

All the visitors enjoyed touring the area and received information from several non coms concerning the history of the corps and the training each of the new Marines had received. It was an awakening to many who had no idea of what their people had gone through to become United States Marines.

The day passed quickly; everyone was directed to the theater where there would be more information presented as well as a short movie of Marine Corps history.

Two marines opened the large roll up door, a cadence was heard..

I don't know, but I've been told,
The Marine Corps is mighty bold.
And up upon the bolden scene,
Stands the United States Marines.

Sound off 1 2,

Sound off 3 4,

1 2 3 4 United States Marine Corps

The only ones with the guts to fight.

They fight all day and stand guard at night.

Sound off 1 2,

Sound off 3 4,

1 2 3 4 United States Marine Corps

Now on land, sea or in the air,

They get the job done no matter where.

So, when they come home from all the battles,

To show off the all their heroic medals.

The Marine Corps is the job for me.

Sound off 1 2,

Sound off 3 4,

1 2 3 4 United States Marine Corps!

Chills ran up the spines of all there to see their Marines.

Sara was wearing a sundress, very tasteful sunglasses and a beautiful straw hat. Many heads turned as she walked by.

The cadence ended before anyone could see the Marines. Then, in perfect step, they marched into the theater. There were four companies graduating, Craig, Otis and Charlie were in 1st Battalion/Alpha Company, the first to march in.

Sara saw him immediately, she was amazed. Although he had been a changed person between the last time she'd seen him in Savannah and the trial, he now marched with a confidence she had never seen in him. Craig's back was laser straight as he marched, his eyes focused directly to the front, never wavering. She was looking at a boy who had become a man.

Howard, Minnie and Grandma saw Craig. Howard instantly noticed several of the new Marines were sporting PFC stripes on their sleeves, his son was one of them. Howard, Minnie and

Grandma all felt a very strong pride for the young Marine, Minnie said, "Just look at him, just look at my boy!" She was crying tears of pride and love.

***

The formalities and introductions of the Drill Instructors finally gave way to the announcement of the afternoon liberty, time to spend with loved ones. Everyone cheered and began making their way through the crowd, finding the persons they wanted to hug.

Minnie hugged Craig so hard he thought his Mom would choke him, Howard next hugged his son and told him how proud he was of him, then came Grandma, Craig was so very glad she had come. "So good to see all of y'all, I've missed you."

"Grandma, how is Sara?"

"Dear, you'll have to ask her yourself. Turn around."

Craig turned, he reached for her hands, "I never thought you could be more beautiful than the last time I saw you, but you are. How are you?"

Sara smiled, "I'm doing good, you look great."

"Thank you."

Craig and Sara gently hugged.

Several minutes passed and the Marines began seeking out their friends and introducing them to one another's loved ones.

Otis approached Craig, both families were introduced, handshakes and hugs were exchanged. A moment later Charlie was walking toward them, "Dad, Chuck, let me introduce y'all to my best friends, if it wasn't for them I don't think I could have made it through boot camp. Otis Jackson, Craig Kirkland, this is my

Dad and cousin Chuck." Otis was first to offer a handshake. It wasn't taken.

Ralph Adcock pulled his son aside and whispered, "What you mean best friends with a darky?"

"Yes sir, one of the best friends I've ever had, both he and Craig are terrific guys, the best."

Seeing the anger rising in Adcock's face, Drill Sargent Morris, a mountain of a man, stepped close, Ralph saw the Sargent's stern expression and removed his hand from Charlies arm. Again, the man whispered, "You got leave coming after graduation, right?"

"Yes sir."

"Don't figure on spending it at home! You understand?"

"Wasn't planning to."

Ralph and Chuck turned and stomped out of the building.

Morris stepped to Charlie, "You handled that very well, Marine. Good Job!" He shook Charlies hand.

Charlie once again approached Craig and Otis. Howard had seen the exchange and shook Charlie's hand. "Son, I've no idea what just took place, but it appears your family just left."

"No sir, my family is still here." He pointed to Craig and Otis, "My brothers are here. Those people who just left are from my past, they are what I once thought I wanted to be. Your son convinced me otherwise when he whipped my butt."

Looking at the size of the young man, compared to Craig's size, everyone's eyes widened. Howard smiled and spoke, "I'll have to hear about that sometime!"

Sara looked at Craig, "He is the second one. Why do you always have to pick the biggest guys to take on?"

Hearing Sara, Charlie asked, "There was another one my size?"

Craig smiled, looked at Charlie, "Bigger they come, harder they fall."

Finally, Charlie was introduced to everyone. All the ladies doted over the big young Marine and hugged him more than anyone ever had. Sara walked to the huge young man and asked him to bend over so she could hug him, she also kissed his cheek. Charlie Adcock blushed.

***

Liberty over, the Marines returned to the barracks. Sitting together, Otis and Charlie asked Craig who the beautiful girl, Sara, was.

"She's a friend." It was obvious Craig didn't want to say much.

Otis pressed Craig to say more.

"What kinda friend?"

"A special friend." Craig turned his eyes away.

"A special friend. Like a girlfriend? You love that girl, don't you, man?"

"Yes, I love her, but it can never be." Craig lowered his face and softly wept.

Charlie and Otis asked no more questions, they knew their friend was hurting inside. The two young men both patted Craig on the back, moved away slightly, allowing him a small amount of privacy. The two young Marines stood guard over their weeping brother, just in case someone had something smartass to say about him.

CHAPTER

39

Dress for Graduation would be Blue Delta Uniforms, blue trousers, khaki blouse and white dress cover. Every man took special care to ensure every crease in their trousers and blouses were perfect and not a wrinkle anywhere. Shoes were shined to perfection, buckles polished to mirror finishes, not a speck of dust nor lint on their uniform or cover. Every Marine worked as a team helping others be sure they were ready.

Forming up, every company marched onto the field, looking sharp!

Sara spotted Craig first and pointed him out. Grandma saw the expression on Sara's face and studied it carefully.

"Dear, what are you thinking?"

"Grandmother, I'm just thinking how proud I am of him and how darn pretty he is. But it saddens me knowing why he's here."

"I agree, dear, but I would choose the word "handsome. We know why he's here and why he chose to be here. Don't dwell on it. Just be very proud of him."

"I always will be."

The ceremony was a beautiful thing to witness for every loved one in attendance. Guidons were retired to the Drill Instructors. The next voice coming through the PA system announced, "The Drill Instructors will now give the final orders the

356

recruits will receive at Boot Camp, and probably the most welcomed!"

The New marines were dismissed, "Hoorah!"

* * *

Hands were shaken, some hugs exchanged, then families and Marines began searching for their loved ones. Once again, same as the day before, Minnie hugged her son so hard again Craig had to ask her to loosen up.

Howard Kirkland stood back and admired the man his son had become, as tears rolled from his eyes, he told Craig, "I have always been proud of you, and thought I could never be more proud, I was wrong, you continue to amaze me." Howard embraced his son.

Sara stood aside as her grandmother approached Craig, the older lady told the young Marine, "You will never know how much I love you; words just are not enough. The kind of person you are, and always have been, has touched me in a way I cannot describe, it goes further than my heart, you have touched my soul. Craig, you are and always will be the only one who can call me Grandma, well, except for Charles." Grandma then hugged the young Marine; she kissed his cheek.

Sara and Craig gently embraced, "You're pretty."

Craig grinned, "Pretty? I don't think I've ever been described as pretty."

"Well, you are!" Sara smiled; Craig laughed.

Charlie, having overheard Sara, had to break in, "Hey, Pretty Boy!"

Craig playfully spoke to the huge young Marine, "I kicked your big ass once, I can do it again if I have to!"

357

"Nope, not again, you showed me your moves." Charlie said while laughing.

By this time Otis and his family had made their way to the group, Otis' mother hugged both Craig and Charlie, she pulled Charlie aside. "Son, I know your family isn't here and I know you have leave starting, you are more than welcome to come home with us. I'm a good cook and will feed you some home cooked meals."

Charlie took Otis' mother's hand and kissed it. "Ma'am, I had expected my Mom would show up today, but I reckon she didn't want to come. But that's alright. You see, I have an aunt who lives in Kentucky, she left Alabama to get away from her brother, my dad, and the rest of the no-good family. She married a man of some means and spends her time training horses on their horse ranch. I've been writing her and explained that I am no longer like the rest of the family, she's invited me to her home. I think I'd like to visit her and get to know her better now that I've changed. But your offer means the world to me."

Mrs. Jackson hugged Charlie and kissed his cheek, "Honey, I think that would be just what you should do. Thank you for being Otis' friend."

"Ma'am, the day Otis and Craig became my friends will always be the best day of my life."

Later, everyone made way to their cars. Craig tossed his duffle in the trunk of his Dad's car and walked to Grandma's. He and Grandma hugged, he opened her door and closed it once she was in. Looking across the roof of the car he saw Sara, she knew to wait until he could open the door for her, she was crying.

Walking around the car, Craig hugged the beautiful young lady, he took her hands and kissed them. Sara asked, "Will I ever see you again?"

"Someday, it's a promise."

Many years later, Craig would keep the promise.

***

The drive was a long one from Parris Island to Anniston, Alabama. Having not driven a car in over three months, Craig asked if he could take the wheel, it felt good to PFC Craig Kirkland to be operating the vehicle.

Following some small talk Howard and Minnie began asking questions about Craig's experiences and his new friends, "Son, when did you meet Otis?"

"He was my roommate in Montgomery, at the hotel, we hit it off immediately."

"And Charlie?"

"Dad, Mom, Charlie was an asshole, it was obvious that next morning in the hotel lobby, he was loud, everyone could tell he was a bully. But when we got to Parris Island the drill instructors instantly targeted him, he broke down. But he still didn't like Otis and me, later he stole Otis cover. Otis caught hell for not having his cover."

Minnie asked, "What's a cover?"

"Headwear, Mom, hat. I have several, all for use with specific uniforms."

"Anyhow, I knew Charlie had taken it and began devising a way to get back at him, opportunity arose one day during a pugil stick session." Craig went on to describe what pugil sticks were and how he'd beaten the bigger young man down, then offered his hand in friendship.

"So, you beat him down, then offered to be his friend?"

359

"And Brother."

"His response?"

"Dad, it was amazing, Charlie looked up at me and smiled, he took my hand and I helped him get to his feet. The change in him was immediate, all for the better."

Howard turned to Minnie, who was sitting in the back seat, "Babe, if you and I have never had anything to be proud of concerning ourselves, we do now. You and I have done right, we raised Craig right. Anybody who can raise a boy these days to be colorblind and who can turn an enemy into a friend, well, we damned sure ought to be proud, we got it right. I am damned proud to be your husband, and one of the parents of our wonderful son."

Minnie leaned close and kissed her husband.

After a while the conversation waned, Craig seemed to go deep into thought.

"You OK, Son?"

"Yes Ma'am."

"Penny for your thoughts."

"Save your penny, Mom."

Howard and Minnie had both seen how Craig and Sara had looked at one another, they knew Craig's thoughts.

***

Craig waited the next day until he heard the choir singing, he silently slipped into the church and sat at the back pew. The minister and choir saw him, but said nothing, not another soul at the service knew he was there.

Craig bowed his head and remembered all the times he'd sat next to Sara during church services and how many times Giles had crawled into his lap and gone to sleep.

How he wished he could turn back the hands of time.

During invitation Craig silently eased out the door.

***

They were waiting on the front porch when Craig arrived home from church. When he turned the corner, Charles, Walter and Cindy all stood, Craig smiled. Stopping the car, he stepped out and Cindy almost bowled him over, she jumped into his arms, legs around his waist and kissed him flush on the lips, "Welcome Home Marine!" The girl saluted as she was laughing.

Charles was next, he hugged Craig for a long time, "Damnit, I've missed your ugly face!"

Craig smiled and told Charles, "My friend, I made another friend named Jackson at Parris Island, a guy named Otis Jackson. Y'all might be cousins!"

"Hey, Shorty!" It was Walter Bradberry speaking, "Your Dad told me you beat the shit out of a guy about my size. That becoming a habit of yours?"

"Well, yeah! Only problem is, it keeps resulting in some big ass people becoming my friends! Maybe they're scared to not be my friends!"

"Well I'm damned sure still scare of you! Now, bring your punk ass over here and give my fat ass a big hug!"

Howard and Minnie were watching from the window. What they saw was the strangest, most beautiful thing, a giant of a boy and their son embracing.

Walter spoke again, "Your Mom invited us all for lunch, you reckon she's got enough to feed a beast like me? Said she's got roast beef."

"Walter, one thing you'll learn about my Mom is that she has an intuition like nobody you'll ever meet. She probably anticipated yall, including you, being here today. I'm betting she will have enough you can have seconds."

"I love me some roast beef."

Craig, Charles and Walter headed toward the house; Cindy leaned back against Craig's car. She put her hand over her mouth, as girls do, and cried. Cindy was worried about what her dear friend might have gotten himself into, and where he might someday find himself. Minnie, looking from the window, saw her.

Minnie met the boys at the door and told them to go wash up and sit at the dining room table, she walked to where Cindy was and embraced the girl, "I know what you're thinking, we share the same thoughts. All we can do is pray."

A few minutes passed, Howard wondered where Minnie and Cindy were. He looked out the front door and saw them, holding one another. Howard eased back inside and occupied the young men with talk of work and sports, giving the girls time for themselves.

***

0400, Craig was awake and dressed in his old boots, jeans and a work shirt. He first wrote a note that he would be back around noon. Locating his old pack in the closet he packed lunch, two flashlights, and three canteens of water. Taking his old .22 rifle, he silently left the house.

Craig was glad his Dad had bought a lot on a hill and that he'd previously swapped out the old automatic transmission for a

four speed, he let the car coast down the hill. Popping the clutch resulted in the car engine starting, he headed toward the forest.

Moving through the woods, each step well thought out before taken, Craig silently moved into the old familiar places he had loved so very much in the years before going to boot camp. He moved like a ghost into the forest.

There it was, the opening to the old mine. Craig stepped into the darkness.

With flashlight in hand he had no problem finding the hidden tunnel, he moved the steel plate and walked into the cavern.

Once inside, Craig stopped and asked aloud, "Why do you keep calling me back here? What is it you want me to find here? Do here? There must be a reason!"

The wind had not been moving that day but suddenly there was a gust, it made the mine sound as though it were moaning, a low, guttural moan.

"I hear you; I just don't understand you. Someday, maybe, I will know."

***

Craig ran every morning and every evening, he worked out and kept himself in shape. The rest of the time he read and studied anything he could find about what to expect next, at least when he wasn't hanging out with Charles, Cindy and Walter.

"When you gotta go?" Cindy asked

They were alone, sitting on the porch, "I had ten days leave till I have to report to Lejeune, and I've used up six of those."

"Take me out, just you and me, the last night before you have to go."

"OK, consider it done. May I ask why?"

"Because I want it that way and you need it to be that way."

She had not been smiling or joking as she usually was. As she left, Craig wondered what was on his friend's mind, he hoped she didn't have any bad news or problems. He would be her shoulder to cry on if she did.

***

"Where to my friend?"

"Let's go get a shake and cruise till dark, then I'll tell you where I want to go."

Two hours of cruising later Cindy told Craig, "Take me down to the river, where you and Sara used to go."

"How'd you know about that place?"

"She needed to talk to someone, I was that someone. She was my friend."

Arriving, Cindy told Craig to open his trunk.

"Why?"

"You have something there that we need, she told me about that, too."

Craig opened the trunk, Cindy took the blanket and spread it on the ground. She lay on it and looked at the stars. Craig watched her, it brought back beautiful memories of he and Sara, he walked to and sat beside his friend.

A few minutes passed, it seemed an eternity. Cindy sat up and told Craig to close his eyes. He did.

She took a bandana from her pocket and carefully blindfolded Craig, he didn't resist. "None of us know when we will

see you again, or even if we ever will. You have been through more than any of us ever will. I want you to do something for yourself. OK?"

"What?"

"I want you to make love to me without seeing me. I want you to see Sara in your mind as you do it."

"I'm not sure about this. I didn't bring anything with me."

"Reach out your hand."

He did.

Cindy placed the condom package in Craig's hand. She gently, softly kissed him. "You are one of my dearest friends Craig Kirkland. I have nothing to give you other than myself, my friendship. Hopefully, you can provide your own memory. Now, make love to me the same way you would if I were Sara, and dream of it being her you're making love to."

Nobody had ever made love to Cindy as Craig did, it was the most tender she had ever been treated. The kisses soft, gentle, sensual. The touches, and caresses were such that she orgasmed before Craig ever entered her. Twice he called out Sara's name, twice Cindy envied Sara.

Cindy knew Craig loved her, she also knew he was not IN love with her, she was his friend and would always remain so.

It was the most beautiful gift a friend could have ever given Craig.

***

Neither Craig nor Cindy would ever speak of their night together. Three times they made love under the stars; each time more beautiful than the one prior.

Each time, Craig saw, in his mind, Sara.

CHAPTER

40

Reporting in at Lejeune, Craig was ordered to Camp Geiger, a satellite of Camp Lejeune. He was immediately ordered to report to Gunnery Sargent Pope.

"Private First Class Kirkland, reporting as ordered."

"Come in Kirkland, sit down."

Craig sat; he was wondering why he'd been ordered to the Gunny's office.

"Kirkland, I've received a call from Sgt. Sanchez over at Parris Island, he seemed very impressed with you. I know Sanchez very well, and I know him to not be easily impressed."

"Sgt. Sanchez taught us well, Gunny."

"Tell me about yourself."

"Born and raised in Anniston, Alabama,,"

Pope interrupted, "Not that part, I don't care where you're from. Sanchez told me your shooting skills were outstanding from the first time you fired your weapon on the range. How is that?"

"Since I was old enough to hold something to shoot, I've loved doing it, it began with a simple little cheap BB gun and advanced to .22, then a 30.06. Gunny, I like to read about things that interest me, so I read anything I could find pertaining to shooting, from outdoor magazines to books that teach the physics of shooting. I know it sounds strange but when I get ready to

367

shoot it's almost as if everything goes into slow motion, my breathing slows, I can feel my heartrate slow, the weapon seems to be as much a part of me as one of my arms. It seems I can feel the trigger releasing the firing pin, then feel it strike the primer. I visualize the bullet leaving the cartridge and traveling through the barrel. I don't really know why it all happens to me in such a way, it just does."

"Remarkable. Tell me how it is you can move so easily, quickly and never make a sound. Sanchez said you spooked the hell out of him in the barracks one night when he attempted to sneak up on you."

"Gunny, most of my life I've spent every minute I could in the forest, and again, I've read more books about stalking and survival than I can count. I learned the basics from books but taught myself the rest about how to move and be silent, to blend in. It's more a case of moving slow to move fast, take what is around you and make it work to your advantage. Again, everything seems to slow down when I am focused on getting from one place to another in such a way as to not be detected. It almost seems I feel, sense, everything in my environment."

"Think you might be up for a test against some of the best?"

"Gunny, the only way to better oneself is to go against the best."

"OK, Kirkland, report to your barracks and get settled in. I'll talk to some others and get back to you in two days."

"Thank you, Gunny."

**

The five sergeants had finished their steaks and were enjoying cold beer.

"I'm telling you what Sanchez told me, he said Kirkland is wicked sneaky, he can exist one second and the next he's gone. Said he's never seen anything like it. Sanchez told me he believes Kirkland might be even better than he is."

"Damn, Bill, Sanchez may be the best I ever knew, he can move like a mist in a fog, totally unseen."

"Exactly, that is why we need to find out if the PFC is as good as Sanchez thinks he might be. You guys up for a chance to find out?"

Everyone wanted in on this test, all agreed.

***

"OK, Kirkland, this is how it will go down. You will be given a map and a compass, you will be dropped off by truck and have ten hours, beginning at 0500 tomorrow, to maneuver to the final objective which will be marked on the map without being detected. Your opponents will be four of the best I have personally ever seen, all sergeants and instructors at this facility. All the sergeants will be armed with weapons that fire a projectile that stings pretty good but will not cause anything worse than a bruise. You will be unarmed, your mission is not to kill, it is to locate the others, mark their locations and evade being killed, if you are hit in any way the test is over. Your opponents will be inserted prior to your entering the area, all have been instructed to remain at least half a mile from your entry point. You can use any personal camouflage you choose to use."

"Sounds like a good test, Gunny."

"You don't seem nervous at all."

"Gunny, I have no intention of losing, but if I do, I will know I lost to the best and will have learned something that may keep me alive when the deal is real."

369

"Good attitude, dismissed."

Craig immediately left the building and began his search for some burlap, he also dropped by the laundry and took some old worn out utilities from the trash that had been thrown out. Ripping strips from the utilities he wove the strips of material into the burlap, it would become his first Ghillie Suit.

***

The Sargent driving the truck received the call at exactly 0500, "Go!"

Craig moved into the tree line.

Ten seconds later the Sargent called Pope, "You won't believe what I just witnessed."

"Tell me."

"I was watching him, never blinked my eyes and he just disappeared. Damnedest thing I ever saw or didn't see."

Pope thought to himself, "Must be pretty good."

Once in the woods Craig took the ghillie suit from his pack and put it on, he used the camo grease and covered every part of his body that was exposed.

At 0700 Craig saw the first one, he'd been watching for a while and saw the man's eyes blink. He saw nothing else, only the blink. He made a mental note of the location and marked the map 15 minutes later, when safe to do so.

Three hours later, 1000 hours, Craig saw the second opponent. The man was in a tree and had a very good view 360 degrees around him. This threw Craig into a longer route than he'd hoped in order to evade being seen. Five hours to go.

One hour later, 1100 hours, the third opponent was seen. The man was lying in a slight depression with a good view of the area. Craig maneuvered around the man and again marked the position.

One mile to go, he had located three of the four opponents. Craig knew the best of the best would be positioned last.

A storm had come through a few weeks earlier and toppled trees as if some strange pickup sticks kind of child's game. The area would not only be difficult to maneuver, it would also offer a perfect place for an opponent to conceal himself.

Once in position, it took Craig an hour to spot the opponent, the man was so perfectly concealed Craig had looked directly at him several times and not seen him. Craig had seen a slight movement. Laying in one position for hours, things tend to go numb, the man had ever so slightly moved his arm in order to get some circulation back into it. Craig began the difficult task of making his way around number four without being seen.

1400 hours. Craig discovered a culvert under the road, he crawled through it and was waiting when the truck came to a stop and Gunny Pope stepped from it. Pope stood next to the truck, his back to Craig who was on the other side of the road.

"I'm pretty thirsty, Gunny. Would you have any water with you?"

Gunny Pope jumped and turned, "DAMN!" What Pope saw was some kind of beast looking at him, and it was smiling!

"About that drink of water, Gunny." Craig smiled again as he asked.

Gunny Pope grinned, "Look in the seat, there's a couple of canteens. Save some for the rest."

371

Pope asked, "Kirkland, what the hell is that thing you're wearing?"

"It's called a Ghillie suit, Gunny. I read about it in a book and figured this would be the first time I needed to try one. They were used some in World War One."

"Well, damned if it don't work, you look like some kinda creature."

"Gunny, here is the map and the locations, along with the times when I spotted the "enemy" Sergeants."

"You not only located them but noted the times as well?"

"I did."

"Damn!"

Although the others had radios, they had been ordered to strict radio silence, Gunny Pope called them all in.

Pope called Sanchez that night and told him about the day. Sanchez got a good laugh, "I told you he's like a damned ghost." Pope agreed!

CHAPTER

41

Training finished at Geiger, leaves were granted followed by almost everyone shipping out for Okinawa where they would all go through jungle warfare training. Almost everything learned would prove to be useless in the months to follow.

It was early 1965 and obvious to everyone something was coming up. Everything took on a new kind of urgency. Something big was coming soon.

***

March 8th, four thousand yards off the coast of Da Nang, Vietnam. Marines were loading into landing craft, upgraded versions of the World War Two Higgins Boats that put men ashore at Normandy. The boats had a ramp located on the bow that would drop and allow the men to disembark.

For some reason the pilot stopped short of the beach, Craig and his group had to begin wading the rest of the way in chest deep water. All had full battle packs and were holding their M14s overhead. Thankfully, they were not under fire. The Vietnamese met them with flowers and signs, "Welcome Marines."

Trucks arrived and transported the Marines to The U.S. Air Base where they would stage and wait for further orders. Those orders came three days later.

Craig's Company were trucked 8 miles from the air base and began setting up a camp. Concertina wire was now everyone's

biggest enemy as they strung it around and set up a perimeter, men cursed each time they received a cut from the wire. Claymore mines were setup and trip flare locations established. The next day the incoming sniper fire would begin, a reminder to the Marines they were now in a war zone. Four nights later, the shit hit the fan.

**

There was one tank in camp, it sat on a hill toward the center of the area. The tank had a large spotlight and would intermittently scan the area.

Although every Marine is a rifleman first, most are also qualified on some type of other weapon, often several other weapons. One of the weapons Craig was qualified on was the M60 machine gun. The M60 is a belt fed automatic firearm, it fires 7.62x51 NATO round. Capable of 500 to 600 rounds per minute the M60 is a formidable weapon when used by a knowledgeable operator.

Twice that night the tank had scanned the area with the spotlight. Around midnight the tank lit the area directly in front of Craig and his assistant gunner. Craig would later describe what he saw as looking like ants coming at him while standing on two legs, he squeezed the trigger as his assistant hit the clackers and set off two claymore mines. People who had made it to the wire began falling in rows as Craig swept the area. The barrel of the M60 began to glow as hundreds of rounds were sent through it.

The enemy continued coming and, in some areas, managed to breach the wire. In Craig's kill zone the enemy would step on dead bodies lying in the wire and use the bodies to help get over it. As one would run at his position, Craig would shoot him down. Little did anyone know, but the enemy had also tunneled under the perimeter and were popping up from the ground with satchel

charges they would throw into bunkers. Many men inside the bunkers died that night.

The fight continued with very little pause until just before dawn. Around first light of day the firing was sporadic. The scene was one of a carnage only the seasoned Marines who had fought in Korea could imagine. Craig and those who had just experienced their first battle were looking at something none of them had ever imagined. Hundreds of dead bodies lay all around them. Craig would talk to his Dad a year later and describe that night. He would end the description with one short sentence, "I killed a lot of people that night."

Later that morning two bulldozers arrived, they dug long trenches and began shoving enemy bodies into the graves. Trucks with bags of lime arrived, the lime spread on the bodies then dirt covered them. It was the most macabre scene Craig had ever witnessed. And this was only the beginning. Before his first tour was over, Craig would be more familiar with death than most people could ever understand.

***

Sargent Jasper Michaels approached Craig's position "How you men doin'?"

"Sargent Michaels, we're good, just cleaning up and checking weapons for tonight's watch."

"You get your Claymores replaced and armed?"

"Got it, Sargent."

"Kirkland, What's your full name?"

"Howard Craig Kirkland, Sargent."

"Come with me."

Craig feared he'd screwed up and was in for a royal ass chewing, but he followed the mean looking Sargent into a bunker and was told to sit.

"I got a friend at Geiger; he and I had a beer a while back and he told me of a PFC who embarrassed the hell out of four of his best instructors. Said the guy is invisible in the bush and can move quieter than a snake on the hunt. He told me any Platoon Sgt. would hope to have the guy in his platoon. He also told me the guy can outshoot most anyone he'd ever seen. Said his name was Craig Kirkland. You ever met Gunnery Sargent Pope?"

"Gunny Pope is a fine man, Sargent Michaels. His recommendation, along with the other four sergeants, got me my crossed rifles."

"Well, Lance Corporal Kirkland, if Pope thinks I need to be happy about having you in my platoon, I am damned sure glad to have you."

"Thank you, Sargent, happy to be here."

"Kirkland, did you know there were more bodies in your kill zone than any others last night?"

"No Sargent, I didn't"

"There were. Do you know why?"

"I can't imagine."

"Well, I can't be sure, but I figure it's because you were aiming instead of going gung ho and spraying rounds anywhere and everywhere. You thought, and you aimed."

"Things were happening fast, I suppose my training kicked in and took over."

"Well, it didn't kick in with a bunch of others cause a couple of em got overrun while they held the trigger down and melted their barrels."

"Mine was glowing."

"But you didn't melt it to the point your weapon failed, you were methodical, fired in bursts and aimed for maximum efficiency."

Craig said nothing.

"Ever kill a man before?"

"No."

"Is your soul OK?"

"I prayed. Yes, it's good."

"Good. Kirkland, soon we will be going out, patrolling in the bush. I hope you're as good as Pope said you are. It'll be a big help to me and a lot of other Marines if you are."

"Sargent Michaels, may I make a request?"

"You can ask. I make no promises."

"I'd like to send a letter to my Dad and have him ship me my rifle from home?"

"Why?"

"We keep getting sniped, I'd like to snipe back. Hard to do with a M60 or M14."

"I'll put in the request to the skipper, it's up to him."

The conversation was abruptly interrupted by another Sargent, "Jazz, Lieutenant wants to talk to you."

"Tell the little asshole I'll be right there."

Craig grinned at the sound of Sargent Jasper Michaels calling his lieutenant an asshole.

"Wipe that grin off your face and go clean your weapon, be sure to put a new barrel on it."

"Yes Sargent!"

***

All over South Vietnam high grounds had been burned off by bombers dropping napalm, burning the vegetation to nothing. New firebases were promptly set up and occupied by the Marines.

Craig's platoon was assigned to one of the more forward bases.

A month later Craig received a package from home, it contained his Winchester Model 70 30.06 and several boxes of ammo.

***

He heard the shot and grabbed the Winchester and binoculars. Climbing atop the bunker Craig lay on his belly and slowly began scanning the tree line. There, slight movement, he guessed six hundred yards, there was no wind. Slowly he lay down the binoculars and made an adjustment to the rifle scope.

Everything went into slow motion, respiration slowed, heart rate slowed, noises became slurred sounds, blinking his eyes seemed to take a minute, the world seemed so surreal. The tree, the man squatting next to the tree, a rifle, in the man's hands, target!

There was music, a child singing. The child was singing a hymn, "Rock of ages, cleft for me,
Let me hide myself in Thee..."

Crosshairs, the eye, crosshairs on the eye. The surprise when the weapon slammed against his shoulder. The head of the man squatting beside the tree, exploding. The music stopped.

"DAMN!" It was Michaels voice. "Pope didn't lie. What a shot!"

"Did he hurt anybody?"

"Nope, but he scared the crap out of some rookie Second LT. He might not come out of the head for a few hours."

***

Craig had taken note of the urgency and accelerated training at Geiger. He had been reading the news and knew things were heating up in Vietnam and figured something was about to happen.

While home on leave, prior to shipping out for Okinawa, Craig had climbed a ladder and located the box he'd hidden on top of the duct work of his parents' home. On his Mothers stationary he wrote a letter and wrapped the box and letter in plain brown paper then returned the package back to its hiding place.

Craig left three days later with his orders for Okinawa.

Three weeks of intense jungle warfare training in the heat and humidity of the island was enough to convince Craig he would soon be in a war zone; he wrote a letter home.

Dear Mom and Dad,

All is well here but I need to ask a favor.

Dad take your step ladder and look about six feet from the furnace toward the garage doors on top of the duct work. You will

locate a package there; it's wrapped in brown paper. Please take it to Mom, she has better penmanship.

Mom, please address the package and see that it is mailed to Sara.

I realize your curiosity is high, but please do not open the package, it is very private.

I love you both and will write again as soon as I can.

Craig

Howard found the package and Minnie did as she was asked. Both wondered what was so secret about it. But both parents loved their son enough that they respected his wish of not opening the package.

***

Grandma accepted the package and noted it was addressed to Sara from Craig, she sat it on the kitchen table and would be sure Sara got it once she came home from school later in the day.

Sara came in and hung her coat in the closet. Grandma was in her bedroom folding laundry, she called to her granddaughter.

"Dear, you have a package, it's on the kitchen table."

Unwrapping the package, there was a letter attached outside the box.

My Dearest Sara,

I hope you will recall the evening you and I went to the jewelry store after I'd asked you to go steady. On that night we looked at several sweetheart rings and I knew the one you liked

best. Afterward you eased over to the case where the engagement and wedding rings were on display, jokingly you picked one out and told me it was the one you wanted me to give you someday.

The next day I returned and purchased the sweetheart ring I gave you on our next date. What you never knew, though, was that I also put the engagement and wedding ring set on layaway.

For several months I made payments on the set and during the week you were on vacation I worked extra hours every day. With the money earned from those extra hours I had just enough to pay off the set and still be able to take you on a date the evening of the day you were supposed to arrive back home. I paid the set off on the evening of August 7th, 1963. I imagine it was about the same time on that date that you were being assaulted. My plan was to show you the set on the evening of the next day when you were to arrive back home, although I knew it would be impossible to give it to you for another couple of years, our parents simply would not have allowed it at that time.

After all that happened, I decided to wait a while to give your body and emotions time to heal before showing the set to you. Then you made the decision that we should not see one another anymore.

By the time you receive this I will either be on my way to or will already be in Viet Nam.

Inside the package this letter is attached to you will find the engagement ring/wedding band set you liked the most. It is yours; I want you to have it. I could never bring myself to return it because it was purchased with love for the most beautiful girl I've ever seen.

Although it is yours to do with as you please I hope you will keep it as a special reminder, that although we can never be together it, along with the sweetheart ring you still have, will

remind you of the last words I spoke to you at the hospital, "Nobody has ever, does now, nor will ever, love you, as I have, do and always will."

With Love,

Craig

Sara was crying so hard she could barely walk down the hall to her grandmother's room. Once there she sat on the bed, handed the older lady the letter and box.

"Oh, Grandmother, he loved me so much, he wanted to someday marry me, why, Oh God, why did I hurt him so bad? I am so very, very ashamed of what I did that week. Why couldn't I have realized how much he loved me and why did I wait so long to realize I was so in love with him? Before it was too late?"

"Oh My" Grandmother replied. She held Sara and cried with her.

Grandma had known about the ring set but never knew what Craig had done with it. She'd kept his secret well.

They had moved about two klicks outside the wire when he saw movement to his left. Smiling as if nothing was amiss, he spoke softly to Michaels, "Were being watched, don't look, our left flank."

"You sure?" Michaels smiled back as he spoke.

"I'm sure."

"How many?"

"I saw three, may be more."

"Be nice to know." Michaels turned his head for a second...he looked back to say something. Craig was no longer there. Michaels whispered to himself, "What the fuck?"

It took Craig twenty minutes to establish there were five Viet Cong. They were moving parallel to the platoon. Craig had moved in a large circle, checking for any other enemy in the area, he was now in front of the five VC, he was waiting.

The M14 set to semi auto, five shots fired, five VC lay dead.

Craig instantly fell behind a large tree for fear the platoon would open fire in his direction, two nervous men did, until Michaels called cease fire.

Craig spoke loud enough to be heard, "Sargent Michaels, there were five."

"Kirkland get your ass back here. NOW!"

"Yes Sargent! I'd appreciate it if nobody would shoot me."

"Everybody hold your fire, there's a Ghost coming through the bush and he's a friendly."

By now the Second Lieutenant had made his way to Michaels, "Sargent, What the hell just happened?"

"Sir, we were being flanked and one of the men noticed. I had no way of letting you know without alerting the enemy to the fact that we knew they were there. Lance Corporal Kirkland observed that there were five enemy and dispatched all of them."

"Where the hell is Kirkland now?"

"Sir, he is standing right behind you."

Neither man had heard Craig, nobody had. Michaels only saw him when he was within five feet behind the LT. Craig, it seemed, had simply materialized. Michaels, in all his days, had never seen anything like it. And, it scared the shit out of the Lieutenant.

"Damnit Kirkland, where the hell did you come from?"

"Over yonder, Sir." He pointed.

"Don't ever sneak up on me like that again!"

"Sorry Sir, sneaking is one of the things I do best."

"That goes without saying. Now, show us the bodies."

The five VC lay in a row. Four had been head shot, one hit in the heart. None had fired a shot. The bodies were searched, weapons and grenades retrieved. One man who liked to think himself a bad ass pulled his K-Bar and was about to cut off the ears from a VC, Michaels grabbed him, "If I ever see you try that again I will break your fucking neck."

***

384

There were no more incidents on the patrol, no further enemy contact. The platoon returned to base.

Later that night Craig was told to report to Michaels bunker.

"Lance Corporal Kirkland reporting as ordered."

"Come on in Kirkland and sit down."

"How long you been in?" Michaels asked.

"Ten months. You?"

"Coming up on twenty years."

"Permission to ask the Sargent a personal question?"

"Granted."

"Why, after twenty years have you only three stripes?"

"Ha! I got busted back to Corporal a while back. I was a Gunnery Sargent. I guess now you want to know why."

"Can't say I'm not curious."

"I caught a drunk Second Lieutenant making unwanted advances toward a very good friend's teenage daughter. Had his hands all over her and she couldn't get away from him. I put my hands, in the form of fists, all over his head. The second time he did it to another man's daughter he got a dishonorable. I wish I'd been there that time, too. Hell, I mighta been kicked back to recruit, it woulda been worth it."

"For reason's I won't mention, I'll just thank you for helping the girl."

"You figure to be a career Marine? Your talents could be a lot of help."

"No. Gonna do my time and go home, I've other plans."

385

"Well, you did a fine job today. You are a natural born leader and your ability to observe and move in the bush undetected is the best I've ever seen, not to mention your talent for shooting. Think about it again when they ask you to re-up. Go get some rest."

Craig was almost out the door when Michaels stopped him.

"Hey, Ghost, if you knew you would only serve the minimum, Why the Marines? You coulda had it easier in another branch."

"I read enough to know I would learn what I need to know better in the Corps than in another branch."

"What's that?"

"Can't say. You'll have to read about it in the papers someday."

"You are the biggest mystery I may ever have met."

"Well, Sargent, I am a Ghost! Ya know?"

"Get outta here."

***

Major Bronson had earned his way in the Marine Corps. Having entered the Corps as a raw recruit Steven Caleb Bronson had worked his way through the enlisted ranks and graduated Officer Candidates School with honors, he was a working man's officer.

"Sargent Michaels request interview with the Major."

"Get your ass in here Jazz. Grab two glasses and pour us a drink."

Michaels and Bronson went way back, they had fought together in Korea, shared the same mud, spilled the same blood.

386

"Your lieutenant came by and babbled something about the patrol yesterday, give me the straight scoop on it."

Michaels went into specific detail about the actions of Lance Corporal Kirkland the day before. He also gave an accurate report on Craig's having sniped the enemy sniper, and the shot he'd made, also the actions the night of the attack.

"I'd been told about him before I met him by Gunny Pope." Michaels went on to describe what Gunny Pope had discussed with him.

"Damn, and you say he's only been in ten months?"

"Steve, if you didn't know he'd been in less than a year you would swear he's a seasoned Marine who'd seen a lot of action. He's a natural fighting man. Hell, he moves like a ghost, in fact I've already popped him with the nickname." Michaels was allowed to call the major by his first name when they were alone.

"Well, I'd hang another stripe on him if he had a year in. But no way in hell the brass will allow it until then. Keep me abreast of him for the next couple of months, if he doesn't foul up in some big way I'll see to it he makes Corporal on his one year anniversary."

"Yes Sir."

"By the way, I sent the papers in three days ago. You'll be getting a pay raise Staff Sargent Michaels."

"Thank you, Major Bronson, Sir!"

"You're welcome. Just don't beat up anymore junior officers."

***

The following two months came and went, Craig's conduct and performance continued to amaze those around him. He was called to Bronson's Command Post and given his Corporal Chevrons with crossed rifles; Craig was officially a non-commissioned officer in the USMC. The lowest rank of non-com, but still a non-com.

CHAPTER

43

The patrol had been ordered to inspect the village northeast of the camp. Enemy activity had been reported in the area. Rice paddies had to be crossed, this would put the patrol in clear view, but had to be done. Everyone was nervous.

Private Harold Limmings had arrived in country only three weeks before and had been processed into Michaels platoon. This would be Limmings first patrol and the eighteen year old private was scared out of his mind, he tried hard not to show it. This patrol would almost prove to be his last.

The men began to slowly work their way across the paddies, some in the water, others dispersed at intervals on the small dikes which separated the paddies. Limmings was on one of the dikes when he was hit.

Craig heard the shot; it had come from the jungle behind the village. Turning, he saw Limmings fall into the water and instantly made his way to the new man. Seeing the hole in the helmet Craig knew the private had been hit in the head. He wasn't moving, everyone assumed he was dead. Today would be the luckiest day Limmings had ever lived.

The bullet had hit at a slight angle, just enough it didn't penetrate both the helmet and the helmet liner. Instead the projectile had made its way around the inside between the helmet and liner and exited at the rear. The concussion caused by the shock had knocked out Limmings, he would later say it felt as

if he'd been hit in the head with a sledgehammer. The bruise made it appear as such.

Other patrols had not been as fortunate. Sporadic sniper fire directed at the patrols had killed a few and wounded others. The camp was also being bothered by snipers, most of which missed their targets but were enough to keep the men on edge. Most of the shots at the camp seemed to be fired by someone less than accurate with their weapon. There were also occasional incoming mortars that interrupted normal operations of the base camp, but those too seemed to be fired by people less than knowledgeable about the operation of their weapon. It needed to be stopped.

Craig approached Michaels late one afternoon, "Staff Sargent, when will I be allowed to go hunting and do what I do best?"

"What the hell are you talking about?"

"I need to be out there." Craig pointed to the jungle.

"I still don't get your meaning."

"What I mean is, the Marine Corps is not utilizing the talents it and I have worked so diligently to develop, enhance and perfect."

"Am I to understand that you want to go out there and hunt the bastards that keep interrupting everyone's sleep?"

"Exactly."

"Honestly, it isn't a bad idea. How many men do you need to go with you?"

"None."

"Alone? Ain't happening."

"Anyone with me will only result in getting my butt shot off, and probably them as well. I move better alone, you know it."

"I know, just don't think the Major will allow it."

Craig simply looked at Michaels for a long couple of minutes.

"OK, OK, I'll talk to him."

***

"Shit, Jazz, have you and Kirkland both lost your minds?"

"Steve, I swear on the cross, I've never seen anything like him. I think he needs at least a chance to see if he can put a stop to, or at least slow down those pissants and their harassment. We can't find em with patrols, I honestly think Kirkland can do it alone."

"What if he goes out alone an doesn't come back, or worse, gets his ass captured? You know what they'd do to him?"

"Sir, I've talked to him enough that I've figured out that something, I don't know what, hurt him bad sometime in his life. He is a mystery who seems to live for only one thing, I don't know what that is either, he just tells me I'll read about it in the papers someday. Look at his eyes sometime, there doesn't seem to be a soul behind them, coldest eyes I've ever seen, and I've seen the eyes of a lot of killers. I believe with everything I am that if he finds himself in a position he cannot escape, there is no way he will allow his capture."

"I'm not sold on sending him out alone, he at least needs a spotter, someone to watch his six."

"Sir, Corporal Kirkland is the only man I've ever known who knows everything around him, 360 degrees, even when he sleeps. Another man with him will get them both killed because he won't

be able to completely concentrate on his mission for worrying about the other man."

"If it was anybody else besides you, I would kick their ass out of my bunker and have em sent back to see a psychiatrist. You know that, don't you?"

Michaels nodded yes.

"When?"

"I'll let him decide and let you know when he goes."

***

Craig had been gathering what he'd needed to put together a ghillie suit, it was stuffed into his small pack.

"OK, Ghost Kirkland, when you want to go?"

"Midnight tonight."

"Weapons?"

"My M70, two .45s and three grenades, frags."

"Not much firepower."

"Don't need much, I'm hunting single people or groups of no more than three."

"How long?"

"Two nights, I'll come in before daylight, day after tomorrow."

"How will I know you're coming in?"

"You won't. If you don't find me in my rack when you make your rounds day after tomorrow, I won't be coming back."

"And suppose our guys spot you and shoot your ass?"

"Trust me, they won't."

"I shouldn't, but I fucking believe you."

"Thanks, Staff Sargent."

"Craig, if they catch you...."

"Jazz, I'm prepared for the possibility, and I'm good with my decision. If, and that's a big if, I don't come back, do me a favor. Look up my Dad when you get back to the world, take him somewhere and buy him a beer, tell him everything. Deal?"

"Deal."

***

"He went out at midnight last night. Steve, I was hidden fifty yards away, watching his hooch. What I saw come out of it looked like some kind of creature, nothing like a man. Wanna know what happened then?"

"What?"

"It turned to me, looked at me, I saw the teeth when it smiled at me. Then it simply disappeared right before my eyes. I'm telling you, Kirkland ain't human."

"When he supposed to be back?"

"Tomorrow morning."

"Report to me when his arrival is confirmed."

"Yes Sir."

***

Craig spent the night silently scouting for signs of men and listening for movement. Shortly before day his ears detected the sounds of twigs softly breaking, he moved in the direction of the

393

sound. The moonless night worked to his advantage, he stayed abreast of the men, none of whom were aware of his presence as they softly jabbered among one another.

Upon hearing the clink of metal Craig determined it was a mortar crew setting up for another day of harassing fire on the camp. He scouted and located a hide that would allow concealment but a good view by which to make his shots.

Dawn just beginning to break offered enough light to shoot, but still dark enough he could move out of the area with the least chance of being detected. His keen ears had not heard anyone else approaching the area.

BOOM! BOOM! BOOM!

Jasper Michaels heard the rifle shots and recognized them for what they were, he'd heard the Model 70 shoot and knew Craig had found targets. It amazed Jazz how someone could fire a bolt action rifle three times as rapidly as he'd heard.

Next, everyone awake saw the explosion. Craig would explain later, after he'd killed the three VC, he had dropped one of his grenades down the mortar tube and hauled ass.

The rest of the day and later that night, Craig hunted, he found no more game.

***

Michaels began his rounds early. He found a ghost sleeping peacefully in its hooch.

CHAPTER

44

A patrol went out later in the day, three bodies and one blown up mortar were found. Craig's kills were confirmed.

The Major peeked into the hooch the afternoon Craig had returned. He'd not wanted to wake the Corporal if he was still resting from his last two nights in the bush. Craig was drinking coffee and cleaning his rifle. Seeing the Major, Craig came to attention. "Sit back down Kirkland. I just dropped by to talk for a few minutes."

"Thank you, Sir. Care for some coffee?"

"Coffee sounds good, you keep doing what you're doing, I'll help myself." The Major poured a cup of the strong brew from the pot sitting atop the makeshift sterno stove. "You had some chow yet?"

"Wanted to get my weapons cleaned first, sir. This humidity is tough on em, some things don't need to wait. Then I was gonna ease over and see if the mess Sargent had anything left."

"Steak and eggs sound good?"

"Yes sir."

"I'll drop by there on my way back and tell him to expect you."

"That's kind of you sir."

"Kirkland, I've seen thousands of Marines during my time in the Corps, I could figure most of them out pretty quickly, you remain a mystery."

"How's that, Sir?"

"You really say very little, and when you talk you do it with a very soft voice. Most Marines bitch, you take things in stride. I've observed you when you didn't know and watched you read your

Bible, so I know you to be religious. You're courteous to a fault and are always helping the new guys, you seem to know what they need before they do. But your eyes are those of a soulless killer, it seems your mission in life to kill. And, you are very good at it. How is it a soft spoken young man from Alabama, raised right and reads his Bible daily could ever become what you have become?"

"Sir, during our lives we are faced with many things that affect us. Those things cause us to possibly change our direction in such a way we may never have considered prior to one, or more, of those things taking place. Life events make us who we are."

"So, am I to assume something happened to you that changed your direction."

"Yes sir, it did."

"May I ask what happened?"

"Sir, with all due respect, It's very personal."

"That's fine, I guess we all have our secrets."

"Thank you, Sir."

"I already know you're good, that's evident from your solo excursion into the bush. Are you as good as Staff Sargent Michaels thinks you are?"

"Sir, please don't think me a braggard when I say what I'm about to say. All my life I have worked to become as good as I could be, either moving in the forests, in this case the jungle, and firing a weapon. I am more comfortable alone in the bush than I am around people anywhere. I feel the jungle around me and become one with it, in tune with it, the jungle becomes my home. Frankly, Sir, I am better than Staff Sargent Michaels thinks I am, and I'm still learning."

"It was against my better judgement to let you go out alone, but Michaels is very convincing. So are you, after having talked with you. Want to do it again in a couple of days?"

"Aye, Sir."

"OK, I'll let you know. Now, finish cleaning your weapons, I'll be sure the mess Sargent knows you're coming. Thanks for the coffee."

* * *

Same as last time, the creature left the bunker at 2400 hours. Once again it stopped, turned and smiled at the man who was hiding, watching. Then, it disappeared. Craig would be alone for five days in the jungles of Vietnam.

The second day Craig was five klicks west of the base, overlooking a village. He heard voices. Twenty minutes passed when five men walked within ten feet of him. He worried they might smell him until he noticed three of the men were smoking. The men continued into the village. Two of them entered a hut.

The two frightened young women were dragged out of the hut, one was very pregnant. While one man held the one who wasn't pregnant, the other took a knife and stabbed the pregnant woman in the belly, then sliced her open, the dead unborn baby fell to the ground. The other men laughed.

Two men ripped the clothing from the other young woman and began to rape her. Craig took aim, in his mind he saw Sara on the ground, the head of the man on top of the woman exploded, next the head of the man who was holding the woman also exploded. Craig began to move.

The three who were still living scattered, hiding behind anything they could find. None hid well enough a ghost couldn't find them. Craig had relocated thirty yards from his original

position, he fired his next shot. Now, there were two. They began running back up the trail.

The ghost allowed the first man to run past the tree he was behind. Suddenly the second man fell, the K-Bar sank to its hilt, the handle protruding from the man's left eye. The first man heard his companion hit the ground; he froze. Two seconds later he was holding his guts in his hands. The man died wondering what the creature standing over him was.

The third day, just before dark, Craig saw three men pushing bicycles along a trail, three shots, three dead men. The bicycles were adapted so weapons and supplies could be tied, attached to them. All were loaded down with weapons and ammunition of all sorts.

The ghost wondered where the trail led, two klicks later he would find out.

The bunker complex was large. Scouting, Craig counted more than thirty scattered throughout the area. Less than fifteen feet from him Craig saw the ground open, a man crawled from the tunnel.

Time to head back, the enemy was planning something big if they'd gone to the trouble of building such a complex area of bunkers and tunnels. It needed to be reported.

***

SSgt. Michaels had taken the platoon out on patrol while Craig had been hunting. The man behind Michaels had stepped on a mine. The explosion had killed the man and Michaels had taken shrapnel, he would soon be in a hospital in Texas for surgery and rehabilitation. Craig would miss SSgt. Michaels but would come to like the Gunnery Sgt. who replaced him.

Gunny Slovenski wasn't as tall as Michaels but his shoulders were just as wide, his biceps bulged, threatening to rip his sleeves, he had a scar across his cheek and if not for his easy smile he might have appeared to be meaner than a cornered crocodile.

"So, you're Ghost, huh?"

"You've talked to SSgt. Michaels?" Craig had just awakened from a five hour sleep. "May I ask where he is?"

"Wounded while you were out, I'm your new platoon Sargent. Name is Slovenski, call me Gunny S, takes to damned long to say Slovenski."

"Welcome to our little piece of heaven, Gunny S."

"Thanks, I managed to talk to Michaels before they shipped his big ass outta here, he and the Major have filled me in about you. I'd already heard some about a ghost, after talking to them I don't mind saying, I am impressed."

"Thanks, Gunny. Now, there is something I need to report to you, and to the Major. I think it's very important." Craig described the bunker and tunnel complex he'd found.

"Damn right it's important. You awake enough to go with me to the CO's bunker?"

"I am."

***

"Major Bronson was glad to see Craig, coffee was offered and accepted."

"Sir, the Corporal has something to report I think you need to know."

"OK, but first tell me how many you got this time, Corporal."

399

Craig gave a description of the five in the village and the three with the bicycles, which he explained had piqued his curiosity about where the trail led.

"Good job. Now, what else?"

For several minutes Corporal Craig Kirkland gave an accurate description of the bunker complex and tunnels. He then marked the location on a map.

"Damn, we had information they were planning something, just didn't know where. How big a force would you guess?"

"Sir, my guess may be wild, but I expect at least three companies, maybe a battalion, Mixture of VC and NVA."

"Good job again, Kirkland. Have you eaten?"

"No sir, just woke and still need to clean my weapons."

"Gunny take Kirkland to the mess and see he gets anything he wants. Have someone clean his weapons."

Craig spoke, "Sir, if it's all the same, I've put in a lot of hours getting my rifle and .45s just right. I'd rather nobody else mess with em."

"Your decision and I understand."

"Thank You, Sir."

"OK, Get y'alls asses outta here. I got some calls to make."

***

Three days later Craig was working with some new guys on setting up their M60 emplacements and teaching them things he'd learned from experience, a lot of which had not been taught during their prior training. He was ordered to Major Bronson's command post.

"Corporal Kirkland reporting, Sir."

"Come in, Son. Take a seat."

"Thank you, Sir."

"Craig", this was the first time Bronson had ever called him anything other than Corporal or Kirkland, "There are times in the career of any CO when he must distinguish between ordering a man to do something and asking a man if he is willing to volunteer. This is one of those times."

"I can understand that Sir."

"Good. Now, I have reported what you told me you found on your last hunting trip. My superiors have made the decision to bomb and shell it, hopefully into oblivion. Some big shit will be dropped on it. You with me?"

"Aye, Sir."

"In order to assure maximum effect, there needs to be an observer calling in both the bombers and the artillery. It'll be extremely hazardous work."

"Sir, may I speak before you continue?"

"You may."

"It'll take two days to get into position, lottsa bad guys roaming around who will need to be left alone so those in the target area are not aware of an observer in the neighborhood. And could I have a new pair of binoculars issued to me? Mine have lost a seal and fogged up."

Smiling, Major Bronson walked to a shelf on the other side of the bunker. He picked up the brand new binoculars his wife had sent him from home and handed them to Craig. "These are from my wife, I'll let her know you appreciate her gift to you."

"Yes sir, please do."

Bronson watched as the young Corporal walked toward his hooch, he prayed, "Thank you Lord, for sending me that damned fine Marine."

***

The bombing and shelling of the complex was the most amazing thing Craig had ever, and might ever, witness. For over ten hours the bombers, the fast movers and the artillery rained down death and destruction on the enemy. Several times coming in much closer to Craig than he was comfortable with, he had moved each time. By the time it was over there was nothing left, Craig had no idea how many hundreds of acres of trees lay in splinters, nor how many dead enemy would be rotting in the heat the next day. Everything was followed by the AC-47s, Puff the Magic Dragon, or Spooky, whichever nickname it was called, they rained down more terror on any enemy in the area who might still be alive. Armed with three 7.62 Mini Guns, each capable of spitting out 2000 rounds per minute. It seemed to Craig that there wasn't a square inch of the area that wasn't hit by a bullet.

Finally, after sunset, Craig began his meticulous return to the base. Knowing there would still be some who had escaped the complex and they would be out for the blood of the observer they knew had to have been spotting, he took extra care and had to listen longer and harder due to the ringing in his ears that wouldn't be gone for a week.

Having taken two days to get into position, it took Craig three days to return. Bronson was worried at the end of the second day.

"Sorry sir," Craig apologized, "had to move slower coming back. They were looking for me, at least those who survived. I had

to evade and change my route several times. Also, I turned the radio off, didn't need bad guys hearing it."

"OK, now that I'm over being pissed off because you had me so damned worried. Good Damned Job, Son!"

***

Craig had lost track of time, it really seemed to not have any meaning to him. He would simply go patrol with the platoon or, more, make his solo trips into the bush and kill people.

"Kirkland, you've been here five and a half months, you are not to leave camp for the next two weeks for any reason. In fact, I do not want to see your face outside your hooch unless you are going to the head or to chow." The Gunny had barked his order.

"Gunny, Why?"

"You know better than to question an order, Marine." Gunny S was smiling.

"Yes, Gunny. But why am I being punished?"

"Not punishment, Son. The Major and I want you to stay alive so you can enjoy an all expense paid trip to lovely Hawaii for your R&R. By the way, Major Bronson picked the place for you, just the kind of asshole he is." Slovenski laughed.

"Well, who am I to dispute the Major?" Craig grinned.

CHAPTER

45

He only had two weeks in which to contact his parents, Charles and Cindy. He hoped to see all of them on his R&R and would be picking up all the costs.

Letters were hastily written; all were received a week later. Sadly, Howard's business was swamped, there was no way he could arrange to be off on such short notice. Minnie feared flying but would do it only if Howard was with her, he had always made her feel safe. Charles was up to his butt cramming for college exams.

Cindy borrowed money from her parents and went on a mad shopping spree for the right clothes she would wear to travel and at the paradise called Hawaii. She would arrive a week after Craig and would stay for two weeks.

***

The last thing Craig did was take his weapons to Gunny S for safe keeping. He knew the Gunny would take care of the M70, M14 and both his .45 Colts.

"Have fun Kirkland! Remember the Four Gets, Get There, Get Drunk, Get Laid, but do not Get in trouble!"

Craig laughed at his platoon Sargent and told him he would do his best.

Hawaii! Island of Paradise. Craig checked in, filled out the paperwork and asked directions to a good bookstore.

"Porn books?"

"No, real books."

"You kidding?"

"I like to read."

"I like to look at pictures."

"Forget it, I'll find a store myself." Craig walked away from the REMF (Rear Echelon Mother Fucker).

Finding a bookstore, Craig purchased three novels and asked directions to the nearest department store where he purchased swim trunks. His upper body had a deep tan from all the time he'd spent shirtless, but his legs were white as a wedding gown, he'd work on tanning those while lying next to the pool, reading.

The week passed quickly. Craig was waiting at the airport when Cindy got off the plane. "Hello Marine!" she kissed him. Make no mistake about it, Cindy had always been a doll, with terrific legs and a butt most men would kill to play with. But her figure had matured since Craig had last seen her, she had gained weight in all the right places.

Craig took note of the heads that turned as he and Cindy walked to the cab waiting for them. "You're being checked out."

"Let em eat their hearts out and be jealous of you."

"Why should they be jealous of me? We're just a couple of buddies hanging out together."

"Well, they would surely be jealous if they knew your buddy has every intention of screwing your brains out as soon as we get me to my room."

Thinking she was joking, Craig laughed.

Cindy grinned a wicked little grin.

***

Craig carried Cindy's baggage and was putting it on the bed. Cindy opened the door and hung the "Do Not Disturb" sign on the doorknob then closed the door, locked it and hooked the safety chain into its slot.

"I've been sitting next to a stinky human all the way from San Francisco, I need a shower and so do you, besides, I need you to wash my back. Get naked."

"Do what?"

"Get naked, you don't have anything I've never seen before." Then she remembered the blindfold she had put on him. "Ohhhh, but I have something you've never seen before. I think it's time you did." Cindy giggled. "Close your eyes."

Craig did as he was told, Cindy undressed.

"Open your eyes."

What Craig saw nearly floored him. Cindy had indeed filled out in the right places. She was beautiful.

"Now, come wash my back, front too, please."

In the shower Craig and Cindy washed one another in the most sensual way imaginable, slowly, methodically. Twice Craig said, "I can't believe I am naked in a shower with one of my best friends."

"Well, if you don't believe that, believe this."

Cindy dropped to her knees and took Craig into her mouth; he came close to fainting. "What the hell do you think you're doing?"

"Well, Marine, if you don't know, you're fixing to get the best lesson of your lifetime! Now, hush."

Craig's knees buckled when he orgasmed, he had to catch himself to keep from falling.

"Wow!" Cindy exclaimed, "I wasn't expecting that much, it must have been a while since you fired that gun."

Cindy washed Craig and told him to get out, she had some stuff on her she needed to wash off.

Still speechless, Craig exited the shower on shaky legs and toweled off.

Finishing her shower, Cindy dried her long hair and climbed into the bed where Craig was still recuperating, she kissed him, tenderly.

Craig said to Cindy, "Why does this feel so not right?"

"We've been friends a long time. We love one another as friends, we've already talked about that. I know you can never be in love with me, and although I could fall in love with you in a heartbeat, I still understand it could never be the same love for me you have for Sara. Are you listening?"

"Yes."

'Good. So, I am willing to accept that and be your friend. But you are a man, I am a woman, I propose we be very good friends, but with benefits. If that is alright with you, Mr. Marine Corps Stud."

"Yes, I suppose. I mean my mind is in a whirlwind right now."

"Well, while you're working things out in your mind, I'd like you to do something for me."

"What?"

Cindy pushed him on to his back and straddled his face. "I want you to do with your mouth what needs to be done to that."

407

"Wait!"

"What?" Cindy sounded exasperated.

"Well, I'm not sure what to do?"

Cindy backed up and sat on Craig's belly, "You have never performed oral sex on a girl?"

"Nope. Cindy you know my experience is, well, limited."

Cindy smiled, "I love you Craig Kirkland. I am going to love being your teacher these next two weeks."

"I just hope I survive."

For the next two hours Cindy would explain the female anatomy in detail to Craig. She would have him look at what she was explaining and have him touch what she told him to touch, and how to. Cindy held up her finger and demonstrated with her tongue what to do to different parts of the female genitalia, then she would have him try it on her. Craig was informed of the female G-Spot, something he'd never heard of, and what to do with it either during intercourse or with his fingers. Finally, Cindy lay back and told Craig to look closely. She reached down and pulled back her hood, "See that little thing under there?"

"Yes."

"Good. Now let me show you something. Cindy reached down and touched the head of Craig's penis. "Feel that?

"Oh Yeah!"

"Well that little part of a woman's anatomy has as many nerve endings, sometimes more, than that big ol thing on the end of your shaft."

"You're kidding?"

"I kid you not! Now, lay back, it's time for your exam."

Once again Cindy straddled Craig's face. He'd been a good student, she orgasmed in less than ten minutes. Cindy fell off Craig and lay there, she was breathing fast and heavy. Craig never gave her time to relax, he was inside her in less than five seconds. The two young people had sex fast and furious for the next hour. Different positions, they loved what they were doing and did it with all their might.

***

"You hungry?"

Craig told her, "Starving."

"I saw a room service menu. I've never stayed any place that had room service."

"If they have Surf and Turf, rare on the Turf, order that for me. You get anything your heart desires."

Craig went to shower, again.

***

"I ordered two steaks, rare, with lobster, a bottle of champagne, I've never had champagne. A half a case of Budweiser and a fifth of bourbon. That OK?"

"Well, I'm learning you're a nymphomaniac, are you an alcoholic too?"

"Nope, but always willing to get a man drunk and take advantage of him, especially if he's a handsome Marine."

"I'm still trying to understand how I will survive two weeks alone with you. Getting sloppy drunk may be my only escape."

The champagne tickled Cindy's nose, she sneezed, but liked the taste. She poured another glass,, then, another.

Craig picked Cindy up and put her inert body into the bed, he gently covered her, pecked her on the cheek and picked up the key to her room as he headed out the door. The Do Not Disturb sign was left hanging on the doorknob.

***

1100 hours the next day, Craig entered the young woman's room. She'd not moved all night. He kissed her cheek, "Wake Up Sleepy Head!"

"Oh My God! What is wrong with my head?"

"I believe it's called a hangover."

"I'm dying."

"You'll be fine after a little while."

Cindy leapt from the bed and ran to the bathroom. Craig heard her throwing up.

"C'mon, let's get you into the tub." Craig helped her into the tub of water he'd already drawn for her and helped her bathe. He brought her some aspirin and coffee but told her to drink some water first as he handed her the glass.

An hour passed, "I am beginning to feel almost human again."

"Another couple of hours and you'll be right as rain. Drink more water, alcohol dehydrates you, water will help."

The more water she drank, along with the aspirin, Cindy began feeling much better.

"Craig, what have you been doing? In Vietnam I mean."

410

"Oh, you know, hanging out at the rear, way behind the lines, doing a lot of paperwork, laundry, stuff like that."

"I know you, you're lying. Tell me the truth."

"Cindy, I've been practicing something." Craig's face took on a very serious look.

"What have you been practicing?"

"Killing people. I've become pretty good at it."

Cindy saw Craig's eyes take on a look that scared her.

"Craig."

"Yeah?"

"Take me to bed, do it now."

He lifted her into his arms and took her to bed.

***

Craig knocked on her door the next morning, he was greeted with a kiss and a surprise.

"Today is nipple day!"

"What?"

"Take off your shirt."

Craig removed his shirt, Cindy surprised him by pinching his nipples.

"Ouch, Damn!"

Cindy giggled, "Sensitive, aren't they? Let me explain. Some women like their nipples pinched, but usually only after they are very aroused. The nipples are very sensitive."

"Yeah, I can tell."

"Most of the time most women want the nipples to be softly touched, licked or sucked gently until they are fully aroused." Cindy removed her top and bra. "Hold up your hands as if you are using your hands and fingers to show the numbers five."

Craig did as instructed.

"Now, take your palms only and touch my nipples, rub the palms of your hands in circles."

Craig, once again, did as he was told.

Cindy closed her eyes and began to moan.

"Good thing?"

"Don't ask, just keep doing it. Oh! My! God!"

Ten minutes later Cindy told Craig, "Suck em!"

Craig obeyed.

Two hours later Craig was wondering if he and Cindy would see any more of Hawaii than the inside of the hotel room.

***

Things settled down and the two friends enjoyed Hawaii as it should be enjoyed. Cindy loved the beaches, although Craig seemed distant, not wanting to talk while on the sands, almost as if he'd rather not be there. They took in the sites and enjoyed exploring the island in the car Craig had rented. Mostly, Cindy and Craig talked.

"I talked to her a few weeks ago."

"Who?"

"Sara."

"I hope she's doing well, how is Grandma?"

"Both of them are doing good. She told me about school and how much she likes it. She told me something else."

"What would that be?"

"Said she received a package a few months ago, from you."

"And?"

"She said it had an engagement ring and wedding band in the package."

"Yeah."

"I just wanted to let you know she had gotten it."

"Thanks. I get letters and cards from her every now and then. I guess Mom gave her my address."

"What do they say?"

"I don't know, I never open them. I just save them."

"Why not read them?"

"I'm just not ready. Besides, I can't afford to become emotionally distracted. It could get me killed."

"Craig, what is it you really do that means you can't even read a letter from the girl who will always be in love with you, even if she and you can never have one another?"

"I told you, I kill people. But I do it differently than what you see on the news. I do what I've always done best."

"Which is?"

"I stalk and I shoot."

"You mentioned practicing before. What has your stalking and shooting have to do with practicing? What are you practicing for?"

The night was perfect, stars filled the beautiful sky, the full moon reflecting on the water. Craig had begrudgingly walked with Cindy on the beach. He stopped and asked her to sit with him.

"You can never speak to anyone about what I am about to tell you. Understand?"

"You know I love you enough to keep to myself anything you ever tell me. Your secret is my secret, forever."

"Only one other person has ever heard what I will tell you, that is the best man I've ever known, my Dad."

"I can think of none better."

"Cindy, I don't know how, but will somehow figure it all out. You see there are many people I love who must be considered, I want no harm to come to those people, you are one of them."

"Go on, I'm listening."

"If you ever hear that I've disappeared, I want you to keep up with the news. What I have in mind won't happen all at once, it will take years to complete and accomplish. You will know I am alive when you hear of the deaths of Oscar Tomlinson, Andy Bohannon, David Clements and Oliver Watson. My intention is to kill all of them, somehow, someday."

Cindy saw Craig's eyes change again. She knew then she was looking into the eyes of her friend who had changed from such a very sweet boy into a pure killer. But a killer who still cared for the few people he loved. What Cindy saw would appear to some as a person with no soul, she knew better, she knew Craig still had a soul, she leaned toward him and kissed him, gently.

Cindy stood, took Craig's hand, "I believe you. Come, let's walk a while longer."

CHAPTER
46

Today would be the last of Cindy's two week stay, she was sad, so Craig planned a fun day for his friend. First, he took her shopping, then on another long drive where she could take all the photos she wanted of the island. Later, Craig had learned there would be a luau and arranged for them to be there.

"I love you Craig Kirkland."

"I love you too Cindy Baxter."

"You know, you've treated me to the best two weeks of my life. I don't think anything will top these last two weeks, ever."

"It has been wonderful, I agree."

"There is one thing I can think of that would make it completely perfect."

"What might that be?"

"If you loved me more than as a friend, if you were in love with me."

Craig was silent, he hugged Cindy, but said nothing.

"Craig, I know, and I understand."

"Thank You."

"But there is one thing you can do."

"That is?"

"Take me to my room and make the sweetest love to me."

The night was spent by the two friends making very gentle love, they talked until sleep overcame Cindy. Craig never slept, he watched his friend sleep and wondered if he would ever see her again. Vietnam was a dangerous place and what he did there put himself at even greater risk. But God help him, he loved it.

Craig watched as Cindy boarded the plane, she was crying when she looked out the window and waved her last goodbye to the young Marine.

***

"What the hell are you doing back here? You had another week left on your R&R!" It was Gunny Slovenski barking at Craig.

"I got bored when my friend went home, not much to do alone. I hitched a ride on a transport headed to Da Nang and found my way back here, home."

"What a fucking foul-up, another week on your R&R and you do not use it.! But hell, it's good to see your ugly face anyhow. Did you have a good time?"

"I did."

"Who was your friend you said visited?"

"A girl I've known most of my life."

"Good! You spent your time with a woman. That's as it should be."

"Yep, Gunny."

"Get laid?"

"Does a fat baby fart?"

Gunny S laughed. "Come on, we'll let Major Bronson know you're back, then get your weapons."

"My old hooch occupied?"

"Nope, well, except for your new roomie, your last one got circulated back home, his time was up."

"What kinda Marine is my new roomie?"

"Ah, he's young and dumb, but seems to hold up well under fire. I think you'll like him, he don't talk much."

Major Bronson reamed Craig for over ten minutes for not using the last week of his leave then told him to get the hell out of his bunker. Just as Craig was leaving the Major spoke again, "Kirkland, good to have you back, get reacclimated with the climate a couple of days then we will discuss your going hunting again."

"Aye, Sir. Will do."

A week later Craig left the camp for six days of hunting. It was good to be in the jungle; Craig was home again.

***

Right at daylight the first day Gunny S heard the M70 bark, twice. Two hours later he heard the same sound, only once, this time further away. A Ghost was haunting Vietnam, killing what it wanted dead.

***

Two months passed, Craig lost count of the hunting trips he'd taken, lost count of the dead left behind, only a few of which were ever confirmed. The enemy had learned of a Marine who was more Ghost than man. It was said he moved like an invisible wind and killed quicker than a tiger. Fear of this ghost ran deep into the enemy ranks.

Craig lay on the hill overlooking the rice paddies, watching the man who seemed out of place somehow. The man was acting suspiciously, continuing to look around. While watching the man Craig's mind wandered back to the little boy sitting atop the old upright piano, singing hymns while the women played the instrument. The crosshairs were on the man's chest, Craig heard the music in his head, "Amazing Grace, How Sweet the Sound." The man in the crosshairs slowly reached into the burlap bag, he had a mine in his hand, a bouncing betty in the man's hand. The M70 spat its death, the man fell. The music stopped.

Suddenly, a breeze picked up, a ghost floated within it. Craig was again on the move.

***

"You need some rest. Stay in a week."

"Aw, Gunny."

"That's an order from the C.O! Your official count is 23 confirmed. How many you think you really have?"

"I'm not sure, I quit counting at forty. May be sixty, seventy. It really doesn't matter. I figure for each one it's one who won't be shooting at any Marines or killing unborn babies and their mommas."

"You're a machine, Kirkland, but every machine needs to be shut down sometime and serviced. You do as the Major ordered, eat good and rest. You hear me Marine?"

Craig stood and offered a clumsy recruit kind of salute, he smiled,
Sir, Yes Sir, Gunny Slovenski, Sir."

The Gunny smiled.

419

Craig lay down on his bunk, he began to sweat but he'd gotten used to it. He slept twelve hours.

***

The monsoons came without warning. Craig had never seen it rain so hard for so long, he knew this would make his work easier. He began planning a hunting trip.

Time had passed quickly; Craig hadn't realized he only had two months left in country until Major Bronson dropped by one afternoon. The major also brought more news, he showed the paper to Craig.

$5000 AMERICAN FOR THE HEAD OF THE MURDERER KNOWN AS GHOST

"One of the men brought this back with him from his leave in Saigon, said they're all over the place."

"Well, Sir, it seems I might be the most popular guy at the prom."

Bronson smiled, "Seems so." The Major then took on a more serious expression, "Possibly too popular. I am very reluctant to allow any more hunting trips."

"Sir, You and I know I am of better use out there than here."

The Major sat down. "You may very well be the most proficient killing machine I have ever seen in this man's Marine Corps, but there comes a time when that just isn't enough. You will have half the damned NVA, VC and civilian population wanting to collect that five grand. They will be pulling out all the stops trying to pick up that rather sizeable piece of change. I'm not sure even with your considerable skills you can last much longer outside the wire. Hell, surviving inside the wire might come to be an issue."

"Sir, there is one guy left, he is a Colonel. I have seen him direct the torture of some people, I know where he lives but have never been able to get the shot and still know I could evade afterward, that's the only reason I never took him out. I'm going to ask you for one more chance. I want him. I want to be the person who sends him to answer to Jesus."

"A Colonel you say?"

"Sir, he is the cruelest motherfucker I've ever seen, and you know I've seen plenty of cruelty inflicted on the Vietnamese people."

"How long?"

"I'll be out two weeks."

"TWO WEEKS?"

"I gotta travel some, then recon, then set it up. Then, I gotta head away from here before heading back because every leaf between there and here will have some asshole behind it wanting to put holes in me, at least for a few days. They will all figure I will be hightailing my ass back here; I'll have to lay low for a while."

"Corporal Kirkland, you have your two weeks. But let me inform you now. This will be your last hunting trip while under my command. Upon completion, if you live through it, you will be sent to the rear where you will remain until you are rotated home. Am I clear?"

"Understood, Sir!"

"Good, just so you understand something else, if they kill you, I will kill you deader. Do Not Fuck Up!"

Craig smiled, "Sir, Yes Sir!" Sir, you reckon that mess Sargent might still have some steak and eggs left?"

"I reckon he better."

"Care to join me for dinner, Sir?"

"Damned right. Let's eat."

It was the first time the Major had hidden and watched Craig's bunker, the sight of the creature's teeth grinning at him when it stepped from the hooch would be a memory the Major would never forget. Craig began his two week hunt two hours before daylight, in the rain.

"Lord, please take care of that Marine, the bastard is well worth it."

***

It took him three days to get close to the Colonel's area of operations, he'd bypassed more than twenty potential targets to get to the place he now found himself.

For two more days he stalked before finding the hide he needed. The Ghost patiently waited.

Once again, a man in the crosshairs of the rifle's scope, the music began, "One glad Morning, When this Life is O'er, I'll fly away," the boy was singing. Everything went into slow motion, it seemed minutes between heartbeats, how long had it been since he'd last breathed? The music stopped, the man fell, lifeless.

***

Major Bronson woke, he grabbed his coffee cup. Beside the percolator were the insignias of a North Vietnamese Colonel. There was a note.

"Thought you might like to have these, Sir."

***

Craig's first night in Saigon was spent getting as drunk as possible. A few days later he found himself getting shots for the clap he'd caught from a hooker he didn't remember ever being with.

CHAPTER

47

"I heard you were back. Good to see you."

"Gunny Pope, thank you, Good to be back."

"Well, truth be known I wanted you here and discussed the possibility with the commandant. He pulled a few strings and made it happen. You will be an asset to this school of infantry."

"I'm flattered, I'll try to live up to your expectations."

"I have no doubt you will. I also have no doubt you will teach some Marines things that may very well keep them alive."

"Hope so sir, too many getting killed over there now."

"Kirkland, the grapevine runs far and reaching among Marine Corps Sergeants, your exploits of the last year are darn near mythical."

"Ah, Gunny, people tend to embellish things they may have heard."

"I've known Slovenski a long time, never known him to embellish. And, by the way, neither does Major Bronson, he and I served together before he went into OCS. We still talk on occasion."

"Major Bronson is a fine man, I would gladly serve under his command anytime, anywhere."

"As would I."

"Well, Gunny, how would you like me to begin here?"

"Since word of you and your accomplishments have gotten here there have been some meetings and discussions about specialized training. I want you to evaluate people and choose twelve you think will be best suited to be trained what you do."

"Gunny, it took me a lifetime to learn what I know, and there is something else."

"That is?"

"It gets personal, looking at a person through a rifle scope and killing that person. The evaluations will have to include psychiatric evaluation. The men chosen must be emotionally stable, ready and prepared."

"This too, has been discussed. There are no less than five psychiatrists on the base. Each man will be evaluated by each of the doctors, if any one of them says no to any of the men, said man will be transferred back to his unit."

"Good."

"How do you want to begin?"

"First thing, I want to watch how they move when they are at PT. First step isn't how strong they are, but more how they move."

"Well alright Corporal Kirkland. You may begin anytime you like. Camp Geiger is yours to roam."

Craig lost count of how many men he'd observed, the count ran into the hundreds, he had a list of one hundred names. Next

came one on one interviews with each of the hundred, the list shortened to fifty.

Fifty men were taken to the range, each was scrutinized, not so much for their target success, but more how they handled their weapons. There was no time to break any bad habits, Craig's list dropped to twenty five. Next, mental evaluations. And then there were twelve.

***

Training began at the combat course. "OK, you have all been selected for specialized training. Your first objective will be to find me and destroy me before I destroy you, simple as that. The area is the size of a football field and has been marked as such, nobody goes outside the area, including me."

One man asked, "Corporal Kirkland, is there a time limit?"

"No, we stay here until I am considered dead, or all of you are considered dead. Honestly it won't take long." Craig grinned.

Craig was given ten minutes head start. The Sargent gave orders. "Each of you were assigned an orange mesh vest, fold it up and put it in your pocket, drop your packs, you won't need them. If you are killed, you are to immediately put on the vest and come back here."

"The only weapon I saw on him was a knife, we've got rifles, seems kinda unfair."

"The knife is rubber, and he won't need a firearm, trust me."

Two hours later there were twelve dejected Marines all asking, "How the hell did he do that?"

"Men, you have all just been formally introduced to Corporal Craig Kirkland, also known as Ghost, you may have heard of him."

With that, what had appeared to be a bush stood and walked toward the men. As Craig was walking, he was removing his ghillie suit. "I really appreciate you all not killing me, those little rubber projectiles the rifles shoot sting bad and leave a helluva bruise." Everyone laughed.

"First you learn the art, real art, of camouflage. Take your weapons back to the barracks and clean the rifles. Always, first order of business after a mission is to clean your weapons, there are no exceptions, you do it before you eat or clean yourself. Is that clear?"

"Aye, Corporal."

"Assemble in front of your barracks in one hour. We will then go on a little scavenging hunt."

***

Behind the mess hall were piles of burlap potato sacks, each man was instructed to pick up three. Next stop, the laundry. A conversation with the Sargent in charge resulted in a large pile of old, thrown out utilities. Each man stuffed a burlap sack with the discarded uniforms.

At the barracks the men used their K-Bar knives to shred the camo utilities into strips.

"What we are about to create is called a Ghillie Suit. The Ghillies were people who worked for Scottish lords and were hired to protect the game on their lands from poachers."

Craig went through the process of weaving the strips of old uniforms into the burlap, how to make sleeves and hoods and attach everything together.

As the men were busy with the Ghillie Suits, Craig began to discuss what their missions would be. "The objective will be to move with stealth and silence in whatever environment you may

426

be ordered into, to stalk your prey and eliminate it with as few shots fired as possible, hopefully only one shot per kill. What you will learn is something that has taken me a lifetime of practice, you will be expected to work hard and absorb all I can teach you in a period of eight weeks. Some of you will fail, there is no shame in failing this training, by just being here you have already demonstrated yourselves to be exemplary Marines, you earned the right to be here. Your missions will serve two purposes, first will be the knowledge that every enemy combatant you eliminate will be one who can never again fire upon a brother Marine, you will, by your actions, be saving lives. Second will be very important, you will be injecting fear into the ranks of the enemy, have him looking over his shoulder at the slightest sound, you will be creating paranoia in the enemy. Understand this, for those of you who pass this training, you will think you are better than you really are, what you will have learned are the most essential basics, in order to be successful you must practice, even on leave, anytime you have spare time. If you are assigned to Vietnam you will be fighting in your enemy's back yard, and he is a very deadly adversary with a desire to kill you, that desire is his only goal in life."

The men continued working on their suits and were told they would be inspected at 0500 the next morning.

***

Craig was pleased with the Ghillie suits and made only a few suggestions. He tossed a Pfc. some steel washers with straps attached, "Strap these to your boots at the toe and heel end and walk across the room as quietly as possible."

Try as he might, the sound was that of a tap dancer stepping easily, the tic, tic made by the washers on the concrete floor was quite audible. "Now, watch and pay close attention. Craig had strapped washers to his boots, he lifted his foot straight up, not

dragging the toe, and reached his leg out about the length of half a step, putting his toe down slowly he then lowered his heal and repeated the process with the next step, this continued until he was across the room, never making a sound. "All our lives we have walked for speed, comfort and efficiency, heel, toe, heel, toe. It's the natural way to walk. Except for stealth, then shorter steps, toe, heel, toe, heel are what works best. You will all practice this until you can cross this room silently. I'll be back in an hour."

"Well, how's it going?"

"Going good, Gunny. They're in the barracks, practicing."

"What are they practicing?"

"How to tap dance without making noise."

"Huh?"

Craig smiled, "Trust me. And tomorrow they will begin learning how to drift across dry leaves, kinda like a ghost would."

An hour later Craig was pleased with the men's process. A few had it worked out very well, the rest still needed a little practice but were making much less noise than he'd expected to hear. "Chow time, with a twist. In boot camp you always ran, everywhere, I remember. This time you will walk to chow, the way you have been practicing for the last hour, even in the chow line. I want it to become second nature."

"Gunny, you sure Kirkland knows what the hell he's doing? Look at the silly ass way he's got em walking."

Gunny Pope grinned, "Cap'n, Sir, you don't recognize that?

"Should I?"

"Absolutely, Sir. Everyone knows it's a tap dance move. Excuse me Sir, I need to go talk to the mess Sargent."

The bewildered Captain stood and stared at the peculiar gait the men were walking. He said to himself, "Tap dance?"

By the end of the week every man could walk through the woods or on pavement without making a sound. Craig ordered them to bring their Ghillie suits and war paint and be at the combat course at 0400 the next morning.

"One word "Patience!" In order to move quickly you must first slow down, become a part of the surroundings. Any hunters here?" Four men raised their hands. "What gives a squirrel away?"

One man answered, "It either barks, runs or flicks its tail."

"And the ones that are the hardest to detect?"

"The ones that don't panic, they remain silent and still or move very slowly."

"Exactly. Time to teach you all how to be smart squirrels."

Every man helped the others apply the war paint as Craig instructed, each man put on his suit. All were told to follow Craig. Within two minutes none could see him or knew his whereabouts until he spoke to them from their rear.

The next ten days were spent one on one with each man, showing him how to become a part of his environment. Craig was astonished that it wasn't the man who'd grown up in the country south of Rankin, Mississippi who performed best, but a young private who'd grown up on the streets of New York. The New Yorker had learned very well and had become so good even Craig worked hard to detect him.

***

Every man was issued 30.06 ammunition and told, "The targets are set at fifty yards, the only way you will progress to one

hundred yards is when you are capable of putting every shot into the targets bullseye. All of you have passed rifle training in boot camp, this is different. If at the end of this training you are not capable of putting a bullet into the eyeball of a man at three hundred yards, you will fail, simple as that. Now, place your M14s on the rack. The commandant has some gifts for you."

Each man was issued a brand new M70 Winchester Rifle with a Leupold 3X9 variable scope. Craig had already zeroed each scope in at the fifty-yard mark, he taught the men how to do the same.

Craig worked with the men and by the end of the day eight of them were hitting bullseye at 100 yards, one at 150 yards.

On each man's rack there was a cleaning kit for the M70s. Every man cleaned his weapon before showering for chow.

The Captain was, once again, standing at a distance watching the twelve men walk to chow, they were all walking weird again. He shook his head and went on his way.

***

Seven and a half weeks passed, time for exams.

First test was the same football field sized area Craig had first taken the men to. In the woods were three men, hidden. The twelve men would, one at a time be required to evade being killed and at the same time locate the "enemy" and mark their locations. Each enemy combatant would relocate after each man.

"Listen up. There are three men hidden in this area. Your job is to locate those men without being detected or killed. Each of those three men are equipped with very powerful air rifles that fire a rubber projectile, it hurts like hell. If you are hit, you fail. If you do not locate all the men, you fail. You will go one at a time, when told to go. No two of you will be in the area at the same

430

time. This test will require two days for all of you to be tested, you will each have two hours to complete your mission. Understood?"

"Aye, Corporal!"

Craig sent the first man in.

By the end of the second day seven men had completed their missions. Five returned to their units, all with very sore bruises caused by rubber bullets.

By the end of the rifle range exam, there were five men left who would pass the course. Craig had already chosen the next class to undergo the training.

CHAPTER

48

Corporal Craig Kirkland had finished with his class on the rifle range at Camp Geiger when he was ordered to report back to the office building where visitors were received. He couldn't imagine who it might be.

There was only one person sitting in the visitor's area, a PFC. The man had crutches beside him. With some difficulty the man stood and extended his hand, introducing himself. "PFC William Spruill, nice to meet you."

"Nice to meet you, too. How may I help you?"

"Cpl. Kirkland, I've heard a lot about you from one of your friends, Charlie Adcock. He told me to look you up if I ever had the chance."

"Yeah, Charlie and I go back a way, went through boot camp together. I've not heard from him in a while."

"That's why I'm here."

"What's up?"

"May I call you Craig?"

"Sure."

"Craig, Charlie was killed a couple weeks ago."

Craig felt the wind go out of him, the pain and shock he experienced was indescribable. He sat, looking down at the floor,

432

unable to speak for fear he would burst into tears, something he'd sworn only the people closest to him would ever see him do again.

A few minutes later Craig raised his head, "Tell me about it."

"Around midnight our base began taking mortars, Charlie was moving about, checking with all of us, making sure we were ready. He knew they would be coming at us hard, and soon. Wasn't long and the trip flares went off, I'd never seen so many NVA at one time."

"Go on."

"Everyone with a clacker began setting off the Claymores, everyone was opening fire. Charlie was still on the move, firing, giving instruction, throwing grenades. Then we began taking casualties and Charlie began dragging men to any cover he could, all while he was still shooting." Pointing at his leg, "Then I got hit."

"How bad?"

"Bad enough to get me shipped back home after a few days in the hospital. It'll heal, but will take a while, and probably get me discharged."

"Go ahead."

"I was laying there, stunned, next thing I knew somebody had me by my collar, dragging me. The mortars and artillery began coming back in, more of it this time. Charlie threw me in a shallow trench and jumped in on top of me. A shell hit close, I heard Charlie grunt, I passed out. They found me the next morning, Charlie was dead. He'd saved my life when he covered me with his own body, he took what would have surely hit me."

"Charlie was a good Marine."

433

"He talked about you a lot; said you whipped his ass in boot camp. Told me it turned his life around. Anytime he talked about boot camp he was always smiling, told me stories about him, you and some guy named Otis. It always made him happy when he would remember those times y'all had together."

"We had some good times."

"Craig, the paperwork has been put in to have Charlie receive the Navy Cross."

"Damn sure earned it."

"They're gonna bury him at Arlington. Figured you would want to know, and be there if you can get a couple day's leave."

"Yeah."

"There is one more thing. For some reason or another Charlie took a liking to me, he trusted me with things."

"I'm sure he had good reason."

"I suppose. About a month ago he gave me an envelope and told me if anything ever happened to him that I was to be sure you got it. Here it is."

Craig took the envelope and Thanked Spruill.

***

Dear Brothers Craig and Otis,

If y'all are reading this, it means I either did something really stupid or made a mistake. One or the other, it means I am no longer among the breathing. Ain't that a bitch?

First, thank you both for having given a damn about me, for teaching me love for my fellow man and for making me a better

person. I really hate what I once was, but I wake each day thankful for who I now am. It would never have happened if not for y'all.

As y'all know, my family disowned me, Otis, just look what you did to this po white boy! HAHA. Except for my aunt and her husband, the rest of my family consists of Two Jar Heads, You Two! Now, before I go any further, I want you to know I've spoken with my aunt about this and she completely agrees with what will be stated next. She even had her lawyer draw it up for me.

I have willed all my worldly possessions to Craig Kirkland and Otis Jackson. Before you get all excited you need to understand you shouldn't plan an around the world cruise and expect to pay for it from my accounts, but there is a little something there for both of you. My aunt has the original will, there is a copy along with this letter.

Except to say I love you both, more than you know, I reckon that is all.

Hope to see y'all on the other side, just be careful and don't make it there too soon.

Semper Fidelis, Charlie

Craig contacted Otis, who was stationed at Marine Corps Air Station Cherry Point, he read Charlie's letter. Both put in requests for, and received, a 4-day leave.

**

"Boy's, just call me Aunt Martha, please."

"Yes ma'am." Both Craig and Otis answered.

Martha hugged them and thanked them for their friendship to Charlie, that he'd spoken so many times about them and told her how much he loved them.

Otis sat to Martha's right, Craig to her left. As the flag was being folded, they both stood at attention and saluted until it had been presented to Martha. Craig and Otis walked Martha to her car and accepted her invitation to dinner at the hotel.

Aunt Martha was an attractive woman in her fifties, very fit from working on her and her husband's ranch. She also had a firm grip when she shook hands, Craig noted it to her. "When you work with horses, you tend to develop strong hands."

"Ma'am," Otis asked, "Why isn't your husband here?"

"Otis, the last time my husband saw Charlie's father he swore if he ever laid eyes on him again, he would kill him. And, trust me, he is quite a man in his own right, he would have no problem choking or beating my brother to death. I feared some of the family might show up for the funeral and I didn't want my husband to end up on trial for killing the heathens, I asked him to stay home."

"But, wasn't he worried about you being here alone?"

"My Dear Otis, the instant I told my husband there would be two handsome young Marines overseeing any protection I might require, he instantly relaxed about my wellbeing. He knew I would be in very capable hands. By the way, he was a Staff Sargent with the Marine Corps 1st Marine Division, The Old Breed, one of the Frozen Chosin. He was with Chesty Puller at the Chosin Reservoir. He asked me to send you a message."

Craig asked, "Message?"

"Semper Fi!"

Martha was also very shrewd and knew the right people to communicate with when she needed some things taken care of, Bankers, Attorneys, Judges, she had friends in high places. Reaching into the small briefcase she'd brought with her to

436

dinner, Martha took out two large manila envelopes and handed both young men one each. "I know people. All you have to do is sign where noted and this is all taken care of."

Craig asked, "Don't we need witnesses, a notary public, something?"

"I repeat, I know people. Now, hush and sign."

A check in the amount of $39,856.72 was handed over, made out to both Craig and Otis. A paper for ownership transfer of a 1965 Chevelle SS to Craig and Otis was signed by both young men. Transfer of ownership of a boat, motor and trailer was made out to both, they signed.

"Ma'am," it was Craig, "I really don't know how I feel about this; Charlie's stuff should be yours."

"Pish Tosh, Charlie loved you both and I don't need anything. He and I discussed this before he shipped out for his second tour. I assured him I would see to his wishes and I am honored to do so."

Craig's voice broke, "Thank you, Ma'am."

"You're very welcome. I've taken the liberty of having the car and boat transported to Savannah, they are being stored in a warehouse there. Rent is paid for a month, the keys to the car are in the glove compartment."

Otis again spoke, "Ma'am, why have you gone to all this trouble for a couple of guys you only met today?"

"Charlie was a mean, hate filled racist bully when he was a child and teenager. The only thing that made him happy was the misery he could inflict on others. He was made that way by my brother, his father. It took two very special young men to change him, and the change was wonderful. Charlie became a loving young man, a person who went out of his way to help others, he

437

went to church services with me whenever he was visiting. He also loved to tell me about both of you, and I cannot tell you how many times he told me he loved y'all. Well, I love you too. How could I not love both of you, for all you meant to Charlie, you mean the same to me. I hope you both realize you have also inherited a crazy, horse loving aunt who lives in Kentucky. I am part of this deal and you had better stay in touch and visit our ranch on occasion!"

Craig and Otis smiled at one another, both stood, saluted, "Ma'am, Yes Ma'am!"

Once Martha finished crying she beckoned the waiter, "Three Bourbons, naked, make em all doubles!"

**

The boat was wider than your typical aluminum johnboat and had a 40 horsepower motor. "Otis, Your Dad likes to fish, doesn't he?"

"Oh yeah, he loves that old Warrior River. He's fed us many meals of catfish he would catch."

"Does he have a boat?"

"Nah, never could afford one, he's got some secret places where he fishes from the bank, some so secret he never took me to em." Otis grinned.

"Well I think he needs a boat."

"OK, how much for your half?"

"Tell your Dad I said happy birthday."

Otis looked at Craig, he nodded his thanks.

The Chevelle was Black. In 1965 Chevy had built 201 of the Chevelle SS models with the new 396 cubic inch, 375 horse power

438

big block engine. Upon popping the hood, Craig discovered Charlie's car was one of them, the odometer showed less than 8000 miles, Charlie hadn't driven it very much.

Otis whistled a long note, "She's a beauty, a Black Beauty, Wow!"

"Otis, a while back, while I was still in Nam, some guy came along and offered Dad twice what he'd paid for my "58", I told him to sell it before the guy changed his mind. He did."

"Well, well, Corporal Kirkland, it seems you are currently without a vehicle and I happened to be half owner of a gorgeous little '65' Chevelle. Could I interest you in purchasing my said half?"

"Possibly.

"Let the haggling begin."

"Got your pencil?"

"You betcha."

"OK, Brainiac, divide $39,856.72 by two."

Otis did the math, "$19,928.36."

"Now subtract $5000.00 from that."

"Sir, am I to assume you are offering me five grand for a used car that cost around three grand when it was purchased brand new? You ain't very good at haggling."

Craig laughed, "Do the math Otis."

"Easy, $14,928.36."

"OK, that is what I'm offering you for your half ownership of the car."

"Damn, white boy, you are the worse at haggling I've ever seen. I swear, you've lost your mind."

Again, Craig laughed. Then, he got serious. "Otis, the GI Bill doesn't cover all the cost for college, there are other expenses. And, your Dad just might need a better pickup truck than he has now to pull the boat. Besides, I don't need much money. And, I'll need even less if I get approved for a second tour in Nam."

"Going back?"

"Hopefully."

"Fool."

"I reckon so."

Otis eyes filled with tears, "Craig, what the hell did I ever do to deserve a friend like you?"

"Reverse it and I could ask you the same thing."

The two young Marines hugged and wept over the loss of Charlie. The next hour was spent cruising in the Chevelle, Black Beauty. They went to the bank where the check was cashed, paperwork on the boat and car were typed out by a nice young lady, signatures properly witnessed and notarized by another.

***

Black Beauty had been a blast to drive, Craig had never experienced such power associated with pressing the accelerator. He'd have to keep himself under control anytime he would be behind the wheel of the lightweight car with the big engine, no way he could afford all the speeding tickets.

Checking in at Geiger and getting himself settled, Craig changed into his utilities and headed to Gunny Pope's office. Approaching the door, he noted the sign beside the door no

440

longer read "Master Gunnery Sargent A. Pope", it now read "Sargent Major A. Pope". Craig knocked.

"Get your ass in here, I saw you walking across the lot."

"Sargent Major Pope, you've moved up in the world. Congratulations."

"Yep, it seems the United States Government finally got around to recognizing my true worth to the Marine Corps." Both men laughed.

"Well Sgt. Major, it took em long enough." Craig grinned.

"Saw you drive in a while ago. New car?"

"Not new, but low miles and it's a dandy. My friend who was killed left it to another guy and me, I bought his half."

"Well, it's about time you had some transportation, a young man of your stature shouldn't be riding the bus home on every leave. Takes too damned long and uses up valuable family time."

"I agree, Sgt. Major."

"Oh yeah, I see you are dressed inappropriately."

Shocked, Craig couldn't imagine what was wrong. He'd checked everything, including the shine on his boots. "My apologies Sgt. Major, would you be kind enough to explain?" Craig was concerned, he'd seen Pope chew out some asses in the past and knew the man was very good at it.

"Go easy, relax and sit down."

Craig sat.

"Fact is, the average time for a Marine to make the rank of Sargent is over four years but are eligible at two years. I told you a few minutes ago that my true worth was finally recognized.

Through the recommendations of several people and the high recommendation of Camp Geiger commandant, the United States Government and U.S. Marine Corps have also recognized your true worth as well, Congratulations Sargent Craig Kirkland." Pope offered his hand, Craig took it and thanked him. "I do hope you realize it is customary for a newly promoted Sargent to buy the first round of drinks on the night of his promotion."

"I've heard. I certainly wouldn't want to break tradition. 1800 Hours tonight?"

"Sounds good."

Craig paused, "Sargent Major Pope, may I change the subject?"

"What's on your mind, son?"

"I know the timing is not good, what with the promotion and all, but I'd like to put in a request for transfer."

"Well, that is a stunner. Transfer to where?"

"Vietnam."

"I'm stunned again, why Nam?"

"I feel my abilities would be better served there than here."

"Have any idea how valuable you are here?"

"Honestly, there are several who have assisted me who could train just as well now."

"I disagree, but you fill out the papers and I'll submit them."

"Thank you, Sgt. Major."

"Craig, does this have any bearing on your friend being killed?"

"Sargent Major Pope, you know me much too well."

Over the next few months Craig's requests were turned down three times. The fourth request was approved. On the third week of January, 1968, Craig landed at Dong Ha in the Quang Tri province. He was close to the DMZ, hunting should be good.

One week later, January 30th, the Tet Offensive began, Dong Ha was surrounded. All Craig could think of was the first battle when his camp had been hit close to DaNang, Déjà vu was the only way he could describe his feelings.

There would be little rest during the ensuing next several weeks as the base was under almost continuous attack, both day and night. Once things calmed, got back to normal, Craig was allowed to go on his hunting excursions. He'd been right, hunting was indeed very good. With each squeeze of the trigger, with each dead body he'd left behind, Craig imagined the person had been the one who'd fired the mortar that had killed Charlie.

Three months later the life Craig Kirkland had known would cease to exist, forever.

CHAPTER

49

The kid was new, only on his second patrol when the tunnel entrance was located. The lieutenant, anxious for glory, medals

and promotions ordered the kid into the cave, the young private began to shake. LT ordered him again to drop his pack and rifle, take a flashlight and a .45 and get his ass into the tunnel, the kid began to cry but began doing as ordered. He moved toward the opening and froze, the terror of crawling into the man-made cave caused the kid to piss his pants.

Craig dropped his pack and told the guy next to him to hold his rifle, he walked to the kid, took the light and .45 from his hands. The LT began screaming at the kid and Craig. Slowly, without a word, Craig turned his gaze to the young officer, his dark eyes showing no emotion as he cocked the hammer of the .45, never lifting it, its barrel still pointed at the ground, the lieutenant froze and took a step back. The two men stared for only a few seconds, the LT began to sweat, he shut up. Craig entered the tunnel.

Craig had crawled in many Viet Cong tunnels, this one was easy, it traveled only 100 meters then exited above ground, no rooms, no branches to other tunnels, he returned and reported what he'd found.

Two nights after the incident with the new guy Craig used his extraordinary ability to move silently, he crept into the sleeping lieutenant's quarters. With his hand over the officer's mouth, in the complete darkness, he ominously whispered to the startled lieutenant, "You are not fit to lead the men of this unit, you will transfer, or I promise you will not survive the next patrol, if you yell, you will not survive this night." Craig crept out as silently as he had arrived, the officer felt something warm, he'd peed in his pants. The next day he requested and was granted transfer to another unit. The day following, he was gone.

Staff Sargent Harold "Harry" Williams had come to be very good friends with Craig, he dropped by for a visit, a bottle of whiskey in hand. "Saw your LT yesterday, came out of his hooch

looking pale as a dead man, I decided to follow him." Harry continued as he poured both men a drink, "He went straight to Major Sam's tent", Samuel Brookshire was a no nonsense Major, "I got close and listened, heard a lot of whining from your LT and even more cussing from the Major. LT said something about someone he couldn't identify sneaking into his hooch, he wanted an immediate transfer, was begging for it. I saw him catching a ride on a slick about an hour ago, looked like he was carrying everything he owned." The Staff Sargent paused for a second before speaking again, "Craig, you know anything about that?"

Craig sipped his drink, it burned as he swallowed, he spoke, "Harry, I'm gonna ask you to forget you asked that and to never ask it again." Harry smiled, reached out with is glass, the two men 'clinked' glasses. Such was the trust between the two friends, they enjoyed another drink.

***

Three days later a runner was dispatched to Craig's hooch, Craig was ordered to Major Sam's command bunker, ASAP. This was never good news and Craig was wondering if somehow Major Sam had found out it was he who had sneaked in on the lieutenant, although the Major probably already suspected. Grabbing his rifle, handgun and helmet he quickly made his way to the Major, expecting a royal ass chewing. With apprehension, Craig entered the bunker.

Major Sam looked at the Sargent and said, "SIT DOWN!" Craig Sat! The Major slammed a sealed manila envelope marked Top Secret on the table and decried, "I DO NOT LIKE THIS SHIT, FUCKING SPOOKS FUCKING WITH MY MEN AND MY COMMAND!" The red faced Major continued, pointing at the envelope, "I have been instructed that THIS is for your eyes only, you are to board a Huey at exactly 0800 hours tomorrow morning, all I've been told is to order you to take with you your M70, one handgun, ammo

for both, seven days rations and water. The chopper driver, AND NO FUCKING BODY ELSE, will have the coordinates where you are to be inserted. You are to open the envelope in private, read the orders, memorize them, and destroy everything by fire, including the envelope, THAT IS ALL I FUCKING KNOW, AND I DON'T LIKE IT!" Craig sat quietly, glad the Major was pissed at someone other than him. When Major Sam was mad it was best to just sit quietly and let him get it out of his system, Craig had once watched him verbally rip into a Brigadier General in such a way the superior officer had no doubt that he didn't, in fact, "know his ass from a hole in the ground." The Major had done so at great risk to his rank, such was the way the man was, he would stand by his principals, and his men, if it meant being busted back to PFC. Craig watched as the man calmed, at least some. "Sargent Kirkland, I have no idea what is going on nor where you are going, and I do not care for it, you are one of the finest marine's, possibly the best, I have ever had the privilege to have under my command and I am pissed off in royal fashion. When outside forces screw with my command and my people it angers me, and to be kept in the dark about your mission just pisses me off even more. Hell, if you get into some deep shit, we won't know how to rescue your sorry ass, THAT, by the way, pisses me off even more. Now, go get your weapons cleaned and ready, check your ammo and rations, open the fucking envelope and do as I said, I will see you back here in one week, Godspeed." The Sargent stood, saluted the officer and returned to his hooch.

Craig opened the envelope, it contained part of a map and written instructions. He was ordered to bring a compass and the items the Major had instructed him to bring, he was to remove all identification and rank from his utilities and leave any other form of ID in his hooch, including wallet and dog tags. Memorizing the instructions Craig folded the map, placed it in his pocket and burned the rest.

At 0750 the Huey landed and refueled. At 0800 Craig boarded and began a mission that would forever change his life.

***

The Huey lifted into the air and flew north for 15 minutes, then dropping to nap-of-the-earth flew east another half hour, Craig heard over the headphones, "Get ready, LZ in one minute". The chopper never touched down, hovering a few feet above the earth, Craig hopped out and made for the closest tree line. Being alone in the jungle was nothing new, he worked best alone.

The instructions had been simple. The map had marked suspected enemy locations, Craig was to avoid these locations and evade any contact with the enemy at all costs. On the map was a small tributary, he would have known it as a creek back in Alabama, next to the creek was marked a bright red dot, he was to make his way there and wait for friendly contact, one man in a canoe, at 2300 hours. If contact didn't show by 2315 hours he was to leave the tributary, hide and evade for seven days and would be picked back up at the same LZ. He would be taken back to the firebase and report the mission a failure, the target had not shown. With compass and map, Craig began moving toward the creek. Twice there were enemy on patrols within 50 feet of his position, he'd waited until they moved on and resumed his trek. Craig arrived at the designated pickup location at approximately 2100 hours and set up a hide, he waited.

His eyes adjusted to the dark, at just before 2300 hours Craig saw a canoe with one man slowly paddling past him on the far side of the creek, he watched as it disappeared around a bend. A few minutes later, his hearing tuned to the sounds of the jungle, Craig heard the very slight sound of a paddle making soft, almost indiscernible splashing noises, he then heard a voice whisper, "Maareen, Maareen." The man paddling the canoe had traveled past on the far side, crossed back over and returned on the side of

the creek Craig was located. Kirkland, with .45 in hand, responded in a whisper, "here."

Craig was instructed to lay down and was covered with reeds and a few dead fish. The man began paddling downstream. Three hours later, not knowing where he was or what was happening, the man stopped paddling, five minutes later Craig heard the faint noise of engines, the sound grew louder. Craig heard the engines slow to an idle and felt wake gently rolling the canoe, then there was a bump, someone said, "come with us please". Uncovering himself Craig was looking straight up at the sailors of the swift boat looking down at him, he passed his rifle to the men and was assisted aboard. The canoe had traveled the creek downstream to where it intersected with a river, water deep enough the swift boat could operate. The boat captain spoke with a southern drawl, "Welcome board sir," when rank is unknown, everyone is sir. "Fresh coffee and an empty rack down below if you wanna get some rest, we gonna be boat riding for a little while." Craig thanked him, retrieved his rifle and went below, the coffee was good, the rack much better.

He didn't know how long the boat had been traveling but having trained his ears to detect the slightest difference in sounds, the sounds of the engines being throttled back woke Craig, he instantly sat up, fully awake. Pouring another cup of the strong coffee he picked up his rifle and went topside, it was daylight now, the boat moving toward a beach, there was a Huey, engine running, waiting on the beach. "Sir", the boat captain spoke, "I'm gonna get us close as I can, till the keel contacts the sand but you gonna have to wade from there, sorry, but it ain't deep, only bout waist deep. I been here before". Craig thanked him for the coffee and hospitality, when he felt the bow touch bottom he eased over the side into the warm water, it felt good, he waded to shore and climbed into the chopper.

448

Once the helicopter was airborn the pilot motioned for Craig to put on a headset, he did and was asked if he'd ever been aboard an aircraft carrier, he replied he had not. Grinning, the pilot said, "Well, this'll be a new experience for you I expect, landing on a nice clean deck instead of some LZ where people are shooting at you". Craig grinned back at the man and exclaimed "I think I'll enjoy that."

The First Officer met Craig as the Huey landed, he escorted him below where there was a head and showers. A Marine "Gunny" then took charge of Craig, "Sir, those boots and utilities look kinda wet and uncomfortable, I have been instructed to place your stuff, cept your weapons, those go with you, in storage in case you need it again and outfit you with new boots and utilities. Sizes?" Craig, still enjoying all the "Sirs," told the Gunny what he needed then used the head and took a nice warm shower, a razor and shaving cream were provided, he shaved, clothing was laid out for him when he finished. Once dressed Craig was escorted to the galley where he enjoyed a very good meal, the coffee was outstanding.

Finishing his meal Craig noticed he was the only person in the room, a few seconds later he heard, "Hello, Young man," it was the Captain speaking. Craig stood, he almost came to attention and saluted when he suddenly remembered nobody on the ship, including the Captain, knew who he was nor his rank, he offered his hand for a handshake, it was received and returned. "Welcome aboard, I wish your stay could be longer, but I have orders to get you on a plane and send you to Hawaii, ever ridden in a F4 Phantom?"

"No sir."

"Well, one is being prepared as we speak. In a few minutes the flight officer will come get you and take you to where you will be suited up in a G-Suit, you look the sort who just might enjoy

449

the thrill of the experience. Your weapons will be stowed on the plane, enjoy the flight." The man stood to leave.

Craig stood and thanked the Captain, shaking hands again.

Once fitted into the G-Suit, Craig was given a 30 minute instruction on what to expect, he was given two barf bags then helped into the rear seat of the fighter. Once strapped into the seat he was instructed to not touch anything, except, as he was shown how to eject if the pilot were to become incapacitated. Craig was told what to expect in the event of an ejection, "You will be shot out the top of the plane by rockets mounted to the bottom of the seat, the seat will separate from you once clear of the plane, the chute will then open and you will drift softly into the ocean, once in the ocean, pull these catches and the chute will disengage from your body, your floatation device will self-inflate, you will be safe until either you drown or the sharks eat you, nothing to it." The man then shoved a helmet onto Craig's head, made the proper connections for oxygen and communications so he and the pilot could talk to one another. Once finished the man patted Craig on the helmet and said, "You all have a nice flight now! Ya hear?"

The experience was nothing Craig could have ever imagined. The plane taxied forward then stopped, within seconds the engines sounded as if they were screaming. Next came the shock of feeling as if everything rear of him was attempting to push itself through his body, his eyes felt as though they had gone flat, then, the plane was in the air, gaining altitude. Craig uttered one word, "Damn", he heard a chuckle, it was the pilot who asked, "OK back there?"

"Yes sir."

"I'm Jack, I don't want to know who you really are but give me something I can call you by, so I don't have to say, "hey you."

Craig grinned and told the captain "Nice to meet you Jack, call me Bill, should be easy for both of us to remember."

Both men laughed, the pilot continued, "I gather from your earlier response to the takeoff it was your first from a carrier."

"It showed, huh?"

"Yep, it usually does, so don't feel bad."

Jack continued, "We will be meeting a tanker shortly, this thing eats a lot of fuel on takeoff and getting up to speed and altitude, you might find the refueling interesting. Other than that, enjoy the view, miles and miles of water, or kick back and nap."

The refueling was very interesting, Craig enjoyed how it all took place and was impressed by Jack and boom operator in the tanker. Craig decided to sleep.

"Bill, 15 minutes to landing." Craig had no idea how long he'd been asleep.

Landing at Hickam Field the plane taxied to where it was directed, a man climbed up and informed Craig he was to keep his helmet on, visor down, he did as he was told. A jeep pulled up driven by a man in shorts, a flower printed shirt and tennis shoes that had seen better days. The man motioned for Craig to get in the jeep. There was only one airplane in the hanger the man pulled the jeep into, the door was then closed. "You can take off the helmet now."

"Hungry?"

"No, where's the head?"

Craig relieved himself and returned to the hanger area where he asked the man for a soft drink, the man snapped his fingers and pointed to another man. The drink arrived a moment later. Craig asked, "What next?"

The man looked at Craig and asked, "After all this don't you have any questions about what is going on?

Sargent Craig Kirkland responded, "Mister, I figure if as much time, effort, resources and money are being used and spent to get one sorry ass grunt this far from where he was yesterday I will just have to wait and see what the hell is going on, and when it's time for me to know someone will tell me without my having to ask any further questions except the one I just asked. What next?"

"Fair enough. In a few minutes a pilot will arrive, he will go over his check list, you and he will board the plane and you will be transported to Buckley Air Force Base in Colorado. You with me?"

"Yes"

"When you land at Buckley the plane will be taken into a hanger with you and the pilot still on board, once there you may disembark the plane. You will be allowed to shower again if you want and change into the clothing provided and waiting, civvies. There will be another man there who will secure your weapons from the plane's storage compartment. A gentleman named Smith will then transport you to a hotel, he will show you a car parked in the lot and provide you with keys to the car, you will also be given a wallet with a driver's license, a social security card and one thousand dollars cash, mostly in 20s, 50s and 10s. You will check into the hotel under an assumed name you will be told by the person who meets you. Once in your room you will find a package on the bed, it will contain all the information you will need for "What Next." Order room service, the food is good, I've been there, and get some rest. By the way, it's a long flight, take some snacks and a couple of sodas." The man threw a handful of change on the table for the vending machine.

The pilot called himself Eddy, he and "Bill" boarded the plane following the check list. This take off was much kinder and gentler than from the carrier, Craig instantly went to sleep. One thing a

452

Marine knew how to do was sleep when he could and stay awake when he had to. Craig had two thoughts just before sleep overtook his thoughts, the sweet lips of Sara Blackmon and the wondering of what the hell could be the next surprise.

CHAPTER

50

The building was nothing special, just one of many dirty old warehouses located close to the railroad yard. Craig parked the car, locked it and walked to the front door. Reaching for the door there was an audible *click*, the door automatically opened, he knew he was being watched. Craig entered, the door automatically closing. Standing alone in the small room he noticed what may have at one time been a receptionist area, probably where some nice lady had greeted people and directed them to the proper person they needed to see, there was no nice lady here now. Using the senses he had trained all his life, he listened, faintly hearing the slightest sounds of footsteps he moved to the door he knew was being approached from the other side, the knob turned, the door opened. A man appeared, the man motioned Craig to follow him.

What lay on the other side of the door was in stark contrast to the exterior of the building and even the dusty receptionist area, walls were freshly painted, floors shined, the ceiling wasn't

cheap acoustic tiles, but rather slick painted sheetrock. Although no pictures adorned the walls the hallway gave the appearance it could be in any high-end office building filled with wealthy executives. One thing was missing, there were no electrical receptacles, Craig wondered where a person might plug in the polisher which kept the floors shined, something most people would never notice.

The man stopped at one of the few doors located in the hallway, unlocked it and directed Craig to have a seat. Inside the room was a simple but well-built desk, three office chairs, one small file cabinet, the phone on the desk had no wires connecting it, fake. There were also no windows, there was one other door to the room. The man left Craig alone in the room, he waited, tuning in his senses. The room had no electrical receptacles in any of the walls.

Through all the years he had been training himself, Craig could count seconds of a minute closer than most expensive time pieces, at 289 seconds, 11 seconds shy of five minutes, the other door opened, a man dressed in street clothes entered. Craig had heard his footsteps two seconds before the doorknob turned.

"Hello Sargent Kirkland, my name is Dyke."

Dyke was slightly shocked by Craig's response.

"Hello Mr. Dyke, why are there no power receptacles?"

"Rather blunt, aren't you Sargent?"

"Just curious."

"Sargent Dyke, if everything goes today as I think it may, I will be more than happy to tell you why there are no power receptacles. Agreed?"

"Sir!"

"Coffee?"

"Thank You."

Dyke poured two cups of coffee and began talking.

"Sargent Kirkland, you are not married, you have no children. At home you have your parents, several cousins, a few aunts you've stayed in touch with. Am I correct?"

"Sir, and three very close friends."

"Ah, Charles Jackson, Cindy Baxter and Walter Bradberry, I should have mentioned them."

Dyke continued.

"Sargent Kirkland, your being here and everything you will hear in this room goes further, much further, than Top Secret, so secret there will never be any record of it having taken place. Should you ever choose to even hint that this meeting ever took place you will be eliminated, and please, never have any doubt this can be done. If you choose to accept the offer presented to you, you will be very well compensated. During the time you are in our employ you will live a good life but will, possibly, be called upon occasionally to perform certain acts you may not understand but can never question else you will be eliminated, you will perform that which is ordered without question. From the moment you agree to assume that which I will present to you, you will cease to exist as the person you are at this moment, you will never allow any of those previously mentioned to know you exist. You can never contact, talk to, speak with in any way shape nor form any of your family, friends or acquaintances. Sargent Kirkland, you will completely disappear, there will no longer be any record of your real fingerprints, those will be replaced by some lost soul from some third world country. Sargent Kirkland, steps to proceed with this process began the moment you were given your last orders and stepped onto the chopper that

delivered you into the jungle where you began your journey here. Should you accept and agree to these terms you will be at our service for a time not to exceed ten years but will always be held to the secrecy of that which is represented until you die. You will be compensated with an immediate ten million dollars, tax free, deposited into several accounts around the world. Are you capable of accepting these terms? You will be given ten minutes alone to consider what you have just been told. If you choose to accept, I will proceed further, if not, you will be returned to the jungle, remain silent about this meeting and report to your officer in command that the target failed to show." Dyke left the room.

Shocked, Craig's mind was in a whirlwind, he knew what this would all mean, giving up every living soul who meant anything to him. He also knew this was the final piece of the puzzle he had never been able to put into place concerning his life's mission. Craig made the decision, yes, but with conditions.

Dyke re-entered the room, sat at the desk and looked at Craig.

Craig began, "Sir, I have chosen to accept your offer but there will need to be some conditions. From the moment I stepped off the bus at Parris Island I have been in training to complete a personal mission I swore to myself at the age of 17 would someday be completed. If you will agree that I may complete that mission I will agree to your terms and will never question any mission I may be ordered to perform in the ten years I am in your employ. Should you not agree to my conditions concerning my personal mission I will return to Viet Nam and no mention of this meeting shall ever be known to any person, anywhere."

Dyke asked, "The Blackmon girl?"

Craig nodded and said, "Yes sir."

If Dyke could smile, he did.

"Thank you, Sargent Kirkland, you just won a bet for me concerning a bottle of very nice whisky."

Dyke reached under the desk and pushed a button, twice.

The door opened, a man appeared and asked, with an accent, "It's good whiskey, yes?"

Dyke answered, "Very, I'll be sure to invite you for a taste." "Sargent, in case you're wondering, my friend and I had a bet that you might possibly have something in store for those who brought harm to Miss Blackmon, I believed you did, my friend did not. I will savor the whiskey."

Looking at Craig, Mr. Dyke continued, "I've read the file and know what those animals did to her. I also have a wife and a daughter, as does the gentleman you see sitting before you." The man simply nodded in agreement.

"Sargent Kirkland, to my knowledge you are the first person in the history of this group to have ever been invited who has ever had any conditions associated with what is typically a yes or no answer to the invitation. Your condition, mission, certainly brings reason for pause on our part. Sargent, we have many people in place all over the world whose jobs are to observe and evaluate persons of interest who may possess certain skills, either natural or trained, you have both. From boot camp it was obvious you were worthy of observing for possible recruitment into this group and the actions on your very first patrol in Viet Nam confirmed we were correct. Since the day following that patrol everything about you has been researched. To say we know you better than you know yourself would be putting it extremely mildly, I too occasionally enjoy the taste of a tart, salty, freshly picked green apple." Craig listened as the man continued. "Although your marksmanship skills are exemplary more importantly is your

457

patience and ability to observe, to see and hear things others miss, your ability to work with officers in planning missions, more than one officer has reported you seem to know what will happen before it does. Your evaluation skills are off the chart. I cannot tell you how many times in your file it is mentioned that you blend into your surroundings, your environment, in such a way it seems you had simply disappeared, this, as you know, has earned you the nickname of "Ghost." How is it your IQ shows you much more intelligent than your high school records show you to be?"

Craig's answer was simple, yet honest "Hated homework, refused to do it and used my exams to keep my grades high enough to pass the classes, sometimes just barely. Sir, at the time other things were more important to me."

"Miss Blackmon?"

"Mostly."

The man with the accent spoke, "Your, uhh, mission, you have plan?"

"Yes sir"

"How?"

"Sir, the plan is to take place over time, several years, one at a time."

"Curious, how you plan any mission?"

"Always in reverse, evade and escape is the priority in planning any mission and even then, an alternate evade and escape is worked into the planning in the event the first plan is interrupted by anything unexpected. Always expect the unexpected and plan for it."

"How many."

"There were five but now only four. The judge who presided at the trial was originally included but I've learned he killed himself after his wife walked into his chambers and caught him with is dick in the mouth of a 17 year old female detainee. There is one more that will be included but I hope to make a plan, a scheme if you will, by which he will die by other people's hands, I will watch him carefully until such opportunity presents itself."

"Who is other one?"

"Samuel Bartolli."

Dyke spoke, "The Attorney, a rotten bastard for sure."

Dyke continued, "Sargent, frankly speaking, you are perfect in every way for the job we have to offer. We are also aware you have top secret clearance; I will remind you that what you've been told goes much higher than top secret. But your personal mission is rather bothersome, as much as I personally believe it should happen, my superiors may deem it a conflict of interest. You are to leave here, go to the hotel we've arranged for you, enjoy a nice meal this evening, check out tomorrow morning and return here at 10 AM. Oh, and I will remind you, you are technically in Viet Nam, make no phone calls, contact no one. We will have an answer for you in the morning."

The room was very nice, Craig ordered steak for dinner, he indulged himself with one drink of whiskey. He couldn't remember the last time he had laid in bed and watched TV, even now it all seemed so very surreal. The last thought Craig Kirkland had before drifting into sleep was the same as every night, it was the memory of kissing Sara's soft sweet lips the night before she went on vacation with her family that first week of August, he had only kissed her one time since, on the day she'd broken his heart. He dreamed every day that somehow, someday he would kiss those sweet lips one more time.

Everything Craig needed had been provided, toothbrush, razor and shaving cream, clothing the right size, he showered, shaved and dressed. It had been the same at the base where he'd landed. All his gear was locked up, boots, utilities, pack and weapons, everything was still at the air base, there would be hell to pay if anyone messed with his weapons. Craig checked out, drove to the warehouse, he walked to the automatic door at precisely 10 AM, it clicked and opened. Mr. Dyke was waiting in the receptionist area, they walked to a different office than the day before, a slightly larger room with two more chairs than the first room. Still no power receptacles in any of the walls.

Craig was offered a chair, he sat. Without asking, Dyke poured them both coffees.

"Sargent we will be joined in a few minutes by the gentleman you met yesterday and two others but first you and I need to talk." Craig nodded yes. "Your condition has created quite a quandary, everyone agrees it should happen, we just cannot have your mission interfering with the missions you may be ordered by us to perform, if there ever are any, everyone also agrees we want you to be a part of our group. You do see how this could confuse the issue, don't you?"

Craig answered, "Yes sir."

"How do you intend to do it?"

"Mr. Dyke, I've had several years to think about that and to plan for it. Due to their actions the night they hurt Sara it is my intention to leave the first two in such a way their families cannot open the caskets, probably done with a rifle in either 30.06 or .308 caliber, sniped, I prefer the 30.06. I may choose explosives although I'm not that well trained in their use, the third will possibly be shown the mercy, if you can call it that, of two .22s to the back of the head, 3 if required. The fourth I have every intention of spending several days with, he will suffer."

460

"Dangerous business, spending time with one. Why do it?"

Looking across the desk at Dyke, Dyke saw, for the first time in Craig, the dark eyes of a killer. "He is the one who set her up to be raped. I want him to experience some of what was done to her."

The side door opened; three men entered the room. One of the men was the man with the accent Craig had met the day before, another was oriental, the last, once he spoke, was obviously British.

The man with the accent spoke first "We hear on speaker, why you not want caskets open?

"Those are the two who inflicted the most pain."

"OK."

The oriental gentleman was next to speak, he did so with only the slightest hint of any accent, most would think he'd been born and raised in the Midwest, his English impeccable. "Sargent Kirkland I've read the files on you and am exceedingly impressed, and young man, I am very difficult to impress. I also realize the life you had planned with Miss Blackmon was seriously interfered with, changed by the actions of a few ruffians, what they did to her was the vilest of things anyone could ever suffer, much less a beautiful young woman. I understand your hatred toward those who committed those ruthless acts. But Sargent I also have my priorities and I need to ask you one question, one most serious question. Are you capable of maintaining an obligation to this group and not allow your personal feelings toward those other people to interfere with that which you may be ordered to do? Without a doubt?"

"Sir, Yes sir!"

The gentleman smiled, "I believe it."

461

In addition to the coffee urn there was also a pot of tea, the Brit poured a cup and sat back down. Sipping his tea, he placed the cup on the saucer, sat it on the desk and contemplated for a moment before speaking, "Your family loves you, they will grieve you terribly. Your Mum, father, how do you feel about that?"

"Sir, I will grieve with them, they just will not know."

"The young lady broke your heart."

"She did but I could not, not love her."

"True love."

"The truest."

"Does anyone else know of your personal mission?"

"If anyone does it would be my Father and Cindy, my friend. Although neither, I believe, think it would actually happen. They also know that when it begins, I must disappear in the interest of self-survival and their protection. This is the one part I have never, in all my planning, been exactly certain how to make happen. You gentlemen have offered an answer to that part of the equation."

"Risky, that they might have an idea."

"Yes, but both are very capable of keeping secrets."

"So, when they hear the news of the demise of certain people, they will probably believe you still live?"

"They might but will not know for certain. I can never allow them to know. It could put people I love in danger."

Dyke spoke, "Sargent Kirkland, please step across the hall, you will find coffee and refreshment, we will be with you momentarily."

The coffee was fresh, the donuts still warm, Craig waited.

An hour passed before Dyke opened the door and told Craig to come with him.

"Sargent Kirkland, we have much to tell you."

"In the early 1920s, following the Great War, WWI, the League of Nations was formed. The League of Nations primary objective was to, quite simply, prevent the possibility of any further World Wars. As you know WWII is the main example of how miserably the League of Nations failed. World War II came about because the League of Nations had not the intestinal fortitude to perform its duties to the world and stop Hitler before he became a power to be dealt with. Politics, diplomacy and pacification were useless. Hitler became allies of Japan and the rest is history. It is estimated that around 70 million people died either directly or indirectly, famine, disease and such, as the result of WWII. In 1942 President Roosevelt along with Prime Minister Churchill and a few other countries formed the United Nations, following WWII other countries joined. More was needed. Occasionally a person or people come along who may present themselves as threats to world peace, once identified as such those people are removed, in one way or another, some are eliminated, killed. Others are removed in such a way that they no longer pose a threat to the initiation of WWIII. One particular General who had the desire to use nuclear weapons during the Korean conflict was removed from duty, it saved his life.

"Following WWII the heads of state for the United States, Great Britain, The Soviet Union and China, leaders of the four world super powers realized the need for back channel communications to prevent any further World Wars. Through those back-channel communications, it was agreed a group of people would always be maintained who, when called upon, would always be ready to eliminate any threats to world peace, to

prevent the next World War. Those chosen would never know who the others were in the event any went rogue and required elimination."

"So, Sargent Kirkland, today you sit before the four representatives of the four leaders of today's world super powers, the United States of America, Great Britain, The Peoples Republic of China and the Soviet Union and are being invited to join a very elite group of people who may, possibly, be called upon to hopefully eliminate the possibility of any further world wars, some may possibly not pose a world war threat but will require elimination for other reasons, world financial, etc. Young man, THAT is some Very Heavy Shit. Will you join us?"

"Have I permission to also pursue my personal mission?"

"As long as it in no way ever poses a threat to this group and never interferes with this group's missions, if there are any. But you need to know one thing, if while pursuing your personal mission you should ever be captured, you will never make it to a court of law? DO YOU UNDERSTAND?" For the first time since Dyke had been in any discussions with Craig, Craig saw the dark cold eyes of a killer looking at him as the question was asked. The two men understood one another.

Having never meant the words as much as he meant them now, Craig answered, "Sir, Yes Sir!"

A pause, a silence filled the room, it was almost deafening.

Dyke spoke, "Sargent Howard Craig Kirkland no longer exists. Within twenty-four hours every record containing his finger prints will contain another person's prints. Sargent Kirkland will fail to arrive at the designated time at the designated rendezvous location and will be reported as Missing in Action, his family will be notified. Sargent Kirkland will never be found."

464

Reality didn't set in, it hit Craig like a pile driver, he dropped his head, tears welled in his eyes, but he wouldn't allow them to spill. The men in the room had seen this same scenario with other young men, the moment they realize they had just given up everything and everybody that had ever meant anything to them. The men silently allowed the young man his few moments of silent grief, one quietly poured him another cup of coffee and sat it on the desk.

Several minutes passed before he lifted his head and asked, "Who am I?"

The Chinese representative opened his briefcase, he took the file from it and handed it to Dyke. "Your name is Gary Wayne Graham, son of John and Patricia (Garner) Graham, both of whom were killed three years ago in an automobile accident, their bodies cremated, ashes scattered in the Coosa River. You were born in Tuscaloosa, Alabama. No siblings. Your mother had one brother, your uncle Robert, last name Garner. Robert was an adventurous sort who worked many different trades and would travel the country seeking the highest wages, he was also very smart with is money and invested heavily in companies and stocks, all of which did very well. You were his only nephew and he loved you enough to have a will, you are his only heir. Robert's only hobby was sailing, he was caught in a storm and lost at sea. The rest is in the file for you to study and memorize. Also, in the file are a birth certificate, driver's license and Social Security card."

"Mr. Graham", it was the Brit speaking, "at any given time around the world there are approximately twenty others much like yourself, those twenty are supported by hundreds more, most of whom have no idea who they are really working for, clerks, secretaries, they simply are at their daily jobs and perform the tasks they are given without question. Then, there are others who you may someday need to contact in order to have access to

specialty items required to complete any missions you may be ordered to perform. One very important point, of the twenty such as yourself, you will never meet nor know any of them. The reason you will never know who the others are is that should you or any of them go rogue or are captured, or frankly, should any of us go rogue, the others will be available and called upon to eliminate the threat. We are not an agency, there are no acronyms such as FBI, CIA, KGB or MI6, we are simply The Group, we answer only to the current world leaders of the four world super powers. In all honesty, we do not exist. Now, on a personal level, every man in this room wishes you all the best on your personal mission, we are sympathetic about what happened to young Miss Blackmon and how it affected your life, those who did what they did are less than human, rabid dogs is the best description I can offer, rabid dogs need killing. But, if your personal mission ever poses any threat to the group you will be hunted down and killed, post haste, do not fail to understand this! Then again, I've given much thought to your mission and think it could very well be a positive, call it, extra training to keep you sharp. We know you've killed, Viet Nam is littered with bodies you have left behind, that was war, your personal mission is anger/revenge killing, do not allow your anger to fog the vision of that which you hope to achieve, if something is wrong, abort the mission until all is right. I must leave now, there is a plane to catch. Wishing you well Mr. Graham, Godspeed!" There were no handshakes, the Brit simply nodded to the other men and left the room.

The Chinese and Soviet representatives had little else to say and both excused themselves leaving "Gary" with Mr. Dyke. Dyke would explain the rest of the process.

"Gary, at this moment you are a very wealthy young man, ten million American dollars have been deposited into several accounts, the locations and account numbers are in the file. For

ten years you may, or may not, be called upon and sent on a mission or missions. Any missions you are ordered to will be funded by means other than your money. Make no mistake, mission definition is to kill somebody, plain and simple. How you choose to do it will be left completely to your discretion, but you will either perform a successful mission or you will die trying. Something you need to know, in the history of The Group there have been several people who have served their ten years and never been called on, those people are living very nice lives as we speak. There have been two who were killed while on missions, they messed up, and there has been one who went rogue, you can guess his fate. I sincerely hope you are never called on, not that I have any problem with some crazed power hungry fool being taken out, but rather if you are called on it means the world is about to be involved in something that could potentially cause the deaths of millions of people or perhaps financial ruin to the world. No sane person wants such."

"You may wonder how much power The Group wields. Remember the Cuban Missile Crises? WWIII was within hours of becoming a reality. The Soviet leader was sent a message he had 5 hours to call his ships back home, to stand down. You see, there are some decisions, especially where the leaders are concerned, The Group must make without approval of the world leaders. Every head of state involved understands that he is not above being eliminated if events concerning his decisions call for it."

Gary asked "Sir, was The Group responsible for the president's assassination?"

"No. Thank Heaven."

Dyke continued, "At the end of your ten years you will be released from any mission responsibilities and wished good will. One thing you can never do though is ever become the person

you were just a half hour ago. You will for the rest of your natural life be Gary Wayne Graham. Understood?"

"Understood"

"OK, you had questions about the power receptacles, or lack of. This building and four others around the world are all similar in many ways. This building, as the others, are probably more secure than the Whitehouse, each building has been structurally enhanced, made as completely sound proof as possible and designed to eliminate, as much as possible, any opportunity by which listening devices, bugs, can be concealed. Think about it, a power receptacle is nothing more than a box with power fed to it which serves an outlet some kind of appliance can be plugged into, the perfect place to conceal a "bug" and all the power required to keep it operating. Really very simple."

"The phone has no wires"

Dyke laughed, "A fake phone idea by our paranoid Soviet friend. Anytime you were in the room alone he was watching you on a TV, yes, we have hidden cameras, he thinks sooner or later someone may try to make a call. Nobody has, but we pacify his paranoia."

"Sir, just a thought, but some fake wires might be a good idea."

"Down to business, the first 6 months of your ten years with us will be spent mostly in this building. As good as you are, you will be made better. You will be under more rigorous training than you ever imagined. The world's best in their fields of expertise will be your trainers. You will be taught ways to immobilize or kill a person with your bare hands, ways you never could imagine. Your marksmanship skills, already exceptional, will be improved upon both with handgun and rifle. By the time you leave here you will know how to kill a person with a bobby pin. You will know the

human anatomy better than most surgeons, well enough that with one thrust of a knife, messy way to kill, will result in almost instantaneous death. Makeup Artists who make the best in Hollywood seem amateurs, they are that good, will teach you how to disguise yourself so even your own parents wouldn't know you. You will live in this building, occasionally will be taken to outside locations for field testing and to firing ranges the likes of which you've never seen, amazing the things that can be hidden below ground. Put simply, Gary, when you leave here in six month you will possess the skills which will make you one of twenty ultimate killing machines."

"At the end of six months you will be allowed to live anywhere in the continental United States. We have crews who build homes, special homes to our specifications. Any idea where you would like to reside?"

Craig replied, "I've visited and enjoy the scenery and serenity of Virginia."

"Of course, Virginia will also put you close enough, yet far enough away from your personal mission, excellent choice. I also find Virginia to be a beautiful place. I'll be back in a moment, have another cup of coffee."

Gone only a few minutes, Dyke returned, "Good news, my contact knows of a piece of land for sale far enough from Lexington, Virginia to offer seclusion but not too far to be inconvenient for your shopping needs, says it has a beautiful view. By this time tomorrow you will be a land owner and work will commence on your home once our contractor is in place. One thing, you can never sell this home to anyone and upon your death it will be demolished. There will be many secrets built into the structure and its immediate surroundings. Any questions?"

"Sir, ten million dollars is a lot of money, I would like to see it grow to become much more money. I've no idea how to do such a

thing and am wondering if The Group can provide a very good financial advisor?"

"We can, but I have to ask, why in the world would you ever need more than ten million dollars?"

"Sir, as you know, my personal mission will result in widows and several children with no fathers, some of those will require some form of financial stability and means to pay for educations. There is also one very special lady whose dreams I would like to help come true, she once mentioned to me her dream of someday owning a nice home on some pastureland and to have a few horses. I've not worked out yet how I can do all these things and remain secret, but somehow I will."

"And that special person would be Sara Blackmon?

"Yes sir."

"And you intend to kill four husbands and fathers but are concerned about their widows and children?"

"Yes sir, they had no hand in what their husbands and fathers did."

"Mr. Graham, the more we talk, the more I like and respect you. We have people in place who can help you achieve all you've mentioned."

Dyke continued. "One more thing you need to know before I show you to your accommodations. Occasionally you will be contacted to return here, you will be physically and mentally evaluated, you will also be evaluated on all you will be trained with during the next six months. I would suggest you keep yourself in shape and continue practicing all you will have learned."

"Understood."

"OK, Mr. Graham, Gary, come with me I will show you to your home for the next half year, I believe you will like it far more than that hooch you've been living in. There is also a bottle of some nice Kentucky Bourbon there, your favorite. It's been a most stressful day and I am pretty sure you could use a drink; I know damned well I could."

Gary Wayne Graham smiled, "Yes sir."

CHAPTER

51

The six months had been hard, harder than anything the Marine Corps training had ever thrown at Craig, the physical aspects of it all had taught him how much more the human body could withstand than he'd ever imagined possible, but the most amazing things learned were what the mind is capable of, the mental training had pushed him to the brink of insanity. Craig realized, in some strange way, after having been to the point of insanity, how clear it was that he was saner than he had ever been in his life. He'd also learned so many other things his mind before could not have comprehended nor imagined possible. He knew the human anatomy better than most physicians and all the points on the body which could cause either instant death or unbearable pain if touched or manipulated in the correct fashion. His marksmanship, already better than most people could ever realize, was even vastly more improved. His eyesight had been corrected, having once been slightly near sighted The Group had a physician perform innovative and yet unapproved surgery on his eyes. Lenses had been implanted, Craig's eyesight was better than what most would describe as perfect. Glasses could prove to be one's demise if light were reflected off the lenses at an inopportune moment. One of his favorite classes had been learning the art of explosives, how they could be made from everyday household items, how to build detonating devices which would bring life to the explosives and death to the person intended to be made dead, he already had a plan for his new knowledge. Wireless devices which would not be available to the public for decades, devices built by employees of The Group for use by Group operatives only. His next favorite class had been chemistry, deadly chemistry. Yes, it had been hard, but he was so

very pleased with all he had absorbed, learned, things he would soon be putting to the test.

Craig would be leaving Denver in two days, heading for his new home in Virginia. Having a desire to drive cross country and see from ground level what he'd seen from the air, Craig had been allowed to shop for a new vehicle, he'd purchased a new Dodge Power Wagon Town Wagon, half 4 wheel drive truck, half station wagon, the thing was a brute and rode like one but it was also tough and would go where most other vehicles wouldn't.

Having plenty of time to get it done, Craig was halfheartedly packing when someone knocked on his door, it was Dyke. "I thought you might want these", Dyke presented Craig with the M70, 30.06 and the Colt .45 which he'd left stored at Buckley. Dyke continued "I know you must be very partial to the weapons, but we took some liberties with them. Our people performed their magic, neither weapon have any markings whatsoever and there is no way to tell they ever did. Both have also been made to accept the suppressors which are packed in the cases with the weapons. The suppressors won't do much in the way of silencing, they will quiet the guns a little, sometimes a little is plenty, but they will suppress the muzzle flash substantially, sometimes that means a lot!" Craig picked up the weapons he knew so intimately and had personally worked hard to perfect. Rifle first, he checked the magazine to assure it was empty, pulled back the bolt he'd spent hours polishing with the mildest polish he could find, toothpaste, he pushed the bolt back into place, shouldered the rifle and squeezed the trigger he had spent much time setting to his preference, 3.25 pounds pull, perfect! The pistol was next, as he was examining it Dyke spoke, "Our people said they've never seen a Colt .45 work as smoothly as that one works." Craig smiled, nobody, even himself, knew how much time he had spent working and reworking every part of the handgun until he had made it as good as it could ever be.

"OK Gary, here are the keys to your new house, in the basement you will find a safe, here is the combination" Dyke handed "Gary" a small piece of paper with numbers printed on it. "The house and outbuildings are very special and contain secrets only you, me and the people who built it will ever be aware of. Inside the safe you will find a booklet describing everything about the house and its internal workings. Before you enter the house, you need to know there is a security system, these are the instructions." He handed the papers to Gary, "do not attempt to enter the house without having read the instructions."

"As I'm sure you realize, being under contract to The Group for the next 9 ½ years comes with certain requirements, one of which is that we must know your whereabouts every day in the event we need to get in touch, agreed?"

"Agreed."

"That new beast you just purchased has had a few items added to it by our people. Hidden inside the vehicle are devices by which we will know where it is every minute of every day, should you ever choose to sell or trade it you must contact us so our technicians can remove the devices. If, and when you purchase any other vehicle in the next 9 ½ years you will call us so our technicians can install devices on it for the same purpose. There have also been added some nifty hidden compartments capable of hiding things you dare not be found, I'm told it would take the person who built the vehicle to know the compartments exist. At least once every day for the next 9 ½ years you will check in with us, before you leave here a technician will explain how to check in and how to know if we require your services. By the way, a Four Wheel Drive without a winch is pretty much useless, sooner or later it's going to be put into a place it won't go, yours has a power takeoff, so we added a winch that'll be very helpful in such cases, on the house! You will be very well versed on anything the techs have done to your vehicle before you leave."

Dyke stood, walked across the room and poured two drinks, he seemed to have something on his mind as he handed Gary one of the drinks and motioned for him to sit across the table, even said, "Please."

"Sir, you have something to say, to add?"

Dyke thoughtfully began to speak, "Everything I want to tell you now is completely off the record. Agree and I keep talking, disagree and I get up and leave."

Craig knew the man had something he wanted to say, "Agreed, Sir."

"Over the last six months I have watched you very closely, taken a personal interest in you. I have seen you excel at things to the point of being superhuman, I know, I've taken this same six-month training and you've far and again surpassed anything I was ever capable of, and I was damned good. You may very well be the absolute best to have ever completed the training, at least the best I've ever seen. I cannot tell you how many times I've wondered where the strength came from, I would see you about to falter, then your eyes would take on a look unlike any I or any of my associates have ever witnessed, yes, I have photos of that look, photos you never knew were being taken. Every time the "look" would expose itself the tenacity to learn, to overcome, became stronger, more resolved. Honestly, when I look at the photos, the face, the eyes, I see the most frightening person I may have ever seen, and I've faced death more than once, I see a man on a mission who will not accept failure, completion of his mission is all that matters. What kept you going? What made you become the only man alive I may hold fear of? What convinced you to not fail? What made you the best I've ever seen?"

Gary looked hard at the man, took a sip of his whiskey and said one name, "Sara Imogene Blackmon."

475

"Deep down", Dyke continued, "I knew it. Have you kept up with her?"

"Some, best I could under the circumstances."

Dyke reached into his jacket and took an envelope, he lay it on the table. "Do not open this until you arrive at your home in Virginia. I will not say what it contains because the information within it came from sources having nothing whatsoever to do with The Group, sources I am capable of utilizing. I think the information will be helpful."

"Gary, I know more than you could imagine, but not everything. What did you do with the engagement ring/wedding band set you purchased? Yes, we even know about that."

"Sir, would I be out of line if I told you it's none of your business?"

Dyke smiled, "No, no you wouldn't be out of line. I respect you saying so. Need I remind you what will happen if you get caught?"

"No sir."

"You asked a while back about financial advisors. Remember?"

"I do."

"Well, those guys are good. That ten million you were paid is now, in six months, worth twelve million. Yeah, they are very good. Keep this up and they may make you a billionaire someday," Dyke laughed. "All information concerning your personal finances is in a separate package in the safe, account numbers, financial advisor contacts, investments info, everything. Another thing, on a cross country drive unexpected situations can sometimes arise, a man should be armed. Since your weapons no longer have any identifying markings and will be hidden in the

storage compartments, you may need a self defense weapon. A brand new, still in the box Colt .45, a box of ammo and an extra magazine will be in the passenger seat of your vehicle, also in the box are the appropriate permits in the name of Gary Wayne Graham. The handgun is stock as a rock, we've not touched it except to clean the cosmoline from it and make it ready for use. Five rounds were test fired through it, it was then cleaned and placed back in the box."

Dyke's voice softened, "Once you arrive at home and learn about the house, I would like you to go check out the garage. You will find a personal gift from me to you for your hard work. It's the least I could do after having plucked you out of the jungle and having you flown half way around the world, not to speak of convincing you to give up all you were and ever had been."

Dyke didn't stay much longer, there just wasn't much else to discuss. The two men exchanged handshakes and Dyke headed toward the door. Dyke opened the door, took a step and hesitated, he looked back, "You get those sonsabitches for what they did to Sara, just don't get caught doing it."

The door closed, Dyke was gone.

Craig whispered, "Yes Sir."

***

The next morning Gary visited all the instructors, going over last-minute details and answering questions, he thanked them for their time and patience. The afternoon was spent with the technicians going over all they had done to his vehicle, including the car phone Dyke had failed to mention. One of the techs handed Gary a note, it was from Dyke and read, "Surprise, every young rich guy needs a telephone in his car! This one is more special than most."

***

Being in no hurry Gary mapped a route from Denver, Colorado to Lexington, Virginia which would take him South through New Mexico, then East through Texas, Oklahoma, Arkansas, Tennessee. He would spend a few days in Knoxville, he knew she lived there with her Grandmother, he just wanted to see her, even from a distance, then to his home in Virginia. The trip would be a long one, over 2000 miles, he would have much time to think and plan. There was another stop to be made. Gary had been given a list of people who could provide items and services which may be required to complete any mission he might be assigned, one of the people on the list was in the town of Searcy, Arkansas. Wanting an identical backup to his personal rifle, Craig dialed the number on the car phone, the man who answered would have a new Model 70 Winchester Rifle, chambered for 30.06, the Leupold scope requested, ready for pickup. Gary would later mount the scope, float the barrel, set the trigger pull to his preference and zero the rifle/scope combination at 500 yards using 165 grain handloaded boat tail bullets. The distance could be recalibrated if need be following a proper recon of the area the rifle was intended to be used. A nice rifle a lot of work would go into.

He had changed his everyday appearance, Gary had grown a moustache and changed the color of his hair, his once high and tight haircut had grown to the style of the day. As many people as there are in the world, he needed to lower the chance of someone he may have once known recognizing him due to some coincidental meeting. There would be many other times in the future he would use the techniques of disguise he had been taught.

It was the Spring season, the world was re-awakening from a cold Winter, flowers blooming, leaves returning to the trees, the weather was perfect for driving with the windows down. Gary enjoyed the scenery as he drove, and thought, and planned.

478

***

Lexington, Virginia was a pretty city with a population of around 7500, small by the standard of many cities, but very friendly and with enough people there would be plenty of goods and services available. Gary followed the written instructions to his new home, what he found exceeded his expectations, the house in the mountains was very beautiful with its exterior of stone work and cedar siding, rustic but very nice. The landscaping was perfect, combining a perfect number of shrubs and native wild flowers, all of which were in full bloom. Gary would learn from the package in the safe that a local landscape gentleman had been hired to perform the work, he would make it a point to meet the man and hire him to continue taking care of it all.

Having read the instruction booklet on the operation of the security system, Gary unlocked the door with one key then located the small box a few feet to the right of the door, with another key he unlocked the box, placed the same key in the switch, turned the key once to the right, back to center, again to the right then twice to the left. A small red light in the box turned off, there was a beep then a female voice was heard, "Welcome Home, Gary." Nice touch.

Finally having time to admire the interior, Gary was amazed. The place was as beautiful as something from a magazine, as the exterior, the inside was also rustic, exposed beams, cedar and stone adorned the walls, the stone fireplace was the center of attraction in the great room. Furniture built from local wood, much of the wood exposed, the rest covered tastefully with nice material. The floors were pine, there were nice paintings on the walls as well as multiple mounted deer and fish, a Kentucky black powder long rifle hung above the mantel. This was a man's home if there had ever been one.

Suddenly his stomach growled, he'd been so engrossed on getting to the house Gary had completely forgotten to stop in

town and pick up anything to eat, he needn't have been concerned. Walking to the kitchen Gary discovered the cupboards full of canned goods, a bin full of potatoes. Opening the refrigerator Gary discovered a thick nicely marbled ribeye, in the crisper were all the makings of a salad, fresh. There was milk, eggs, cheese, everything he might need for a few days as he got himself settled in. There was cold beer, he opened one. The kitchen was so well stocked and everything so fresh Gary realized someone had known where he was and when he would arrive. The knowledge was somewhat unsettling, but it was the life he'd be living, might as well accept it.

The basement was finished as nicely as the main level, it contained workout equipment and weights, a pool table, a well-stocked bar, and a safe. The combination was used, the safe opened, he removed the envelopes and returned to the main level. Walking out the back door revealed a very nice grill, Gary used the charcoal provided and started a fire, went back to the kitchen, seasoned the steak and prepared a salad.

As he enjoyed his meal Gary was also reading the information about the house, it was indeed a very special house. He would never have guessed while he was in the basement, but it was built over a sub-basement. Finished with his meal, dishes washed and put up, Gary took the instructions and went back downstairs. Inside the cabinet holding the cue sticks he located the hidden latch, pressing the latch he pulled the cabinet forward revealing steps, turned on the lights and walked down, what he discovered was amazing.

There was equipment for handloading ammunition, two large gun safes, combinations had been in the paperwork, the safes containing an array of weapons, rifles, shotguns, handguns, all in various calibers and gauges, knives, explosive materials and everything to build any sort of detonating device he might choose, there were suppressors for several of the weapons. Checking each

weapon closely, there were no identifying markings on any of them. There were also two small TV sets, turning one on offered a clear view of the front of the house, switching channels offered differing views of other parts of the exterior. There was also a door, Gary opened it and followed the tunnel to another set of stairs.

The door latch was nothing high tech, should one need to take this route in a hurry he wouldn't need to be fumbling with anything more complicated than a door knob. Opening the door pushed the large tool cabinet attached to it forward. The garage was total darkness except the light from the tunnel, no windows. Gary located the switch and turned on the lights. Sitting before him was a beautiful 1968 Pontiac GTO, Dyke's "Personal Gift." Raising the hood revealed the engine with its 4-barrel carb, looking inside Gary saw an envelope in the driver's seat, keys in the ignition and a four-speed shifter, a car phone was mounted to the console, he knew there would also be the devices which would be tracking the car's location. Gary opened the envelope.

Hello Gary,

I hope you like the car, it's registered to you, tag and registration paid for, as well as 6 months insurance, you pick it up then, you can afford it. As much as I know you like that beast you drive, you are also a handsome young man, a rich handsome young man, and need something other than that ugly ass truck to drive. Pontiac builds a very nice automobile; the techs made this one even better. The techs have added some things to the suspension in order to make it stronger and drive better, the engine has been taken apart and reassembled with much stronger parts, they tell me it also makes much more horse power than the stock motor, although it doesn't appear to have ever been touched. Under the dash, to the right of the steering column you will find a button, I don't know how it works but they tell me if

you have the engine at full throttle and push the button it will feel almost the same as you felt on takeoff from the carrier, some kind of gas called nitrous oxide which is hidden under the rear seat. One of the younger techs called the car sexy. I never saw a car with boobs and a nice ass so I wouldn't know about that. The phone can be dismounted and plugged into any cigar lighter in any vehicle, take it or the one from your beast if you should ever drive anything other than your vehicles, which I fully believe you will be doing soon. By doing this we can keep track of you and you will have the means for your daily check in. Both your vehicles are made to be theft proof by any means other than a tow truck. If that should ever happen, we will know within minutes and it will be the last theft the thief ever makes.

Now, you will live the rest of your life at the location you currently reside. I highly recommend you get out and meet the people in the area, make friends, attend church and become active in the community, hell, coach little league if you want to. Let it be known about your wealthy uncle who left you all his money and that you love to travel, often for weeks at a time. Gary, I know you love Sara but you are a handsome young rich guy who is single, meet some of the young single women and date them, you don't have to fall in love and I know you won't, but you also are not living under the disguise of being a priest, so don't act like one. Other than that little Vietnamese hooker who gave you a case of the clap, yes, we know about that, we also know about your friend Cindy, when is the last time you were laid? You know by now your house is bugged, but every man needs a place for privacy, his own space, your bedroom is that place. There are no cameras nor hidden bugs of any kind in your bedroom, trust me there are some things we don't care to see. We may be very sneaky, but we are not perverts. But if you happen to have a naked young lady anywhere else in the house it'll thrill the hell out of the techs.

I told you this once, will say it again, I honestly hope we never have need of your services but if we do you will be notified. If you ever have any questions, you have the number.

Best wishes on a good life young man, you've earned it.

Dyke.

PS: Don't get any tickets, insurance rates for that little GTO are already outrageous!

PS: AGAIN: Burn this letter, NOW!

He couldn't help but smile at the letter, Gary figured it was about time for a haircut. No better place to start getting to know people than a local barber shop. It would also be a good way to enjoy his first drive in the GTO. Hopefully tomorrow would result in gaining a few new friends. He turned off the lights, closed the door and made his way back to the main level of the house. Suddenly tired, the bed comfortable, Gary slept for 14 hours.

***

Gary would later open the envelope Dyke had given him right before he'd left Denver. There were listed names and current addresses of people, people Craig Kirkland was very interested in.

CHAPTER

52

Tommy Williams' father was Associate Pastor at the Baptist Church about two blocks from campus. Kenneth had visited with Tommy a few times and enjoyed the services, he had also seen a girl who looked so very familiar, but he'd not been able to place where he might have met her.

**

Christmas Season, holiday parties were common around the campus of the University of Tennessee, most too wild for Kenneth's preference, especially those at the fraternity and sorority houses. He was invited to many, but usually had a good excuse to politely decline. But, when Tommy mentioned the Young Singles Department were doing a Christmas program at the church with refreshment afterward and asked if he would like to come, Kenneth readily accepted.

Although the young people performed all the Christmas Hymns beautifully, Kenneth wasn't really listening, he was staring at the beautiful, petite girl in the first row of the choir. He absolutely could not take his eyes off her, he knew they had somewhere met, he was positive they had met.

Everyone stood and applauded the choir; they had been outstanding. The Minister of Music invited everyone to the downstairs dining area where refreshment would be served.

Tommy and Kenneth were enjoying their punch when someone tapped Kenneth on the arm, looking to see who it was

he was greeted by the gorgeous petite girl holding a small plate containing a slice of pie, "My Grandmother taught me to make pecan pie. I would enjoy an honest opinion, if you don't mind, Sir."

Making all the correct sounds and faces, Kenneth savored each bite, the pie really was delicious. The girl told him to wait there, she would be back. She turned, disappeared into the crowd. A few minutes later she reappeared with two cups of coffee, "Would you care for a breath of fresh air? It's warm for this time of year and nice out."

Kenneth accepted the offer.

She spoke, "I had to rescue you, half the girls are plotting how to find out more about you. We are all approaching marriage age you know, and prospects are growing smaller each year in the number of handsome available young men." They laughed.

"Well, I do very much appreciate being rescued, especially by such a lovely heroine, but it isn't often I've had opportunity to be approached by so many ladies at one time, it's a bit overwhelming!"

"You're welcome, but now I find myself in a very awkward position."

"How so?"

"It goes far and beyond my personality that I approach people, especially not men, I mean, I even very rarely date. And most of my dates, what few there are, are with friends, not people I would ever consider anything other than a friend. Frankly, I am usually very timid about such things."

"I find it difficult to believe you don't get asked out a lot."

"Oh, I have my share of offers, but usually try to find a nice way of refusing."

"If I may, you didn't seem timid when you asked me out here for some air."

"Well, let me tell you, it took a lot of courage that I didn't know I had, and I was nervous as everything when I was walking across the room with that pie in my hand. I still am nervous, but I needed to meet you."

"Well, if you don't mind my saying, I came here tonight specifically TO meet you. I also felt the need to know you."

"Why?"

"Because I have the darndest feeling I've seen you before. I don't mean the times I've visited church services, but before, before. Get my drift?"

"That's good, because I have the same feeling. Is it possible two people can have the same déjà vu moments at the same times?"

"Must be, because it seems to be happening."

"We must get to the bottom of this mystery! Where are you from?"

"Born in Memphis. Dad's company transferred him here when I was just a little kid, before I started school, been here since. You?"

"Originally Anniston, Alabama. I came to live with my grandmother in 1963. What about other family members?"

"Paternal grandparents in Memphis, Maternal grandparents in Savannah."

She smiled. Kenneth noticed and asked, "What?"

Grinning she replied, "I wish all mysteries were this easy to solve."

"Mind letting me in on it?"

"A few years ago, your maternal grandfather had surgery in Savannah. You took him to the park across the street from the hospital. While in the park you noticed a lady having some difficulty while pushing a girl in a wheelchair up the hill to the exit of the park, you offered your assistance. You noticed the girl had been crying and told her she was pretty. Your name is Kenneth Allison, I will never forget it and had hoped one day we could meet so I could properly thank you."

"And your name is Sara! I remember!!"

Sara offered to shake Kenneth's hand, "Sara Blackmon, a pleasure to meet you again Kenneth Allison."

Kenneth took her hand. The instant Kenneth shook Sara's hand he had a feeling he'd never felt before, a simultaneous chill and warmth, feelings of happiness and joy filled his soul, his heart rate got faster. Kenneth had no idea what it meant.

"Sara noticed something suddenly different and asked him if he was OK."

"Yes, just suddenly, for some reason the cat got my tongue. I'm sorry, it's so very nice to finally meet you again Sara. Before I lose courage, may I see you again soon?"

Sara laughed, "Kenneth, I know I shouldn't say this, but if you hadn't asked, I would have. In fact, let me just go ahead and do it, would you care to join my grandmother and me at her home for lunch tomorrow after Church Services?"

"I would be honored. But, will it be OK with your grandmother? And, what should I bring?"

"Grandmother will love it; she enjoys watching a man eat a good meal. By the way, I hope you like roast beef, Sunday is roast

beef day. Bring nothing other than your appetite. But just in case, she loves yellow roses, if any can be found this time of year."

Unbeknownst to Sara, Kenneth's dad had a friend who owned some greenhouses.

***

Grandmother opened the door and saw a handsome young man holding a dozen yellow roses, "Oh, those are beautiful, Sara will love them!"

"Mrs. Blackmon, these are for you!"

She feigned a blush and thanked the young man, "And you are Kenneth?"

"Yes Ma'am."

"Call me Grandmother, please."

"Sara is upstairs changing. Coffee?"

"Thank you Ma'am."

Kenneth and Grandmother chatted. Neither knew Sara was eavesdropping. Wanting to ask the lady something before Sara came into the room, Kenneth abruptly changed topic, "Grandmother, I realize it's uncommon for someone to ask this these days, but may I have your permission to see Sara? Date her? If she will accept my offer of course. I will always let you know where we will be and have her home at the time you require."

"Kenneth, you've no idea how delighted I would be that you continue seeing my granddaughter."

Sara was beaming. It was all she could do to wait another few minutes before entering the room.

***

The year was 1968, Kenneth was a senior, Sara a Junior, they continued to see one another throughout the school year. Both also had jobs and would work dates in to fit around their schedules. Many dates consisted of sitting across from one another at Grandmother's dining room table while they both studied or were working on papers. Happiness meant being together, even if working or studying. On more than one occasion Grandmother had gone to the kitchen in the early morning hours for a glass of water and found Kenneth sleeping with his head on her table or lying on her sofa, she always covered him and gently kissed him. Grandmother was watching her granddaughter fall in love again, it was a beautiful thing to behold.

***

Kenneth Allison graduated in the top ten of his class with a degree in Mechanical Engineering. One of the top engineering firms in Knoxville had a job waiting for him. Kenneth's life was coming together for him in ways he could never have believed. A beautiful girlfriend, college behind him and a terrific job where he could advance and build a future. God was so very good to him; he knelt each night and gave his thanks.

There was only one thing that bothered Kenneth. Each time he would approach Sara on a possible life together, she would tend to back off and tell him, "We'll talk about it later, I still have another year of school." And that would be that, conversation would end as she would change the subject.

***

"Grandmother, I'm falling in love."

"I know dear, I've been watching it happen. I just wondered when you would admit it."

"It scares me."

"I understand how it would."

"Grandmother, Kenneth has never been anything other than kind to me, he shows me more respect than I feel I deserve. Not one time has he ever made any sexual advances toward me. I mean, sure we've kissed and held one another, I liked it, but nothing more."

"He's a very nice young man, Dear, a gentleman."

Sara continued, "He wants to talk about a future together, that scares me, and I tend to back off. I don't want to hurt his feelings, but I get frightened. I also know he is more than a gentleman; he is a gentle man as well."

"You still have a lot of love inside your heart for Craig, don't you?"

"I will always be in love with Craig, although it's believed he's dead, I still strongly believe he is alive, somehow. But even if he is, we can never be together, although he has forgiven me for what I did."

"A complicated situation, you are in love with a man who may be dead and falling for one who is very much alive. Have you any idea how many girls wish they could have even one man in their lifetime to love them the way you now have two in your heart?"

"Complicated. Yes."

"Have you a plan."

"No ma'am, I get so frightened. I hope you can advise me."

"You're right, you do need to finish school, no doubt there. But if you really think you are falling in love, which I think you already have, don't push him away. There will come a day, not right now, when you will have to tell of everything. And Dear, I

491

mean EVERYTHING, Craig, the assault, how you came to be at the place you were assaulted, the trial and most especially, he will absolutely have to know you cannot give him any children. What I'm saying is, be honest with the young man, he deserves it."

"Yes ma'am, I understand and agree."

***

With his new job came enough money Kenneth could take Sara to nice places and enjoy treating her to things he couldn't while he was in school. Even Grandmother was invited to join them at some events Kenneth knew she enjoyed. He so very much enjoyed treating them both to nice things and places.

Winter came and went; everyone was so happy when the first days of Spring like weather began in late February. Days would warm then a cold spell would happen, but the cold spells became shorter each time. Spring was trying to happen in the South. And, Sara's graduation date was approaching.

He'd been working long hours on a project and asked his boss for an afternoon off, that he had some personal business to take care of. His boss was extremely pleased with what he had seen of this young engineer and his outstanding work, "Absolutely, take the afternoon off, you deserve it."

Kenneth called Grandmother.

"Of course, Dear, you can drop by here anytime."

***

She greeted him with a hug and kiss on is cheek, same as always. "Come in, let's go to the kitchen I was just starting a grocery list, I'll fix you a glass of tea."

"Thank you, Ma'am."

Moving her list aside, sitting the tea on the table, she sat down, "What's on your mind on such a nice afternoon?"

"Grandmother, Sara will be graduating soon."

"Isn't it wonderful?" Grandmother beamed; her smile showed even more enthusiasm.

"Absolutely, it's terrific. But there is something I must ask you."

"You seem so serious, Dear. How may I help you?"

"Grandmother, I love Sara, deeply. I am here today to ask your permission to ask her to marry me. I pray you will say yes and pray harder that she will say yes."

Grandmother sat in silence for a few seconds as she studied the young man across from her. Finally, she stood and walked around the table, "Stand please."

Kenneth stood; the older lady embraced him.

"My most dear Kenneth, I can think of no other person I would rather have marry my Sara than you. I have come to love you. Combined with my love for you, I have also come to respect you as a wonderful man. Yes, you have my permission to ask Sara to marry you."

Breathing a sigh of relief, "Whew! I thought when you said nothing for a few seconds you were going to run me out of here. I love you, too!"

The laughter was easy, and good. They sat for a while and enjoyed talking.

***

Three weeks before Sara's graduation. Grandmother was so proud of Sara and thankful to the Lord for how far her

493

granddaughter had come. She had also prearranged with Kenneth that she would be out one evening, visiting with her attorney friend.

Sara answered the door, "Hey, come on in, Grandmother is gone to visit her friend, but we have some leftovers, hope you're hungry." They hugged and pecked lips.

She was done with classes and already had her grades. Sara had done extremely well and would be graduating with honors, she was ecstatic! She and Kenneth talked of their day as they enjoyed dinner. Kenneth helped clean up afterward and poured them both another glass of tea.

"Sara, there is something we need to discuss, please."

"Something wrong? You look so serious."

"Nothing wrong, may we go sit in the living room?"

"Sure." Sara was wondering what Kenneth was being so serious about.

They sat on the sofa, "Sara, do you remember the night we met, actually for the second time, at the Christmas program?"

"Yes."

"Something happened that night that I could not explain."

"I remember you got suddenly quiet and dizzy."

"There was more to it than that, but it took me a long time to figure out what it was."

"What was it?"

"Love."

"Huh?"

494

"When we shook hands, when I touched your hand, I felt as if everything in the world had suddenly become right, I was overwhelmed with a peace, a warmth, and a chill. It was the most wonderful feeling I had ever experienced, and I didn't know why until a long time afterward. Sara, when I touched your hand, I fell in love with you, I just didn't know it then."

"Oh My." Kenneth was the second person who had told her the same thing.

"Kenneth rose from his seat, knelt and took the ring from his pocket, "Sara Imogene Blackmon, will you honor me by becoming my wife?" He opened the box containing the ring. The reaction he saw was not what he had expected. Sara began to cry.

**

"Kenneth, I am in love with you but there is much you need to know before I accept. I will ask you to remain silent and let me talk. It may take a while and if, when I finish, you leave and I never see you again it will break my heart, but I will understand. OK?"

Kenneth pulled up a chair and sat directly in front of Sara. "You have the floor."

"For the next two hours Sara talked in detail about everything, beginning with Craig, and then her infatuation with a boy named Oliver. She told of Oliver asking her to his place and her wanting to go there again after having been with him the day before. Sara was as forthright and honest as she had ever been. She told of the humiliation of the trial, how she was made to look like a slut, which she had been for ever having gone to the place with a boy she'd met on the beach that week. She told of the gang rape and beating. Sara talked of breaking Craig's heart, that she had sent him away and how he had been listed as Missing in Action in Viet Nam, later presumed killed in action, but that she would always be in love with him. Kenneth was told that she

495

could never have children. For the whole of two hours she spilled her soul to the man who had just asked her to marry him. The only other people she had opened up to so freely to had been Craig, Zoe and Grandmother."

Then, there was silence.

Kenneth stood, "Excuse me for a minute please."

Sara sat alone with her thoughts, she may have just lost the person, the other person, she was in love with.

He walked slowly back into the room.

"With all the coffee I had at the office and the tea I've had since I got here, I've been about to bust the last 30 minutes."

Sara looked at the man, she was dumbfounded.

Kenneth once again knelt on one knee, "Sara Blackmon, if you're through talking, Will you be my wife?"

She held her left hand for Kenneth to place the engagement ring on, then leapt into his lap, knocking them both to the floor. Sara kissed Kenneth and said over and over, "Yes! I love you!!!

***

Grandmother was a sneaky old dame. She had raised a window slightly open so everything could be heard as she was standing outside, looking in and eavesdropping. This had been way too good to pass up! Her heart was filled with love and joy for Sara and Kenneth.

***

Only a few months prior to Sara and Kenneth becoming engaged, word had been received that Craig was MIA, a month later he was presumed Killed in Action. No remains were ever recovered.

Sara graduated in 1969, she and Kenneth would plan their wedding for April of 1970.

A Bridal Shower was planned by Sara's friends, Minnie was invited and would attend. After all the guests had left, Howard walked into the house and presented Sara with a very special gift.

The wedding was beautiful, the bride beautiful and glowing with happiness, the groom thankful for the wonderful woman with whom he would spend the rest of his life.

Leaving the church for their honeymoon, the bride and groom climbed into the beautiful 1965 Black Chevelle Super Sport and pulled from the parking lot.

As he'd handed Sara the keys all Howard had said at the shower was, "He loved you, I think he would have wanted you to have it."

***

Nobody recognized the old man who had quietly eased into the sanctuary and sat alone at the back of the church. The old man smiled.

CHAPTER

53

He could hardly believe his luck when his orders were that he would be sent to Germany, most of his basic training buddies were going to Viet Nam following AIT. Andy's orders would first send him to Camp Knox, Kentucky, he would learn to drive a tank, then on to Germany where he would guard West Germany against a communist invasion that would never come. For the most part he would find himself drinking beer and screwing the gorgeous local women. The time Andy served in the Army were the best times of his life.

Following Army life Andy came home to South Creek, he was still detested by most of the people his age, so he zeroed in on the younger more gullible women. Needing a job, Oliver's dad avouched for him. Oliver's dad had purchased a great portion of McKinney Construction when the original owner found himself up to his ass in gambling debts, a recommendation from Mr. Watson carried a lot of weight. Andy got the job and began the process of learning to operate heavy machinery, he became very good at it.

Widow Brantley was an attractive woman in her middle 40s. She'd married a man 20 years her senior who, it was rumored, had passed away while his wife was astraddle of him in bed one evening. People joked he had died with a smile on his face. Mr. Brantley had left his wife several hundred acres, a very nice home and a couple of barns. There were cattle and horses, she loved the horses but there wasn't enough open pasture to suit her, land needed clearing. A call was made to McKinney.

The area Mrs. Brantley chose had a small spring fed stream running through one corner of the property, the stream had never gone dry and would serve the small lake, pond, she wanted to include in the project. The entire area was mapped out, work would begin with the loggers, no need to burn perfectly good lumber and pulp trees when someone was willing to pay for them. Next, a rather large front end loader would come in and dig up the stumps, many of the hardwood stumps would also be sold, the burled woodgrain within them was highly prized by woodworkers, others would be burned. Once the land lay bare the machines would begin shaping and smoothing it into something beautiful, the dam for the lake would be built. After all this was complete the land would be sown with grasses chosen which would be best for the animals to graze upon. Fences would be built; it would be gorgeous.

Work progressed, the loggers finished the tree removal and left the site. As usual the land was a mess following this kind of work, next was stump removal. A rather large front end loader was delivered one afternoon by a tractor trailer rig. The driver and a young man who'd followed him in his car began removing the binders and unloading the machine. Mrs. Brantley was watching the process and took note of the handsome young red headed man with the deep dimples and nice, slim physique, she introduced herself, both smiled as they shook hands. The spark of attraction was immediately lit in both.

Mrs. Brantley enjoyed spending hours at a time each day watching the work, and the young man operating the machine. Friday of the second week's work, workday done, Andy was walking to his car, waiting there was Ella Brantley. "If you don't have any plans for the evening, I have cold beer and two nice T-Bones ready for the grill. I hate to dine alone. Care to join me?"

"Ma'am, I don't have any plans but I'm kinda dirty and sweaty. I would enjoy having dinner but I need to go clean up first and change clothes."

"Not to fear, you can shower at the house. As far as clothes, we would often have people my husband did business with who would unexpectedly have to stay over for a night. We have closets full of clothes with varying sizes, I'm sure we can find something."

"Yes Ma'am, sounds very nice, I appreciate it."

Andy watched her every step as she walked to her vehicle. Ella's walk was akin to a well rehearsed dance, every move perfect.

The only other house Andy had ever been in as nice as the one he was currently standing in had been Oliver's parents' home, this place was beautiful. He was shown to a large bathroom just off a very large bedroom, in the bedroom were two closets, a dresser and two chests of drawers, Ella told Andy he should be able to find something to wear. Dinner would be very casual, shorts would be fine.

Following his shower Andy found a nice pair of shorts, a pullover shirt and a pair of brand new low top sneakers that fit perfectly. He went to present himself for dinner with the lady of the house. Ella heard him coming, she turned and saw him, "Perfect, you found something, I thought you would. Care for a beer?"

"Beer sounds great, Thanks."

"Let's go sit by the pool a while, we will also be having dinner out there, too nice an evening to waste."

Following an hour of chit chat, and mild flirting from both sides of the conversation, Ella fired up the grill and checked the potatoes she had baking in the oven. Dinner was delicious, best

steak Andy had ever eaten. Salad was made from items fresh from the garden. He had no idea what kind of cheese Ella had used on the baked potatoes, but it was something he wanted more of.

Andy helped clean up and put the dishes in the washer. Ella thanked him and told him to help himself to another beer, they went back outside. After a while Ella suddenly stood, "Let's take a swim!"

Caught off guard Andy mentioned he had no swimsuit. Ella pulled off her shirt and bra, "Honey, there is nobody way out here except you and me, you don't need a swimsuit." She dropped her shorts and panties just before diving into the water.

Andy had seen women older than himself naked, he had never seen a woman Ella's age with a body so perfect. Now that he'd seen it, he wanted to touch it. Within seconds there were two nude bodies swimming in the pool.

***

He'd been married briefly to a pretty girl younger than himself; Andy had gotten her pregnant, a baby girl was born. Three years into the marriage the girl had grown sick of him chasing every skirt that would raise, she'd left him. Her parents had shunned her, most friends wanted nothing more to do with a "girl with a reputation", she was struggling. A young single mother trying to support herself by doing housework for people who would allow her to bring the baby to work. She received no financial help from Andy, he never came to visit his child.

***

Andy never knew how much fun sex in the water could be, the buoyancy of the bodies allowed things that gravity didn't allow on dry land or in a bed. Sitting on the side of the pool while reaching down to fondle floating breast was terrific, especially

while receiving some of the best oral sex he'd ever had. Ella finally suggested they move to the master bedroom.

Following twice having orgasmed, Andy needed time to recover. Ella reached into the bedside table and produced some things she enjoyed, some buzzed, some oscillated, one rather large one thrusted, she came twice more by the time Andy was ready to play again.

Exhausted, he left the house around midnight. The house being at the back of the property, the well-kept gravel driveway was very long.

Andy didn't see the man hidden in the trees who watched as he drove past.

***

For two months Andy and Ella enjoyed themselves whenever she wanted, one day she made a proposal to the red headed young man, "Andy, I really like sex with you, I think you like it with me, I want to make you a deal."

"I'm listening."

"You move in here, you will have your own room, I will replace that clunker you drive with a very nice pickup truck of your choice, good food and drink all you want. You can even go out and meet with those little hotties I'm sure you have lined up wanting some of you, as long as you use condoms and don't give me something I do not want. You will have all the nice clothes you want. But you will be at my beck and call, anytime I want to be serviced you will provide such service even if you have something else lined up, if I want you, you will cancel other plans. You will keep your job and go to work every day. With no expenses, and being a kept man, all of what you earn can be spent on anything you so desire. There may, on occasion, be invited another person, a man or a woman, you may or may not be invited to join the fun,

503

the one thing you will not do is become jealous of it whether participating with us or not. Deal?"

"I love the idea. Deal! How you feeling right now?"

"Horny!"

Life became very good for Andy Bohannon. It just wouldn't last long.

***

Amazing, the damage a ping pong ball filled with C4 explosive can do, add BB's to it and the watermelons were ripped to shreds, Gary was impressed.

For six months Gary had been making recon trips, learning Andy Bohannon's habits and learning the lay of the land. He'd learned there was a well kept road on the timber company's property adjoining the parcel where the new pasture was being built, the road was about twenty feet from the property line. Perfect, not too far to drag an unconscious man.

Gary learned that on Saturday evenings it was on schedule that Andy drive to Hiram's Bar where he would spend the evening. On more than one occasion he'd seen Andy come out of the bar with some young girl and get in the pickup truck, the girl would disappear. Andy would light a cigarette, lay his head back and enjoy. Eventually the girl would reappear, usually wiping her mouth on her sleeve.

***

In the sub-basement Gary had all he required for what he was about to build, a miniature bomb with a radio controlled detonator.

First thing to do was split the ping pong ball very carefully, he used a scalpel. With the use of quick drying glue, the entire

insides of both halves of the ball were lined with BBs and set aside. It had taken much experimentation to build the detonating device small enough to be placed inside the ball and leave enough room for the BBs and C4, enough C4 to do the job. The battery had been his biggest challenge, finally one of the contacts on his list shipped to him the tiniest batteries he'd ever seen, they worked beautifully. Work went about assembling the detonator and imbedding it in the premeasured sphere of explosive, this was then glued into half the ping pong ball, installation of the battery and final placing of the other half of the ball would take place while the victim was unconscious. The last thing Gary wanted was to have a completed bomb in his truck and it pick up some form of wireless signal, completion would take place at the scene.

Friday night Gary loaded all he would need for the next day, the day would be a long one. Gary would leave home at 2AM, the drive would take around ten hours.

The truck was well hidden from view on a lesser used timber company road, not far from where Ella's driveway met the main road. Branches had been placed over and around the truck, in case the timber company overflew the property. Gary picked up his small pack and the suppressed .22 magnum, he eased into the woods and waited at the most perfect hide he had located on prior recon missions and still make the shot required.

Shortly before dark Gary heard a car slow and turn off the main road, there were two young men in the car as it passed him. Loud music was blaring, both men were sipping beers as the car drove by. This was a new development, always expect the unexpected, Gary could abort or wait and evaluate the situation, he chose to wait.

Sun setting, it became more dark than light. Gary heard the pickup truck coming down the drive, he'd learned the sound of its custom exhaust. At just the right moment Gary fired the small

caliber rifle, about 100 feet down the driveway the truck stopped, the left front tire flat. Andy turned the ignition off and exited the vehicle, he was cursing as he kicked the tire, never aware of the man in the woods no more than ten feet off the driveway and moving toward him.

Andy had not seen the muzzle flash because of the suppressor, nor had he heard the mild "Pop" of the suppressed rifle because of the loud country western music on his radio.

Gary had initially planned to strike as Andy was removing the flat, the two young men who had come past earlier changed his plans. He would wait until the spare was installed, make his attack and throw Andy into the truck, he would transport him to the other area, finish his mission and hike back for his own vehicle. Improvisation! Gary did not want Andy's truck to be blocking the drive when the young men left.

Andy tightened the last lug nut on the wheel, glad to be finished with the task, he let the truck down and pulled the jack from beneath it. Just before he stood there were two blows, one to each side of his neck, Andy fell to the ground unconscious. Gary had landed the blows to Andy's carotid arteries perfectly; he jabbed a syringe into the shoulder and pressed the plunger. The mild sedative would keep the victim asleep for the time required to do what had to be done. Shouldering the sleeping man Gary tossed him into the bed of the truck, started the truck and drove to the timber company road behind the new pasture.

Andy had been living well and had gained a few pounds, Gary was breathing hard when he'd finished dragging the limp male to the tree at the edge of the pasture. He placed the man in a sitting position, his back against the red oak, took two sets of handcuffs and connected them to Andy's wrists and the length of chain around the tree. From his pack Gary removed the two halves of the ping pong ball, inserted the battery in its tiny holder then

506

glued the ball together with the quick setting glue, he waited a few minutes for the glue to cure then opened Andy's mouth and inserted the ball. A small alcohol swab was used to dry the moisture from Andy's lips, they were then glued together with the same adhesive that had been used on the ball. The head was tilted forward to prevent the man from choking. Gary waited.

About an hour passed when Andy began waking, he was moaning and trying to raise his head. Gary waited another half hour then used the smelling salts he had brought. Waving the salts under Andy's nose the man snapped his head back in rebellion from the foul scent, Gary did it again and slapped the man, "Wake up man, we need to talk!" Andy's eyes opened wide, he tried to speak but his lips wouldn't work, and something was in his mouth! Startled, his eyes moving in all directions he finally saw the man. "Hi Andy, it's been a long time."

"I know you can't talk but you can nod or shake your head to the questions I am about to ask you. Do you understand?"

Andy nodded.

"Andy, the reason you cannot speak is that I have glued your lips together with some very strong cement, OK?"

The man nodded.

"Now, I will ask some questions and try to help you understand what this is all about. You need to know these things."

"First, I am now known as Gary, in times past I was known as Craig Kirkland. Does Craig Kirkland mean anything to you?

Andy shook his head

"So, you've forgotten my name. I'll remind you in a few moments. Do you remember Sara Blackmon?"

Andy looked at the man, his eyes very wide.

"I knew you would remember her; this is about what you and your other sadistic friends did to her. By the way, I was at Oscar's funeral and saw you there. I am who killed him."

Andy began to struggle, he thrashed about until he had no more strength to try and escape. Having fallen over, Gary lifted him back into place and asked, "You Finished?" Andy simply looked at the man.

"OK, I was also at the trial where you and the rest of the ilk were set free due to your friend Oliver's dad having bought off the judge and jury. I remember as you stood in front of Sara, you grabbed your crotch, humped and waggled your tongue at Sara. Then, all of you laughed at Sara, her parents and at me, at least until I hit Oscar, then you ran like scared puppies. At that moment I decided someday I would kill you all and would have that day if they hadn't stopped me, I was her boyfriend, Craig Kirkland. With me? Remember me now?""

Andy nodded.

"Because of what I learned from Sara's testimony, from the medical reports, and from what she was able to tell me, there are two of you who will be so mangled your coffins will have to be closed, Oscar was one, you are the other. Clements will probably be shown at least some mercy if I learn from him what I think I will, his body will be fine for an open casket, and Oliver, well I have a special surprise for him. So, Andy, you can see I've planned this out well. Agreed?"

The doomed man simply nodded.

Taking the transmitter from his pack he showed it to Andy "This little device is really very neat, I push a switch to activate it, then push another switch which will send a signal to a detonator that will set off a small explosive charge. Surrounding the charge are a couple hundred BBs. All of this has been installed into a ping

pong ball that is currently inside your mouth, behind your lips that are glued shut."

Andy looked at the man with eyes begging for pity.

"Sorry Andy, you hurt Sara and showed no pity to her or her family, nor me. None will be shown you."

"Now Andy, I've not tested this on any human being, only on watermelons. Once it's done, I will come back and take a quick look at the results, knowing the results may serve me well in my current vocation. I'm moving off a safe distance now, you have time to pray if you want to, I highly suggest it. My only regret is that you will not suffer. Bye, Andy."

Gary moved into the woods and behind a large tree, he pressed the switches.

In a millionth of a second the detonator set off the explosives sending the BBs in all directions, out the face, up into the brain and soft tissue, cartilage and bone disintegrated. BBs entered the brain and instantly destroyed it, many exiting the back and top of the skull. From the eyebrows down there was nothing but a gory void where a face had once been, for some reason the blast had directed itself somewhat toward the left, that side of the head was missing. Andy Bohannon was very dead, his face and parts of his head scattered around a semi circle 50 yard radius.

Andrew Bohannon would die on August 7, 1976. Thirteen years exactly from the date of the gang rape of Sara Blackmon.

It took an hour of careful movement to return to his truck. Gary removed the branches covering the vehicle and left the area well before daylight. He had a long drive ahead.

***

Ella Brantley had invited the two young men who had been working on the new fence to spend time at her pool that evening,

she figured if Andy was going to have fun she might as well do the same. When she heard the sound, she had her mouth full of one nineteen year old young man, she was on her elbows and knees, the other young man was taking care of business from the other end. She thought "Oh well, probably someone poaching a deer."

***

The man delivering the seed for the pasture arrived early. Looking across the field he saw something looking like a man sitting next to a tree, he went to examine. What he saw caused him to leave four eggs, bacon and two biscuits on the ground. After he recovered, he ran to the main house and asked to use the telephone. Ella let him in and quickly drove to the new pasture, seeing the body she knew it was Andy, she'd bought the clothes. Ella instantly knew what the sound had been.

***

One month later Alice Chance Bohannon heard a knock on the door of her beat up old mobile home. The man introduced himself and told her he was an attorney, he asked if he could come in. An hour after hearing all the man had to say and signing the papers, Alice and her daughter got in the car with the man.

The house was quaint, two bedrooms, one bath, wood siding and a small screened in front porch. The house was in a nice quiet neighborhood and it belonged to Alice, no mortgage, paid for. A monthly allowance would be provided as long as she was single, the child's education paid for if she went on to college. Alice cried tears of joy.

***

The closed casket funeral was attended by few, Andy's mother and a very few old friends.

***

510

The letter was short.

Gary,

Nicely done! Good work!

Dyke

CHAPTER

54

Fourteen years after almost emotionally destroying Sara on the witness stand Sam Bartolli decided to expand his business. Having a cousin who was a "Made Man" with one of the Chicago syndicate families, Sam gave him a call.

"Roberto, long time no talk. How've you been?"

"Hey Sammy, Good in the windy city. You OK?"

"Doing great here but need a vacation. Thought I might fly up and visit with you all soon. I would love to see Aunt Maria and discuss the possibility of getting with you on some business ventures, if you're interested."

"Always interested in new ventures. Mom would love to see you as well, she misses talking to your mother, rest her soul."

"Great, give me a few days to tie up some loose ends and I'll book a flight and make reservations for a place to stay."

"Just let me know when you will be here. No need to reserve a room, you can stay with us, we've plenty of room and Mom will enjoy keeping you well fed with her wonderful Italian recipes."

"Thanks, talk soon."

Craig listened to the recording. Chicago was nice this time of year.

**

The flight was very nice. Bartolli was picked up by Roberto and taken to see the family he'd last seen at his mother's funeral. Warm greetings were extended by all, especially by Aunt Maria, Sam had been her sister's only child and he held a special place in her heart.

Once inside, wine was served while everybody caught up on everyone's current lives, memories were exchanged, most happy, a few sad. The house had the aroma of something wonderful, Aunt Maria had already begun preparing a surprise meal. Good homemade Italian food was something Sam had missed dearly since his mother passed away.

The home was located a few miles outside the city in a very nice wooded area. Not far away, on a hill in the woods, sat a man. The man had a camera with a long lens, photos were taken. All Craig had to do now was install a few devices, strategically located, by which to hear and record conversations. Recon had begun.

**

Roberto waited two days before talking business. He'd let his mother and sisters enjoy their nephew and cousin. Business was one thing; family time was another.

"So, Sammy, how's the lawyer business these days?"

"It's OK. You know I only have one client and other than that thing with his son a few years ago it's typically boring. Pay is alright but I've been thinking about raising my standard of living, expanding the work I do."

"I heard about the kid, what became of the girl?"

"Last I heard she was in Knoxville."

"What kind of work you do for Watson."

"Make sure all his real estate deals go smoothly, not all are straight forward and sometimes research has to be done in order to convince the seller he wants to sell, and at the price offered. I also clean up some money on other deals the cops might not find to be exactly up to their standard of legal. I've set up a couple of companies and run funds through them and some off shore accounts."

Roberto laughed, "Clean up money huh?"

Sam grinned, "It's the best kind."

"So, what did you have in mind? You mentioned business ventures."

"As I said, I have a desire to better my standard of living and would enjoy taking on some work for you and your associates. If, of course, they're interested. I was thinking having an attorney all the way down in Georgia, quite some distance from their home network, could serve to ease some of the attention their local attorneys might have on them."

"That isn't a bad idea. But you know I'll have to take the idea to my superiors."

"Absolutely, wouldn't have it any other way."

"OK, let's get back home. If I keep you away from Mom very much longer, she'll be mad. And, Sammy, everybody likes clean money."

The devices in the car had performed perfectly. Every word sent to the transmitter located on the vehicle's chassis, every word transmitted to the man's ears and recording device. Craig smiled as he began hoping the "superiors" would accept the offer.

They would!

Craig flew home two days later, after learning Bartolli would be in Chicago for another week. The man's office and home needed visiting, there would be more conversations to be heard.

***

Howard Kirkland had grown up poor, he'd worked hard to overcome a life of poverty. The man had often spoken to his son about many times not having shoes to wear and the times he did have shoes they had been hand me downs and already worn out. Howard, as a child, made himself a promise that someday, somehow, he would never have to worry about walking anywhere barefoot again. He achieved that goal.

Years later Howard heard of an all volunteer, non profit charity that, by donations, would help less fortunate children have new shoes once a year. Having checked on the validity of the charity Howard began, when he could, to make donations to The United Craftsmen Children's Shoe Drive.

Craig began devising a plan. The plan wouldn't happen quickly, but, if it worked out the way he was hoping, the charity

his Dad had contributed to just might, possibly, benefit from Bartolli and those he would soon be working for. Time would tell.

***

A month later, Roberto called Sam, "Roberto, Good to hear from you."

"Sammy, how's the weather in Georgia? If it looks good, I might come visit."

"Weather is great, can't beat Spring of the year in Georgia."

"Great, I'll book a flight. Can you pick me up in Atlanta?"

"Absolutely, just let me know the date and time."

***

Craig was listening to the conversation currently taking place in Bartolli's car. Following greetings and pleasantries Roberto got down to business, "I spoke with my bosses, they've agreed to give your proposal a try."

"Outstanding, I'll not disappoint them."

"It's better to never disappoint them."

"Understood."

"OK, Sammy, before I continue, we need to discuss your fee."

"Usual fee is ten percent of the initial investment, plus cost, travel fees and such. Most of the time, not always, interest and dividends will result in a return greater than the fee and costs. For example, last year, just one initial investment of 1 million, cost my investor my fee of 100 thousand plus 5 thousand my costs. Three months later I placed into the client's accounts a total of One Million Three Hundred Thousand Dollars, every dollar clean as a whistle. Now, remember, world finances change, I cannot always

515

promise such a return. On occasion something might happen that could cause just breaking even to be considered good. But I can show how every dollar, both received and returned was handled.

"OK, sounds reasonable."

"Another thing, since your people have decided to give me a try, I will not charge any fee on their first investment, except costs."

"Excellent. Are you prepared to begin immediately?"

"Yes."

"OK, Sammy, we're going to start small. Yesterday a man flew down and checked into a hotel in Atlanta. The room is a double, there is a key waiting for you at the desk. You will find a gym bag in the room, inside the bag is One Hundred Thousand Dollars cash. The man is already back in Chicago, you will find his key inside the Bible, top drawer of the bedside table closest to the window. With me?"

"I'm with you."

"You are to spend the night and check out, tomorrow, turn in both keys, his and yours. I will stay at your place a few days. Once you get home tomorrow you can show me around, what I saw flying in was very lovely, I'm looking forward to seeing more."

Bartolli would be on the road a lot today. After dropping Roberto off and showing him around the house he left for a return trip to Atlanta. Bartolli entered the room and found everything as Roberto had described. He checked out the next morning, gym bag and money in his trunk, he enjoyed the drive home.

The safe in the basement was very substantial, the best money could buy. Once the money was in the safe, Bartolli and Roberto packed some soft drinks and headed out for a tour of

Bartolli's beloved Georgia and a visit to the best barbeque joint in the southeast. Roberto had never known what real barbeque was, he loved it.

"Tell me about the case that involved your client's son. I read about it in the papers and saw it on the news."

"What you want to know?"

"Were the kids guilty?"

"Oh yeah, Guilty as hell. I'll tell you this, if the shoe was on the other foot and that pretty little thing had been my daughter, I would have been calling you asking for some family assistance. I mean, she was over sexed, there is no doubt, but those four boys did rape and beat her that night. They're all a bunch of assholes, especially Oliver, my client's spoiled ass kid. One of them, his name was Oscar, was such an asshole someone killed him, blew his head damn near off with a high powered rifle. They've no idea who did it. Another one by the name of Andy was found with his face blown off by some kind of explosive, he was a smart ass little prick. But I did what Watson paid me to do, bribed the judge, paid off and threatened the jury, made the girl look bad and got the boys a not guilty."

A few days later Roberto boarded a flight home to Chicago. Bartolli went to work moving money, he'd divided the money into separate amounts and deposited into separate accounts and paper businesses. Two months later Bartolli checked into the same hotel where he'd initially picked up the gym bag. The next day the same man who had delivered the gym bag left the hotel with a bag of money totaling One Hundred Fifteen Thousand Dollars. Roberto's friends were satisfied.

Over time the amounts of cash gradually increased into the millions of dollars.

***

For more than a month Bartolli was either on an airplane, crisscrossing the country, or in a rental car driving the trips that took less than a day to drive. He had lost count of the hotels he'd spent the night in, always leaving with either a gym bag or suitcase filled with cash. By the end of the three weeks his safe held the largest deposit to date, Fourteen Million Dollars. The lawyer had his work cut out.

In the time since he'd begun working for Roberto's bosses Bartolli had not only laundered close to a billion dollars for them, he'd also managed to earn them a profit that averaged twenty percent, the people liked him. He had worked his ass off and was badly in need of a vacation. Having never visited the homeland of his ancestors, Bartolli decided to visit Sicily. Plans were made, he'd be gone for three weeks.

Bartolli's home was equipped with the best security system and surveillance equipment money could buy. The attorney never had any concern about leaving his home or the money located there.

Had he known Craig Kirkland now, all those years since he'd last seen the boy who'd shed so many tears in the courtroom, Bartolli would have had many concerns. Craig was the last person on Bartolli's mind as he boarded the airplane.

***

Craig had listened to live and recorded conversations between Bartolli, Roberto, mob bosses and many others. He had watched hours of recorded visual films made by equipment he had access to that wouldn't be marketed for another ten, or more, years. The equipment had been created by geniuses who worked for The Group. With other equipment the same people had created there wasn't a security system in the world Craig couldn't override and manipulate, stuff so futuristic it never ceased to amaze him. With all the years of self-training and that

518

training having been enhanced through time in Vietnam and by instructors at the group, Craig could move almost anywhere and not be seen nor noticed.

He'd been in Bartolli's home several times, making test runs, practicing. Twice Craig had opened both safes, Bartolli had needed to have a second one installed. There had been no need for safe cracking expertise, although he possessed it, he simply turned the dials. The camera's he had installed had shown the man putting in the combinations, Craig had memorized the numbers, including that Bartolli always left the dials set to the number 1 after he closed and locked either safe.

On this night Craig had knowledge how much mob money was deposited in the safes; he had heard Roberto and Bartolli making the arrangements. But he wasn't sure how much Bartolli had in his own personal safe. Enough money can become a heavy load, Craig calculated a minimum of three trips inside and out in order to empty the safes. It'd be a long night.

He entered the house at 11 PM, first order of business was to remove all the equipment he had concealed in Bertolli's house. Craig left nothing behind for anyone to discover. Next, he opened the safes and began placing the stacks of bills into the oversize backpack he'd brought, it would require five, not three trips, mob money plus more Bartolli personal money than he'd considered. But he always allowed for the unexpected, always expect the unexpected. Craig also found a stack of Bearer Bonds in Bartolli's safe. This was a pleasant surprise, more money, less weight.

Craig closed the safes and locked them, turned both dials to the number 1. The drive from South Creek, Georgia to Lexington, Virginia would be a long one, too long after a hard night's work. Craig would stop and rest at a safe place owned by a man he only knew as, Gee. Gee didn't talk much, he usually only asked two questions, "What do you need?" And, "When do you need it?"

Gee was expecting Craig, he never spoke, simply handed Craig a key to the small house next door.

***

Home, always good to get home, Craig pulled the truck into the garage and closed the door. He had money to count. Four hours and two pots of coffee later, having counted the funds twice, Craig was satisfied with his final calculation. Cash plus bearer bonds came to a total of Thirty Three Million Two hundred Thousand Dollars. Bartolli had done well. What Craig was looking at in front of him was more than enough. For the next two weeks Bartolli would purchase many high dollar items, cars, boats, even a private airplane and beach house in Panama City, he just wouldn't know he was doing it.

During his six month training for The Group one of the things taught that Craig had become an expert at was the art of forgery. He could sign anyone's signature and no expert in the world could tell the signature wasn't that of the original person. Craig went shopping, spending Sammy's money, signing Bartolli's name.

***

Sam was exhausted when he got off the plane, it had been a long flight, he checked into a hotel and spent the night in Atlanta. Even after sleeping ten hours the drive home was tough, jet lag was doing a number on his entire system. After a strong drink, Bartolli lay down in his own bed and slept another eight hours.

Waking, Sam made coffee and a light breakfast although it was the wrong time of day for the meal, he felt improved. A shower made him feel even better, he decided to go downstairs and start dividing his latest receipt. Time to get back to work.

Bartolli checked the dials, both still set to the number 1, he opened the safe containing the mob money. The safe was empty, Sam gasped. But it was OK, he had enough personal money in the

other safe to cover it, he felt suddenly nauseous upon opening the other safe. "Oh My God!"

CHAPTER

55

In a panic, Bartolli grabbed his keys. He ran every stop sign and traffic light on the way to his office, there were records there, secret records he hoped had not been stolen. The money being stolen was bad enough, the records would make it all much worse.

He burst into his office, going straight to the safe, nothing had been touched. Everything in the safe was as he'd left it. Bartolli's next move was to call Roberto.

"Hello."

"Roberto, Sam."

"Hiya Sammy."

"Roberto, something very bad has happened."

Hearing the desperation in his cousin's voice, Roberto asked what.

"The money is all gone."

"What the fuck you mean, gone?"

"I mean it's all gone. Someone stole it from my safe."

"When?"

"I don't know."

"Why the fuck don't you know?"

"Well, it had to have happened while I was on vacation the last three weeks, in Sicily."

"You mean to tell me you left fourteen million bucks in your safe unattended for three weeks? You stupid son of a bitch!"

"But, I, But..."

"Just shut up. I'll call you later."

Chills ran up Roberto's spine, he'd been who had avouched for Sam. Roberto also carried responsibility, he made a call, asked for a meeting, it was of utmost importance.

**

Matteo 'Matty' Cancio was happy being second in command of the organization. He had worked his way up and the position demanded much respect. Matty liked Roberto and decided to meet with him other than send someone, it'd been a while since he had talked to the up and coming, young man. The day was very pleasant, Matty liked hotdogs and knew a guy in the park who made the best. Roberto was told where to be, and when.

"Roberto, always good to see you"

"Matty, it's an honor to see you again."

"Come, I'm hungry, let's get a bite. How is your beautiful mother?"

"She is very well, Sir. She will be pleased you asked about her."

The two men sat on a bench away from the other people in the park, they enjoyed their meals.

Finished eating, Matty turned to Roberto, "Now, tell me what is so important that you required a meeting?"

"Matty, do you remember my cousin in Georgia?"

"Well, I never met him personally but know of the work he does for us and I am extremely pleased with his results."

"Sir, he's had a problem with the last deposit we made to him."

"Explain."

"Someone has stolen the money, all of it."

"Well, this is bad news. How did it happen?"

"The best we know now is that someone came into his house while he was on vacation and took the money from his safe."

"He keeps it in his home?"

"Yes sir."

"Careless."

"I agree, Sir."

"You are to pack immediately and go to Georgia. Find out what you can and keep me informed, I will take your calls anytime. Roberto, you realize that amount of money, although to most sounds like a lot, is only a very small percentage of what the organization earns."

"I do."

"But stealing from us has consequences. We can never allow people to think they can get away with such a thing. Understand?"

"Yes Sir."

"You will find out who took it, call me and I will instruct you how to handle it."

"Yes sir."

***

The telegram had arrived while Roberto was meeting with Matty, it was sealed in an envelope. Roberto rushed home to pack and book a flight to Atlanta, his sister gave him the envelope.

I am a friend. Your cousin has recently been noticed making several expensive purchases. There is a safe deposit box in the name of Samuel Bartolli at First Savings and Loan of The South in Atlanta. Combination to box is 0807.

0807, August 7th.

Roberto's mind was spinning, he would be asking Sammy about his recent expenditures and they both would see what was in the box. Roberto thought, "Holy Mother, surely Sam knew better than to rip off the people he was working for."

The flight booked, Roberto made the call, "Sammy, pick me up at the airport at 2AM."

***

"Sammy, how'd they get into your house?"

"I don't know, I checked everything. There is nothing broken so they didn't force their way in."

"Don't you have a security system?"

"The best money can buy. No alarms were set off, even the surveillance recordings don't show anything."

"And the safe? What kind of condition is it in?"

"Perfect, and there are two, both perfect."

Sammy pulled into the hotel parking garage, Roberto got out, "Been a long day, we got some talking to do but I want to get some rest first, clear my head."

The men checked in to adjoining rooms. Roberto was asleep in seconds.

Sammy didn't rest, wondering what else would be asked of him.

***

"Good coffee, Sammy. Thanks for ordering."

"You're Welcome."

"Sammy, stealing from the organization is serious business, it carries some serious consequences. I've been told to find out who did it."

"OK, where do we begin?"

"First Savings and Loan of The South."

Just before entering the building Roberto said he would do the talking; Sam was to do as told. Bartolli was suddenly very nervous.

Roberto approached a nice middle-aged lady who asked if she could help.

"Yes Ma'am, my cousin has been keeping some items here for me in a safe deposit box while I've been out of the country. We'd like to get them please. The box is in the name of Samuel Bartolli.

The lady stepped away, Bartolli looked at Roberto, "I don't have a safe deposit box here, never have."

"We'll see."

The lady returned with the sign in book and the original signature card to compare signatures. Sammy signed where she told him. Signatures were compared. "We have a match. Your box is 1122 Come with me gentlemen."

1122, November 22nd, the day Craig had asked Sara to go steady.

The lady used a key to unlock the bank's portion of the lock. After showing the men where they could have privacy, she left. Roberto rolled the roller combination's numbers to read 0807, he heard the click of the lock releasing.

Inside the box were several receipts and titles for some very nice automobiles, one for a private airplane, two for boats, a deed to a house in Panama City Florida and a deed for property in Savannah. Everything requiring a signature had been signed by Samuel Bartolli, including a bank account in the Cayman Islands.

Sam's blood ran cold, the man had never known fear as he was experiencing at that moment.

"Sammy, this is not good. You have some serious explaining to do."

"I swear, Roberto, I do not have a clue. If you think I stole the money, why would I have called you?"

"You're a smart guy Sammy, maybe you called to throw me off."

"I swear on my mother's grave; I did not take the money."

"Sammy, let's take a trip to Savannah."

***

The property turned out to be a warehouse, a very nice warehouse. The door once again required a combination. Not

527

knowing what else to try, Roberto put in the same numbers as the safe deposit box, 0807. It worked. "You need more imagination, Sammy."

Inside the warehouse were a 1936 Cadillac LaSalle in mint condition, a restored 1935 Duesenberg SSJ, a 1960 Bentley S2, a 1963 Corvette Split Window, a 1958 Corvette Convertible and a 1960 Porsche 356B T5 Roadster. There were also two boats, one was a 35-foot boat intended for salt water trolling, the other a beautifully restored 1928 26 foot Chris Craft Triple Cockpit mahogany boat. All matched the receipts Roberto was holding. "One thing for sure Sammy, you got good taste."

"Roberto, I've never seen any of these cars or boats. I swear! I swear!"

"Well, Sammy, Let's get back to your place. I got a guy who can do some checking on things for me. I also want to talk to that bank in the Caymans."

The drive was long, and quiet.

***

The money in the account had been wire transferred from a bank in Savannah into an account in the name of Samuel Bartolli, Ten Million Dollars.

Roberto's contact had done some checking, all vehicle, boat and property purchases had been done over the telephone and overnight mail. Paperwork had been delivered to an address in South Creek, Georgia, Bartolli's address.

"We got problems, Sammy. I got to make a call."

Craig had removed all the equipment from Bartolli's house, but he'd tapped the phone at a junction box down the road.

One hour after Roberto had talked to the Cayman Island bank, the money had been transferred, thirty minutes later it was transferred again.

A lot of kids would be wearing new shoes soon.

***

"Sammy, it hurts me deeply to know you would do what you did. You didn't have to; you were making a lot of money. You didn't have to steal from us."

"Please, Roberto," Bartolli pleaded, "Please believe me, I've been set up."

"Why would someone set you up?"

"I don't know, I've caused a lot of people a lot of trouble over the years. Maybe it has something to do with what took place at Tybee, the rape, maybe it was one of the girl's relatives." At that moment, Sammy remembered the look he'd seen on Craig's face, the cold eyes, "Or maybe it was the boyfriend, You remember I told you about Oscar being shot, I bet it was the boyfriend, Craig something, can't remember his last name!"

"Sammy, it's been what, fourteen years? He would have come for you before now. You're reaching too far."

Roberto and Sam were back at the warehouse where the cars and boats were stored, it was night.

Two men walked in.

Nobody in the building had any idea there was a man in the building next door, watching, recording everything.

***

"Sammy, because you and I are related, I am not expected to do anything to you, that's what these men are here for."

Bartolli felt a sudden shiver of fear, he peed his pants. Sam knew he was going to die, he hoped it would be fast.

It wouldn't be.

Sammy was stripped naked and tied to a chair. The men took turns hitting him until he passed out.

Sam woke to a pain so agonizing he'd never thought could exist. One of the men was injecting small amounts of acid under his fingernails with a syringe. Sam tried to scream but he had been gagged, a ball of rags in his mouth. One of the men grinned as he asked, "Good stuff, huh, Sam?" Bartolli could only watch as his fingernails disintegrated before his eyes.

The men waited, allowing the acid to do its work. Sam was crying. One of the men left the building, he returned later with sandwiches and drinks. As the acid was doing as expected, the men sat and casually enjoyed lunch. Sam fainted.

The next day, Sam lost his toenails the same way he'd lost the nails on his fingers.

By the end of the third day, Sam had no ears.

On the fourth day the men told Roberto what was about to happen. Roberto requested the men do it with no pain. Sam was, after all, his first cousin. An IV was started, something injected, Sam fell asleep.

The pain was excruciating in his legs. Sam woke to see, on a table in front of him, feet. Sam knew the feet were his, he smelled the awful scent of burned flesh. Looking down confirmed what he already knew. There were very tight tourniquets around his legs, the ends of his legs burned, but his feet were no longer attached to his legs, they were on the table. Sam begged for death.

"Soon."

For two more days pain was inflicted on the crooked attorney in such ways Sam wouldn't believe possible to survive. The use of needles, knives, power tools, chemicals, salt and hand tools. The men were experts. By the end of it all Sam had no teeth, he was blind, had no feet, hands nor ears, his genitals had been burned to a crisp with a blow torch. There was only one thing left to do.

Roberto leaned close to his cousin, "Sammy, you ready?"

All Sam could do was nod, yes.

Sam heard a chainsaw being started.

All ever found of Sam Bartolli was his head, sitting atop the mailbox at his home.

***

A letter addressed to Roberto was delivered a month later.

Dear Roberto,

I am very happy to know you took care of Sam. Good Job.

Something you might want to know though, is Sam didn't take the money. I took the money, I set him up. You and your people did the rest.

What you also didn't know is, I have most of his last week on film. Everyone's face is on film. Everything you did to Sam is on film. Conversations of you talking to Chicago are on tape. There area also hundreds of conversations recorded over the last couple of years between you, Sam and your bosses.

I imagine about this time there are several FBI agents enjoying listening to those conversations and looking at the films.

531

I visited Sam's office two days after you arrived in Georgia. There were a lot of records in his office safe concerning money transactions. The FBI accountants must absolutely be having orgasms.

Have a Nice Day

**

Roberto walked out the back door, sat down on a loveseat in the garden, he put a pistol in his mouth and pulled the trigger.

There was no way he would go through what he'd seen Sammy put through.

**

Bob Carpenter was a bear of a man, huge in stature, his heart just as big. Bob had been asked to take over the charity when its founder had lost his life in an automobile accident. The charity helped children, The United Craftsmen Children's Shoe Drive.

The man had worked diligently and for hours on his own time, volunteering his time and efforts to make the charity grow that it could help more children.

The attorney knocked on the door, "Are you Mister Bob Carpenter?"

"Yes sir, what can I do for you?"

The attorney introduced himself and informed Bob of his anonymous client who had read about the Shoe Drive and would like to donate, all Bob had to do was sign a receipt, he did.

Handing over the envelope the attorney waited as it was opened.

Bob first gasped for air, then he fainted.

The first thing Bob saw upon coming back around was the very frightened face of the attorney, "Sir, are you OK?"

"Does that check read Ten Million Dollars?"

"Yes sir, it does. Are you OK?"

Before the man could react, Bob wrapped him in the biggest hug he'd ever experienced!

"Sir, my client sends his best wishes that his donation will be of help."

***

Craig opened the letter.

Gary,

I understand you have decided to involve yourself in the legal profession.

Glad to hear things are getting A-Head.

Good Job,

Dyke

CHAPTER

56

He answered the car phone. A package would be delivered in two days.

The delivery truck arrived; package delivered.

In the basement of the house the package was opened, it contained a key to a Richmond Airport locker.

A lovely day, nice day to take the GTO for a drive to Richmond.

***

The small travel bag had been opened in the basement of the house. Mostly containing junk, old clothes, rags, to disguise it as being full, at the bottom was a manila envelope.

The man in the photo appeared to be in his early 40s, nice looking, dressed well and in style, other photos of the man fishing, playing tennis, normal activities a man might enjoy, were included. Close examination of the direction of the belt buckle, the necktie knot and the arm wearing the wristwatch showed the man to be left handed.

The letter gave last known location of the man. A note, "Gee can provide you with any supplies you may require."

***

The house sat on a slight rise, surrounded on all sides by wide open fields where the land had been cleared and made into pastures. Cattle lazily grazed and enjoyed sunning themselves, occasionally wading into a pond to cool off.

The closest cover were the woods about a quarter mile away from the home, through the woods was a ten feet tall electrically charged fence. Guard dogs roamed the area inside the fence.

Once, while up a tree with his spotting scope, the wind had suddenly changed direction. Three of the dogs put their noses to the air and moved in Craig's direction. Only the fence kept them at bay as they began to bark an alarm. He couldn't fault the dogs;

they were only doing as they had been trained. Armed men, alerted by the dogs, came from the house and drove across the field for closer examination. Craig left the area in search of a better place to do that which he'd been ordered to do.

The road to the house was over three miles long, Craig had examined every inch of it. There was one bridge over a small creek. This would be where it would happen.

For two weeks Craig, dressed in his Ghillie Suit, had watched and waited. The only times the luxury armored vehicle left the house it had the target inside and was always escorted by two other vehicles. All other traffic had been people in pickup trucks either taking care of errands or farm workers coming to work or heading home after their day was done.

Craig put in a call to Gee, he placed his order.

***

The assassin had no idea what the man had done or was planning to do. He had simply been issued an order the man was to die, and it was his job to get it done.

Harrison Thomas Wellborn III had once been a member of the Elite British MI6 but had become disenchanted with the way things were done and had gone rogue. Wellborn had made the decision the world needed to be made right, in his opinion, and damn it all if it caused another world war. After all, he thought, the world needs a good dose of chaos on occasion.

Wellborn had made many contacts through the years and for this job he reached far into the underworld for just the right people, those who could build very special devices of the nuclear type. Money had been acquired through likeminded people and five devices the sizes of a suitcase had been ordered.

Intelligence had determined that the devices were to be placed in five cities and would all be simultaneously triggered. New York, San Francisco, Moscow, Beijing and London wouldn't stand a chance in hell of recovering for many decades. Millions would die instantly, those would be the lucky ones. Depending on the wind, hundreds of thousands of others would suffer lingering deaths from radiation poisoning delivered from the fallout.

Unknown to Craig, there were ten other people around the globe who had been assigned ten other targets.

***

The packages from Gee arrived two days after having been ordered. It would require Craig three days to transport his equipment and set up the ambush. Then, he would wait.

The third day of watching the road finally resulted in the heavily armored vehicle and its escorts arriving at the scene.

The lead vehicle crossed the bridge. The instant the armored car's front wheels were on the bridge Craig pressed the small remote control switch; the bridge disappeared from under the car. Nose down, its front wheels in the water, there was no quick escape for the vehicle's occupants.

Both the lead and trailing vehicles stopped, armed men quickly exiting and looking for someone to shoot, they saw no one.

Craig hit the clackers as rapidly as possible, four Claymore mines exploded. All six men from the lead vehicle fell, dead or dying. The same process was followed with the other clackers and all the people who had exited the trailing vehicle were killed.

Cautiously, Craig approached the vehicle. He heard Wellborn screaming for someone to "DO SOMETHING!"

The driver's door opened, the man had a pistol in hand, he was hit with half a magazine from the Uzi Craig was carrying. A second man attempted to escape from the front passenger side, the 9MM rounds from the remaining half of the Uzi's magazine ripped into the man. Craig dropped the magazine and clicked another in its place.

Knowing people at the farm would have heard the noise, Craig worked methodically, but quickly as he attached the shape charges he'd made from the bottoms of champagne bottles and C4 plastic explosive. One attached to the fuel tank, one each on the car's rear windows, the armoring would never stand up to that which it was about to be subjected.

Craig looked in the window and saw Wellborn, he confirmed his identity, the belt buckle, wristwatch confirmed the man in the car to be left-handed. Craig compared the face looking back at him to the photo he had memorized. Harrison Thomas Wellborn III was seconds from meeting his maker.

From a distance Craig hit the switch. Looking back, the last thing he saw in the flames was the burning silhouette of a man who had thought world chaos would have been a good thing, no matter how many had to die. He'd been wrong.

The search for him was organized quickly, on the ground and in the air. But, even those in the helicopters couldn't locate a Ghost who didn't want to be found.

***

The water from the jug in his truck was warm but tasted good after his ten mile hike through the woods, Craig savored very swallow. A stop at a small store a few miles down the road for gas and snacks, he set out on his way home, but with a detour.

Craig had a new mission to plan, it would begin with a visit to a church in Huntsville, Alabama. The minister of the church was Pastor David Clements.

CHAPTER

57

If any description of pity would be shown it would be exhibited toward David Edward Clements. David would still die but his death would not leave his face marked or torn away, his death would be as painless and instantaneous as possible, he would know it was about to happen and be given time to prepare himself and to have a last prayer for his soul.

***

David had done well in seminary and had earned a reputation as a good minister. He was a gentle, soft spoken, caring man but could on occasion bring forth a voice that could preach Hell Fire and Brimstone to the congregation of Baptist, something they needed every now and then. Working as youth minister at a couple of churches, then associate pastor at two more, David prayed daily for a church of his own, a church with a sign out front stating David E. Clements-Pastor.

June Holloway was not a pretty girl, somewhat buck toothed and had to keep her hair long so it would cover her slightly oversized ears, but she was cute and had a nice figure, a smile that was always genuine and would cause anyone who saw it want to smile back at her. Above all, she was very nice, always courteous, if one word could describe her it would be "Bubbly." David had met June is last year of college, the two hit it off and began dating steadily. Although David had little funds by which to take her very many nice places, he was working two part time jobs to meet his college tuition, they spent many days and evenings together on river banks or picnicking, just loving being with one another. They often spoke of David's dream of having his own church and how wonderful it would be. Although they were falling in love, would kiss and hold one another, there was never any mention of sex and neither made any moves that would indicate any desires for sex. June was a virgin and would be until her wedding night, as far as she knew, David was as well. Although David still prayed daily for forgiveness for his participation the night of August 7, 1963 at Tybee Island, he never told June about it nor that he'd had sex. Others who knew him now had no idea what he'd done.

A year after college David and June were married. The ceremony was very nice, but small, mostly family and very close friends. Fourteen months later a baby boy was born to the proud couple. Finances were tight, but they managed with some help from the church and David's parents. Three years following the birth of their son they welcomed a beautiful baby girl into their family. Two years later a search committee whose own pastor had retired visited the church where David was associate pastor, his own pastor knew beforehand of the visit and asked David to deliver the Sunday sermon. David had prepared a beautiful sermon, the committee asked him to visit and preach at their church the next week. The family made the trip to the small church located a few miles outside Huntsville Alabama, David

delivered the best sermon of his life, a vote was taken, a salary amount offered and accepted. The sign in front of the church the following week would read, David E. Clements—Pastor. His dream had come true, his prayers answered.

Life was very good for David and June, the children were beautiful, church membership was increasing monthly, so much an annex had been built and his salary increased. Life was perfect, until the day he checked the mail and found a newspaper his father had sent from South Creek. The headline read, "OSCAR TOMLINSON KILLED". The article went on to explain an ongoing investigation, a high powered rifle, killed at home, body discovered by friends, no suspects yet, the things such articles usually said so soon after a crime had been committed. At first a chill ran up David's spine, he wondered if it had anything to do with the Blackmon girl, maybe someone she knew, a family member possibly? Then he stopped and remembered that Oscar could be a bully and there was probably a list of people from his past who wouldn't mind hearing of his demise. David tossed away any thoughts of the killing being associated with Sara; he threw the newspaper in the trash.

As the church membership grew so did the funds in the bank account. A committee began a search for some property, somewhere to build a few small cabins and pavilions to be used for picnics, retreats or even for families to hold reunions, all of which could be rented to other churches or families for their use and the rent would help cover maintenance costs. Property was found and the complex built, it became one of David's favorite places and on Thursday of each week he would go there alone and write his next sermon in the peacefulness of one of the cabins. He especially liked it during Winter when there was never anyone around.

Time had passed since his father had sent the newspaper, there was another in today's mail. The small-town newspaper

541

headline shocked David, ANDREW "ANDY' BOHANNON FOUND DEAD. This time the article included gruesome comments, explosives, face blown off, body identified by fingerprints, ongoing investigation, no suspects. It was what David read about halfway into the article that made his heart begin to race. "Police have stated they are looking into the possibility that Bohannon's murder may be connected to the still unsolved murder of Oscar Tomlinson and the rape trial of Sara Blackmon." The article then mentioned the trial and listed all four boys' names. "The police have been in contact with authorities in Alabama and are requesting their assistance in the investigation." There would be no hiding it from June any longer, tonight they would talk.

David called June and asked her to let the kids visit a neighbor for dinner tonight, that he and she needed some time alone, he had something to discuss with her. June stated, "You sound so serious, something bad happen?" All David could say was "yes, we need to talk about it."

He was sitting alone at the kitchen table when she walked in, his face in his hands. June poured two glasses of iced tea and sat down next to her husband, she put her soft hand gently on his arm, David patted her hand and looked at her. "I am about to tell you something about me you never knew, you never would have suspected, something awful. What I about to tell you is something I did a long time ago that I ask God daily to forgive me for. I hope you can also forgive me once you hear the story." By now David was crying, tears flowing down his cheeks as he continued, "June, do you remember our wedding night, how awkward we were the first time we had sex?"

"Yes." She was blushing.

He continued, "You were a virgin, I know that. You thought I was a virgin as well, I wasn't. There had been one night several years ago that I have regretted every day since, I lost my virginity

542

that night in the most awful way imaginable." David was sobbing now, his body shaking, trying so hard to continue talking, trying to tell the wonderful woman he loved so very much the hardest thing he could ever admit to her. It was several minutes before David could speak again, finally, with his wife looking at him, touching his arm so kindly, he spoke, "It was a Friday night, August 7, myself and three other boys committed gang rape, physical and sexual abuse on a beautiful 16 year old petite girl while we were at Tybee Island. Her name was Sara Blackmon and we did things to her that night you can never imagine, you could never imagine me doing. I discovered today two of the other boys have since been murdered, you can read the newspaper article if you want, my name is in it."

June removed her hand from his arm and with her other hand covered her mouth, she was shocked! June then did something she had never done nor considered doing, never thought possible of herself, she drew back her hand and slapped David so hard he almost fell from his chair. He looked at her and told her, "You've no idea how much I deserved that."

"Tell me everything you bastard!"

For the next hour David talked, June listened. He detailed how Oliver had enticed Sara to the cottage the boys were staying in, that Oliver's father owned, how at first Oliver and Sara began having sex while the rest of the boys were hidden in the bathroom watching. He then told of how they had quietly come from the bathroom and Andy started touching Sara's breast, she'd had her eyes closed as Oliver was giving her intercourse, how Sara then opened her eyes and at first seemed OK with Andy being involved then suddenly struck by the realization of what was happening saying, "NO". She had tried to stop but they held her down. David said, "I began not wanting to be a part of it and told the others to let her go. They taunted me and told me I was a wimp. I will never forget Oscar telling me, "Your mouth says one thing, the front of

your pants is saying you want it", I had an erection." David continued, "They spread her legs while one held his hand over her mouth, I was told to pull out my penis and stick it in her, I did as he said. And I orgasmed in her."

The room was quiet for a few moments.

June told him "go on."

"Sometime during it all something happened to her, it was as if her mind had left her body, she went into some form of stupor, her body went limp, eyes open, the only time she made a sound was when one of the boys would scream at her asking if she wanted this or that, if she didn't answer they would hurt her, slap her, pinch her breast, they would do something to hurt her until she would simply say yes. I will never forget the sound of her voice, almost as if it were a recording, she really had no idea she was saying anything. Oscar had found a small garden trowel, he poured cooking oil on the handle and rammed it into her anus then he told me to get myself some of that tight little asshole, he had it ready for me. I committed sodomy on a poor defenseless teenage girl. After a while the realization of it all hit me, I came somewhat to my senses and went outside, I cried. I could hear the other three laughing. I have no idea what else they did to her or put in her. A while later they all came outside and began making fun of me. We had all started drinking beer earlier in the day, they continued the drinking. I went inside and saw her laying there, she was pitiful. There was blood and semen coming from her vagina and anus, her face splattered with semen, some of it mine, a cut on her lip was bleeding. Her breasts and buttocks were bruised and she had a black eye. I somehow got her to the bathroom and put her in the tub, just as I did, they all came back in, shoved me out of the way, they all urinated on her then went back outside."

June was crying now but told David to "Keep talking you sonofabitch."

544

"I bathed her the best I could, her hair was very short, so it was easy to clean. I dressed her and used some washcloths in her pants to absorb some of the blood. She could walk, barely, if assisted but her mind was still in some form of stupor. I helped her back to the road, I hoped she could find her way back to where her family was staying."

"When I returned to the cottage the others were packing the car and told me to get my things, we were leaving. I did as I was told. All the way home to South Creek they all continued to threaten me if I ever said a word about what had happened. Knowing these boys, I feared for my life."

"Someone found her the next day. Someone else recognized her as the girl who went into the cottage with Oliver the night before, they knew we had all been there. The police picked us up, we all kept our mouths shut and Oliver's dad bailed us out. There was a trial, but Oliver's dad is very wealthy and powerful, he bought off the judge and jury."

"Now two of the four of us have been murdered. I remember her having a sweetheart ring, I remember her boyfriend being at the trial, I wonder if it could be him who is killing us all off. I think she had a brother; it could be him. I left South Creek immediately after the trial. Now South Creek has found me, something I had hoped would never happen."

June took the newspaper and silently left the room, she read the article then burned the paper. Surely nobody this far from South Creek Georgia would ever learn of this. Two years passed with no more news, life had slowly gotten back to almost normal, except for intimacy. June refused to let David touch her in any kind of sexual way, she found what she sometimes needed with the owner of the printing company that provided services for the church.

***

545

Typical North Alabama weather for January, drizzling rain, temperature in the low 40s with enough wind to make it seem colder, it was the third Thursday of the month. The kerosene heater combined with the fire he'd built in the cabin's fireplace were beginning to make David feel better, coffee in the percolator smelled wonderful. He took the items from his brief case, his Bible, legal pad, two reference books and placed them on the table with his pencils. David always wrote his sermons in pencil, it was better to erase than scratch through with a pen if changes were required, neater and easier to read.

The coffee was ready, David poured a cup and added his usual cream and sugar. He began writing this week's sermon. The topic this week would be forgiveness, a subject dear to David's heart. Engrossed in his work he had not heard nor seen the man standing in the doorway between the bedroom and where he was sitting.

"Hello David."

For some reason David wasn't startled, he simply looked up and saw the man with a handgun pointed at him. He closed his books, lay down his pencil and dropped his head. The man slowly moved across the room, walked behind David, poured himself mug of coffee then came around and sat across from the minister.

"I'd like to talk with you a while." The man sipped his coffee. "Good coffee, Thank you."

David raised his head and looked first at the gun, it wasn't big, but the suppressor made it look menacing. Then at the man, one look at the man's eyes made David shiver. "Yes sir, how may I help you?"

"David, we're going to talk about something that happened a long time ago involving a girl named Sara, something that involved you and your friends."

"May I ask who you are?"

"Surely, a man should know to whom he is speaking. These days I'm known as Gary, I was once known by another name, Craig Kirkland."

David thought for a second, "I've seen the name, or heard it, I can't remember where."

"Do you read the newspapers? Especially the weekly list of "Nam" casualties?"

"Yes! I remember, wasn't Craig Kirkland killed in action a few years ago? I always remember the men from Alabama."

"The papers also list those missing. Craig Kirkland is Missing in Action, presumed dead, his body will never be recovered. You might also remember me from another place, although I'm not sure you would remember my name from back then."

"Where might that be?"

"The trial, I was sitting with Sara, my parents, her grandmother and her parents. I'm surprised you didn't remember my name from then, especially since I was made to testify for the defense."

"You're her boyfriend!! I do remember!!"

"Correction, was."

David's eyes widened, "You killed Oscar and Andy!?"

"Yes."

"How? The papers never said in detail."

"Oscar was shot in the head with a 30.06 rifle, Andy died as the result of a small amount of C4 explosive in his mouth doing what explosives are meant to do."

"Oh, My Lord."

"David let's talk. You know I was at the trial. What you do not know is that I have ways you would never understand if I told you to access other things, other things being police reports, medical reports, those sorts of things. I also know what Sara told me after it all took place and she was in the hospital, at least what she could remember and could talk about."

"Are you going to kill me"

"That's the plan."

"Then why should I tell you anything?"

"Two reasons. First, you want to, you want to open your heart and spill your soul to me. Second, what you tell me will directly determine how you will die, if your body will be recognizable or not, if you will die painlessly or if you suffer. The decisions will be based on what you tell me. David, to sum it up if what you tell me confirms what I already suspect, your family will have opportunity to say their last goodbyes to you with the casket open, the others did not have such opportunity. By the way, David, you and I enjoyed a very nice conversation a while back."

"How? What?"

"Remember the nice older Irish gentleman who stopped by the church while you were cutting some roses to take home?"

"Yes."

"That was me. Thank you for showing me around the church, the inside and grounds surrounding the buildings are very lovely."

"You? How?"

"I've learned a few things the last few years that are very beneficial to my current occupation. Disguise being one of those things."

"What is your occupation?"

"I'm an assassin."

David was speechless, he sat with his mouth open and stared at the man.

"Snap out of it, David!"

"Did she tell you I helped her? Cleaned her up?"

"She told me what she could remember, said she pretty much blacked out sometime while she was there, she said angels took her away, but she remembered bits and pieces of someone bathing her and helping her get dressed. From what I have seen of you, I believe that person may have been you. Tell me about it, all of it."

For the next half hour David talked, he talked about the entire week. David told of how he and the boys and first met Sara and how Oliver had spent time with her alone every day and had taken her to the cottage the day before. David told of how the boys had planned how they were going to have him lose his virginity, how Sara would be at the cottage again that night. David then went into great detail about the evening it all took place, what they had done, what he had done and how Sara had suddenly gone into a stupor, but it didn't matter they all still had their ways with her young body. David told how they, all of them, had sodomized her multiple times, of the things never intended to be used for sexual pleasure as they were brutally shoved into the girl's body. He told of coming in to check on her afterward and seeing her, how pitiful she was, the blood and semen coming from her, the semen on her face, even the feces between her legs, she had finally soiled and wet herself. David spoke of the

indignity of the others urinating on her when she was in the bathtub. He told of finally cleaning her as best he could, dressing her and taking her back to the main road.

David then spoke of his family and how much he loved them.

"You are blessed with a beautiful family, David, I hold no ill will toward them, I am honestly sorry for June and your children. In about a month June will be contacted by a man, an attorney, the attorney has no idea who I am other than a wealthy secret benefactor who occasionally helps widows and orphans. A trust will be set up which will take care of June until she remarries, for life if she remains single. The fund will also take care of your children until they reach the ages of 18, if they choose to attend college the fund will cover the cost involved. Much the same has been done for the others."

"Thank You." David began crying, he sobbed harder than he ever had. Craig allowed the man his grief.

Finally, after a while, David's sobs began to subside. Craig asked him if he would like to pray, and would he like another cup of coffee, David said yes.

As David was praying aloud Craig got up under the pretense of pouring them both coffees.

Finished, David said "Amen." Craig said "Amen," then shot David twice in the back of the head with the suppressed .22 caliber pistol, he reached around and moved the Bible, not wanting it to be soiled by the blood. Craig picked up the brass, washed his coffee mug and put it in the cabinet, he turned off the heater and percolator, the fire was already dying down and would burn itself out soon. The handgun, suppressor and brass would be given to the Tennessee River.

David had been the only one Craig had ever briefly considered allowing to live. The thought had been fleeting and

was forgotten as quickly as it had appeared. But, because of what he'd done for Sara after the fact, it was decided his casket would at least be open at the funeral. This was the only mercy Craig would ever exhibit any of the people who had inflicted such pain on the girl he loved.

Leaving by the back-door Craig Kirkland, aka: Gary Wayne Graham began, in the rain, the two mile walk through the forest to where he'd parked the rental car. The rain would wash away any sign of his ever having gone through the woods.

***

One month later June received a phone call from an attorney who requested a meeting with her at her home, she agreed. The news the man brought was truly a blessing.

***

In Nashville, Tennessee, two weeks after David E. Clements body had been discovered, a newspaper would be delivered to the business address of Oliver Calix Watson. There was no return address, only postal markings showing the Alabama newspaper had been mailed from Minneapolis, Minnesota. Oliver had received two other newspapers, on two other occasions, both sent from different cities.

This newspaper included a note typed on the index card stapled to the front page. "Oliver, I'm looking forward to meeting you."

***

The letter was short.

Gary,

Nice to hear your work is making excellent progress. Well Done.

Dyke

CHAPTER

58

It had been dangerous and tedious work to tap Oliver's' phones both at his Nashville office and his home. But the work had been worth it, the information was invaluable. Travel schedules were the bonus.

Craig had been following, listening to, photographing and filming Oliver for nearly a year. Patience was a must in Craig's work but by sending the newspapers of Oscar's, Andy's and David's deaths he had essentially warned Oliver of his impending doom. In many ways Oliver became more cautious, in others, more paranoid. Paranoia can often work to the oppositions advantage.

A hunter's every move is very slow, he realizes while he is moving it is more difficult to see any prey which may also be moving. The eyes scan, but do so in a smooth, calculated slower than normal movement, often stopping to study something suspicious, possibly to detect the flick of a deer's ear, or the one foot that may be slowly pawing at an acorn. Even the prey become aware of the hunters in the area and learn quickly to move slow in order to prevent being detected or to detect the hunter first. But as with any living creatures, both man and animal can allow anxiousness or fear to create a paranoia, once it strikes, it is difficult to control. What may be thought as careful routines can often become unwanted habits, movements become more rapid, and the eyes dart from object to object, person to person, and most often fail to see things and people in between. A paranoid person can be, and often is, his worst enemy.

It had been over two years since Oliver had received the last of the three newspapers, the one reporting David's murder. For months he'd been fearful anytime he was outdoors or even walking past a window with the curtains drawn back. After a while he thought the fear had subsided, when, in reality, it had morphed into paranoia, Oliver failed to recognize the change, the difference, his became a habitual state of paranoid. The hunter took notice and his stalk began.

Not only had Craig tapped the phone lines, he'd also tapped into the home and office security systems and included several hidden devices of his own as well. He could literally follow Oliver and his family's lives on TV screens or on recordings which could be observed anytime he liked. Oliver and his family were being watched and recorded 24 hours a day, 7 days a week. And none of them had any idea.

In his occupation Oliver traveled many places, one of his favorites was Chattanooga. Not only did the business own many properties and was expanding in the area, Oliver also enjoyed the company of some young women there, one of whom was a young lady who reminded him so very much of the girl he'd met at Tybee Island in 1963, if their pictures had been side by side most would have thought them to be sisters. Yes, Oliver liked this girl a lot! What Oliver didn't know was that someone else had taken note of his Chattanooga trips and the amazing similarity of the young lady and the 16 year old version of Sara Blackmon, the likeness was so striking it had taken Craig by complete surprise.

Although the girl looked so very much like Sara had when she had been sixteen, she was 3 years older, her name was Lucy. Oliver had helped her find a job with one of the several local companies he owned. Lucy had been itching to move out of her parents' home and had told Oliver of this. As it happened, Oliver owned a small parcel of land with a quaint little home on it his wife knew nothing about. He would be more than happy to "rent"

the house to the young lady for a small monthly fee. The small monthly fee was that she would be available to him anytime he was in Chattanooga, paperwork was only a formality.

Craig heard the call, "I'll be coming down on Friday, arriving mid-morning. After checking in at the hotel I'll pick up some steaks and go on out to the house."

"Do I need to leave work early?"

"No, I have several calls to make and will be tied up with business all afternoon. You stay at work till quitting time. I know about how long it takes you to get home and will have the hot tub up and running when you get there. We can relax a while before dinner. I'll leave later and stay at the hotel Saturday and Sunday, I have potential customers to entertain on the riverboat this weekend. Big money people from Europe who requested me personally."

"OK, going to be great seeing you."

Every word was being listened to. The man listening smiled, "Perfect!"

***

Carrying the groceries, wine and whiskey, he unlocked the door and entered the house, placing the paper sack on the table he went to get a small bag containing a few clothes. The wine needed chilling, lobster and steaks needed refrigerating, he returned to the kitchen. All he heard was a "pfft", then felt the sting as the dart struck home. He spun around, the man hit him. All went dark.

Within minutes, the truck that had been parked behind the house pulled onto the road and headed toward Anniston, Alabama. In the back, laying bound, gagged, drugged and covered with a tarp, was Oliver Calix Watson, Multi Billionaire.

***

Gradually, he began to wake, the shot he had been given contained strong chemicals. Eyes closed, head slowly rolling side to side he seemed to dream about coffee, yes, he could smell it. Next came the chill, he was cold, he groaned. Slowly, ever so slowly, he raised his head, briefly opening his eyes, he thought he saw a man, then eyes slowly closed again, so tired, so drowsy.

On his wrists were shackles attached to cables routed through holes drilled into the arms of the metal chair. The cables then ran through pulleys attached to the legs of the chair and then to two manual boat winches, one each left and right about five feet from the chair. The chair was welded to what looked like train rails. Both ankles were shackled with chains welded to the rails.

About 30 minutes later he could hold his head up and eyes open, speech was still slurred.

"Just take it easy, you're getting there. I know you're confused right now."

With each passing minute he was becoming more alert, and frightened, he realized he was naked, humiliated to be sitting naked in front of another man who was being so casual about everything.

"Care for some coffee, I put a pot on when I saw you beginning to wake. Cream and sugar, am I right?"

"Yes, where am I?"

"Oh, let's chat a while, get to know one another, actually I already know a lot about you. I think we need to get acquainted more then I will explain everything to you in detail. Cigarette? I brought your brand." Coffee and a lit cigarette were placed on the small tray.

As the man stooped next to the winch on the right side and released the catch Oliver snatched his arm but there was only so far he could pull, it stopped abruptly with just enough slack he could reach his face.

"It has a stop on it, it'll only allow enough slack for you to eat or drink."

"Now, enjoy your coffee and cigarette."

"For a kidnapper, why are you being so nice?"

"You consider someone who would shackle you naked to a chair as someone being nice?"

"Well, no. I need to pee."

"Go ahead. I guess with the anxiety and such you failed to realize the bottom of the chair has a hole in it about the same size as a toilet seat, there's a bucket underneath. More coffee?"

"Yes. Who are you?"

"We'll get to that later. First, I want to talk about you, you've done well in life. Being a crook like your father has reaped you many of the same benefits, even more. Good Job, Well Done."

"Feels like something is pinching my nutsack."

"Oh, that. Pay attention, I'll explain. See that device sitting on the shelf over there? You might remember old timey telephones that had a crank on the side, it generated an electrical charge when the crank was turned. The device on the shelf is something similar, except I built it and it puts out a stronger charge of electricity than the old phones. It won't kill you, but it'll get your attention. Allow me to show you."

"SWEET MOTHER OF GOD PLEASE DON'T DO THAT AGAIN!"

"The wire from it goes to a clip I attached to your balls. Hurts doesn't it?"

"OH JESUS!"

"Now, you are Oliver Calix Watson, son of Thomas and Alena Watson. You are the CEO of Watson and Associates, Real Estate and Mortgage Lenders. You have a beautiful wife and two children, boys, live on a 500-acre piece of prime property not far out of Nashville where you enjoy raising and training horses. You are 35 years old and a multi billionaire. I must tell you, as good as your father was, you are far better. Oliver, you are brilliant beyond description, damned shame you didn't put your intellect to work doing good instead of bad. You would have still been extremely wealthy but just think of how much good you could have done. By the way, before you and I finish our business together you will give me your account numbers."

"Bullshit I will!"

The man turned the crank, several times.

The bucket did its job.

***

"You OK?"

The shocks to his genitals had been so strong it took Oliver several minutes to recover, he was still breathing heavily. He simply nodded his head.

"You're doing all this for money? I can pay you whatever you want, just let me go."

"Not about money, at least not for me. Everything I take from your accounts, stocks, whatever, will be given away. I have no personal need of your money."

"If not for money, why? Who are you? Where are we?"

"One question at a time, where we are! When I was a boy, I discovered this place, it's an old abandoned mine, we are deep underground. All my life I continued to be drawn to this place, it was amazing, but I continued to return and explore. A friend was with me when I first discovered the entrance, but I came back and found the area we are now located, you and me. I never told my friend about it, curiously I felt he didn't need to know. For the last few years I've returned many times and brought in the equipment you see here and made all accommodations in preparation for your arrival. You, Oliver, are the guest of honor."

"So, you got me here, what are you going to do with me?"

"First, I intend to torture you, gain the information concerning your finances. Then it's my intent to kill you. You may well be begging me to before I do."

"My God Man, You're a maniac."

"Frankly, Oliver, I may be the sanest person you will ever have met."

***

"Hungry? I am. I make a mean omelet."

"Yes. Who are you?"

"In due time. While I'm cooking, I want to tell you more about yourself."

"Sure, why not. Not like I'm going anywhere, some maniac who takes great joy in shocking my balls has me chained to a chair!"

The man laughed, "Your arrogance is funny."

"You enjoy speaking down to and using women, including your wife. Your hobby seems to be rough sex with younger women, some still in high school. They don't report what you do because you pay them to stay quiet. You ever thought about fishing for a hobby? Very relaxing. Anyway, what you do not realize is, you are not alone in your sexual desires, your wife tends to enjoy other men when you are away on business. I'll show you films later of both of you."

"You have pictures?"

"And movies. Oliver, I cleaned your pool one day while you were away. Your gorgeous wife was sunning in her pink bikini, she was horny and gives a terrific blowjob. Typically, I wouldn't have accepted her offer, not my style, but did just so I could tell you about it and watch your reaction. I wanted you to experience knowing the woman you love had someone else's dick in her mouth!"

"You son of a bitch, I'm gonna kill you!"

"Oliver, look around, you have it all backwards."

Oliver struggled with the shackles, to no avail.

"Eat your omelet before it gets cold."

The rest of the day was spent talking about Oliver and the mine. Twice he was asked for account numbers, Oliver laughed and received shocks to his genitals.

Later in the evening drinks were poured from a bottle of bourbon.

"I may be planning to torture and kill you, but there's no need to be rude. Enjoy your drink, we have a fun day planned for tomorrow. You will also learn who I am."

After tidying up, the man said goodnight and walked further down the mine shaft to an area he'd prepared for himself. Oliver had long since given up any ideas of escaping the shackles. He didn't struggle.

Oliver woke to the smell of fresh coffee and bacon frying. He peed and didn't care.

"Hope you slept well. How you like your eggs?"

"Over easy."

Three eggs, bacon and coffee were placed on the tray. The cables given slack in order that Oliver could feed himself. Once finished his arms were pulled back down tight to the arms of the chair.

"I know you haven't been awake long but I'm going to let you sleep a while longer. I have some things to prepare for our day and want them to be a surprise for you." Oliver felt the needle enter his shoulder. In seconds, he was asleep.

An hour passed; Oliver began to awaken.

"Good stuff isn't it? I gave you a mild dose."

Suddenly Oliver's eyes sprang open wide! He was face down, strapped and chained tightly to a table with his legs spread wide.

"What is in my ass?! Oh God, it hurts!"

"Oliver, I happen to be very handy with my hands. I can build almost anything I choose to. In this case it is an apparatus with a fake penis attached that simulates the thrusting of a male having intercourse. What you feel now is the fake penis, a very large fake penis, in your rectum."

"Oh God, Oh God. Hurts!"

Pulling a chair in front of Oliver, the man sat down, looking at Oliver eye to eye.

"I was once known as Craig Kirkland, most who know me now call me Gary. I am a very highly trained assassin and am employed by people you could never imagine exist. But it is not they who have sent me on this mission. This mission, you, will be the culmination of much work which has taken place since 1964. Years of planning which have included military training, first hand stalking and killing people in the jungles of Viet Nam, then further training by others who are experts in the art of death. The idea was conceived the instant you, your father, Andy, and Oscar laughed at Sara Blackmon, her grandmother, her parents, and me following the trial your daddy bought and paid for. David did not laugh, he was shown at least some mercy, you will not be shown any respect nor mercy. Understand?"

"Oh Lord, Oh God, I remember, on the beach she said she had a boyfriend, his name was Craig, then heard your name again when you were sworn in. I remember how Bartolli ripped into you and Sara, how you tried to get at him, how you knocked Oscar down. Please forgive me, please, please!" Oliver was crying.

"David told me something I had never known. Oliver why did you, Andy and Oscar have to pee on her?"

"I don't know, I don't know, we were all drinking."

"Oliver, did Sara cry? Did she beg you and your friends to stop hurting her?"

"Yes, YES SHE DID. I'm so sorry, please don't do this!"

"Feel what Sara felt! Oliver, get fucked!" Craig hit the switch.

Even a killer could never have imagined the sounds of the screams he was hearing come from Oliver. It took an hour for him to pass out.

It was the pain that caused Oliver to lose consciousness, no angels were there to carry him away.

***

The electricity running through his male organs abruptly brought him from his state of unconsciousness, he screamed.

"Wake up Oliver, our day has just begun. May I ask you something?"

The answer was weak, "yes."

"You are a 35-year-old man in very good condition, you screamed for an hour before fainting. How long did a 16 year old girl scream and beg before she passed out?"

"At least as long, maybe longer. What is that smell?"

"Your bowels lost control. You are laying in your own shit the same as Sara was once you and your friends finished with her. David told me; he confirmed the police reports."

"She wanted it."

"No Oliver, she wanted you. You were everything I wasn't, Sara told me the whole story of meeting you and spending time with you that week. You had it all, looks, intelligence, a great physique, an athlete. Nobody like you had ever shown her the attention you showed her that week. She was so very flattered she became infatuated, she wanted you, she wanted sex with the best looking boy she'd ever met. She did not want a gangbang and certainly didn't want to be gang raped, beaten, bitten, burned or tortured. And she damned sure didn't want to have her insides ripped apart with a broom handle to the point she could never have children."

Oliver said nothing.

563

"How about those account numbers and location?"

"No."

Craig reached for the machine's switch

"WAIT!!"

"Numbers and locations! Now!"

"My wife and kids will be left with nothing!"

"No Oliver, there will be plenty left for your wife and children. I have no desire to leave them destitute. They will be very comfortable for the rests of their lives."

"I, I can't."

The machine was turned on, in addition Craig turned the crank of the other device. The combination of being sodomized while his balls were being electrically shocked was more than he could stand. This time the screams were several octaves higher and many decibels louder.

Craig didn't let it last too long; he wanted the man conscious of everything. He held the straw to Oliver's lips, "drink."

The water was good, helping sooth the throat sore from screaming.

"Get something to write on."

Craig wrote as the man talked. There were two overseas accounts.

"I have some calls to make in order to check the validity of the information you've given me. I'll see you tomorrow."

"What? Where are you going? Are you going to leave me like this? In my own shit?"

"Yes Oliver. That is precisely what I am going to do."

Oliver began to cry and beg.

"Oliver, I want you to lay there in your own shit and remember. Remember what you did to Sara Blackmon. I want you to remember her pleas, how she begged, how she cried. Remember how all of you sat and drank beer, laughing, after having left Sara laying in her own shit and piss while bleeding from her vagina and rectum. Remember how four strong boys beat up a beautiful young woman then pissed on her. Then I want you to start remembering other account numbers and locations, stock market accounts. This can all go on as long as I want, or until you have a heart attack. Think about it. Remember! I'll see you tomorrow."

The lights went out, total darkness.

Oliver heard footsteps disappearing into the darkness, he cried for his mother.

***

He had never known when it had happened, the smell of coffee was the first thing he realized, he was back in the chair.

"Good morning Oliver."

"How did I get back here, in the chair?"

"I'm sneaky."

"What now?"

"Breakfast, I've had a long night and traveled some. I'm hungry, French toast sounds good. What say?"

"OK."

"The accounts verified, good job. Some two hundred million dollars.'

"I know."

"Neither account any longer exists. It would take a team of accountants over ten years to realize they ever did."

"What? How?"

"I know things, and I know people who can make such things happen. You see, I am no longer the skinny, dorky looking, silly, teenage boy with braces and horn-rimmed glasses who was once described to you by Sara. I have, for lack of a better word, evolved. Enjoy your breakfast."

It was unimaginable how badly he was hurting. By now, relieving himself in front of Kirkland was no issue, there was no humiliation. Oliver would pee when he needed to and couldn't control his bowels if he'd wanted to. It just happened.

"You killed Andy, Oscar and David. You were really the one?"

"Yes, you received the newspapers?"

"Yes. How many more will you kill?"

"Originally there were to be six, but that changed."

"Who were the other two? I mean, after me and the other three."

"The judge and your father."

"The judge is already dead."

"I know."

"Will you go after my father next?"

"No. As I said, that changed. I have something far more painful in store for him. Something that will hurt him worse than you are hurting now."

"What?"

"Not ever having known what happened to the son he loved more than he loved anything else. Oliver, your body will someday be located, at least what little will be left after the rats find it, but not until I want it to be. Your father will wake every day of the remainder of his life wondering if that will be the day he will see his beloved son again. It won't be, you will be very dead, but he won't know. Your father will never know the closure of knowing what became of you or of attending your funeral. Some things are worse than death. He will suffer for the rest of his life. He should never have laughed after the trial. He should never have paid off the judge and jury."

"By the way. You heard of Bartolli's demise at the hands of the mob?"

"Yes."

"Well, I always wanted something special for him. I did some checking and found he had relatives in the organization. So, I set him up and let them do the dirty work. I watched it all happen with great satisfaction. Trust me, you should be happy you are with me and not with people like them."

"So, what happens today."

Craig stood and walked to the shelf, he cranked the handle. Oliver screamed.

"Well, we can do a lot of that, we can get you back on the table and let you enjoy more sensual time with my machine, or I can introduce you to a few of my other tricks."

"Oh Lord."

"There is another option."

Oliver looked at Craig.

"Two hundred million is just a fraction of your worth. Tell me how to access more and I will allow you a day of rest."

"Fuck you!"

The needle stung as it entered Oliver's arm, his eyes slowly closed.

***

The dosage was lowered considerably, meant more to scare Oliver than anything else. Oliver dozed, but never really slept. He roused to find a portable movie screen set up in front of where he sat.

"Let's watch a few home movies, Oliver! I made some popcorn, want some? Popcorn and movies are made for one another."

The projector was turned on.

"Look Oliver, it's you. Isn't that sweet how you're helping that nice young lady out of her clothes, you are such a considerate guy. What is she? Maybe 17 years old?"

Oliver closed his eyes.

Craig noticed, "Close your eyes again motherfucker and I will relieve you of your damned eyelids. Now, WATCH!"

Seeing the knife which had seemed to appear from nowhere, Oliver opened his eyes.

After an hour of seeing himself with multiple young women, performing acts most married couples would never even consider

with their own spouses, the reels were changed. It was time for Oliver to see his wife in action.

Craig stated, "That is interesting. Wonder how three men and one woman accomplished it? Oliver, you are more sexually experienced than I, can you explain it? I still can't believe what she just did with those guys. Help me out here man, explain it to me!" This went on for another hour.

Oliver, I am now going to show you one I really gave a lot of thought to, I almost didn't do it. But you see, I want you to hurt, terribly and emotionally. I want you to feel hate in its purest form because somebody is hurting someone you love. Then I will explain the consequences which were later paid for what you are about to see.

The next film was short, but explicit. It showed a man who worked for Oliver, and Oliver's youngest son. Oliver thrashed, pulled, he screamed, cursed and cried.

Craig allowed the film to finish. He rewound it, put it away, and allowed Oliver his time.

Finally, silence.

"There is one thing I hate more than I hate a rapist, a molester of children. That man died the day before I came for you, I saw to it. He also knew why he was dying, I told him. Oliver, the film was made via remote and hidden cameras. It was not something I had expected. I want you to know something, had I been close enough to have stopped it from happening, I would have. But your revenge has already been taken care of."

Oliver genuinely meant it when he said, "Thank You. I believe you."

"Oliver, I'm tired and in need of a nap, you probably need one as well. Let's rest today. Big plans coming up soon."

***

The next few days were filled with the horrors of a person trained in the ways of torture and death; Oliver Watson was nothing more than a shell of the human being he had once been. None of this surprised Craig, as far back as Viet Nam he'd witnessed those who gave misery were the ones who could take misery the least. Account numbers and stock accounts, all worth more than two billion dollars, had been given. All had been confirmed, money had been moved, accounts closed and made nonexistent.

"Almost time to say my last goodbye Oliver."

"How will you kill me?'

"Slowly, you will watch as it happens. Are you ready?"

"Is anybody ever?"

"Sometimes. Sara told me she was wishing for death just before her mind shut down and removed itself from what was happening, before what she described as the angels carrying her away. Yes, sometimes people are ready."

Picking up the scalpel Craig made two small incisions, cutting just enough, in just the right places. The blood would flow and could not be stopped, he placed buckets to capture the flow and so Oliver could watch the blood leaving his body.

"Oliver, you are going to bleed to death. It will take a while but there is nothing you can do to stop it from happening. You can, however, watch it happen by seeing the blood run into the buckets. Close your eyes and let it happen, or watch it and hope it will stop, which it will not. Choice is yours."

"There is one more thing I want you to know before this is completed, today is August 7th, the time is 8:15 PM. Exactly 19

years, to the minute, same date, same time, since you and the other thugs were in the process of raping and torturing my Sara."

"Craig, I'm so sorry. Please, please tell Sara, I'm sorry."

"No Oliver, I won't do that. I won't do it because I don't believe you would ever have felt any remorse if you had never met me."

The blood stopped flowing, the heart stopped beating, there were no breaths.

The person who had caused so much heartache, so much sorrow, the man who could have done so much good had he not chosen evil, was dead.

Craig Kirkland turned off the lights, sealed the hidden entrance to the tunnel and walked to his vehicle. The pain he'd been occasionally experiencing in his back caused him to stop and catch his breath. Maybe he'd see a doctor soon.

***

A week later the letter arrived in the mail.

Gary,

It's great to hear you've been performing some part time work.

I do understand something is missing but I also have no doubt, with you on the job, it shall someday be located. I am looking forward to learning how you do it.

Congratulations.

Best Wishes,

Dyke

CHAPTER

59

The pain in his back had grown worse, he was now hurting in his belly as well. Occasional bouts of nausea would hit with no warning. Craig finally made the call.

***

Although his time was up with The Group, Craig was still expected to contact them if any health issues arose, there was a reason for this. The Group didn't want some physician drugging one of the employees, past or present, to the point things might be said which should not be heard.

Within an hour of his call, a private airplane was on its way. On the plane was a doctor who would begin examining Craig while he was being flown to Denver where there was a medical team and proper equipment to treat almost anything imaginable.

For the next week Craig would be poked, prodded, stuck with countless needles, X-rayed, scanned by every machine available at the time. So many blood samples had been taken he wondered how there could be any left.

***

Dyke was still working for The Group, he had instructed the lead physician, Dr. Leon Harris, to report only to him.

Dr. Harris knocked on Dyke's door.

"Dyke, the news on Graham/Kirkland isn't good, Pancreatic Cancer."

"How far along is it and has it spread?"

"Won't know for sure unless we go in, take some biopsies and look around."

"You're positive about your diagnosis?"

"Well, without the biopsies I can't be 100%, but I've seen enough of it. And with all the other tests, I'm 99% sure."

"What are his chances?"

"Even with chemo, and we have meds made in house that the FDA won't know about for another 10 years, good stuff, and from what I know and have seen, not good. In fact, I'd say very bad."

"Can he have a drink? Last time he and I were together, years ago, we had a drink."

"I can't promise it won't make him sick, but if you like him I'd recommend you and he have a drink together. Just one."

***

There was a knock on the door, it was Dyke.

"Hello Sir, it's been a long time, please come in."

The men shook hands, "Hello Gary, aw, hell with it, I'm going to use your real name. Craig, it has been a long time."

Dyke noticed the whites of Craig's eyes had taken a yellow tint; he was becoming jaundiced. From his pocket Dyke produced two whiskey miniatures, "Let's have a drink." Dyke poured the whiskey, glasses were clinked.

"Craig, Doctor Harris came by my office today, we talked about you."

"Well, Sir, if he came to see you first and you came to see me while bearing whiskey, I would guess what you're going to tell me isn't good news."

"Your guess would be correct."

"Mr. Dyke, I've had some time this week, between tests, to visit the library here, I've done a lot of reading, medical books. Based on what I learned, and on my symptoms, I would diagnose myself as having advanced pancreatic cancer."

Dyke sat looking at the younger man.

"Sir, according to Dr. Harris, would my self diagnoses be correct?"

"Your diagnoses would be exactly correct."

"And my chances according to Dr. Harris?"

"Even with treatment, not good. He did mention going in and taking biopsies, see if and how far it's spread."

"Sir, I'm going to turn down Dr. Harris' offer, I think it will do no good to biopsy or treat with chemo. May I make a request?"

"Absolutely."

"I would like to request medications for pain and the other symptoms. Let me continue to function as long as possible. I know how to start an IV and can do that to myself if the doctor recommends intravenous. You see, Sir, my mission is not yet finished, I still have a few things on my agenda before I face God and answer for all I've done. Still some things I want to do for a few people."

"Would one of those people be a lady named Sara?"

"You know me too well sir, yes."

"And do you have a plan for when it's time?"

"Honestly, now that I know what is happening to me, and a good guess what Dr. Harris will prescribe and hopefully provide, I've just come up with a plan for when it's time." Craig spent the next few minutes explaining how it would end and asked Mr. Dyke's approval. Dyke agreed and approved.

***

Dyke changed the subject, "I'm curious, how much money is there?"

Craig grinned, "Honestly, I'm not exactly sure. Its spread all over the place, in banks all over the world, in stocks, bearer bonds, and some things I don't understand. I'd need a couple of days to make some calls and sit down with a calculator to be sure. But, just guessing, and especially with the help of the people you put me in touch with when I first came on board here, I would guess somewhere around Three Billion. The folks you put me in touch with are absolute magicians at placing money where it will grow, and even better at making it grow and not be affected by taxes, or at least not too badly affected."

Dyke let out a long whistle, "Wow! What will become of it?"

"I plan to give it all away, first to some people who are very special to me, the rest to good charities."

"Seems I read a charity received a very large donation shortly after that lawyer's demise."

"The Children's Shoe Drive charity did very well. It was Chicago mob and Bartolli's money. They'll receive at least one more nice donation."

"Good Job, I like your style."

"This leads me to another request."

576

"OK?"

"The individuals who will be receiving from the funds will need help. None of them know how to handle what they will suddenly be receiving, same as I was unprepared to handle my pay from The Group. May I provide those people with the same list of contacts you provided me?"

"This could be a tad tricky. I'll run it past my compatriots, but I'm leaning toward giving approval. I'll contact you with an answer in a few days."

"Thank you, sir."

"You know Craig, you were contracted with us to be on standby, ready at any time if required. We only called on you one time, you performed perfectly. Most who contract with us never go on any missions in their ten years. That's how we like it, it means problems get worked out through diplomacy and we aren't needed. But you went on several other missions, personal missions, you also performed perfectly on those. Are you pleased with the results of having inflicted your revenge on those people?"

"I've often thought about it, sir. Revenge is an awful thing, the Bible tells us, "Vengeance is mine, Sayeth the Lord." "I like to think I was the tool he used; it helps me maintain my sanity."

"And Oliver, the torture you inflicted on him?"

"God help me Sir, I loved every scream that came from him. That's one I pray about, daily."

***

"Sir, there is one more thing."

"That would be?"

577

Craig handed Dyke a note with Charles Jackson's name and number written on it. "I know you keep up with things, a lot of things, and people, very closely. Would Thomas Watson be one of those people?"

"Because of your connection with him, yes."

"Then you know he is also very sick."

"Yes, couldn't happen to a more deserving sonofabitch."

"If you will, when you learn of Watson's death, please call Charles and tell him you are Dyke and then these words, Thomas Watson is dead."

"Happy to do it. May I ask why?"

"It will be Charles' notice that he will be going fishing at Reelfoot Lake."

"I know you well enough to know there is more to it than that." Dyke smiled, "But I also know the crappie fishing is terrific at Reelfoot, and the scenery is beautiful. I'm sure Charles will enjoy himself."

***

Craig was flown back home the next day. Dr. Harris had provided him with medications he would need to continue functioning and the promise of more anytime he needed them. All further medications would be delivered by courier.

Two days of phone calls and the use of a calculator resulted in there being more money than Craig had first thought, Three Billion Four Hundred Thousand, total.

CHAPTER

60

She had always loved horses but could never afford one. The one hundred fifty acres was perfect. Everything perfect, including the home, barn and other outbuildings. The smaller attractive caretaker's home was set away from the main house. There was a ten acre spring fed lake stocked with catfish, bream and bass, and plenty of pasture land surrounded by hardwood forests. Picturesque didn't begin to define how perfect this place was. Most importantly, there were horses.

The caretaker was a very nice man in his 50s. He had calloused hands, the dark, ruddy complexion of a man who worked outdoors for a living, his face sported the fullest mustache Craig had ever seen and the man's smile was as genuine as his firm handshake. "Julian Bandy, most folks call me "Handy". Dad called me Handy Bandy from the time I was born, it stuck, most folks have no idea what my real name is," he grinned. "Hop in the jeep, I'll be happy to show you around."

The man was easy conversation, he explained that he and his wife, Betty, had worked for the current owners more than 20 years. Both children were married and lived in other states, he bragged how proud he was that the kids had earned their way through college, they'd been raised with good work ethics and held down jobs while also making good grades. Handy beamed when he spoke of his children. For an hour they toured the property before returning to the house. "Come on in, it's a real nice place, Mrs. Harris designed it herself." The place was beautiful, designed by a woman but with a man's touch as well, not dainty, not rugged. Perfect!

"Handy, what kind of stock are there?"

"Right now, there are 8 horses, two of those will be giving us some babies before long, 32 head of cattle, be getting some babies from a few of them too, some of them are steers that'll be ready for the packing house soon."

"May we see the horses?"

"Yes Sir, I got em all in the barn when I knew you were coming."

Craig was amazed at the way Handy and the horses reacted to one another, the love between man and animals was instantly obvious.

"Are they gentle enough to be around a small woman and children?"

"Most are, I raised most of em from babies and taught em manners. Mamie over here", he walked to a stall and was greeted by a beautiful mare, "she can be a tad stubborn and hardheaded, takes a little firmer hand, more a man's horse." He looked at the horse, "Aint that right girl?" Almost as if the horse understood, she shook her head, Craig and Handy laughed. The two men and lady realtor walked outside. Craig asked the realtor for a few more minutes alone with Handy.

"Handy, I'm very wealthy, not a brag, just a fact. I've also decided to buy this place."

"Figured you were worth something or you wouldn't be looking at it."

"Exactly. Thing is, I am also very sick and, honestly, I'm dying. I won't be around long enough to enjoy the place."

"Then, Sir, why buy it?"

"There is a family that is very special to me, a married couple with two daughters. I intend to give them this place as a gift."

"Damn! Oh, sorry, Betty fusses when I cuss. That's a mighty fine present."

Craig grinned, "It's OK, I've been known to cuss a little myself."

"Yes sir."

"Handy, you love those horses and this place, don't you?"

"Sir, those horses, well, they are like children to me and Betty. You know how people love their dogs or cats?" Craig nodded. "That's how we feel about those horses. Four legged children."

"Have you and Betty discussed plans for when this place sells."

"We talked about it; reckon I'll find another job."

"What's your pay?"

"Paid taxes last year on twenty five thousand. Not too bad I don't guess for a dumb ol man who never finished high school."

"Nothing dumb about you Handy. I know people, don't sell yourself short."

"Thanks, sir."

"Well, it just doesn't seem right, taking a man away from his children, even four legged ones. So, for a ten thousand a year pay raise and annual raises each year afterward, would you and Betty be willing to stay and continue your current employment?"

"Ten Thousand a Year? Raise?!"

"Is it enough to convince you to stay?"

"Oh Lord all mighty sir. I never had no desire to kiss a man. But you're close!"

Craig laughed out loud, "I'll settle for a handshake to seal the deal."

***

Unknown to anyone, Craig was once again in disguise, it was subtle, but enough that no one he'd met today would recognize him once he removed the disguise.

The realtor was shocked when Thomas Alan McGuire said three words, "I'll take it."

"No counter offer?"

"Nope, I'll take it for the price being asked. To whom should the earnest money check be made and have you the contract for me to sign?"

"Wow! This has never happened to me. Yes, I have a contract you can sign." She told Craig who to make the check to, "I'll have to confirm funds before we proceed any further. You understand I hope."

"Of course, are the phones working in the house?"

"Yes, all utilities are."

"Good, let's go in, you can call the bank."

"Excellent idea Mr. McGuire."

"Once you've confirmed the check is good, we need to sit down, I have some things to tell you and some instructions on how to deed the place."

***

"What I'm about to tell you must be kept in complete, total confidence, you can tell absolutely not one person. Do you understand? If you do not understand the entire deal is off."

582

"I do understand."

Craig went on to explain to the young realtor everything he had told Handy. By the time he was finished there were tears flowing down the attractive young woman's face, streaking her cheeks with mascara. Craig handed her his handkerchief.

"I am so very sorry. How long?"

"Not long, but please don't feel sorry for me. I've lived through and survived more things I should never have survived than most could ever imagine. I've lived an adventurous life."

"How do you want this handled?"

"It will all be handled by an attorney from here on. You tell me what information you require for the sale papers and deed process to be correctly filled out. I will see that you receive what you need, through the attorney, you and I will never have any further contact. You and the attorney will both swear to this secret and work together so everything not only goes smoothly but is also a surprise. On the date of closing they will be brought here having no idea that the day is anything other than an invitation for everyone to enjoy horseback riding and fishing in the lake. They will learn differently, of course."

***

The letter his secretary brought was still sealed, it was marked PRIVATE. There were two sheets of paper in the envelope. The first sheet contained three words,

TEN TWO FOUR

Charles gasped, how could this be possible? He looked at the second sheet.

My Dearest Friend Charles,

I am at a place in my life which will soon be requiring your services.

Expect a call Tuesday at 11 AM, at that time we can arrange a discreet place we can meet and discuss my legal needs.

Imperative you do not discuss this letter to anyone.

Not knowing what your retainer fee is I have enclosed a check. If more is needed, I will be glad to pay the additional amount you require.

Kindest Regards

**

Charles found the check filled out for the total of $5000.00, it was signed by a Vincent H. Christy.

The following Tuesday, Eleven AM, Charles answered the phone, "Yes, Mount Cheaha is beautiful this time of year, Mr. Christy. I know the overlook well, 2 PM is good."

Anticipation having gotten the better of him, Charles arrived a half hour early. The old man sitting on the bench with his camera nodded a greeting, Charles acknowledged with a slight wave. Neither man spoke.

Two PM exactly, Charles heard a voice he knew well, "You're looking very well, my dear friend. Thank you for responding to my TEN TWO FOUR."

Charles stared in amazement at the old man's face, a face he had never seen, speaking to him with a voice not belonging to it. "My God, Craig, I would never have known it was you!"

"When a person is required to keep people believing he is dead there are certain things he learns to do. One of those things is the art of disguise, it seems to have worked."

"Yeah, Very damned well! I don't know if I should hug you or punch you."

"Honestly, if you punched me, I would understand. A hug would be much more pleasant."

The two friends embraced.

***

"I've kept up with you over the years. Last time I saw you was at my parent's funeral after the accident. I was in position that I could watch the graveside service, but where nobody would know I was there."

"Damned drunk driver piece of shit. Somebody killed him a couple of weeks later. He deserved it, not only for killing your parents but I also learned he was abusive to his wife and kids."

"Yeah, I read about it." Craig told the truth; he had read the newspaper article about the man's murder. He had read about it the day after he'd put two bullets in the man's head. No mention was made about the trust funds set up to care for the widow and children.

"No suspects the cops can nail it on, even though the guy had plenty of enemies. If they ever do catch the killer, I will represent him free of charge."

***

"There are so many things I want to know about why you disappeared, where you've been. Hell, why expose yourself now?"

585

"I realize you have many questions. I cannot answer most. I worked for people who do not exist, you have never heard of them and never will. I was recruited during my second tour in Nam and the only way to perform my job effectively was to go missing in action, later presumed dead. I gave up everything when I took the job, but by accepting the job it also opened opportunities for other things I had been planning for several years. That is all I can tell you. I hope attorney/client privilege applies here, because you can never speak of what I just told you nor the fact that you and I have met or communicated in any way."

"Mr. Christy, attorney/client privilege does apply in any prior, present or future communications we may have had, are having or will ever have."

***

"Over the years I have received four newspapers, all sent from different cities. In each of the papers were articles concerning the four boys who hurt Sara. Three were killed, one is missing. I also saw on the news a report about the head of the attorney for the boys being found on his mailbox. The FBI, I heard on the news, received a package with a shitload of incriminating evidence concerning the mob. Should I ask if you know anything about those newspapers, or the attorney?"

"No, some things you and I should not discuss."

"I'm going to tell you something, then I will never broach the topic again."

"Go on."

"I visited your Dad when I received the first newspaper, he read the article and smiled. He looked at me and said something."

"What?"

"He told me, "The boy is alive, Craig is alive, he has begun his mission, this article proves it to me. I don't know when or how, but the others will die as well. He will not stop until his mission is complete.""

Charles continued, "I tossed it off as just some redneck getting caught screwing his buddy's wife, or something like that, and figured his buddy killed him. I never gave any thought that it might be you. Then the second paper came, and the third. I showed them to your dad each time a new one arrived he took great joy in reading the articles. Your dad would smile and look at me, all he would say was, "I told you so." "I wish he had been alive to see the last one, the one about Oliver Watson having gone missing."

Craig said nothing. Anything he said about the killings or even discussion of the topic could place Charles in a bad position if anything was ever suspected.

"The cops questioned me, hell they questioned anyone who ever knew you, your parents, Cindy, my parents, everyone! They wanted so badly to pin it all on you, but damnit, their prime suspect, according to The Marine Corps, was missing and presumed dead. They even questioned me as if they might have thought it was me. Which was absolutely laughable, like some overweight lawyer is capable of doing all that had been done."

Charles waited for any reaction, there was none.

"OK, end of this topic. No further conversations concerning it shall evermore take place. Now, Vincent, how may I be of service?"

"I'm dying, Pancreatic cancer."

"Damnit man, why don't you just slap the hell out of me. Did you have to be so fucking blunt about it?"

"Sorry, wanted to get that part out of the way as quickly as possible."

"Well, it damned sure worked. How long?"

"Not long, but there are some things I need you to do for me, legal things. Also, there are some people I have permission from that you may contact who can assist you. There are sums of money, stocks and bonds the likes of which even you have no idea how to handle without those persons' assistance." Charles was handed an envelope containing a list of contacts. "It is my intent to give away everything I possess, this includes all money, stocks, bonds and a farm I recently contracted to purchase under another name."

"How many names and faces do you have?"

"As many as are required. Now hush and listen."

Charles hushed.

"The farm, along with all live stock, house, barn, everything is to be deeded to some nice people." Another envelope was handed to Charles, "These are the names and current address of the people. This is to be a complete surprise to them; you and I will work out details on the surprise."

"Here is the real estate person's card. Very nice young lady. Do your lawyer thing and get her all the details concerning the new owners of the farm that she will need for the sale. You will prepare all the closing papers and deed. Do this without telling anyone why. There is also a gift to them which will be in the form of money, stocks and bonds which total almost one and a half billion dollars.

"SWEET JESUS MAN, I HAVE NO IDEA WHAT TO DO WITH SOMETHING LIKE THAT!"

"Lower your voice, Charles, take a deep breath. Stand up and walk around for a minute. While you're doing that please grab a couple of drinks from the cooler in the passenger seat of my car." Charles calmed, he smiled at seeing the familiar label on the drinks.

Craig continued, "I know you have no idea how to handle it. That is why I gave you the list of people."

"Who are they?"

"Do not ask, simply trust me that they will gladly help."

"OK."

"Got all that?"

"Got it. Anything else?"

"One more thing. Sometime soon you will receive a call from a man who will introduce himself as Dyke, nothing more. He will say four words then hang up. What he will say is "Thomas Watson is dead."

Charles raised his eyebrows, "How do you know this?"

"I've kept up with him, he's as sick as I am and won't last much longer."

"OK. Then what?"

Charles was handed a large manila envelope with more than enough stamps attached to cover postage. The envelope was addressed to Detective Jake Brighton, Tybee Island Police Department. He was then given a smaller envelope.

"Inside the smaller envelope are reservations at Reelfoot Lake for an all-expense paid week of accommodations and guided fishing. The reservation is four months from now, both Watson and I should both be dead by then. But if you have not received

the call from Dyke you will need to postpone the trip to a later date. Take the large envelope with you, drive, do not fly. Somewhere around half way between your home and the lake, drop the envelope in a mailbox. Just before mailing it, moisten a cloth with alcohol and wipe the envelope as best as you can, all of it, and do not touch it again with your bare hands. This is extremely important, you should handle it, after wiping it down, with gloves on. Understand?"

"Yes, no fingerprints."

"Exactly."

"Charles, do you still have the maps you made of the mine?"

"Yep, keepsakes of yours and my times together."

"Listen to me and listen closely. There will come a time when you may be approached about any knowledge of the mine. Lie and say you do not. Burn every map you made, keep nothing remotely associated with the mine. This is of the utmost importance to protect you, as well as my identity."

"Why would someone ask about the mine?"

"You don't need to know at this time. But do not visit the mine, stay out of the area completely and do what I just said to do. You will learn later why you will be questioned about the mine, trust me."

"I trust nobody more. I'll burn the maps as soon as I get home."

***

"I never would have put you and Cindy together, but I'm glad it happened. How did it happen."

"Weirdest damned thing. I picked her up one day as I had hundreds of times, just gonna hang out like we always had. Then, I don't know, maybe it was how the sunlight hit her hair, for the first time ever, I noticed how very beautiful she was. I pulled over and just took time to really study her, she looked at me and asked what was wrong."

Smiling, Craig asked, "What did you tell her."

"I told her I wanted to kiss her."

"And?"

"She said, "Well, it's about damned time!" She laid one on me! One thing led to another, we began dating, going steady, screwing, and let me tell you, I knew she had experience more than me, but DAMN she taught me some really good stuff!"

Craig laughed! He made no mention he knew what his friend was talking about.

"So, next thing you know we got engaged, waited a year after I finished school, married, had kids, the American dream."

"How does she like the silver antique tea set?"

"How do you know about that?"

"She always admired the one my Mom had. I located one almost identical, I gave it to y'all as a wedding gift, anonymously."

"Cindy told me it was almost identical to the one your Mom had. She loves it."

"I was also at the wedding. It was all I could do to keep from laughing when you began to stutter during your vows. You were a nervous wreck!"

"You were there? You sneaky asshole!"

"Yep, it's something else I'm pretty good at."

"I believe it. I still remember you sneaking up on me in the woods."

"Charles, you can't tell her about me."

"I know, that will be my toughest attorney/client privilege ever. She loved you, we all did."

"I love you all too, always have."

The call from Charles had been wonderful, they'd not talked in a couple of years. He would be in Knoxville for a few days, staying at a client's home about an hour's drive from downtown and had permission to invite friends for a nice day of horseback riding and fishing. Kenneth had heard Sara speak of Charles many times and was very much looking forward to meeting the man.

The girls were especially excited, the only horses they had ever ridden had been at the State Fair Pony Ride. Kenneth and Sara had adopted Ellen, now 7, as a newborn. One year later Mary, now 8, was adopted. In a twist of fate, Mary was a year older than Ellen, having been two years old when adopted. Kenneth took great joy in seeing the confusion he could create by introducing his oldest daughter as their second child and the youngest as their first.

In the many years Sara had lived in Knoxville she couldn't remember ever having been in this part of the county, it was beautiful. Pastureland mixed with woods. Many small lakes dotted the area and the homes were gorgeous, she was already enjoying her day and it had only begun.

Charles, having seen the car turn onto the long drive, walked outside to greet the Allison family. He was beaming when Sara stepped from the car, "My God Sara, you are still as beautiful as the first time I saw you, possibly more beautiful!" Sara blushed, she hugged Charles tightly, kissed his cheek and introduced him to

Kenneth and the girls. "Charles, I can't tell you how honored I am to finally meet you, Sara has spoken highly of you so many times."

"Kenneth, I am an attorney, please don't set the standard too high and expect me to meet it." Both men laughed.

Sara was looking around, "Charles, this place is absolutely beautiful. Your client must have done very well for himself."

"He has done exceedingly well, with outstanding advice from his tax attorney of course." Charles joked. "Come in, I know you being a female, you are busting to see the inside of the house."

As they entered the house Charles heard Sara, "Oh My Goodness, this is more beautiful than I imagined. Is it all this nice?"

"Yes. I'm told by the caretaker, Handy, a Mrs. Harris, the original owner, personally designed the house."

As they toured the house Charles watched Kenneth and Sara very closely. It was obvious they loved the house; it would be interesting to see how they felt about the property. Finishing inside the house they all stepped outside and took in the view across the pasture to the lake, the view was breathtaking.

The girls had asked several times about the horses. Charles suggested they all head toward the barn and meet Handy. Such was the caretaker's personality that within minutes every member of the Allison family felt as though they had known him for years. As Handy was introducing the girls to the horses and allowing them to feed some apples and carrots, Charles spoke to Sara and Kenneth.

"I want everyone to enjoy themselves today and have a very special time. We will have roast beef sandwiches for lunch. Oh, and the best apple pie you ever tasted, Handy's wife Betty makes it. I'm sorry, thinking of the pie caused me to forget where I was

going. Anyhow, after lunch I would like some time alone with both of you. I have a business proposition a client has asked me to discuss with you. Betty and Handy have already volunteered to watch the children for a while so we can talk. You need not worry about the children; they will be in most excellent hands."

"Yes, of course, but who is your client?"

"Can't say at this time, Attorney/Client privilege thing."

"We understand. OK."

Handy busied himself saddling five of the horses, four of the gentlest and one stubborn mare named Mamie for himself. He asked Kenneth and Sara if they rode. It had been many years since she had, not as long for Kenneth.

"OK, Miss Sara, your husband and I will both have the reins of your children's horses tied to our saddle horns, you will have your horse to yourself, that OK? She's a sweet girl, you will like her."

"Yes sir Mr. Handy."

And off they went, girls swapping between giggling and asking questions, Kenneth and Sara smiling. The dogwoods and redbuds were in full bloom, the woods were stunning. They all stopped as Handy pointed to another pasture, mixed among the cattle were several deer. Handy spoke, "They come out and feed on the tender new grass every Spring. This is one of my favorite places on the property." Handy, sworn to secrecy, never spoke of the property having been sold. He had also been told the people he was with would be the new owners, they just didn't know it yet. He already liked them all, especially the children, it would be wonderful having children around again.

The two-hour ride had been one of the most wonderful times of their lives. Relaxing in a beautiful environment, breathing

in the sweetness of the country air, it was something Sara had dreamed of all her life.

At the barn the men helped the children down, Sara dismounted and rubbed her butt. "Mr. Handy, I can never thank you enough for showing us this beautiful place and the wonderful horseback ride. But I am kinda glad we didn't ride any longer, I'm a bit, uh, tender."

Handy laughed, "Yes Ma'am, it takes a while to get used to it."

Charles, having a fear of horses, had used the excuse of having some business calls to make. He walked into the barn, the children began telling him of the ride, Sara once again hugged him. Charles was so happy for Sara, he still never knew exactly what she'd said to Craig in the hospital room all those years ago, but he felt nothing but happiness for how far she'd come from the broken girl he had last seen.

"Lunch? Miss Betty has cooked some terrific roast beef for sandwiches. Y'all hungry?"

Inside the house everyone met Betty Bandy, it was obvious Betty was pure sweetheart as she hugged both girls and Sara. Betty had also been informed of what would happen today and was overjoyed but kept her secret and didn't let on. "Girls, after lunch would you all like to go fishing with Handy and me for a little while?"

Both girls' eyes lit up, "YES MA'AM!!"

Nobody had any idea how Betty seasoned her roast, but it was unique and without a doubt the best any of them had ever tasted. The pie was even better, Kenneth and Charles had seconds.

Sara helped Betty clean up. The two women were at ease with one another.

***

Charles moved his briefcase to the dining room table, he asked Sara and Kenneth to join him there. Before joining her husband and Charles at the table Sara prepared everyone a fresh glass of tea.

"OK, where to begin? I know y'all are confused about all of this, but everything will be revealed to you in just a short while."

Charles continued. "Sara you asked who my client is. I still cannot tell you, not right now, before this afternoon is over his identity will be revealed to you and Kenneth. Be patient. But first there are other things that need to be explained. What I can tell you about my client is that he is the wealthiest person I've ever met, and I've met a lot of wealthy people. The difference in my client and many other people of wealth is that he is also very generous and has an extremely soft heart for children and women, he has helped several women and children over the course of the last few years. Y'all with me?"

"Yes."

"Sara, my client knows everything that happened to you on Tybee Island and at the trial. I apologize for bringing up such an unpleasant memory but it's necessary in order that you fully understand what is happening."

"Kenneth, I assume you know?" It was more a question than a statement. "I apologize for that as well; I should have been sure before I spoke of the subject."

Kenneth nodded, Sara told Charles, "No apologies needed, Charles, I have put it all behind me and Kenneth knew everything before we were married."

597

"Thank you, Sara. Now, my client has taken a very special interest in you from the time it happened and all through the years. He has kept up with you, Kenneth, and the children, he always wanted to do something very special for you. Therefore, you are both here today for the special thing he has decided to do."

"What?"

"You will find out in just a few minutes. We are awaiting the arrival of a lady who should be here any moment."

Minutes later the doorbell rang. "Sara, Kenneth, this is Mrs. Donna Wisely, she works in real estate." Everyone shook hands, Sara brought Donna a glass of tea.

"Sara, Kenneth, you have both been invited to this place today because your signatures will be required as new owners of this house, the land it sits on, all 150 acres, all livestock, plainly put, the whole kit n kaboodle. What we have here is a real estate closing!"

Kenneth said nothing, he simply sat with his mouth open.

"Charles Jackson, I know you always loved a practical joke, you better not be!"

"Dear Beautiful Sara, I do love a good practical joke but even I would never be so cruel as to tease you about this. It's real."

Sara looked at Donna. Donna was smiling and nodding yes. Sara felt faint.

"Sara, Sara, please don't fall out of your chair", it was Charles talking, "that would just ruin all this happy I'm feeling right now!" Sara took a long drink from her tea, Donna refilled Sara's glass for her.

Kenneth had finally recovered, "Sara, Charles, I hate to put a damper on everyone's happy feelings, but there is no way we can even consider this, we can't afford the property taxes on such a place."

"Kenneth, one thing at a time. This day still has some very big surprises in store for you and Sara."

The closing went smoothly. Emotions alternated between crying and laughing. At the end of it all, everyone hugged. The Allison's owned a beautiful home and property, they had also been made aware of Handy's pay raise and future raises, all while having no idea how they could pay him anything. Donna had just earned the largest commission of her young career; she was ecstatic as she left and headed for her office.

Another person was so happy he had shed tears listening to the joy in Sara's voice. He was about a mile away, stopped on a side road, listening to the entire conversation. The transmitter had been placed in Charles' briefcase. He also knew what would be said next would bring the level of happiness down a few notches. Charles had more to inform the Allison's about his client.

***

"Guys, there is something else I have to tell you, it will be very difficult for me to speak the words and it will sadden you as well. I need a drink, anyone else?"

Kenneth and Charles both poured whiskeys, Sara stayed with tea.

"Sara, Kenneth, my client is dying." Charles had to stop and hold back the tears. Sara and Kenneth thought Charles must be extremely close to his client.

"My client has only a few weeks to live, at best. He so wanted to do this very special thing for you both. Kenneth, he

599

admires you as a husband to Sara, a father to the girls and as a good man, this place is as much a gift to you as to Sara. Before he passes on, he intends to give away everything he owns, most of it to you two." Charles reached into his case and handed Kenneth some papers. "Kenneth, As an engineer you are very good with numbers. Give those a quick glance."

The papers were account numbers, bonds and stock holdings, all of which were in Kenneth's and Sara's names. There were also two papers, each with the girl's names, those were trust funds which had been set up especially for the children.

"OH MY GOD!"

Shocked by his outburst, Sara looked at Kenneth.

"If I added these anywhere close to correctly in my head, there is at least one and a quarter billion dollars in these accounts."

Charles grinned, "Actually just a shade under one and a half billion. But whose gonna quibble about a quarter billion or so?" He laughed.

"Charles, I don't think my heart can handle any more surprises today."

"Well, Sara, Kenneth, there is one more. But before it is revealed I must tell you both, what is about to happen next can never be spoken of to any person, nobody, for the rests of yours and my life. This is not a request, it is imperative that you keep the secret as long as you live, people's safety, including yours, could depend on it. Your benefactor wanted to see you both in person. He will be here in a few minutes."

Handy had seen the real estate lady leave. Now there was another car coming up the drive, he didn't recognize it and hadn't

expected anyone else. As the car drove past, Handy got a look at the driver, he looked familiar. The car pulled behind the house.

***

Sara had stepped to the bathroom, powdered her nose and put on new lipstick.

"Honey, how do I look? Oh, never mind, you will tell me I look OK even if I don't. Charles?"

Charles, having had his second double whiskey by now, looked at Sara, "My dear, you have never been more radiant, absolutely stunning."

"You're drunk."

"To the point of total and complete honesty. Yes, Radiant is exactly the right word to describe you."

***

Everyone heard the car stop behind the house, then the sound of its door closing. Unseen down the hallway but heard by all was the backdoor of the house opening, then the sound of footsteps.

The sound was something Sara would never forget, the timing of each step, how it sounded when each foot sat down on the floor. It was a gait she had heard hundreds of times as it came down the corridor to her room in the hospital. Some things had not changed over the years, the sound of those footsteps was one of those things. She stood.

He entered the room and stopped.

Kenneth watched curiously as his wife slowly walked to the man.

601

"I knew you were alive, I felt it. Many times, I felt you were close, but I could never see you, I just knew you were there, somehow, looking after me and my family. You were, weren't you?"

"Many times, yes. Several times you looked at me but didn't know me."

She reached out her arms. They embraced one another, not as friends, but as two people in love. Tears ran down the cheeks of both.

"Kenneth, allow me to introduce you to Craig Kirkland." Sara introduced the two men, both of whom she was in love with.

"Craig, you've no idea what an honor this is for me."

"Sir, I feel exactly the same toward you."

They sat at the table, Craig across from Sara so he could take in as much of her beauty as possible in the time they had.

"Charles, would you pour me a drink please?"

"Sure you should? Meds, I mean."

"Skipped em today."

The whiskey helped.

***

We have much to talk about and not much time to do it. I'm sure you both have questions. Some I may not be able to answer.

"Daddy sent Grandmother some newspapers."

"Some things I can't discuss in front of my attorney."

"I'll go see if the kids are catching any fish. You all don't need me around for a while anyhow." Charles left the house.

"I thought he might. I wish I could see her; I love her so. But it's impossible and she cannot know I am alive."

"Three dead, one missing."

"Yes."

"Will he be found?"

"Yes."

"Is he, gone?"

"As dead as Abraham Lincoln." Craig explained about Oliver's father and wanting the old man to hurt.

"Oh Craig."

"Sara, I know you never would have wanted it handled in such a way, you are too kind for that. But after what they did to you and when you were dealt such an injustice by a crooked Judge and jury, then they laughed. I changed. By the way, did you know the judge is also dead?"

"You?"

"No, he beat me to it. Killed himself when his wife caught him with a teenage female inmate."

"I saw on the news about that awful lawyer, Bartolli. And that the FBI received information that led to the downfall of a lot of Mafia people. Was that you?"

"Let's just say I helped it all along."

"Where have you been?"

"Joined the Corps, went to Viet Nam, came home and was stationed at Camp Geiger, training people. While at Geiger I received word that a very dear friend had been killed during an attack, I requested to go back. I was on my second tour when I

was recruited by some other people. From there I cannot tell you anymore due to the secrecy and nature of the work."

Kenneth wanted to ask something, "You told Sara you were looking after us sometimes?"

"I was around more than you realize."

"Were you around the day that man snatched our Mary from the playground at school?"

"If anyone shouldn't believe in coincidence it should be me, but that day was one. I had been on a job and detoured so I could come through Knoxville, I wanted to see y'all. I love your children, they're beautiful. I stopped by the school hoping to catch a glimpse of them and from across the playground I saw the man grab Mary and put her in his car. I got in my vehicle; it took me longer to find him than I had hoped. Luckily, I spotted him and followed his car to the house he took her into. I went in and got her."

"They said his neck was broken."

"Yeah. I'm, let's say, pretty good at that kind of thing."

"Mary said it was an old man with white whiskers."

"Disguise, something else I'm pretty good at. I was at yall's wedding. It was beautiful."

"At our wedding?!!"

"Yes. The poem you chose to recite before your vows was a wonderful choice, beautiful."

"Oh My!"

"May I say something?

"Please do, but first let me thank you from my heart for saving Mary."

"I never began life wanting to be who I am today, but when what happened to Sara took place, I made it my life's mission to destroy the people who had done it. I've succeeded in completing that mission. Kenneth, I want you to know something, not a second has passed that I've not been in love with Sara, deeply in love. The last words I spoke to her at the hospital, Sara do you remember?"

Sara was crying, "I could never forget them, especially after I knew I'd broken your heart."

"Kenneth, the last words I spoke to Sara were," "Nobody has ever, does now, nor will ever love you as I have, do and always will." "Well, I was wrong."

Craig continued, "Sara, there is one man who has loved you, loves you now and will always love more than I, I've seen it in his eyes, he is your husband. And I am so very happy that you two found one another. Your love for one another completes me."

Kenneth responded, "Craig, I've always known Sara was in love with you, it was accepted and there were never any feelings of jealousy. It was something I knew going into our marriage, something she had explained. All I can say is we've both, you and I, been honored to have shared a love for the same wonderful woman and I can think of no better man to have shared it with. Thank you for being in both our lives."

"Time is short, there are some things you need to know. Charles has a list of contacts you and he will need to talk to. The kind of wealth you just came into is not as easily taken care of and protected as you may believe. Be sure to call the people on the list. They are expecting to hear from you, Charles will help. Once I leave here today, I will never contact you again. I will die soon,

there will be no funeral or memorial service, I will simply be gone. All I ask is that you pray for my soul."

Craig continued, "Sara, do you still have the rings?"

"Yes, I could never part with them. I cherish them."

"If you don't mind, I would like your girls to have them when they are old enough to understand when you tell them who they are from. In the list of people Charles has is a jeweler, I have instructed him on what to do with the rings. This is your decision, but also a request from me. The jeweler will charge nothing, he is a friend and will do the job as a favor to me."

Both Sara and Kenneth were crying.

"Kenneth I now have one last request of you."

"Craig, whatever I can do, I will."

"If Sara will allow me and with your permission, I would like to kiss her, one last time. Every night since the last time I saw her it has been my last thought before going to sleep, kissing her, one more time."

Kenneth looked at Sara, she nodded.

"I'll leave you two alone." Kenneth walked outside, closing the door behind himself.

No words were spoken, the kiss said it all.

***

His secretary was opening the mail the next day when she came across an envelope marked "PRIVATE", it was addressed to Charles, she took it to his office. Inside the envelope was a storage compartment key and directions. Charles was to have his secretary immediately drive him to the compartment. He did as the note instructed; the note had made it clear this was URGENT.

Opening the compartment door revealed a near perfect condition 1968 Pontiac GTO. On the seat was an envelope containing some papers, a title to the car, and two sets of the car's keys. The title was now in Charles name. The papers were accounts, also in his name, totaling 40 million dollars.

There was a note,

Dear Charles,

Hope you like the car, she's a sweet ride.

Enjoy the other gifts but remember to help someone else along the way as you have always helped me.

I can never thank you enough for showing me the love you always have, the love of a brother. Please know, I loved you as much.

Best Wishes

***

The package arrived by special courier; it was addressed to Sara.

The rings were identical, the marquis diamond from the engagement ring had been accurately cut in half. One each of the halves were now mounted on each ring. They were beautiful.

There was also a sealed envelope.

My Garden of Life is very large and beautiful.

Filled with wonders and light.

As large as the garden is, there is only one flower

607

Constantly in bloom, its beauty so bright

Dear Sara,

The One Flower in My Garden is and always has been, you.

***

Someday, Sara would give the girls the rings. She would tell them of a boy named Craig, and of the love they had shared for one another.

**

Several charities enjoyed receiving very handsome donations.

Charles had received a call, he decided to take a trip to Reelfoot Lake.

**

Dear Detective Jake Brighton,

Enclosed you will find a smaller envelope, please do not open it until instructed.

By your receiving this letter it means I have passed away. It also means answers to questions involving unsolved cases you and others have kept open for several years. I regret the frustration I caused you, please accept my apology. I also regret not telling you who I am, at least not directly but I know you have a very good idea. The reason I will not identify myself is really very simple, there are elements still out there who would and could bring harm to innocent people I don't want harmed, people I was once very closely associated with. Once you think about this, and the people involved, you will understand.

Sir, I am writing you that you can finally have answers to two murder cases which took place at South Creek, Georgia, one in Huntsville, Alabama and one missing person case in Chattanooga, Tennessee.

Oscar William Tomlinson. As you know Oscar was killed by a rifle shot to the back of his head. I understand the bullet was never found, please allow me to help. The bullet was a handloaded 165 grain boat tail, 30.06 caliber. The shot was made at a range of 300 yards. Inside this communication you will find a

sketch, a map of sort. The sketch will detail exactly where I was when I fired the shot and exactly where Oscar was standing when he died. I would suggest you take the sketch and examine the area; a trained sniper will also be able to assist you and will confirm it was the best setup for the shot.

Andrew "Andy" Carlton Bohannon. I blew his head up with a small bomb. The bomb consisted of a ping pong ball lined with BBs for maximum damage and filled with a small charge of C4 explosive, placed in his mouth and his lips glued shut. The charge was set off by radio remote. As Andy was leaving the house, I waited for him to pass where I was hidden and shot his tire with a suppressed .22 Magnum. Once he finished changing the tire I then knocked him out and injected meds to keep him sleeping while I transported him to where he died. Much experimentation was required to perfect the small bomb. I was extremely pleased with the final effects.

David Edward Clements. His biggest mistake in life was choosing the wrong people he wanted to be friends with during his teenage years and allowing them to dictate his actions. I almost allowed him to live, but it was only a very brief thought. He, too, had to pay the price. But from some things I had learned, as well as conversation he and I had just before I killed him, I chose at least some mercy. His body would be left in such a way his casket could be open, his family could have their last goodbyes.

I imagine the Huntsville police will be interested in reading this communication, feel free to copy and send it to them. Frankly, I don't care if the South Creek police ever know this letter exist although I imagine you will send them a copy as well.

Oliver Calix Watson. The worst of the bunch. Please open the smaller envelope now.

(Jake Brighton dumped the contents of the envelope onto the table, photos!)

Detective Brighton, In the photos you will have a positive identification of Oliver, he and I spent several days together, he suffered much pain, humiliation and indignity, the same as he once inflicted upon another person. The photos will show much of what he experienced. God help me, I enjoyed every minute of his pain and misery, every scream which came from his mouth, but above all, I enjoyed watching him die slowly.

I kidnapped Oliver at his mistress' home just outside Chattanooga and kept him sleeping with injections. He was transported to an area close to Anniston, Alabama where I had located an old mine entrance a few years before and had set up a place in the mine just for him. The mine entrance is well hidden by natural plant growth, but you will find good coordinates and a map as a separate part of this communication.

Before I proceed, I suppose you are wondering why Anniston? Honestly, because it was once the hometown of the real victim in all this, Sara Blackmon. I thought it somehow symbolic Oliver be found there. I also thought it symbolic that Oliver, Oscar and Andy each die on August 7th, the date of the assault on Sara Blackmon. Due to logistics issues, David died during the Winter.

That said, there is also a map of the inside of the mine, follow it very closely. You will find a very well-hidden entrance to a secondary tunnel behind some abandoned equipment, all this is marked on the map. Inside the secondary tunnel, you will find Oliver, or at least what is left of him. You will also find all the equipment I shared with Oliver, he was, after all, the guest of honor.

Oliver died by loss of blood. I have studied the human anatomy and probably know it as well as some surgeons, better

611

than most. I have also studied the art of killing and was, at one time, extremely good at it. After situating Oliver in such a position he could watch his blood flow from his body and into buckets, I used a scalpel to make small incisions on both his wrists. He simply bled to death. I left the tunnel, sealed it and have never returned.

Why I did all this. I sat and watched the trial and have never seen such an injustice as was dealt Sara Blackmon. I saw how she was humiliated and treated like trash. I saw a judge who could have, and should have, allowed a much fairer trial but had been bought and paid for by Thomas Watson's money, as was Watson's evil attorney, Samuel Bartolli. I saw a jury that voted either by fear of Watson or took his money in return for a verdict of not guilty. But the reason I set forth to kill them was because of how they acted toward and laughed at the entire Blackmon family following the verdict. I made it my life's mission to destroy them all. I had also included the judge as a target, but you know how he met his own demise, and why.

Initially it was my intent to kill Thomas Watson as well. After much thought I decided a much greater pain would be more applicable, the pain of wondering where his only child might be. This is one of the reasons I didn't outright kill Oliver where he would be located until a time of my choosing, I wanted his parents to suffer, especially his father. Noted previously, I chose to bring suffering to Oliver as well. And suffer he did.

Good bet Anniston Police Department will be very interested in obtaining a copy of this letter.

The murder weapons? You will never find them, except the scalpel, I imagine it is still in the mine. The rest of the weapons were disassembled and scattered in rivers and lakes all over three states. Don't even bother, it would simply be a waste of your time, time I've already taken enough of.

It was arranged with people prior to my death to mail you this communication following the death of the elder Watson. I died first, cancer got me, but I had learned Thomas was also ill. I did not want him going to his grave knowing where his son was. I wanted to deny him having any closure. Therefore, you are receiving this letter now, because Thomas Watson is dead.

Once again, I deeply apologize to you and all the other law enforcement agencies and departments for the time you've all invested in your investigations. I also apologize for not revealing my identity. I don't know if you can close the cases now, or not, based on this letter and not having proof of my death or who I am, something which cannot ever be revealed to you. You simply have my word.

Respectfully and With Kindest Regards,

Justice

He finished reading the letter, "Holy Shit!"

Jake grabbed everything, jumped from this desk and ran to the Chief's office. Without knocking he barged in, "Sorry Chief, you have got to see this!!"

Chief Richards read the communication, he looked at the photos, "Holy Shit!"

"Exactly what I said!"

"Get your ass to Anniston as quickly as possible. Say nothing about this, call nobody about it. I want you to show up on their doorstep with this."

"Chief, should I? I mean, no crime concerning Oliver here. He lived in Nashville, went missing in Chattanooga and now his body is supposed to be in some mine at Anniston, Alabama. What the hell can I do in Alabama?"

"Not a damned thing legally, but you can be there when he's found. It all began here and by God, we will be represented. Let Anniston PD call Chattanooga, I'm sure they will contact Nashville PD as well. "

"Yes sir."

"Jake, you know who did this, don't you?"

"Without a doubt sir, Craig Kirkland did it all. But how the hell can anyone prove a man supposedly dead for years and claims to be a dead man now has been killing people?"

"I'd like to shake his damned hand! Off the record of course."

"Sir, off the record, Me Too!"

"Get home and pack your bags to be gone for a few days. Stay in contact, report in and let me know if I can be of any help from this end. See ya when I see ya!"

Jake quickly made copies of the papers and used the copying machine to make copies of the photos. He headed home, 20 minutes later was on the road toward Anniston, Alabama.

***

"Chief Thompson, thanks for seeing me without an appointment, sir."

"Professional courtesy, Detective Brighton. How may I help you?"

"Sir, are you familiar with the missing person case concerning Oliver Watson?"

"Oh yeah. Billionaire goes missing it makes the news, bigtime. Why?"

"I have in this envelope information leading me to believe his body may be in your jurisdiction?"

Chief Thompson read the letter and looked at the photos. "Holy Shit!"

"Yes sir."

"I remember the trial. The sonsabitches raped that girl sure as hell. Every damned one of them should have gone to prison and be getting buttfucked every day in the shower."

"Yes sir."

"Map appears to be something a military person would make. I got a detective who served 20 in the Marine Corps, got wounded in Nam, bet he can read it better than you or me.

Thompson picked up the phone, "Tell Michaels to get his nose outta the sports section and come to my office, now!"

The man knocked but didn't wait to be told to come in, the door opened. Jake had seen some mean looking people in his time, but former Gunnery Sargent Jasper Michaels looked mean enough to take on any grizzly bear ever born. The man even looked mean when he smiled!

Thompson made introductions, "Jazz, can you read this map?"

Taking a few minutes to study the map, the man nodded, yes. "I know the location pretty well. I help a buddy who is a scoutmaster, we've taken boys on hikes through there. Pretty woods. Why, what's up?"

"Read this. It was sent to Jake. He brought it directly to us."

A few more minutes passed, "Holy Shit!"

Jake noted, "Yeah, that seems to be the general consensus."

"I knew that area had been mined but thought they were all sealed up."

"It appears a person found one that wasn't. But keep in mind, this could be a wild goose chase. Yall know how some idiots can be."

Jazz asked Jake, "Got any boots?"

"In my car."

"Grab em and meet me out front. We need to drop by my house for some decent flashlights and I need a compass."

Thompson spoke, "If you find anything, don't touch. Call me and I will get forensics down there. Chattanooga will also need to be contacted and I expect, and because it involves a kidnapping across state lines, the damned feds will want to poke their noses in, which I could do without but will have to be tolerated. Jake, thank you for coming here and bringing us the information. Please remember, you really have no other reason to be here, but I am allowing you to participate, albeit limited, because I know you worked the investigation when those animals raped and hurt one of our local kids. I also know the DA and you presented a damned good case. For those reasons I am permitting you to continue with us, just be careful, observe and stay out of the way. OK?"

Jake shook Thompson's hand, "Thank you Sir, Yes sir."

***

"Remember me saying I helped my scoutmaster buddy?"

"Yes."

"He knew the girl's family. Said she was one of the sweetest kids he'd ever met, always smiling, said she was beautiful. Can I say something off the record?"

"Yep."

"If I knew who killed the bastards, I might just have to look the other way."

Jake looked at the man, he nodded in agreement.

Jazz stopped the car, looked at the map. "Looks like somebody I might have trained."

"Huh?"

"The person who drew the map. Just like I would have trained a Marine to do."

617

'Ah, OK."

"Grab one of those canteens and hook it on your belt. We got a way to walk. Let's go, Jake."

Several times Jazz stopped and looked at the map, took readings with his compass. They may or may not adjust the direction they were headed, all Jazz would say was, "Let's go." An hour and a half in, they stopped. The map was checked again. "Well, if there is a mine entrance, its right around here somewhere."

Twenty minutes of searching revealed nothing. Jake sat down, leaned back against a tree and was taking a sip of water from the canteen. With his head tilted back, looking across the container, he spotted something not quite right, a dark spot behind some bushes on the side of a hill.

Jake screwed the cap on the canteen and put it back in its sheath. He walked up the hill. Behind the bushes was the entrance to a mine. "Jazz, I got it!!"

Jazz came running, "Looks more like an airshaft than an entrance. Let's see what's inside, hope you aren't claustrophobic."

The map of the mine was amazingly accurate and detailed. The abandoned equipment was located, behind it the opening sealed with stacked stones and a steel plate leaning against them. The men went to work, they soon had the opening unsealed.

"Your jurisdiction Jazz, you first."

The men entered the tunnel, shining their lights around, inspecting the area, a moment later Jake heard Jazz, "Yep, I'd say he's about as dead as dead is."

What Jake saw was a partially rat eaten body, the rest was almost as if it was half mummified. It was lying face down on a

618

table, arms still shackled, hanging down over buckets of something resembling tar, legs with shackles to the table and straps, now loose, across the torso. There was no stink of death, that had long since dissipated. One thing Jake recognized, he had seen the same gold necklace with a diamond studded crucifix hanging proudly around the neck of Oliver Calix Watson while the boy had sat meekly at the defendant's table. Speaking more to himself, but aloud, Jake let his thoughts out, "Well, you finally got what you deserved. Didn't you? You smart ass little sonofabitch!"

"I'd say he did, Look at all this stuff in here. Damn! Somebody worked a while getting this place set up. And if they crammed that in him," Jazz pointed at the dildo still attached to the machine, "he hurt a while, and bad!! I've seen some big dicks, never anything the size of that thing. And it wasn't an easy task getting a sleeping body all the way here. Musta been one helluva man to do it."

"And determined."

"Absolutely. Let's go outside and hope this portable radio will work." Jazz called in, the radio worked, "Put the chief on."

"Thompson, Talk to me Jazz."

"Put together a crew, Chief. We need generators, portable lights, a lot of lights, all the extension cords that can be rounded up. Might as well put some of those trustees to work, let em earn their meals. Call forensics and tell em we got a lot of fun in store for em, we got one very dead piece of shit just waiting for them to play with. I expect the coroner might want to get into this game as well so he can tell us the dead person is dead and get his name in the newspaper. As far as any other calls, those are your decision."

Jazz gave the Chief the location of his car and said he and Jake would be waiting there to guide everyone in. He also asked for some burgers, fries and milkshakes, the two men were hungry.

619

"By the time they gather up everything and get down here ought to be just about the time we get back to the car. Let's go, Jake."

***

The coroner arrived, "Let's get this done, my daughter has a piano recital this evening."

"Shut up Harry, we'll get to it as soon as Detective Brighton and I finish eating."

"How far is it?"

"Bout a mile, maybe a little more."

"Shit!"

Jazz looked at the man's shoes, "Yeah, Harry, those penny loafers are perfect for a little hike through the woods."

Finished eating, Jazz gathered everyone together and barked out orders, he walked to the last man in the group. The old man was wearing a jail uniform, he appeared to be frail, "Lester, you OK to make a pretty good little walk in the woods?"

"Yes sir, boss."

Jazz handed the old inmate a roll of orange ribbon, "Lester, I want you to tie some of this around a tree every 20 feet or so, it'll mark the path for others who need to come in. Understand?"

"Yes sir, boss."

"If anyone else tells you to do anything else you tell em to check with me. OK?"

"Yes sir, boss."

Jake had been watching the exchange between the detective and the trustee. Pulling Jazz aside he asked about it.

620

"Jake, old Lester ain't got anything or anybody, he gets himself in trouble so we will throw him in jail. At least that way he has a warm place to sleep, something to eat and can get a shower. Old bastard fought in World War Two, he has three Purple Hearts and two Navy Crosses. I've read his action reports, he should have been awarded the Medal of Honor. He is a Marine, I am a Marine, and any mother's son thinks he's gonna fuck with old Lester will answer to me."

"I understand. You also understand, if they fuck with Lester and have to deal with you, I've got your back. I don't think you need it, but just in case."

Jazz grinned, "Let's go, Jake."

They all hiked to the mine opening with Harry complaining, Jazz telling Harry to shut up and Lester giggling at the two men. Lester tied the ribbon as he'd been instructed to do.

Harry Smith pronounced the body dead.

Jazz couldn't resist, "Well, no shit Harry. You gonna cram your thermometer up his nonexistent ass now and give us the time of death?"

The corner was seething, "I will expect the body to be at the morgue by no later than tomorrow morning!"

"You can expect any damned thing you so desire. The body will be removed from here when I say so. Get off my crime scene!"

As soon as Harry had left, Jake asked Jazz about his dislike for the man.

"Harry is a pompous ass who thinks he is more important than he really is. He is crass and undignified when dealing with the families of those he pronounces dead, he has no sympathy and shows none. I also take no pleasure in dealing with people who

gain so much joy messing with dead people, and Harry loves it, way too much."

**

Before anyone else was allowed into the area Jazz had sent in the forensic team to look for fingerprints. "Jazz, we got a gazillion prints. The guy either didn't care or is one very stupid individual."

"He isn't stupid, more like brilliant."

"How you figure?"

"Just look at this place. He was smart enough to bring all this stuff in here without being seen, and it took a lot of trips. Smart enough to set everything up, build the table and chair. He brought in plenty of food and provisions, set up a bank of 12 volt batteries with that little thing to convert the voltage so he could have lights and run the percolator. He cooked on a camp stove. He did all that and managed to capture and transport his victim from Chattanooga to Anniston by road then from wherever he left his vehicle to here. The guy was brilliant, you'll never find any match to those prints."

"Why you say that?"

"Because he didn't mind leaving them for us to find. If he'd cared, he would have worn gloves. Somehow, he knows his prints are not on record anywhere. I know you've got to try and find a match, but it'll be a waste of time. Y'all find anything else?"

"From the number of paper plates and plastic ware in the trash they were here several days. Still enough canned goods to last a couple more, plenty of water in some jugs for a few more days. Only blood we found is in the buckets and I'm betting some of that mess on the dildo is blood. He must have shocked the guy a bunch, too."

"Shocked? How you mean?"

"Electrically, let me show you."

The instant Jazz saw the device he knew what it was. "I've seen one, a guy I knew in Nam built one. He took great delight in rigging it to different things and shocking the snot out of unsuspecting victims, got me with it once, knocked the crap outta me. Said he learned how to build it from a magazine article."

"Well, this one had the ground wires attached to the chair and table, the hot wire is run to the victim's crotch. No telling how many times he turned that crank and knocked the victim's nuts up into his watch pocket, so to speak."

"What else?"

"The machine he used to screw the guy is a work of art. The guy could patent it and make millions off horny housewives. Although I ain't sure how many would want a dildo that big, some might, but I expect most would want something more comfortable. The guy must have absolutely destroyed the victim's rectum and probably did some internal damage. The victim hurt like hell, I mean worse than bad, he also shit all over the place, dried up feces all over the table. Oh, we also found a scalpel," the officer pointed, "it's on the table over there, same place we found it."

***

"Give me your car keys, I'll have someone deliver your car to wherever you're staying."

Jake handed over his keys, "I haven't had time to find a room yet."

"OK, no need to. I got a spare room you can use while you're here, you look old enough to be house broken. I'll have your car

brought to my house. Let's go, Jake. We both need some shut eye."

Before leaving for the long walk in the dark Jazz instructed an officer to call the chief and request enough trustees and tools to clear a path from the road to the mine wide enough for golf carts and have four carts delivered. Jazz was tired of walking.

The walk out seemed longer than before; the two detectives talked.

"The girl have anyone close enough to her who might be capable of killing the other three and doing this one like he did? Family or friends?"

"Only one, but he's presumed dead."

"Tell me about him."

"Boyfriend, a kid named Kirkland. See, the girl went with Oliver voluntarily to his place, she had no idea the other boys would be there or what they had planned for her, she thought it would only be Watson. She told her boyfriend about it, broke the kids' heart. Then he had to sit through the trial and listen to Sara tell about the whole week, again. He was forced to witness for the defense and told things he really didn't want to tell about the relationship he and she had. The defense attorney went too far one day as he was questioning Sara, it took me and another cop to stop the kid before he could get to the guy. But through it all, the kid still loved Sara, and you could tell she still loved him. I did a lot of studying, asked a lot of questions and learned he had expert survival and woodsmanship skills, self-taught. He was a crack shot, also self-taught. From what I learned after she broke his heart, he changed, became a loner, he was afraid to be close to anyone because he didn't want to be hurt again. They said instead of going out like other kids, movies, ballgames and such, he took up running and working out, said he went from being a

624

skinny kid to someone who could have been a star athlete, if he'd wanted to. Graduated high school, joined the Marine Corps. On his second Nam tour he was sent on some secret mission and never returned. He was reported MIA and later presumed dead.

"Marine, huh?"

"Yep, oh, I found out that somebody in Nam nicknamed him "Ghost". Said you could be talking to him, turn your head and when you looked back, he would just be gone, he could disappear like a ghost. Ever hear of a Marine like that?"

Jazz showed no emotion, "Heard of him."

"Well, he would have been, and really has been our only suspect. Except he's dead."

In the darkness Jazz smiled and remembered what he'd told Jake earlier about turning his head. It seemed there was a Ghost who had not died in Viet Nam after all. Thinking to himself, "Good Damn Job Craig."

***

The officer told Jazz, "FBI took all the carts. They're at the mine now."

Using his radio Jazz called his man at the mine. "Me and Detective Brighton are about to start walking in, I expect a cart to be headed our way and meet us. Re-phrase, there better By God be a cart headed our way, NOW!"

Jake looked at Jazz, "Saw it coming, didn't you?"

"Hell yes, just didn't expect em to get here this quick. I misjudged."

The officer again spoke, "Chief called, said he talked to Chattanooga, they are sending one of theirs. Chief knows the guy,

said you would like him and have no problems from him. Also, Chief has been getting calls from all sort of news people, some national, he said you should be expecting them to start showing up anytime."

"This party just keeps getting more fun all the time. Let's go, Jake."

***

They were easy to spot, they all were wearing brand new jeans and boots. Jazz approached an FBI agent, he offered no introduction, "If any of you want transportation to and from this crime scene, provide your own, The Anniston Police Department is not a fucking taxi service. What the hell are you doing on my crime scene?"

"We're here to take over this investigation."

"Got papers from a federal judge stating so?"

"No."

Jazz turned to one of his officers, "Go outside and bring in three more officers. I want these people escorted off this crime scene. If they give you any trouble arrest and handcuff em, charge them with obstructing an investigation."

The officer smiled, walked to the tunnel opening and whistled.

All three agents began to say something, Jazz interrupted, "Boys, let me explain. You will leave here now with my officers or you can resist. If you choose to resist you need to pray my officers can get you dragged out of here before I can get to you. If I get to you first, I will take great joy in ripping your heads off and pissing down your neck holes."

There was no resisting, "We'll be back with that court order."

"I'm sure you will be. Bye!"

"Where the hell is Brad?"

The young officer heard his name and came running from down the tunnel, "Yes sir?"

"Brad, go outside and call your Uncle Chief. Tell him the FBI has been tossed off this crime scene until they can provide a court order directing them to take over this case. Tell Uncle Chief to call every politician he's ever played golf with, hunted with, fished with or ever even shook hands with and slow the FBI down for as long as possible. Got it?"

"Got it!"

"Jazz, you know they're gonna win."

"Aw hell Jake, I know it, I don't like it, but I know it. At least I got to have my fun with it, though."

***

Three days later the FBI got their court order. By now there was really nothing more for the Aniston PD to learn from the scene. All Golf carts had been removed from the area and every dealer within a hundred-mile radius had been informed, they were all more than willing to double their prices if some "certain" people showed up to make any purchases. Oliver's body was laying in the morgue, positive identification had been made by dental records.

A request from the FBI to Chief Thompson for manpower to remove everything from what had become known as "Oliver's Mine" was turned down. "It's your case, you man it", had been the chief's reply. He had also, as politely as he could, given them directions to hell and wishes for an enjoyable trip.

It was late in the day, "Jake, you know, it isn't as if we all hate the FBI, hell, we need the FBI. The problem is how they act when they show up. Strutting around as if they are all God's gifts to law enforcement, barking orders, just taking over as if the rest of us don't know a damned thing about how to investigate and are nothing but their peons to be used as they see fit. THAT is the problem! If they would exhibit some humility and courtesy, there isn't a law enforcement officer alive who wouldn't welcome their agents and the help they could offer. I guess they just can't help being egotistical assholes, must be a job requirement. I expect you'll be headed home in the morning, let me buy you a steak and a beer. I'm off duty, Let's go, Jake."

Two weeks later a crew was sent in. Forms were built, concrete poured. The mine would have no more visitors.

***

Not far outside South Creek, Georgia, there was a small farm. Retired Sheriff Jeff Edmunds and his wife lived there and enjoyed the quiet life. Jeff had only one official duty to perform, more a promise than a duty, and was wondering if he would live long enough to finally know it could be performed.

The man who now held the office Jeff once held called before he drove to the Edmunds place. Arriving there, he enjoyed a few minutes with the folks then asked Jeff to take a drive. Jeff opened the envelope he was handed and carefully read its contents.

"So, whoever it was finally got around to getting the last one."

"Yep, appears so."

The next day Jeff Edmunds drove to the bank and removed a package from the safe deposit box. Without opening the box, he

drove to a place on the back of his property and watched the box and its contents burn until only ash remained.

Jeff Edmunds made three phone calls. Each of the women thanked him for keeping his promise of secrecy.

CHAPTER

64

The pain had let him know it was time. He loaded the syringe with what he knew would be the last of the pain killer he would ever need and placed it in the machine. Next, he connected the tube from the machine to the IV port in his arm, he lay on the bed. Picking up the phone he dialed the number, when the person answered all he said was, "It's Time."

With his finger on the button that would activate the machine to press the syringe plunger, Howard Craig Kirkland uttered his last words, "Oh Sara, How I've loved you so." He closed his eyes; he pressed the button. First came the feeling of warmth, then euphoria, then sleep. Craig never felt his heart begin to slow, he never knew his breathing was slowing, they simply did until there were no more breaths, no more heart beats, he'd left this world.

***

It had been two weeks since Craig's visit with Sara and Kenneth, the couple were on their way to dinner at Sara's favorite restaurant. Suddenly Sara was overcome, she gasped, put one hand to her lips, the other to her heart. The sudden onset of shocked grief was nothing she had ever experienced, she screamed, "HE'S GONE!!"

Startled by his wife's sudden outburst Kenneth stopped the car and asked her what was going on. Sara responded, "Please Kenneth, take me somewhere, take me somewhere and just hold me." Kenneth drove to a little league ballpark not far from where they were and parked in the empty lot. Sara was crying as

Kenneth took her in his arms and again asked what was wrong, Sara told him, "Craig is gone, he's dead".

"How could you possibly know?" Kenneth asked.

"I felt it, felt it as I've never felt anything before. Kenneth, I heard him tell me he loved me. I don't understand it, but I know it's so."

Kenneth held the only woman he'd ever loved, the same woman he knew was loved by another man, a man he knew his wife also loved, a man he deeply respected. He told her, "Honey, I believe you."

For the next hour she cried, Sara's small body was wracked with sobs stronger than she could believe possible, she never would have imagined the eyes could produce so many tears.

All the years she had carried the shame of the lust for some boy she had met on vacation, all the years of pain her lust had caused the man who had once been her boyfriend, all the pain that had been imposed on her that night because of having put herself in the place she had put herself, all the dirty things that were done to her that night, all the humiliation of the trial that followed, how a sweet boy had changed and became a stone cold assassin, all the lives that had been affected, all the years before and especially after that night her mother had never shown her anything but indignation and disdain, all the times her father could have helped but didn't, everything Sara had carried with her for so many years spilled from deep within her in screams, sobs, tears. That night the tears washed Sara's soul.

It all happened while being held by the kindest, most gentle man she had ever known. The man Craig had told her was the only person who could ever love her more than he had, did and ever would, her husband, Kenneth Allison.

***

Three hours after Craig had made the call a van pulled up to his house, his remains were put into a body bag, placed in the van and driven to a crematorium. The ashes were transported to a helicopter which would fly over the Virginia mountains Craig had come to love, they were scattered into the wind.

There would be no trace of one of the most lethal men who ever lived.

Within seven days the house was no longer there, topsoil had been brought in, grass and trees were planted. In a few years the forest would once again reclaim the area.

***

A dozen yellow roses were delivered the day after he died.

"To Grandma, With My Love"

THE END

DISCLAIMER

This is except for Bob Carpenter and The United Craftsmen Children's Shoe Drive, a charity which provides under privileged children an opportunity to shop for new shoes. The United Craftsmen Children's Shoe Drive will also receive a percentage from the sale of this work of fiction.

Bob Carpenter is the CEO of The UCCSD and my friend.

ACKNOWLEDGEMENTS

Teresa, my beautiful wife. Thank you for always being the wonderful person you are and always have been. You are my reason, my inspiration and my main proofreader. You are also beautiful, after more than forty six years since our wedding, more beautiful than ever. Having need for someone to create Sara's physical appearance on, I chose you at the age of sixteen. You are and shall always be The One Flower In My Garden.

Mr. Carl Miller who waded ashore at DaNang in 1965 and your experiences while in Viet Nam were invaluable to this book. I can never thank you enough for your help. Thank you for your Service, Sir!

And to my friends who continually offered their love and encouragement to continue writing this story. I love you all.

Made in the USA
Columbia, SC
25 June 2021